Thorn:
The Tree

Copyright © 2014 by Peter Garth Hardy.

Library of Congress Control Number:		2014902349
ISBN:	Hardcover	978-1-4931-7180-4
	Softcover	978-1-4931-7179-8
	eBook	978-1-4931-7181-1

This is a work of fiction. Names, characters, places and incidents either are the product of the author's imagination or are used fictitiously, and any resemblance to any actual persons, living or dead, events, or locales is entirely coincidental.

This book was printed in the United States of America.

Rev. date: 02/14/2014

To order additional copies of this book, contact:
Xlibris LLC
1-888-795-4274
www.Xlibris.com
Orders@Xlibris.com
552054

Thorn: The Tree

Peter Garth Hardy

CONTENTS

Dedication

This book is dedicated to
to all those souls
sincerely seeking
the Truth

"Ask, and it will be given to you;
Seek, and you will find;
Knock, and it will be opened to you."
Matthew, 7:7

Prologue

Paxton was born on Christmas Day in the holy town of Bethlehem, Pennsylvania. He was a hippie child, or more precisely, he was a hippie's child. He grew up with The Grateful Dead. He travelled the country with them, actually, first in his mother's belly and later in the saddle of her ample left hip.

He read at an early age. Not that he was a genius, mind you, but he had to find ways to entertain himself while his mother sold organic whole foods and acid at Dead shows. He would be left in someone's car or tent, sometimes with other hippie children, before and after the show, but Mary always took him inside for the music.

Paxton progressed rapidly from bedtime stories to newspapers to novels and pretty much anything he could pick up on the road. This was most of his education until he was accepted at The University of Maine at sixteen years of age. The gaps were filled in by the numerous and varied characters in his mother's supporting cast. It was a fine education, if SAT scores were any judge, because that was the only supporting document he had filed with his application for college, unless one counted the recommendation from his mother's shaman, Dr. Jack.

It was Orono where Paxton met his best friend, his first lover and Thorn, in that order, only separated by a couple of years. That's when the real craziness began in his already colorful life. That's when Paxton discovered he could move things with his mind, talk to dead people and predict the future. It is also when Paxton discovered he was a prophet for the 32nd Coming of Christ.

But this story is getting ahead of itself. Let us start at the beginning. Not at the beginning of Paxton's natural life, of course, but the beginning of his supernatural one. Let us join him as he hikes to the summit of Blueberry Hill on the afternoon of October 15th, 1999.

ONE

Heading for the Light

Time has stopped, for the moment.
    criss-crossed grass shadows still,
        weaving the sun's descent
           into the tapestry of twilight.
Two suns in the sunset,
    one staunch and stable,
        one faltering and flighty.
Melt together and vanish,
    into the water.

I thank you, All,
    for this wonderful life,
And I thank you, All,
    for this beautiful sky.
Day and night perched
    upon the setting sun.
As we head into the Light,
    and we head into the One.

Which son will rise up tomorrow?
One born of unique thought,
    original creation,
Or one just drifting along
    the currents of history?

How will he react to
    what he sees as reality?
Stepping off the well-worn path
    into the unknown,
        or quiet acquiescence?

Yesterday overtaking tomorrow,
    in a string of tomorrows,
        defining who he is
           and who he shall become.

Face up, against
    the winds of change
Will he set his jaw
    and clench a fist,
Or take a running start
    and throw himself along?
Carried away by the breeze
    with the last of the autumn leaves,
    to a place that
        he knows not where.

Here. Hereafter.
There. Thereafter.

Paxton inhaled the crisp autumn air as he placed one hiking boot in front of the other upon the increasingly steep, dirt road. He counted as his feet logged one, two, three, four steps. He exhaled through his nose while trudging another one two, three, four, five, six steps. He observed that there were more steps upon his exhalation, but was otherwise unwilling to comment on the matter. In fact, he was trying not to think at all. This was an exercise in walking meditation. In an attempt to clear his mind he visualized a still pond with nary a ripple upon its unbroken surface.

Paxton had dubbed this place Blueberry Hill because of the profusion of blueberry bushes at its crest. Not the most imaginative name, he would grant you, but having never discovered its true name, if in fact it even had one, Blueberry Hill had sufficed.

"Be here, now. Be here, now," repeated the mantra inside his head, but Paxton was having a hard time focusing upon the present moment. Climbing this hill again was like dredging a rake through the silt that had settled upon his memories of this place. How many years had it been? Three? Four years. His mind conspired to pull his attention backward to the last time he had made this climb, a guitar slung across his back, Tucker and Annie in tow.

It was the last happy time the three roommates had shared together. Tucker had carried an enormous backpack full of picnic supplies upon his broad shoulders. Annie's woven bag full of paper and paints was tiny by comparison. She and Paxton had worked on Tucker the entire hour-long climb and finally succeeded in convincing him to take psychedelic mushrooms for the first time in his young life.

Those few afternoon hours had stretched into oceans of distorted time. They drank bottles of red wine and feasted upon apples and strawberries. Paxton sang every song he could conjure while his friends cavorted and danced rings around the enormous old oak tree in the center of a field of blueberries at the summit of the hill. They had all taken turns painting pictures on paper, then on the tree, wildflowers and eventually on each other as their clothing became superfluous. Then they had made love, the three of them together in a natural extension of the love they all felt for one another. Natural that is, until they were no longer peaking and the hangover, both physical and moral, set in. There was nothing natural about their relationship after that.

Tucker had the most virulent reaction in the aftermath of that strange afternoon, taking pains to assure his roommates that he was not gay. Annie slept with him again just to shut him up. If Paxton was going to step up to the plate, that would have been the time to do it. But Paxton didn't step up. He did quite the opposite, pushing his two best friends further and further away with his jealous tirades. He was barely speaking with either of them when they all graduated from the University of Maine a month later.

Paxton wanted to put as much distance between himself and his former roommates as possible, so he joined the Peace Corps and spent the following three years teaching high school mathematics in a small desert town in northern Kenya. It was here that he discovered not only that he liked to teach, but that he was reasonably good at it. He also discovered that he was not very adept at doling out discipline. His colleagues typically delivered their punishments with a large cane. Refusing to follow suit, Paxton had settled on making the wrongdoers carry water up the hill to his house. Such castigation was especially humiliating to the boys since it was well-known that carrying water was women's work.

His Kenyan counterparts had considered his reluctance to use the cane a weakness, but Paxton was quick to point out that after his miscreants had carried four or five buckets of water up the hill they wished he had used the cane on them instead. The other teachers made their students cook and clean and carry water for them as a matter of course, so his argument never did hold much water, so to speak.

Although he knew that he wouldn't have to use the cane back home, high schools in the United States were fraught with their own discipline problems. Paxton determined that he was better suited to teaching at the college level. After a year of traveling through Africa and Asia, he eventually found himself back at the University of Maine, working toward a PhD in Mathematics.

Paxton shook his head forcefully to derail this backward-traveling train of thought. He had just come to the point where the road turned sharply to the east as it skirted the upper reaches of Blueberry Hill. It was here that the foot trail, which led to the hill's crest, branched off from the main road. The trail was overgrown from years of disuse and he had trouble finding its trace. He wondered if anyone at all had used the path in the four years of his absence. The casual hiker, unaware of the trail's existence, would easily miss it. Still, it was hard to imagine that other adventurous college students had not discovered the trail as he and his friends had done. Paxton hesitated only a moment before abandoning the road and bushwhacking his way through the trailhead.

Within fifty feet the trail opened up and Paxton observed telltale droppings and tracks indicating that deer and other smaller animals were still using this path. He concentrated upon his hiking boots as he maneuvered over and around half-buried boulders and protruding pine tree roots. Like many of Maine's forests, this one was predominantly evergreen. Occasional oak, maple and birch trees commingled with the conifers, their leafy, orange, red and yellow-dipped paint brushes pointing toward the cloudless, autumn sky.

It was merely a matter of minutes from the logging road to the crest of the hill. As he neared the last little rise that would take him to the top, the squatting junipers and stunted evergreen trees gave way to a field covered in withering lupine and blueberry bushes. Neither blossom nor fruit could be seen anywhere in the dun-colored meadow, which had taken on both the fragrance and hue of the pre-harvest hay fields he had passed on his drive from campus. The path took a sharp bend around a rather large boulder and then scrambled up a steep but short scree before ending abruptly at the base of an old oak tree.

The tree stood anchored in the center of the meadow, and dominated Paxton's field of vision as he crested the hill. He had often marveled that it had not only survived but prospered atop this little knoll, given the rocky soil and exposure to the elements. Having long ago crowded out any and all competitors, the oak was the only tree to be seen in the meadow, except for the short, wind-blown pine trees encroaching upon its edges. Paxton estimated the tree's age at one hundred years, give or take a decade, but he and Tucker had never taken a core sample to verify this guess, though they had talked about doing so several times.

The oak stood forty to fifty feet tall and its branches spread at least that wide. Its garment of leaves sloped gently inward towards a pointed crown, giving the tree's foliage the overall shape of an inverted acorn. Extending at right angles from its trunk, massive lower limbs seemed to uphold the oblong globe of leaves, like Atlas stooped beneath the weight of the world. The oak was anything but stooped, however, and looked more like a bodybuilder flexing his muscles in some prearranged pose. It stood atop that hill as a conquering king surveying his territory. Having already endured a century of brutal Maine winters, his posture was one of defiance, fists clenched against Mother Nature.

Yet for all its raw strength, the tree had always symbolized peace to Paxton. There was a time during college that he used to climb Blueberry Hill almost every weekend, though it was an hour-long drive from campus. He liked to take his problems to this tree. He would sit under its canopy for hours, thinking, reading and even sleeping. He was always at ease with himself and his world when he sat under his favorite tree and his problems somehow worked themselves out beneath its shade.

He absent-mindedly wiped a tear from the corner of his eye, not even aware of the motion of his arm, so enchanted had he once again become by the spectacle before him. The tree was resplendent in deep oranges and yellows, the reflection of the late afternoon sunlight forming a golden halo around its edges. The leaves, rustling in a cool, autumnal breeze, seemed to beckon him to come and rest beneath their protective canopy.

Paxton strode up to the tree and patted its trunk in greeting, a habit formed long ago when he had been a much more frequent visitor. He walked a full circle around the tree, staring upward into the patchwork of light and shadow interwoven amongst its leaves. Then he took a seat in a familiar bole formed where one enormous root bent away from the trunk, diving into the earth.

In an attempt to distance himself from his melancholy, Paxton closed his eyes and focused upon the sounds of the natural world around him. He could hear the leaves whispering above him, and a pair of chickadees somewhere in the tree, warning each other to prepare for the coming winter. His cheeks were dried by the slight breeze in a matter of minutes, but he did not notice, for he had fallen into a light sleep and had begun to dream.

Paxton's dream commenced where his waking mind had powered down. He found himself once again walking up the path toward the top of Blueberry Hill. He heard his name being whispered simultaneously from all directions. He turned this way and that, searching for the source of the voices. He could see no one, either on the path or in the woods, and decided he was listening to the trees dance in the strong wind which must surely be ushering in a thunderstorm. Indeed, the sky was dark and the air heavy with impending rain. Lightning flashed from somewhere in front of him and he wondered if the oak had been hit.

Still he could hear his name being called, more loudly now as he climbed higher. Dark faces began to form in the shadows of the trees surrounding him and he realized that the voices he heard were coming from their leafy lips. Frightened, he took off at a trot toward the top of the hill, the rising cacophony of voices spurring him onward until he was running full speed through the forest. Having left the path somewhere behind him, he crashed through the underbrush, darting between the trees like a running back avoiding tacklers on his quest for a touchdown. He lowered his shoulder and ran straight through the last defender, a pine tree no taller than himself, before reaching the end zone of the meadow.

No fanfare greeted him at the top of the hill. On the contrary, the wind died down abruptly when he burst upon the field of blueberries, and the silence was broken only by his wildly beating heart and ragged breathing. The electric air hung heavily all around him as he doubled over, hands upon his knees, trying to catch his breath. After he had recovered sufficiently to raise his head, the air in his now full lungs immediately deserted him again as he gasped in astonishment at the sight before him.

A single beam of light had broken through the dark cloud cover and fallen squarely upon the huge, old oak. The tree seemed to both absorb and reflect the light, giving it the appearance of a giant light bulb, illuminating the entire meadow in its iridescent glow. Lightning struck the meadow behind the tree, but Paxton barely flinched at the deafening thunder which followed closely on its heels. A strange feeling of peace settled upon him as he moved slowly toward the tree, where he knew he would be safe. He walked up to the oak and laid his hand upon its cracked and variegated trunk.

"Hello, Paxton," he heard distinctly, from a spot almost directly above his head. He was startled by the nearness of the voice and peered up into the branches of the tree for its owner.

"You're not going to find what you're looking for up there," said a decidedly masculine, yet not ungentle voice. "Nor will you find it anywhere outside yourself."

"Who's there? Where are you?" shouted Paxton, his peaceful feeling shattered by the disembodied voice. He whirled around to see if someone had followed him up the trail. Seeing no one, he raced around the tree and then once again searched its boughs for the person that must surely be hidden there.

"I'm right in front of you, Paxton," he heard in his head. He could not pinpoint from which direction the voice was coming. It seemed to materialize in his mind, bypassing his auditory system altogether, though he was able to distinguish intonation in the speech.

"Who are you?" challenged Paxton.

"I don't know who or what I am. I know only that I am."

"What is *that* supposed to mean?" asked Paxton.

"Do you know who you are, Paxton Stevens?"

"How do you know my name?"

"I've been acquainted with you for a long time."

"Then you've already answered your own question," observed Paxton.

"Because I know your name? A name is far from an identity. 'A rose by any other name would smell as sweet.' And my question was not 'Who are you?' but 'Do you know who you are?'"

"Of course I do!"

"Tell me."

"I am the person you must surely see standing beneath this tree."

"I do indeed see a bag of bones beneath me," Paxton heard inside his head, spurring him to search harder amongst the tree's branches for his inquisitor. "But what about the part of you which is separate from your physical body? What will survive when those bones are buried six feet beneath the ground?"

"I don't know what happens to us when we die," stated Paxton, irritably, "and I'm getting tired of this interrogation. Why don't you come out and show yourself?"

"I can't come out, or go anywhere for that matter, even if you weren't standing on top of me!"

Paxton looked downward, realization coming to him slowly, but gaining momentum as he stared at his feet. Startled, he pushed his upper body forcefully away from the trunk of the tree, jumping backward off the root upon which he had been standing.

Paxton felt a sharp pain in his left foot accompanied by the brief image of a puff adder striking him with lightning speed, sinking its venomous fangs into his ankle. His rational mind had just enough time to refute this anachronism before the snake was gone and the more familiar and less acute pain of pins and needles began to travel the length of his leg as though it were being awakened from a deep slumber. The thudding pain in his foot was repeated a second and third time before the rest of his body was also roused to wakefulness with a start. His sleepy eyes focused just in time to avoid the fourth kick aimed at his foot by the dark shape now looming over him.

"Wake up, buddy!" a strangely familiar voice spoke down to him. "Don't you know this is private property?"

Not quite sure whether or not he was still dreaming, Paxton stared upward into the brooding eyes of his former best friend and replied, "Tucker, is that you?"

TWO

Hey, Diddle Diddle

You think you're so clever,
with your supersonic planes,
artificial hearts,
and computer brains.
You can see inside the atom,
gaze off into outer space,
and you can vanish in a moment
leaving nothing but a trace.

You debate over abortion,
homosexuality.
You can clone a human being,
but is he just like you and me?
Your greatest minds are busy
creating plasma TV,
while your greatest cities vanish
in the rising of the sea.

Hey, diddle, diddle
Nero's tuning up his fiddle.
Who cares about the burning,
we've got "Malcolm in the Middle."
The Pats are in the Superbowl
the new "Survivor" is here,
just sit down on your sofa
and grab yourself a beer.

Your leaders take your money,
for their God and your country.
The gap keeps getting wider
between wealth and poverty.
Though they feast upon the masses,
they're never fully sated,
but they'll perish with the rest
in the wasteland they created.

Hey, diddle, diddle
Nero's tuning up his fiddle.
The sky is getting heavy
or so says Chicken Little.
We're suckling our babies
as the Horsemen gain their saddles,
then we'll cheer those sons and daughters
as they ride off into battle.

You go to work each morning,
Just focused on the day.
You come home in the evening,
you got nothing much to say.
You'd give everything you have,
so your kids can have it all.
Maybe they will pay attention
to the writing on the wall.

Hey, diddle, diddle
Nero's tuning up his fiddle.
The cause of our ambivalence
is something of a riddle.
We gather at the Coliseum,
the gladiators fight,
and the hole keeps getting bigger,
full of ultraviolet light.

Hey, diddle, diddle
Nero's tuning up his fiddle.
Who cares about the burning,
Nero's tuning up his fiddle.
Hey, diddle, diddle
Hey, diddle, diddle
Hey, diddle, diddle
Hey.

“Paxton?” asked Tucker incredulously.

“Yes it's me!” replied Paxton testily, jumping to his feet. “Would you quit kicking me?”

“What are you doing here?” questioned Tucker.

“I could ask you the same thing!”

“I summoned you here!” the words registered in Paxton's mind, without ever having passed through his auditory canals.

“What?” they both responded in unison.

“What do you mean you summoned me?” asked Tucker.

“I didn't say that,” Paxton replied.

“Then who did?” challenged Tucker.

“I did,” a deep, masculine voice responded once again in their heads.

“How are you doing that?” asked Tucker.

“I'm not doing anything,” Paxton defended himself, “but I'm going to find out who is.”

Paxton peered upward into the tree, shading his eyes against the setting sun with his open left hand. He watched the light flicker through golden leaves fluttering on the slight but steady breeze but he saw no sign of a human silhouette.

“There must be a tape recorder hidden here somewhere,” he mumbled to himself, walking a full circle around the tree. His search ended when he stumbled into Tucker's hard shoulder, eliciting a grunt of disapproval from his old friend.

Paxton rubbed his temple as he peered upward into the blue eyes of the slightly taller man and asked, “What *are* you doing here?”

“I'm working,” Tucker replied tersely.

“Like hell,” Paxton scoffed. “Doing what?”

“If you must know, I am surveying this forest for potential harvest.”

“Thomas works for the logging company which is going to cut me down,” remarked the disembodied voice once more.

“Are you hearing that?” asked Paxton, noticing that Tucker's lips hadn't moved.

“Hearing what?” came Tucker's noncommittal response.

“That voice,” continued Paxton. “It said, ‘*Thomas works for the company which is going to cut me down.*’”

“I did hear that,” admitted a visibly relieved Tucker. “Where is it coming from?”

"This is too weird," said Paxton, shaking his head. "I was dreaming when you kicked me awake just now. I was dreaming that I was communicating with this tree. But this doesn't feel like a dream anymore."

"This is no dream, Paxton," verified the tenor tones inside his head. "Nor was the other, really. It was more a vision. You were not sleeping but in a light meditative state. I first wanted to appeal to your subconscious mind so as not to frighten you too badly, although I'm afraid I've done just that."

"I'm, I'm not scared," stuttered Paxton, taking a few inadvertent steps backward.

"What is going on here?" asked Tucker, his wide eyes betraying his own fear.

"You two are having a polite conversation with an oak tree," came the response. "Why are you so surprised? This is not our first conversation, Paxton. You and Annie both communicated with me the last time the three of you were up here."

"That was real?" thought Paxton to himself. He did indeed remember lying upon one of the oak tree's lower branches in communion with the tree for what had seemed like hours, but he had been tripping on mushrooms at the time!

"And you used to talk to the vegetation you trimmed all the time, Thomas, back in your landscaping days," continued the strange voice.

"Yeah, but it never talked back to me," answered Tucker. "Hey, wait a minute! How do you know about my landscaping job? How do you know my name, for that matter?"

"Oh, I know a lot about you, Thomas. I have been tuned into your soul's frequency ever since your father brought you up here when you were four. Your signal was so strong that it woke me from a deep meditation, long before you reached the top of this hill. I've been following your life ever since."

"What do you mean you've been tuned into my soul's frequency?" questioned Tucker.

"Every soul vibrates at its own distinct frequency, not unlike the different frequencies at which radio waves are transmitted," explained the tree. "It's possible to tune into another soul's frequency, just as you can tune a radio dial to receive a certain station's frequency. It is somewhat harder to accomplish, however, and takes a good deal of practice and meditation."

"If what you say is true," reasoned Tucker, "then you must know everything there is to know about me."

"I do know quite a lot about you, Thomas, but not everything. Your signal becomes weaker as the distance between us increases. And I can really only pick up whatever signals you may be transmitting, which is limited to the outreach of your conscious mind, for the most part. There are thoughts and emotions buried deep in your subconsciousness that I'll probably never be able to reach, unless you first dig them up yourself."

"Tell me something, then," challenged Tucker.

"Tell you what?" replied the tree.

"Tell me something about myself that only I know. Prove to me that you really can tune into my soul's frequency."

"My doubting Thomas," the tree mumbled, followed by something akin to a sigh. "Let's see . . . . You wear boxers instead of briefs."

"I could have told you that," interjected Paxton.

Tucker shot Paxton a withering glare before he concurred, "You're going to have to do better than that!"

"Okay, you asked for it. When you were in the fourth grade, you got a lesson in compassion when you put a Dumbo valentine into George Hostetler's valentine bag. You wrote on it, 'This looks just like you, George.' George was the fattest boy in your elementary school. Because he was so much bigger than everyone else, he was somewhat of a bully, so you felt justified in giving him such a horrible valentine. When your mother overheard you telling one of your brothers about it, she was mortified and made you promise to replace the valentine in George's bag. She stood over you as you wrote out a nicer message on a Mickey Mouse valentine, your personal favorite.

"It took you a few days to actually pull the switch. You sat in the front row staring at George's valentine bag, which was taped to the chalk ledge of the black-board with the other bags, wondering how you could exchange the two valentines without being seen. You waited until everyone had gone outside for recess one afternoon, fished around in his bag until you had found the Dumbo valentine and then you replaced it with the new one. On Valentine's Day, after everyone had opened their valentines, George approached you with a radiant face and gave you a big hug, thanking you for the valentine and telling you that it was the best one he had gotten. You spent a lot of time afterwards, pondering over the incident. You marveled over the power you had to affect someone else's life, and you felt so much better about having made George happy as opposed to having made him mad at you."

Paxton could tell from the incredulous look on Tucker's face that the story was true. But there was something else bothering him. He had noticed during this last exchange that Tucker's lips hadn't moved at all. Paxton could *hear* Tucker's thoughts just as clearly as he *heard* the tree's voice. He thought to himself, "How is he doing that?"

"He is not doing it, I am," the oak tree answered Paxton's unspoken question.

"Are you also tuned into my soul?" asked Paxton mentally.

"The frequency coming from your soul is just as strong as Thomas' frequency, but I haven't been acquainted with you for quite as long. I have been communicating with you since the first day that Thomas brought you up here. You sensed my presence, you just never tried to talk back to me, except for that day when you and Annie hung out together in my branches."

"But how is it that Paxton and I can hear each other's thoughts, too?" Tucker broke in with his own mind.

"I'm bridging the gap between your two minds by lengthening the frequencies with which you transmit and receive information. You could do it on your own, if you practiced at it enough. But I can't wait for that to happen."

"And you're a tree," stated Paxton. "This is too weird."

"You thrive on the weird, Paxton. Here is your chance to step outside the boundaries of the normal and into the paranormal. You've been on a vision quest for some time, now. Your striving for spiritual awareness is about to come to fruition."

"Is this a vision, then?" asked Paxton.

"No, I can assure you that I am quite real. But I can help you to find your vision."

Paxton turned to Tucker asking aloud, "Can you hear all of this or am I going crazy?"

"If you're going crazy, then we're going crazy together because I can definitely hear him, too."

"Do you have a name?" asked Paxton, turning back to face the tree.

"You can call me Thorn."

"*Thorn?*" Tucker chuckled. "Why *Thorn*? You're an oak tree!"

"I am quite aware of the fact that I have no thorns," the tree replied, unamused. "Still, I find myself drawn to them, perhaps as a moth is drawn to the flame. Thorns are a recurrent theme in my dreams and in some way as yet undecipherable to me, I believe that thorns hold the key to one of my past lives."

"I don't believe in past lives," stated Tucker with confidence.

"Of course you don't, Thomas, but you will. I am going to take you both to a place where we can examine each other's past lives. Once there, I am hoping you will be able to assist me in discovering who or what I am."

"You don't know who you are?"

"Do you know who you are, Paxton? I could tell you that I am this oak tree. That would be easy enough for you to understand, grounded as you are in your illusion of time-space reality. You identify people as the bodies or the personalities they possess. Just as you identify objects by their physical forms. This tree is just the shell in which I am encased. You have a fully functioning body, but is that who you really are? When that shell has outlived its usefulness, will you cease to be, or will you find another shell in which to live?"

"I like to think that there is something after this life," admitted Paxton.

"As well you should," agreed Thorn. "I am interested in my essence, the pure energy that you would call a soul. I have not always been this tree, nor will I remain a tree for much longer. I have been able to catch glimpses of my past lives, and future ones, but I cannot seem to get close enough to examine the stories in more detail. I'm hoping that one or both of you might be able to do so."

"Is that why you *summoned* us here?" asked Tucker, emphasizing his disbelief that such a thing were even possible.

"Exactly," Thorn confirmed. "My time inside this tree grows short, but so too does your time in this reality, as you perceive it to be. We all have our parts to play in the coming events."

"What coming events?" asked Tucker.

"The End of the World!" interjected Paxton dramatically.

"You're not still preaching that, are you?" returned Tucker, turning toward him.

"Not preaching, but only because I no longer have an audience," admitted Paxton with a smile. "I still believe it's going to happen."

Ever since reading *The Late Great Planet Earth* after a Grateful Dead show in New Orleans, Paxton had been fascinated with The Apocalypse. His young mind devoured anything he could find on the subject, from the *Centuries* of Nostradamus to the Book of Revelation, though this latter had been harder to come by considering the crowd his mother ran with. He fully expected to witness humanity's impending doom, a fact he was happy to share with anyone who cared to listen, but he had never been quite ready to shout it from the rooftops.

"So now you're going to tell me that the world is coming to an end, too?" asked Tucker, sarcastically.

"I would never do that," said Thorn. "'The End of the World' is somewhat of a misnomer, don't you think? Do you seriously believe that human beings have the tools and technology with which to completely destroy the Earth? Even could you succeed in wiping out all of the life forms on Earth, new ones would eventually appear and follow their own evolutionary courses, which would probably be considerably different from the ones which have resulted in modern-day humans.

"Although it does appear that she's in for some cataclysmic changes, the Earth will come through them just fine. It's the human race you should be worried about. This planet has been around for four and a half billion years, while *homo sapiens* have been here for only a few hundred thousand, arguably. Mother Earth has little to fear from human beings. She will continue along her own evolutionary course until the sun becomes a supernova and explodes, about five billion years from now."

"Okay, take it easy, Thorn. It's only a figure of speech," Paxton apologized.

"I guess it's just a pet peeve of mine," said Thorn.

"*Trees have pet peeves?*" thought Tucker with some humor.

"This one does," Thorn responded to his unspoken commentary. Paxton found it interesting that not only was he privy to Tucker's thoughts, but he could also feel his former friend's growing anger at Thorn's continual intrusion into their minds. If Thorn were aware of Tucker's increasing resistance, however, he paid it no heed as he continued his own diatribe.

"Visionaries from many different traditions and religions have prophesied The End of the World. These prophets haven't seen the end of the world so much as the end of their own traditions and beliefs. The Book of Revelation predicts not the end of the world but the end of Christianity. Nostradamus couldn't see very far into the twenty-first century, not because there was nothing left of humanity, but because he couldn't attune to the common consciousness connecting all those who survive."

"If we're not to call it The End of the World, what should we call it?" Paxton asked. "The Apocalypse? Armageddon? The End Times?"

"Of those I'd choose the latter, but I prefer to think of the End Times as The Beginning Times. For with every ending comes a beginning, and the new beginning coming to this planet will be an amazing one. Although, as with many changes, this one won't be affected without some amount of upheaval. How about The Metamorphosis?"

"What of this metamorphosis?" Paxton continued to question. "What will it entail? Will humankind survive it?"

"As far as I can tell, yes. The current human population on Earth will be decimated during The Metamorphosis, but humankind will not be wiped out altogether. The Metamorphosis is a change, not an ending. This is a very exciting time in both the evolution of the Earth and of humankind. You, and everyone else on this planet, chose to be incarnated at this precise moment so that you could be a part of these changes, but only a small percentage of you will be able to participate in the formation of the New World Order."

"Will Tucker and I still be here?"

"Even if I knew the answer to that question, I doubt that I would tell it to you. We are all going to leave these particular physical forms behind someday, but I believe it does us more harm than good to know when that day will be. Are you afraid of dying, Paxton?"

"Yes, I'm afraid of dying. Isn't everyone? I believe in an afterlife, but that remains one of the great mysteries of this life. It could very well be that the only thing waiting for us at the end of this existence is nothingness."

"I'm not afraid to die," lied Tucker, believing in his own fallacy. "I don't know what happens to us when we die, nor do I care. The only thing I have control over is the way in which I live my life. Let the afterlife take care of itself. I'm more concerned about the fate of humankind in general. We've come so far as a race, I'd like to believe that we are not going to have that progress obliterated."

"You've come so far in some respects, but are merely infants in others. Your intellect has grown faster than your collective spirituality, which is why you're faced with destruction in the first place. The Metamorphosis will bring those two realms back into balance. Much of your architecture and technology will be destroyed. On the other hand, quantum leaps will be made in the psychic and mystic aspects of your existence. Some of this will result from the merging of the physical and spiritual realms during the coming upheaval, but most of this insight will be brought about by a new teacher come to Earth. A teacher that will unite all the peoples of the world as one and usher in a new and golden era on this planet. A being whose teachings and influence will be even more far-reaching than Jesus the Christ!"

Paxton thought about the implications of this last prediction. Anyone who could unite all of the people of the world under one ideology would be a powerful person, indeed. Even the teachings of Christ, which had evolved into the most populous world religion to date, had not succeeded in uniting all of the people of the world underneath its umbrella, though this was not for lack of effort. His train of thought was derailed by Tucker's next comment.

"You mentioned that Nostradamus couldn't see very far into the twenty-first century. Please don't tell me you're one of these Y2K fanatics!"

"Humans will weather Y2K just fine," Thorn assured him, with something akin to a chuckle. "But many of the world's prophets, both past and present, pinpoint *this* time for the birth of the next great Messiah. The 'signs of the time' are upon us."

"What signs?" questioned Paxton. "How do you know all of this?"

"All in good time, Paxton, all in good time," soothed Thorn. "It's getting late. You two had better get a move on if you want to get back down this hill in the daylight. Unless, of course, you're prepared to spend the night."

Paxton looked up from his reverie, amazed that the sun had already set behind the ridge of hills to the west. How long had he been sleeping beneath Thorn's branches?

"I'm not prepared," admitted Paxton.

"Me either," Tucker agreed. "I hadn't planned on staying this late. I don't even have a flashlight for the walk down."

"But how can we leave?" inquired Paxton.

"It's easy," offered Thorn. "You bid me goodnight and promise to come back in the morning with your camping gear so we can continue this conversation for the rest of the weekend. I'll start by telling you my life story and we can go on from there."

"I'm game if you are," Paxton agreed immediately.

"I guess so," Tucker assented somewhat more reluctantly.

"Then it's settled," Thorn confirmed. "I'll see you both up here bright and early tomorrow morning."

At this exclamation, Paxton felt the sudden emptiness in his mind caused by Thorn's withdrawal. He stretched out his hand to touch the trunk of the tree in farewell and said out loud, "Good night, Thorn."

Paxton stared at the back of his former roommate as he picked his way carefully along the narrow trail that led down to the logging road. Tucker seemed mostly unchanged in the four years since he had last seen him, although he had taken on every appearance of the lumberjack that Thorn had proclaimed him to be. He stood at a little over six feet tall, his broad shoulders and muscular back clothed, but not disguised, by a thick, red flannel shirt. His close-cropped, curly black hair was covered in a black, woollen cap, though it was not nearly cold enough to need one on this mid-October afternoon. One could easily imagine his huge hands hefting a double-edged broad-axe, though Paxton was more used to seeing them clutching a basketball.

They had met on the fieldhouse courts in the first few weeks of their freshmen year. Both of them were reasonably good at the game, Tucker because of his size and Paxton because of his quickness. They formed a fast friendship that began to extend itself to meetings off the court. By the end of their sophomore year, they had both had enough of dormitory living and decided to rent an apartment together. They chose the first one they looked at, an upstairs apartment with three bedrooms near the center of Orono.

Needing a third roommate, Paxton suggested Annie Parker, an art education major from his dormitory that he had gotten to know quite well over the previous two years. Tucker had met her a few times at various parties and had no strong objections, so the three of them moved into 58 Middle Street in the fall of their third year at college.

Tucker's appearance from out of thin air had dredged up bittersweet memories that Paxton had long since buried. Tucker was the best friend he had ever known, and Annie was the only woman he had ever really loved. Had it not ended so badly, from his point of view, he might have been able to look backward with more humor. In any event, they had all known their trio couldn't go on indefinitely. None of them escaped the pain of their parting, though at least Annie and Tucker had each other for solace, while Paxton retreated into the shell of his solitude.

Tucker was the first to speak, but only after they had broken through the underbrush and onto the wider logging road and they no longer needed their full concentration upon the placement of their footfalls.

"Was that for real?" he asked.

"Your guess is as good as mine," Paxton offered. "I would have bet that we were being filmed for *Candid Camera* except that the majority of our conversation happened only in our minds."

"And we were hearing the same things!" Tucker agreed.

"And we could also read each other's thoughts! It was just too weird. Are you going to come back up here again tomorrow?"

"We promised Thorn, didn't we? I have some camping gear at home."

"I could pack us some food. I just went grocery shopping yesterday."

After a silence which went on long enough to become uncomfortable Paxton changed the subject asking, "How long have you been back in town?"

"About a month," Tucker responded. "My grandmother got me this job with B & G Lumber. Apparently she and the owner are old friends."

"What does Annie think about being back in Maine?" broached Paxton

At the mention of her name Tucker stopped dead in his tracks and turned to Paxton with a quizzical expression on his countenance. He asked, "You don't know, do you?"

"Know what?"

"Annie is dead. She and our son Camden died in a plane crash about a year ago."

"What?!?" Paxton, who had continued on a few steps now wheeled around and looked up at Tucker, who seemed even taller since he was standing slightly uphill.

"Flight 396 from Portland to Raleigh. You didn't hear about it? It was all over the news." "I don't get the news," admitted Paxton.

"Of course you don't."

"Tucker, I'm so sorry," Paxton said, reaching his hand out to touch Tucker's elbow.

"It's old news, now," grunted Tucker, shrugging him off to continue his descent. Paxton followed him for a few steps before stopping again at a sudden realization.

"I saw her, you know," he declared. "It must have been the day before she died. She and Camden came up to Orono for the afternoon. We had a picnic down at Webster Park and took Camden for a swim in the Stillwater."

Tucker stopped and turned in one swift motion, the jealousy plain upon on his face. Paxton almost flinched as those angry eyes came to bear upon his face.

"Don't look at me like that!" Paxton said, his own anger galloping forward in challenge. "What do you have to be jealous about? Annie was completely in love with you. I must admit, when she called me out of the blue like that, I half hoped she was dissatisfied with your marriage, but that just wasn't the case."

Tucker deflated like a balloon at this comment. Paxton watched the anger melt from his face before Tucker hung his head down, breaking their eye contact.

"Did she say anything about me that day?" asked Tucker sheepishly, his gaze once again fixed upon his hiking boots.

"She said a lot about you," Paxton answered, his anger also receding. "She said you were stubborn and bull-headed and she told me how mad she was that you didn't come up here with them to visit your parents. On the other hand, she also told me how completely happy she was in both marriage and motherhood. I could see that happiness for myself in the way her voice became animated and her face lit up when she talked about you and Camden. But the truth is, I did most of the talking. Annie wanted to know everything about Kenya and my travels afterward. I don't usually have such a rapt audience for my Peace Corps stories so I took full advantage."

Paxton remembered that afternoon as if it were yesterday. They had sat on a blanket in Webster Park for hours, drinking wine and talking. Camden had worn himself out swimming and running around and took a long nap under the shade of a maple tree as they talked.

Paxton had prepared himself for a wide range of negative emotions, from jealousy to anger to sadness, but what he experienced was a meeting between two old friends. Their conversation had been open and easy and as they renewed their friendship Paxton wished that Tucker had come with her to Maine. There was no mention of the love he still felt for her, but it was understood between them. She kissed him on the cheek when she left, and he had hugged her until she whispered in his ear, "I have to go."

Annie and Camden flew out of Portland the following day. Paxton was as oblivious to the plane crash as he was to any other noteworthy news. He didn't own a television, nor did he read the newspaper, preferring to live in the peace of his ignorance. The world was going to hell, as far as he was concerned, and it depressed him to keep track of its decline on a daily basis. Annie told him she would contact him again, after she had talked to Tucker. When the weeks turned into months and there was still no word from her, Paxton had figured that Tucker put a stop to their renewed acquaintance.

The two men continued the rest of their descent in silence until they were almost back to Route 15. They reached Tucker's truck first, parked in the gully off the dirt road at a spot wide enough so that he did not have to worry about obstructing access to the hill.

"Where are you staying?" asked Paxton, as Tucker unlocked the cab and deposited his backpack upon the front seat.

"With my grandma for now," Tucker responded, "until I can find a place of my own."

"Why don't you come over for dinner tonight?" offered Paxton, running his fingers along the

B & G Lumber logo on the passenger side door. "We could have a few beers and you can meet Claire."

"Is this a girlfriend?" asked Tucker, raising both eyebrows.

"I guess you could call her that," Paxton admitted, "but we've been taking it pretty slowly."

"Why not?" Tucker agreed. "It is Friday night and I could definitely use those beers after what just happened."

"Yeah," began Paxton with some hesitation, "about that. I've been thinking that I might not mention this to Claire just yet, until we figure out what's really going on."

"I'm down with that. I might just want to forget about it myself. Where are you living these days?"

"I'm back at UMO, working on my PhD, if you can believe that," answered Paxton. "I'm renting a house on Parker Street, not far from our old place. If you go down Mill Street to the end and make a right onto Broadway, it's the first street you come to on the left. My place is the third house on the right."

"It'll take me at least an hour to get there. First I need to return this truck and get my own."

"Sounds good," said Paxton, patting the door of the truck and backing away. "See you then."

THREE

Do You Want To Be My Friend?

A child approaches another fearlessly,
"Do you want to be my friend?" she asks.
I can't hear the reply.
But they walk off together, hand in hand.
Lost in their own little play space.

If only it were that easy
        for the rest of us.
I imagine myself walking up
        to a complete stranger.
"Do you want to be my friend?" I'd ask.
What would he say?
What would he do?
Would he laugh at me?
Hit me, or take my hand?
Would he be afraid of me, or
        would I be afraid of him?

I cannot act in such a way.
I have too many
convenient categories
To file away the strangers
I brush up against.
Race. Age. Weight. Sex.
Religion. Intelligence.
My daughter has only one—size.
She has found another little person.
"Do you want to be my friend?"

As Tucker's truck cruised along I-95 on autopilot, his mind was awash with memories, questions and conundrums. Had he somehow imagined today's encounter with Paxton and Thorn? Of all possible explanations, this was the most troubling to him, for it meant that he must be going insane. He had never before questioned his own sanity and did not really know how to proceed in that direction. He felt perfectly sane in all other aspects of his life. Did insanity come upon a person all at once as a result of some upheaval in one's life, or did it work its way into the subconscious slowly and insidiously, like rust overtaking iron exposed to the weather? He supposed the latter was more likely, and also less comforting.

Could he have dreamed the afternoon away, lying in the shade of the old, oak tree atop Blueberry Hill? That was also certainly possible, though if it were true, it was a dream unlike any other he had ever dreamt. He discounted this explanation also, for it still pointed in the direction of his mental faculties gone awry. He did not remember either falling asleep or waking up beneath the tree, and he had not slept away a whole afternoon since he was in college.

Was it some sort of practical joke orchestrated by Paxton? Could he have hidden a two-way radio transmitter somewhere in the tree? No, Thorn had known too many of the intimate details of his life for that to be true. He had never told Paxton the story of George Hostetler and the Dumbo valentine. Nor did he keep a journal where someone could have read his innermost thoughts. And that still wouldn't explain the mental communication between he and his old friend.

Was Thorn for real, then? Had he actually come into contact with a soul encased in a tree and spent the afternoon in conversation with it? He found this hard to believe, as well, but he liked this explanation a whole lot better than any which cast aspersions upon his sanity. He decided to proceed on the basis that Thorn was real, and reserve further judgement until he and Paxton returned to Blueberry Hill in the morning. Having drawn this conclusion, his mind drifted backward to a time when he drove this stretch of highway toward Orono as a younger man.

Tucker received his degree in Forestry from the University of Maine in 1994, but he began his college career as a Mechanical Engineering major, at the bequest of his father. He could still hear his father's voice in the back of his mind preaching, "An engineering degree will put you on the first rung of the ladder of corporate management."

Tucker quickly discovered, however, that he was neither mechanical nor engineering and he changed his major to forestry at the end of his sophomore year. His father had cut him off financially as a result of this decision, but by then Tucker had already discovered that he could, with hard work and a little help from Uncle Sam, put himself through school. He and his father had yet to mend that fence, though he had to admit that his father had been right about one thing—jobs for foresters were few and far between.

Thoughts of college were always inexorably linked to Paxton and Annie. He had proposed to her on the very spot that he had chanced upon Paxton this very afternoon. She accepted without hesitation if not without reservations, and they had made love for hours, their cries drowned by the tree's wildly flailing limbs, animated by a gale which seemed to have arisen from their passion itself. Afterward they lay half-asleep in each other's arms, neither of them wanting to go home and face Paxton, who cared just as deeply for Annie.

As they had feared, Paxton was crushed by the news. He announced shortly thereafter that he was joining the Peace Corps and he was in Africa on the day they were married.

After graduation they moved to Annie's hometown of Raleigh, North Carolina. Tucker had once asked her why she had come all the way to Maine to go to college. She had replied in her slight Southern accent, "Art is a state of mind. It can be studied anywhere. I wanted to see what all the fuss over you damn Yankees was all about. Maine is about as damned as you can get!"

Annie had fallen in love with Maine's rugged beauty, but she could never get used to its bitterly cold winters, which sometimes held on so long they relegated spring to three weeks instead of her rightful three months.

As a Maine Yankee in Sir Walter Raleigh's Court, Tucker had about as much a chance of getting hired by the North Carolina Forestry Service as he did of usurping Jesse Helms from his seat on the Senate. Instead he took a job as a landscape architect, which in this case was really a glorified title for 'mower of lawns.'

Regardless of his title, Tucker found that he liked his job. He was outside all day long and the exercise kept him in great shape. He found that there was no end to the variation with which he could mow the same lawn, and he enjoyed watching the wide variety of lush, Southern flora grow green and thick during the long summer months.

He especially loved the magnolia trees, with their thick, waxy leaves and pungent white flowers. He would take the large magnolia blooms home to Annie at every opportunity during the late spring and early summer. They would last for a couple of days in a bowl of water, where they did battle with the fragrances emanating from dog and diaper. Tucker also discovered that magnolias are great climbing trees. He spent many a lunch break wedged between trunk and branch, twenty feet above his various implements of urban ground vegetation containment and control.

He could even rationalize, when he cared to think on such things, that he was somehow making use of his forestry degree. "This is field work," he would delude himself into believing, as he pushed his lawn mower down one long row after another, sweat streaming through every pore of his body, adding its moisture to the already overly humid summer air.

Annie taught art at Millbrook Elementary School, and they got by well enough on both of their incomes, even managing to salt away nearly enough money to travel to someplace exotic on the honeymoon they had never really taken. That particular nest egg was fried when Camden came into their lives. He was an accident, but not really a surprise, the night stand housing their condoms residing just a little too far out of reach on many occasions.

Annie had picked out the name Camden, despite Tucker's reservations about naming their son after a seaside town in Maine. Annie explained that Camden was a Gaelic name meaning 'from the winding valley,' which could refer to the Crabtree Valley where he was born. Tucker had joked that he preferred to think of Camden's point of origin as being the winding valley between Annie's legs. She had laughed out loud, and he had allowed himself to be won over.

Tucker made the transition to fatherhood without hesitation, forming a deep bond with his son which he had never felt with his own father. He stayed home with Camden for the first year of his life and the two of them were inseparable. Annie liked to tease him, complaining that the only reason they kept her around was because of their affinity for her breasts, which had grown to twice their normal size during her pregnancy and stayed that way until Camden was finished nursing. Money was tight during this time, but there was always food on the dinner table. This was sufficient for Tucker, since everything he loved was seated around that table every evening.

He had gone back to work with strangely mixed emotions. It felt great to be outside and exercising again, but he hated having to drop Camden off at day care every morning. The three of them quickly filled in the niches of their daily routines, however, and three years passed in the blink of an eye, or so it seemed to Tucker now. They had been the happiest years of his life, a happiness which ended as abruptly as a slamming door when steel met flesh and bones in a field outside of RDU International Airport.

Tucker had yet to forgive himself for not being on that plane with Annie and Camden. She had begged him to take her back to Maine so that Camden could meet his grandparents. Tucker had refused. He and his father hadn't spoken since college, though he did talk regularly with his mother on the phone when he knew his father was at work. He told Annie that if his parents really wanted to see Camden, they could come down to North Carolina.

Annie's decision to take Camden up there herself prompted the biggest fight of their married life. Although they had reconciled after a fashion on the night before she and Camden left, the tension between them was still palpable as he drove them to the airport the following morning. He hadn't even told her he loved her as she kissed him goodbye. The last image he had of his lost family was of Camden turning around to wave to him as they disappeared through the boarding gate.

To dispel this parting sequence, which had already played across his mind countless times, Tucker concentrated on happier memories. He tried to picture Annie lying there beside him in the afterglow of their lovemaking. He visualized her long red hair cascading across his broad chest and her thin fingers interlocked in his own. She had always appeared so petite, so fragile next to his muscular frame. Possessing a deep well of inner strength and a boundless supply of energy, she would never have been described as fragile by anyone who had spent five minutes with her. But she proved to be just as fragile as the other one hundred and forty-seven passengers aboard flight 396 which came to rest several hundred yards from the runway it should have touched down upon.

Though he wasn't a passenger on that flight, Tucker still hadn't recovered from the crash. He had spent the next several months in an alcoholic fog, unable to muster the energy for anything more strenuous than the short walk to Mitch's Tavern each afternoon. He would still be sitting on the corner stool, staring at his own sour expression in the mirror behind the bar, if it weren't for the paranormal encounter he had experienced one late summer evening. To this day he still wasn't sure whether it was a vision, a dream or a hallucination, but he and Annie had spoken in their bedroom that night.

"I forgive you, Friar Tuck" she had said, using her favorite pet name for him. "And I love you."

"I love you, too!" Tucker had wailed, tears flowing freely from his suddenly sober eyes.

"If you truly loved me," she had responded, "you would stop acting like an ass. It's time you started living again. You need to find your smile."

They talked of other things, but this was the only part Tucker could remember with absolute clarity. The encounter was too insubstantial to prove the supernatural, but too real to pass off as a dream. Regardless, Tucker made up his mind the following day to leave Raleigh for good.

The actual departure had taken considerably longer than had the decision. Tucker sold or gave away most of the possessions he and Annie had accumulated. He said his goodbyes to the friends he had neglected since her death, and the memories he hoped to leave behind. After clearing his debts, Tucker took what was left of the settlement from the airlines, loaded their little red truck with his clothes and a few pictures and headed West.

Tucker began to come alive again after crossing the mighty Mississippi River. He fell in love with the Rocky Mountains and the Pacific Northwest, and eventually ventured as far north as Alaska. After traveling about as far away from Maine as he could get in his truck, Tucker turned around finally, and headed slowly back to the only place he had ever considered home. He had come back to his roots, and to the best friend he had ever known, apart from Annie.

Tucker did not resist the tears running relay races across his cheeks. There had been a time when he would have struggled to keep them from flowing. One of the unwanted legacies his father had left him was the notion that real men don't cry. It was Annie who had taught him how to cry, both in her life and in her death. He hastened to wipe them away with the palm of his hand, however, when he realized he was coasting down Middle Street and would soon be pulling into Paxton's driveway.

The apartment was exactly where Paxton had said it would be. He parked his car behind a maroon, Subaru wagon with a Gore 2000 bumper sticker in the corner of its rear window. After extricating himself from the cab of his Truck, he walked the short distance to the porch. He knocked loudly upon the screen door in the hopes he would be heard above the sound of Jerry Garcia spilling through the open door and windows.

"Is that you Tucker?" Paxton called from some inner room not visible from Tucker's vantage point. "Come on in."

As the screen door banged shut behind him he heard the patter of small footsteps on the hardwood floor. He turned his head in time to see a small girl running toward him from the opposite corner of the living room, her wispy blonde hair trailing out behind her.

"Are you my new daddy?" she asked enthusiastically, crashing into his leg and grasping it in her baby bear hug. Tucker picked her up and held her at arm's length a moment, before sitting her down in the crook of one arm.

"What have we here?" he asked with dramatic flair. The girl bit her finger and looked at him shyly from beneath her long, brown eyelashes.

"Oh, so now you're shy," he added, tousling her hair with his free hand.

"Elizabeth, he is not your daddy!" said the more mature female voice entering the room. The voice was followed by a tall woman in a floral print dress. Her long, black hair was braided loosely down her back and she wore an uneasy smile as she strode into the room.

"I am so sorry," she apologized. "Elizabeth is a little confused right now."

The girl turned to him and smiled. "I've been waiting for you," she said.

"You have, have you? What's your name?"

"Beth, and I'm three years old," she answered, thrusting three fingers at him for emphasis.

"Nice to meet you, Beth. My name is Tucker, and you must be Claire," he said, extending his free hand toward her. "Paxton didn't tell me you had such a beautiful little girl."

"She's my niece," commented Claire. "But now I'm her legal guardian."

"My mommy and daddy are in heaven," interrupted Beth. "Aunt Claire is my new mommy."

"Her parents died in a car crash a few months ago," Claire explained.

"I'm so sorry to hear that," Tucker said, looking down upon Beth with pity.

She smiled up at him, and then turned to Claire with a puzzled expression on her tiny face, "He's not my new daddy?"

"No, Elizabeth, he's not your new daddy. I told you I'm not married anymore."

"Do you want to be my friend?" asked Beth, turning back to Tucker.

"Of course I'll be your friend, sweetie," he answered, setting her on the floor. "What do you want to do?"

"There's cookies in the kitchen," she offered.

"Let's go!" Tucker agreed enthusiastically, following her down a narrow hallway toward the rear of the small house.

—

Claire Harrison had wanted to be a lawyer since she was a young girl. Her grandfather was a lawyer and she had always been impressed by his stately mannerisms and expressive dignity, qualities she attributed to his profession. She would sneak downstairs late at night during his visits to listen from the next room as he regaled her parents with trial stories covering a vast array of criminal acts from shoplifting to murder. After she had grown older and expressed her interest in the law, he had even begun to take her to court with him during her summer breaks, but only when he wasn't prosecuting particularly perverse criminals.

While other children played post office or doctor, Claire and her best friend Molly pretended to be lawyers on opposing sides of a trial. Brothers and sisters, when they could be talked into it, served as clients and witnesses. Teddy bears proved superior in these roles, however, because they could be counted on to do exactly as they were told. Stuffed animals also stuffed the jury box, but it was Claire's mom who usually decided the outcome of the trials. Eventually she grew weary of the inevitable fight her decisions caused and she retired, or else she was promoted to the Supreme Court.

Molly went on to become the mother of six in their hometown of Yarmouth, but Claire pursued her dream with the single-mindedness with which she tackled every challenge thrust upon her. She was awarded a partial scholarship to Harvard Law School and paid the rest of her tuition through the tips she earned as a waitress at a high-priced restaurant in downtown Boston. She also amassed a few student loans, which she managed to pay back within the first few years of her employment as a Public Defender in Portland.

Claire hadn't become a lawyer for the money, but rather because of some vague notion that her life could make a real difference in society as a whole. It was for this reason, and because she wanted to be closer to home, that she had turned down several lucrative offers from well-established law firms upon graduation and went to work for the state of Maine.

She entered into her new role as defender of the weak and downtrodden with great energy and enthusiasm, but it wasn't long before she began to grow disillusioned with her job. Finding creative ways to keep Portland's criminals out of jail did not satisfy her hunger for social justice. She became increasingly dissatisfied with her work, and by extension with her life, which was her work.

She met Michael Carson in a bar near her office on Congress Street, after a long day of soul-searching. A former client had requested her services that morning, after he was arrested for the rape and murder of a thirteen year old girl. Scarcely a year had passed since she had plea-bargained his sentence down to one year plus time already served, for the rape of a fifteen year old girl. Though there had been a preponderance of circumstantial evidence, the girl could not identify him in a line-up, nor were her parents anxious to have their daughter become the focus of a high profile rape trial. He had been out of jail barely two months before Claire found herself in the unenviable position of defending this man again, though this time his list of offenses included murder.

Claire rarely drank alcohol, so she was already feeling the effects of her two glasses of wine when Michael took the bar stool next to hers. They quickly discovered they had something in common as Michael was also a lawyer. She was immediately attracted to his rugged good looks and did not resist his attempts to draw her into conversation.

On the contrary, by the time she finished her third glass of wine, she had told him not only about her involvement in this most recent case, but also about her growing disillusionment with her role in the justice system. She admitted that her efforts more often resulted in the release of guilty criminals due to technicalities, than in ensuring the freedom of the innocent. She revealed that her guilty conscience had been the cause of many a sleepless night. Their conversation was so relaxed and natural that it seemed to Claire as if they had been friends for a long time.

Michael spoke passionately of the environment and the need for people to come forward in its defense before it was damaged beyond repair. He told Claire of an organization he had just founded called The Society for the Protection of America's Wilderness and Nature, or SPAWN. He jokingly asked her if she would like to come work for him, as he was going to need some good lawyers to go after the companies and industries which were the most flagrant polluters of New England's air and water. Though she laughed at his proposal, she couldn't help but be impressed by his knowledge of the law and his passion for his cause.

Their conversation continued over dinner at a nearby restaurant, before Claire asked Michael to take her home. They saw each other every night for the next week, and within a month she had indeed quit her job and joined Michael's team.

They were married that same year and SPAWN became the focal point of their marriage. Claire worked to expose those companies in violation of federal anti-pollution laws with the same tireless energy which she had once injected into her role as public defender. The difference was that now she had found a cause she could sink her teeth into, and she worked every day alongside a man whom she respected, admired and loved.

They were very happily married for almost five years, before Michael began to press her about having children. It was not something that they had talked much about in their first few years of marriage. When the subject had come up, they had both agreed that they might like to have children *someday*, but they were too busy to even consider becoming parents at the present time. That *someday* had come sooner for Michael than it did for Claire. It was not that Claire didn't want to have children, but she wondered where she would ever find the time to be both a mother and a lawyer, and she certainly was not going to give up her career to become a homemaker. Claire finally relented, and the tension in their marriage vanished.

Now that they were actively trying to create a baby, their lovemaking increased in frequency, if not quality. They took every opportunity their busy schedules allowed them to make love. The office became their love nest, as they usually worked late into the night there, and returned home in the early morning hours exhausted and wanting nothing more than to grab a few hours of uninterrupted sleep in their bed. No sooner had the last secretary gone home on many nights, than they were naked on the couch in Michael's office or a desktop, trying to make Claire's belly grow.

Her womb never did get any bigger, however, and after a year of trying to conceive, they went to the doctor to see if anything was wrong. After several months of testing, it was determined that Claire was sterile. Her doctor concluded the culprit was chlamydia, a bacterial infection she had contracted during college. She hadn't experienced any symptoms in the early stages of the infection and she had waited too long to seek treatment for the symptoms once they had become evident.

Michael was crestfallen and Claire was surprised at the depth of her own disappointment. Michael tried to be as supportive as possible, but grew increasingly distant as the months passed. Claire mentioned adoption, but he wanted no part of that. They consoled themselves with their work, and the office walls no longer heard either their cries of passion or their laughter.

One night Claire came home earlier than expected from a trial in Connecticut. Michael was not at home, and she walked the few blocks to the office to surprise him with the news that she had won the trial, which involved the dumping of toxic substances into the Connecticut River by a large chemical corporation.

His office light was on, and Claire let herself into the building as quietly as she could. She opened the door to his office to find him lying naked on his couch in post-coital bliss with their receptionist. They jumped up and scurried around the office for their clothes, but Claire merely closed the door softly and walked slowly out of the building and into the night. She walked the dark streets of Portland for many hours before coming home to find Michael waiting for her at their kitchen table.

"Claire . . ." he fumbled, "I'm sorry that you had to find out about us this way, but Sheila and I have fallen in love . . . We plan to be married . . . I want a divorce."

Claire cut him off with outstretched hand, as if he were oncoming traffic and she was a cop at the intersection of their lives.

"I don't want to hear anything more about you and Sheila," she said. "I'll grant you a divorce on one condition. You turn SPAWN over to me and the two of you move far away from here."

"But Claire . . ." he began.

"That's all I want from you, Michael. You can start a new organization wherever it is you end up."

Michael reluctantly agreed to her terms, and he and the receptionist moved out to California, where he found other wars to wage. They had already had two children in the three years since the divorce. Claire still maintained contact with him, mostly for professional reasons. As the years passed, she found that she could forgive him, though she couldn't share in the happiness he had found in the family she couldn't give to him.

Claire took over the reins of SPAWN, which had grown considerably since she had cast her lot beneath its auspices. At its inception, SPAWN consisted only of she and Michael and one secretary. Today it boasted ten full-time employees and a host of volunteers. As there were now two other lawyers on her staff, Claire's focus had shifted to the necessary, if tedious, job of administration and fund-raising. The focus of SPAWN had shifted as well. While her lawyers still argued cases against the destroyers of the environment, most of the organization's time and energy was spent in educating the public concerning the possibility of impending environmental crisis and in lobbying both the state and federal government to pass more stringent laws to try to prevent that crisis.

SPAWN also changed locale in the first few months after the divorce. There were too many memories of Michael housed inside the walls of the old office, which had begun to close in as SPAWN continued to expand. Claire took her headquarters north to Bangor. She had considered Augusta, where she would be closer to the state legislature, but chose Bangor instead, because of its proximity to the University of Maine, where she hoped to recruit volunteers.

Also, Claire had decided her next battle would be waged against the clear-cutting which was systematically destroying the northern Maine wilderness, and Bangor was closer to the scene of the crime.

It was at the university that Claire met Paxton. She recruited him, actually, from her booth outside the Student Union on Earth Day. He had agreed to help disseminate information on campus. Claire suspected that his willingness to help stemmed more from his attraction to her than from any deep commitment to her cause, but she would take the help where she could get it. He worked for her intermittently over a few months before he got up the nerve to ask her out, and it was almost another year before she agreed. Their first date was a picnic at the ornamental gardens on campus, and it was the first date Claire had been on since her divorce.

Claire had been determined not to let anything serious come of their dating. She found Paxton attractive, intelligent and funny, but she still wasn't ready to become romantically involved with him or anyone else. As she looked across the table at him now, she realized for the first time how deep her feelings for him had grown. She had become more involved in their relationship than she cared to admit, either to him or to herself.

Her gaze lingered on Paxton only a moment before her thoughts were interrupted by the laughter coming from Paxton's other two dinner guests. Claire joined in the infectious laughter as the child who had become the daughter she could not conceive, and a man employed by the environmental rapist she was currently trying to bring down, held a conversation about Barney the dinosaur.

"Paxton tells me you work for B & G Lumber," said Claire between mouthfuls of the vegetable stir-fry Paxton had concocted for dinner. They sat cross-legged on the floor around the coffee table in the living room because there weren't enough chairs for the four of them to eat at the kitchen table.

"That's right," answered Tucker, looking up from Beth, who had insisted on sitting in his lap through most of dinner. Their almost untouched plates of food languished in front of them. Beth had eaten too many cookies to be hungry, and Tucker was clearly enchanted by the little girl.

"I've only been there a few weeks," he continued. "I'm still trying to get a feel for the job."

"What do you do there?" she pressed.

"Not much of anything, yet," Tucker laughed. "I spent the first two weeks in the office doing paperwork and I finally got out into the woods these past couple of days. I've been trying to get a feel for the lay of the land at the next big job site."

"Are you a tree-cutter?"

"No. Not yet, anyway. I've been charged with making sure the tree-cutters are nice to the environment. It seems some tree-*huggers* are suing the company over the rights to log that particular forest."

"Were you aware of the fact that you're dining with the chief tree-hugger?" questioned Claire flatly, the sudden animosity in her voice taking Tucker aback. "My organization is going to stop you from destroying that forest."

"Paxton neglected to mention that," stammered Tucker, glaring at Paxton, who had taken renewed interest in the stir-fry on the plate in front of him.

"Oh, did I not tell you what Claire does for a living?" he asked, feigning innocence.

"Must've slipped your mind," Tucker commented.

"Nor did he tell me very much about you," said Claire, looking across the table at Paxton.

"What are these?" broke in Beth from across the room. She had squirmed out of Tucker's lap as his attention was diverted and was exploring the confines of the room. She stood in front of several strange-looking sculptures, huddled together beneath the window. Each one was mounted on a piece of plywood with a small plaque in one corner bearing its name.

"Those are my garbage sculptures," Paxton exclaimed. He jumped up to show Beth his creations, only too happy to change the topic of conversation.

Paxton had proudly shown Claire his sculptures the first time she had seen his apartment. They were made from materials that most people throw away, but Paxton had explained that he had learned to recycle everything in Kenya, and was still having a hard time parting with his trash now that he had returned stateside. 'The Tree of Life' was made from cardboard cereal boxes with aluminum cans painted red for apples. 'The Castle' was sculpted completely from egg cartons, except for the plastic figurines that stood atop its ramparts. Beth picked up one of the knights for a closer look.

"That one is extra special because it has a bunch of little people living in it," Paxton pointed out as she handed him the knight. "Have you found the princess yet?"

As Paxton sat down next to Beth and opened the castle door, Claire turned back to Tucker and asked, "Just how do you propose to be *nice* to the environment as you clear-cut all of its trees?"

"We replace the trees," countered Tucker, on the defensive for the moment.

"But you don't replace the forest," interrupted Claire. "Your breeding ground is planted in nice straight lines of white pine and spruce, destroying the biodiversity necessary to support wildlife. And before the roots of those trees grow deep enough to prevent it, the top layer of soil is washed away by the spring melt, further hampering the forest's ability to regenerate itself and choking the fish in nearby lakes and streams."

"Take it easy," said Tucker, glancing hopefully at Paxton, who was ignoring him. "I've only just started working there."

"Sorry," said Claire, who realized she was gearing up for a familiar lecture. "But you must realize that the company you work for is causing irreparable harm to Maine's forests."

"I'll admit that a selective cut is a much better method for removing the trees, but aren't they well within their rights to clear-cut on privately owned land? Correct me if I'm wrong, but didn't the people of Maine vote a few years back not to ban clear-cutting?"

"That decision was bought and paid for by the big paper companies," Claire responded. "When it looked like we might actually succeed in banning clear-cutting in Maine, they sat up and took notice. If Maine banned clear-cutting, then other states might follow suit, and they couldn't let that happen. They scared the people of Maine into thinking that most of the jobs in the lumber industry would be gone if our referendum passed."

"The reason it didn't get passed," interjected Paxton, "was because Jonathan Carter was unwilling to compromise. The wording of his proposal was too restrictive and all-encompassing. He probably could've gotten the people of Maine to vote for a ban on clear-cutting land owned by the large paper conglomerates, but his proposal also covered the few acres of timberland owned by the private landowner, and no one is going to vote to let the government tell them what they can or cannot do on their own property."

"What is the big deal, anyway?" asked Tucker. "The northern Maine wilderness is vast and almost limitless."

"That's exactly what the paper companies would like everyone to believe," Claire pointed out. "But there are very definite limits, which will be reached sooner than you think at the present rate the forests are being clear-cut. And the tract of land your company is about to clear-cut is not in the northern Maine wilderness but south of Guilford, right here in our own backyard!"

"Why are you guys fighting?" asked Beth, who had walked over to the coffee table and was standing between them.

"We're not fighting," answered Claire. "We're just having a discussion about trees."

"Oh, I love trees!" she said. "Can we go for a walk?"

"I don't know," Claire replied. "I have to help clean up these dishes."

"Please!"

"I'll take her for a walk," said Tucker, "if it's okay with you, Claire."

"Yeah!" shouted Beth.

"I don't know," Claire repeated. Claire was not so sure she wanted Beth to go off alone with this man whom she had just met and who worked for her enemy. She arched her eyebrows at Paxton, but didn't receive the support she was looking for.

"Let her go," he said. "They'll be fine."

"All right," Claire relented, "but it'll have to be a short one. It's getting pretty close to your bed time."

"Okay, Mommy," said Beth, giving her a big hug.

After Claire had bundled her into her jacket, Beth grabbed Tucker's hand and started pulling him toward the door.

"Where are we gonna go?" asked Beth, as they were walking out the door.

"I thought we'd go down to the river . . ." was the last thing Claire heard before the door closed behind them.

"Where did you pick him up?" asked Claire, as they gathered the dinner dishes and carried them into the kitchen.

"Tucker was my best friend in college," Paxton replied. "You really could've been nicer to him, you know."

"I *was* being nice to him! Whenever I think about those trees they're going to cut down it makes me furious. How did he end up taking a job with B & G of all places?"

"He just moved back to Maine. Apparently his grandmother knows one of the owners of the company and somehow got the job for him. I got the feeling that he's not that excited about the clear-cut either."

"But he works for the people who are going to do it, and that makes him part of the problem, friend or no friend."

Claire took a seat at the kitchen table as Paxton filled the sink with hot water to wash the dishes. Noticing the clenched teeth and hard eyes of the woman she saw reflected in the kitchen window, Claire forced herself to relax. She drained the rest of the wine in her glass and attempted to change the subject.

"I'm a little worried about the two of them taking a walk so late," she mentioned, not wanting to come right out and say she didn't trust Tucker.

"They'll be fine," answered Paxton. "Tucker is great with kids. He used to have a little boy himself."

"He used to?"

"His wife Annie and their son Camden died in an airplane crash about a year ago."

"I didn't know that," stated Claire flatly. Having recently experienced the death of her sister she felt sudden empathy for Tucker and regretted her harsh tone from their earlier conversation.

"How could you?" asked Paxton.

Claire rose from the table and grabbed the dish towel from the handle on the oven door. She began to dry the dishes and they worked together in silence. Paxton glanced sidelong at her a number of times, but Claire did not return his gaze. Her thoughts were on her sister, Hannah, and the funeral she had attended for her in Chicago this past summer.

"So you're a mom, now," Paxton said finally, breaking Claire's self-hypnotic state.

Claire didn't answer, but set the dish towel down on the countertop and began to weep. Paxton gathered her into his arms. All of the hardness was gone from her now, as she yielded to his embrace and rested her head on his shoulder, crying softly.

"Let's leave the rest of these dishes," he said, gently leading her into the living room. "I'll get them later."

Once they were seated comfortably next to each other on the couch, Claire regurgitated all of the anxiety she had swallowed over the past two weeks. "What am I going to do? I don't know anything about being a mother! I'm ecstatic to have Beth with me, but I'm scared, too. It's such a huge responsibility. What if John's parents are right? What if I am unfit to be a mother? What if I screw this up?"

"You're not going to screw anything up," Paxton soothed. "You'll be a fine mother. You just have to get used to the idea. It's all so new to you right now."

When she had calmed down somewhat, Paxton prodded, "Tell me all about Chicago. How did you end up with Beth? I didn't even know you were being considered for custody."

"Neither did I! It came as quite a shock to me, too! They named me as legal guardian for Elizabeth in the event that something should happen to both of them."

"What did happen to them? You didn't say too much about the funeral when you came back this summer. I figured you didn't want to talk about it, so I didn't press you."

"It was awful," Claire replied, taking his hand. "They were killed in a car accident. No other cars were involved as far as anyone knows. They skidded off the road during a thunder storm and hit a tree. John was driving. They had a double funeral, and both sides of the family were there. In some bizarre way it reminded me of their wedding, even down to the crying. All of my sisters were there. They started bickering almost as soon as the funeral was over. I had Elizabeth to shield me from it for the most part. She clung to me all through the funeral, and the reception afterward."

"Why didn't you bring Beth back with you after the funeral?"

"John's parent's suppressed the will. His sister found out about it and turned the will over to the courts. Apparently his parents wanted to raise Elizabeth themselves. They still do, but they don't dare take me to court now, after trying to keep the will a secret. They tried to convince me I was not ready to be a mother, instead. It almost worked, too."

"That's ridiculous," scoffed Paxton. "You're going to be a great mom!"

"I wish I could share your confidence," Claire smiled at him as she began to list her weaknesses. "I'm divorced and I have almost no experience with children. I'm way too busy with my work to take care of a three-year-old child. I don't even have any toys in my house!"

"I was all ready to give her up to his parents before they pushed me too far. The more they told me how unsuitable a parent I would make, the more I wanted to become one. And then there was Elizabeth, following me everywhere like a shadow and calling me Mommy. Someone must have told her about the will before I ever got there."

"I think it's cute that she already calls you Mommy."

"Me too," Claire confessed, "but there's also something very strange about it. Elizabeth accepted me so easily, both at the funeral and on this last visit to Chicago, even though she hardly knows me. I was her godmother, but the last time I saw her was well over a year before the funeral and I'm pretty sure she doesn't remember that."

"Well, you're pretty easy to like," Paxton said, moving closer to her on the couch.

"I don't know a whole lot about three-year-olds," Claire responded, ignoring his advances, "but it seems to me that she has adjusted to the loss of her parents much too easily to be natural. I'm afraid she's repressing her feelings, but I don't know what to do about it. Maybe I should make an appointment for her with a child psychologist."

"Maybe you should make an appointment for yourself with a mathematician," he commented, finally gaining her full attention. "I missed you. And I was kind of hurt that you didn't call me while you were gone."

"I'm sorry," she replied, putting her hand on his knee. "I had so many things that I needed to sort out, and I didn't want to burden you with them. I missed you, too."

Paxton ran the fingers of one hand through the hair at her temple. She leaned toward him and their lips met tentatively, before Claire reached her arms behind his back and pulled him closer to her. She had missed Paxton more than she would care to admit. Now that she found herself safely enfolded within his arms, she was able to relax for the first time in weeks.

Paxton's tongue parted her lips as he leaned forward and lowered her gently back onto the well-worn sofa. He followed her body with his own, cradling her beneath him as he supported himself on his elbows. They were still locked in this embrace when they heard Beth's voice outside, followed by the tramping of Tucker's boots upon the wooden porch. Claire pushed Paxton forcefully from her and onto the floor. They both scrambled quickly into sitting positions, Paxton stretching his feet out under the coffee table and resting his back against the opposite side of the couch from where Claire now sat.

"We went over a bridge with train tracks!" said Beth excitedly, running across the room and into Claire's arms.

"You took her over the trestle?" asked Claire incredulously, jumping out of her seat. "What are you, crazy?"

Paxton had taken Claire there once. It was an old steel railroad bridge across the Stillwater River. She had crossed it fearfully, clinging to Paxton's arm as they stepped from one railroad tie to another. A train came just as they reached the other side, and she had refused to walk back across, making him take her the long way home across the roadway bridge further upriver, which at least had a sidewalk attached to it for pedestrians.

"I carried her across on my shoulders," admitted Tucker, chagrined. "It's not a big deal. Trains rarely come through here at this time of day. We looped around through Webster Park and stopped at the IGA on the way home."

"I got a lollipop," Beth said, taking it out of her mouth as proof. "Want some?"

"No, thank you," said Claire, making a face. "We have to get going."

"Your jacket's in the bedroom," Paxton stated, interpreting the movement of her eyes as she scanned about the room. "I'll get it."

"I'm sorry you were worried about us," said Tucker in a conciliatory tone, when Paxton had left the room. "I won't take her out there again."

"*You won't ever get the opportunity to take her out there again,*" thought Claire, but she didn't say anything. Paxton returned with her jacket and helped her on with it. She kissed him lightly on the cheek, her glance conveying that she wished she could kiss him properly. He winked at her.

"Thanks for dinner," she said. "Elizabeth, what do you say to Paxton for that nice dinner he made for us?"

"Thank you," she said mechanically, and then ran over to hug Tucker goodbye. "Can we play again tomorrow?"

Claire answered the question for him, saying, "You won't see him tomorrow, Elizabeth. We're going to get you settled into your new room, remember?"

"We're going to paint it pink," she told him.

"That sounds wonderful," Tucker responded. "I'm sure it will be a beautiful room. I hope I'll see you again soon, sweetie."

"Would you like some help painting?" Paxton offered.

"No, but thank you for offering," Claire returned, her gaze still fixed upon Tucker. "I think we can handle it."

Paxton walked outside with the girls and helped Beth into her car seat. He kissed Claire again as she climbed into the driver's seat and he waved to them both as they pulled out of the driveway. Claire stole glances at his shrinking form in her rear view mirror until she turned onto Broadway and he was no longer in sight.

FOUR

A Tree Is In Deep Meditation

A tree is in deep meditation
Surveying its own vegetation
Majestic in its isolation
A study in sense deprivation

Rooted in the same situation
It welcomes some slight variation
A bird for polite conversation
A squirrel planning tree immigration

A red, gold and green conflagration
Commemorates fall's celebration
Each winter's four month long vacation
Brings spring and a new incarnation

An expert at cohabitation
Reproducing without copulation
Seeds with genetic information
Ensuring species preservation

Believing in predestination
Assured of its own soul's salvation
It lies down without hesitation
To make way for the next generation

"What are you thinking about?" Tucker asked Paxton, breaking a silence which had lasted for the better part of the hour long drive to Blueberry Hill. Apart from exchanging pleasantries, both men had been absorbed by their own thoughts since Paxton had climbed into the cab of Tucker's truck.

"What?" asked Paxton, looking up suddenly and coming dangerously close to upending the mostly untouched cup of coffee between his legs.

"Or should I say *who* are you thinking about?" Tucker amended his question, also looking up and meeting Paxton's eyes. A moment of complete understanding passed between them, as if they had both just realized that they were still privy to each other's thoughts. They looked away just as quickly and Tucker's eyes once more focused on the road spread out before him.

"I'm thinking about Claire," said Paxton. "I can't believe she has a kid, now! I've never been with anyone who had a kid before."

"Beth's an amazing child," observed Tucker. "She's incredibly perceptive for a three year old."

"I'm not knocking Beth. I just don't know if I'm ready for instant fatherhood."

"Don't knock fatherhood, either. It was the best thing that ever happened to me. But aren't you getting a little ahead of yourself?"

"Maybe, maybe not. Things have been getting progressively more serious between us. I'm still not sure where it will lead, but now she comes as a package deal with Beth."

"What's the story behind that?"

"Claire's sister and her husband were killed in a car accident this past summer," Paxton explained. "Claire was Beth's godmother and she was named legal guardian in their will. She went to Chicago to attend a reading of the will and she came home with Beth."

"Claire seems pretty uncomfortable in her new role as mother," Tucker observed.

"I think she had pretty much given up on ever having children. Her first husband left her because she's infertile."

"I'm sorry to hear that," Tucker said, and then fell silent a moment. It was his turn to feel sympathy for Claire, whom he had been predisposed to dislike, mostly because of her open animosity toward him. He found her to be very one-dimensional, and had never felt comfortable with people who could see only one side of an argument.

"What do you think of Claire?" Paxton asked, as if he were once again inside Tucker's head.

"I don't think she likes me very much," commented Tucker, diplomatically.

"Don't take it personally. It's the company you keep that she doesn't like. She's pretty obsessed with her impending case against B & G at the moment."

"She's definitely very pretty," Tucker admitted. "She also seems really familiar to me. Did she go to school with us?"

"No, and even if she had gone to the University of Maine she would have graduated before we got there. She's ten years older than us."

"Really?" asked Tucker, surprised. "I never would have guessed that! I'll have to try to figure out where I've seen her before. It's bugging me."

Tucker was still wondering about Claire as he pulled off Route 15 and onto the dirt road at the base of Blueberry Hill. He parked the truck out of sight of the main road and disembarked. After checking to be sure the doors were locked, he strapped himself into the enormous pack containing his camping equipment and quickly caught up to Paxton, whose pack was of a size more familiar to the typical college student.

"I feel kind of silly carrying this huge pack up there," admitted Tucker. "I'm not so sure I'm going to want to spend the night if the only thing we find at the top is an old, oak tree."

"Ditto that," agreed Paxton. "I only brought one bottle of wine and that's not even going to get us through lunch!"

They both laughed and whatever tension there may have been between them seemed to be gone for the moment. They were still at a loss for conversation, however, and walked along the gentle upgrade of the logging road with only their increasingly labored breathing disturbing the mostly silent woods. Tucker's curiosity finally got the better of him and he looked back over his shoulder and slowed his pace a little to let Paxton catch up to him.

"Did you tell Claire about Thorn?" he asked.

"Even had I wanted to, I didn't get the chance," answered Paxton between breaths. "Beth came as a complete surprise to me and she was just about all we talked about while you two were on your death-defying walk over the trestle."

"Yeah, in retrospect that might not have been the best place to take her," admitted Tucker.

"You think?" countered Paxton, smiling over at him. "Besides, what was I going to tell her? That we met a man inside a tree?"

"It sounds pretty crazy when you say it like that!"

"It was pretty crazy!" Paxton concurred. "Do you think he'll still be there when we get to the top?"

"Why don't *you* tell me! You're the one who arranged this practical joke!" accused Tucker with good humor.

"Not I, said the fly!" countered Paxton. "What about you? You've been traipsing around these woods for the past couple of days. You've had plenty of opportunities to arrange all this."

"Yeah, like I knew you would be up here yesterday, so I buried my mind-reading equipment beneath that oak tree so that I could scare the crap out of you!"

"I wasn't scared!" lied Paxton.

"Neither was I!" Tucker joined him.

"Anyway, we'll find out what's going on soon enough," offered Paxton. "Here's the trail."

They walked single-file along the steep and narrow foot trail that would take them to the top of Blueberry Hill, both of them breathing heavily enough to preclude more conversation. When they finally achieved the meadow, Tucker stopped to remove his pack and let it fall heavily to the ground as Paxton continued onward into the shade of the massive tree.

Tucker sat down upon his pack a moment to catch his breath, but his eyes never left Paxton, searching for some tell-tell movement implicating his complicity in this charade. Though his rational mind reasoned that the technology to transmit and receive thoughts didn't as yet exist, he half expected to see Paxton reach into some hollow in the tree and flip a switch to turn on his equipment. As far-fetched as this might be, it wasn't any stranger than the alternative, that Thorn actually existed and was waiting for them to renew yesterday's conversation. He watched Paxton remove his own pack and pat Thorn's trunk a few times before he hefted himself up and lumbered the last few strides to Thorn's side.

"Good morning, Tucker," he *heard* the now-familiar timbre of Thorn's voice in his mind. Paxton turned to him with wide eyes as if to confirm that he, too, was privy to the conversation.

"Good morning," he answered aloud, suspending his disbelief for the moment.

"Isn't this wild!" Paxton exclaimed. "He's still in there!"

"Where would you expect me to go?" materialized in their minds simultaneously.

"Nowhere, I guess," answered Paxton. "We just weren't sure if you were real or not."

"And are you sure now?" pressed Thorn.

"I, I guess so," stammered Paxton. He continued to qualify his response but Tucker did not hear the words clearly as he walked slowly around the tree, peering up into the crisscrossing patterns of light and shadow. He was surprised to realize he was looking for some type of face in the network of leaves and branches above him. As he stared at a bole on the north side of the tree, a face formed from the shadows enveloping a large knot where one of the tree's thick lower limbs connected to its trunk. Two deep set eyes seemed to be peering out at him over a widely grinning mouth. Low laughter sounded from somewhere in the recesses of his mind. He blinked his eyes rapidly a few times and when he looked up again, the image had faded and he could see only what appeared to be a deep scar from a wound long since healed. He was about to ask where the scar had come from when the oak broke into his thoughts.

"You won't find a countenance," the tree said, "although I can see yours plainly enough. My sight is not the same as your sight, of course. My sight is made possible by tapping into the life-force all around us."

"I think this would be much easier for me if you had a face," replied Tucker aloud. "At least then I would feel like I'm talking *to* somebody."

"You could sit underneath me in meditation," offered Thorn. "Then we could converse completely in your head."

"I don't think so," replied Tucker. "That would be even stranger."

Tucker still had trouble believing that he was actually talking to a tree, but at the moment he could come up with no better explanation. He looked past the tree to the edge of the meadow where small spruce trees were attempting to push themselves skyward.

"Does every tree around here have a consciousness?" he thought the question without turning around to face the oak.

"Yes and no," Thorn replied. "All forms of life are connected to the universal consciousness. Very few of these trees have a personality as I do. Certainly all the trees you see around you are sentient of their surroundings. They can feel cold and warmth, pain and pleasure. Not every tree can communicate with you as I am doing, at least not in your present state of spiritual awareness. Could you become more enlightened you might be able to communicate with these trees, though they may not have very much to say. I, on the other hand, have a lot I want to say to you."

"What sets you apart, then?" challenged Paxton. "How is it that we can talk to you but not to any of these other trees?"

"The same thing that sets you apart from the other almost six billion human beings on this planet!" Thorn returned. "The unique circumstances of my birth, all of the experiences I have encountered since that birth and all of the memories, knowledge and wisdom I have acquired as a result of those experiences. Would you like to hear more about my life?"

"Of course!" Paxton answered.

"I'm all ears," Tucker agreed, and then realized the absurdity of this statement given the fact that his ears were less than useful at the moment.

"Why don't you both get comfortable?" offered Thorn. "I'm going to tell you a story."

Paxton gave Tucker a glance as if to say, "How long can this possibly take?"

Tucker merely shrugged. They took seats on opposite sides of his trunk, leaning up against his rough and variegated bark. Thorn remained silent until they were settled.

"Close your eyes and relax," he said finally. "I'm going to tell you a story."

"I can't say for sure how old I am. I didn't begin to keep track of linear time until I heard my first radio transmission in the 1920's. Time is circular in the natural world. The sun rises and sets each day. The moon changes phases completely each twenty-eight days. The earth revolves around the sun every three hundred sixty-five and one quarter days. I had seen many winters come and go before I ever learned about calendars.

"In the beginning I knew only darkness and light, cold and warmth. I could feel the wind caressing my branches, but I had no inkling from whence it came. My whole existence centered on growth. I didn't know why, but I knew I had to push upward and outward as quickly as possible. Autumn is my favorite time of year, now. Back then I hated it, because the cold weather was a sign that I would have to curtail my growing until the spring, which seemed like such a long time to wait. The first time I can ever remember dropping my leaves I thought my world was coming to an end. I knew nothing of death, but the world grew cold and I became despondent. As the days grew shorter and shorter I became more and more sleepy. Eventually I fell into a deep sleep, from which I didn't awaken again until the following spring.

"After many seasons, I began to feel quite strong. My roots had spread out along the ground to anchor my ever increasing height. Each spring I burst forth an impressive display of leaves to feed my growing form. I started to receive complete sunlight and felt the rush of the bare wind, broken only by my opposition to it. Only then was I able to divert some of my attention from my perpetual growth and begin to wonder about the world around me.

"I knew that other beings existed in my world. I could feel the roots of other plants intermingling with my own. At first I did my best to try to strangle any that I came into contact with. These other roots were a threat to my water supply. It wasn't until much later, when I grew more confident about my survival, that I learned how to share with the smaller plants surrounding me. I even found that I grew more heartily on the water being filtered through their tendrils.

"I also felt the patter of tiny feet upon the exposed parts of my roots, and later in my branches. One spring a chickadee and her mate took up residence amongst my branches. I could barely feel their light steps upon my rough exterior, but I could sense the life force emanating from them, even as they slept in their nest at night. I became obsessed with them, focusing my attention on their vibrating hearts, charting their course as they capered among my fresh, new leaves. I could think of little else that whole spring, and I grew very little that season. I don't know if it was caused by the miracle of the birth of their chicks or by my intense meditations on their existence, but one day, early in the summer I suddenly found my consciousness inside the father bird.

"That was my first out-of-trunk experience! Imagine living half of your childhood inside a dark box and then one day being suddenly thrust out into the world in which you now live. I was able to see and hear for the first time. My consciousness floated out upon the air on the wings of that tiny bird and I experienced motion. I felt his bond to his mate and chicks. The instinct to protect and provide for them was even more powerful than the instinct for his own survival. And I saw myself for the first time through his wide and unblinking eyes.

"I tried to communicate with him, but found that I could not, at least not as we are communicating now. He was very open to my suggestions, however, and soon I had him flying outside his natural range so that I could explore beyond the realm of this hilltop. I ignored his body's pangs of hunger and thirst, just as I caused him to ignore his responsibilities to his family, and the mother bird had to leave the nest unguarded so that she could search for food for herself and her family. It was only a matter of days before I had taxed his undernourished heart beyond its capacity and it ceased to beat in mid-flight, causing us to plummet toward the earth from our cruising altitude several hundred feet above these hills.

"Just as in a dream where you are falling from some great height but you wake up before you hit the ground, my consciousness was thrust back inside this tree long before the chickadee's body ever made contact with the Earth. After three days in the sun and moonlight, I was disoriented by the utter darkness which enfolded me in my natural form. When I realized where I was, I tried in vain to reconnect with my erstwhile host. I could detect not so much as a flicker of the life which had so recently had his indelible imprint upon it.

"I had not yet determined that I was the cause of the bird's death, and it was not long before I turned my attention to his mate. It was much easier for me to merge with her consciousness, having already performed the trick once. She resisted my presence more than the father bird had, probably because her determination to provide for her family was stronger, but in the end she met with a similar fate. Now that I had experienced the outside world through their senses, I couldn't get enough of it, and I went through each one of the chicks in turn. I caused two of them to fall out of the nest before I realized they weren't capable of flight. I sat with the third one as he slowly starved to death, staring at the sun for so long that his newly opened eyes were blinded before he died.

"After the bird family's demise I felt loneliness for the first time in my life. I missed the patter of the parents' claws upon my bark and I felt trapped inside the dark prison that had become my existence inside this tree. I spent a long winter in contemplation over my newfound knowledge. The little I had learned of myself and my world only served to raise more questions than I could hope to answer with the limited sensual input I received during those cold months. I wondered why the world grew cold and then warm again at regular intervals and what the landscape looked like during this cold period. I scanned the limited range of my awareness for signs of other animal life, and although I could sense the presence of other creatures from time to time, these encounters were fleeting and lacked the connection I was able to establish with the chickadees.

"I no longer needed my winter's nap in preparation for the growing season to come, and I had begun to spend most of the winter in what I would now call a deep state of meditation. This self-hypnotic state was not that far removed from the winter's slumber of my youth, except that I was fully cognizant of the variations in temperature and light and the changing pressure of the snow upon my limbs as it gathered and melted and then gathered again. That particular winter seemed to stretch on forever and it was with much elation that I greeted the longer, warmer days of spring.

"I had thought long and hard over my encounter with the chickadees the previous year. I had established that I was the cause of their untimely deaths. I resolved not to repeat the same mistake should I be afforded a similar opportunity. This decision was based more upon self-interest than any type of moral standpoint. I knew nothing of guilt or remorse at this point, and it wasn't until much later that I learned of compassion for the other forms of life surrounding me.

"I connected with a squirrel that spring, and although his legs were more limiting to my education than were the wings of the chickadees, I got to know my own physical form much more intimately as he climbed throughout my branches. This time I merged with his consciousness only a few hours each day, and I tried as much as possible not to influence his decisions, though I couldn't help but convince him that my branches would be an excellent place for him to make his home.

"The squirrel stayed with me for two summers, until he was caught in the jaws of a red fox one evening at twilight. I'm afraid his death was my fault also, as he was distracted by a mole track that I was very keen on examining. My consciousness was transferred into the fox as the squirrel was in his death throes, and I stayed with him for a time, until he reached the outer limits of my range and I was suddenly and forcefully pulled back into this tree.

"In the years that followed I shared the bodies of many animals, insects and even the other plants in this meadow. After many summers of practice and many winters spent in meditation, I found that I could expand my awareness into the whole of the natural world around me. In this way I could see through many eyes at once, and hear through many ears, and my presence was less intrusive to any single organism. I became a great observer of the workings of Mother Nature, and nothing happened on this hill, or any of the surrounding hills, as my range widened, that I didn't know about. I learned the languages of the animals and the plants, and began to communicate with them. When I thought I had learned everything there was to know in the daily drama of life and death, I turned my attention to the sky and contemplated the mechanics of the heavens.

"I looked upon the sun and moon with awe and reverence, just as did humankind in her infancy, until she discovered how they worked. I, too, lost some of my awe when I discovered I could chart the motion of the moon through her phases, and the motion of the Earth through the change in seasons. I calculated the revolution of the Earth by observing the relative motion of the stars and the planets. With this mystery exposed, I thought I had reached the extent of the knowledge the natural world had to offer. I reigned as Supreme Being in my ever widening circle of influence for many years, and would have been content to do so for many more had not humans intruded upon the scene.

"I had encountered humans in my forest twice, since becoming cognizant of my surroundings. I wasn't able to establish a firm connection during either of these two brief encounters, which bothered me, but humans were such infrequent visitors to my kingdom that I paid them little heed. I began to grow more curious as my eagle flights took me farther afield and I discovered roads, cars and houses, which I eventually attributed to humans. My curiosity was soon to be amply satisfied as they marched full force into my forest, bearing axes and saws, horses and carts and provisions for their war against the trees.

"It was more a slaughter than a war, this mob bent on mass destruction against an army of pacifist trees. The woods were filled with the death cries of the many trees that were felled by the lumberjacks, who paid them no heed. I was sure that they would eventually assault my ramparts, and I came face to face with my own mortality for the first time. I realized that I did not want to die, and I summoned all the powers of nature at my disposal to try to muster some sort of defense. The animals of the forest ransacked their provisions and attacked the men in their sleep. Trees began to fall in unexpected ways, injuring men and damaging equipment. Despite these minor setbacks, the destruction continued almost unabated.

"As the days turned into weeks and then months and they still hadn't reached farther than half-way up these slopes, I felt increased hope that my stretch of woods might be overlooked, after all. I scanned the places they had already been and discovered that the forest itself was no worse off for the selective trees they had cut down, though the trees which were taken had a differing opinion, no doubt. When they moved off this hill and on to the next and I no longer feared for my continued existence, I began to examine these human creatures a little more closely.

"They were so different from the animals of the forest. Their minds were much more complex and harder for me to connect with. I was able to merge with a few of the lumberjacks for short periods of time, but none of them were open to my powers of suggestion. I didn't know if this was just because I couldn't speak their language or if I really couldn't break through the mental barriers which were not present in the animals I had previously come into contact with.

"For all their differences, I found that their motivations were not so far removed from the woodland creatures. They thought about food and shelter and warmth, love and reproduction and their families. They also thought about many things which I did not comprehend until much later, such as money and sports and beer. I was just beginning to learn the rudiments of their language when they moved out of my forest completely, leaving a dirt road and thousands of tree stumps in their wake.

"Despite the damage they had caused, I was sorry to see them go. The forest seemed so empty without their loud presence and I grew lonely for their company. It was only a matter of a few years before they returned to my forest, this time through the air waves. Radio had been discovered, and soon I was receiving transmissions from as far away as New York City. I didn't know what they were at first, and I could only understand bits and pieces of the broadcasts with my limited knowledge of the English language. The little English I had picked up from the lumber-jacks was enough to get me started, however, and I taught myself the language after countless hours of radio programs, which grew more frequent and elaborate as the years went by.

"My range widened as communications technology improved. Soon I was picking up radio programs in other languages. Deciphering these other languages kept me busy for a number of years. Being a tree, I could devote all of my free time to the endeavor, and all of my time is free time. Today I am proficient in all of the major languages of the world, at least all of the languages that are broadcast over the air waves. Satellite technology has opened up even the most remote parts of the world to me. Nothing of consequence happens on this planet anymore that I don't know about, but back then I was just beginning to learn about the things which concern humans in their world and I began to drink in the knowledge heartily.

"With the onset of television my mental pictures were enhanced and corrected by the visual images which now accompanied the broadcasts I received. Television really opened my eyes to the world of humans, so to speak. For many years I stayed tuned into all the channels I could access. Talk about your sensory overload! No need for a remote control here, I could watch every channel simultaneously. Eventually the information I was receiving became redundant, and I became a lot more selective in my choices of programming. Nowadays I rarely tune into anything except the news, and even that has become redundant, for the most part. Maybe it's my age, but these days I much prefer the silence of my solitude to the ever present chatter and wide variety of background noise which seems to be an integral part of most of human existence.

"I need this silent space for my meditations and musings on the great metaphysical questions of existence and the meaning of life. I may have never voiced these questions had I been left to my own devices, but once they were raised in my consciousness by humans, I have never been able to let go of them. Who am I? Why am I here? What is the nature of God? Where do we go when we die? Humans have been asking these questions since before they knew they were humans. Your various religious traditions have been founded upon the different ways of answering these questions. I have become a scholar of philosophy and theology, and quantum physics when I can get it, because I am interested in answering these questions for myself.

"Most humans believe what they are told to believe by their parents, religions, and societies. There have been relatively few free thinkers amongst your numbers and when you do encounter one every century or so, you tend to dispose of them with great dramatic effect. Burning these dissidents at the stake or hanging them upon a cross are wonderful reminders to the masses of the dangers of free thinking. In these modern times you are much more humane in your dispensation of justice, and the gun works quite nicely as a means of silencing these prophets, or devils, as the case may be.

"As far as I know, I am the only one of my kind on this planet. I have been educated by humans, but I don't share kinship with any one of your many tribes. As such, I have been able to examine your differing schools of thought with much more objectivity.

"Still, I have been influenced by my human education into believing that I was once human, and will be reborn as a human again someday. I have a consciousness such as only humans share upon this planet. I believe I also have a soul, though why it is encased in this form I can only speculate. My latest theory espouses reincarnation and explains my life inside this tree as just one of many incarnations which my soul has experienced. This notion isn't without its drawbacks, but it goes a long way toward explaining how I've come into being. And there's been no one here to dispute my position for many years, until now. You two will no doubt have something to say on the matter.

"Which brings me to the here and now. Here we all are and now you have some understanding of who I am and how I came to be a sentient tree."

FIVE

Spiritual Surfing

From beneath
the constellation
of Sagittarius
I set sail
in search of
a new world.

Eschewing
the peace
and safety
of my ship
I leaped
over the rail
a surfboard
under one arm
hoping for
the ride
of a lifetime.

The cold
dark waters
of the cosmic sea
enfold me
threaten to
overwhelm me
before I discover
balance.

Held aloft
by faith
I ride through crest
and trough
as wave upon wave
of energy
propel me
ever toward
the distant shore.

"**I**'m done with my story," said Thorn, breaking the silence of the last few minutes. Paxton had become increasingly enchanted as Thorn's long soliloquy unfolded. He had barely noticed that Thorn was finished speaking, until the spell had been broken by his voice, like a hypnotist snapping his fingers to bring a patient back from a trance.

"That's an incredible story, Thorn," said Paxton, opening his eyes and stretching his arms above his head. "How do Tucker and I fit into it?"

"That is an excellent question, Paxton. Unfortunately, I don't have an equally excellent answer. I'm sure our destinies are intertwined, I just haven't been able to establish to what extent, as of yet. Predicting the future is an inexact science. Do you believe in astrology?"

"Not really," Paxton replied, "but the horoscopes are fun to read. I recognize some of the standard Sagittarian traits in myself, but the different profiles, and the associated horoscopes, for that matter, are so generalized as to be applicable to a wide range of people and situations. I guess my scientific mind has a hard time accepting that the events of my life can somehow be directly related to the time of my birth."

"Oh, but they are related. Everything in the universe is interrelated. The energies that compromise our universe are like the currents of the ocean. They are in constant motion as they ebb and flow throughout the cosmos. And just as the currents of this world's oceans have been charted and mapped, so can the energies of the cosmos be charted and mapped, though it is much harder to do so. The science of astrology attempts to chart these currents, and through their study, to predict where the currents are going. The better the astrologer, the more detailed the map and consequently the more accurate the prediction."

"Astrology is somewhat of a lost art," Thorn continued. "Many of today's astrologers only touch the surface of the water. They chart the major currents and hence can only deal in generalities. It is possible, however, to delve deeper and to make more detailed maps which enable the scholar to see these energy patterns more clearly and in much more intricate detail. You'd be surprised at some of the insights you could gain about yourself if you had your chart read by a qualified astrologer. Unfortunately, there aren't too many of those about these days."

"I don't believe that for a moment," interrupted Tucker.

"What exactly don't you believe?" asked Thorn.

"I don't believe that my whole life is predetermined by the coincidence of the date of my birth."

"Perhaps it's not a coincidence, Tucker. Perhaps you get to choose the circumstances of your birth based upon the spiritual lessons you feel you most need to learn in any given lifetime. Whether or not you then make any spiritual progress during that lifetime is dependent upon the choices you make after that birth. In this way your life is not predetermined. You've merely chosen a general direction in which to travel. There are still choices to be made, but having chosen a general current to embark upon, it is hard to fight against that current. The best you can hope to do is to learn how to surf. Have you ever tried surfing, Tucker?"

"No, I haven't."

"I tried it once," answered Paxton. "I wasn't very good at it, I'm afraid."

"Describe the experience to me," prodded Thorn.

"It's a lot harder than it looks, I can tell you that much. The first thing I had to learn was how to catch the wave. You have to time the start of your ride just right so that the wave will carry you along rather than just break over top of you. You also have to pick and choose which wave might be a good one to attempt to ride. If you pick too powerful a wave you can really get hurt and if it's just a swell you won't get a very long ride out of it."

"After a while I got pretty good at picking and choosing my waves, but then I had to learn how to keep my balance on the board. Good surfers make it look so easy, but I found it to be far from that. At first I couldn't even stand on it for longer than a second before losing my balance. Finally I got to where I could stay up for a few seconds at a time and by the end of the day I even managed one longer ride of about thirty seconds or so."

"You've just described the spiritual quest, Paxton," stated Thorn perfunctorily.

"How so?" asked Paxton, confused.

"Picture a new soul being tossed about by the waves of energy in constant flux throughout space. When one is tired of being tossed about by the waves, one desires to be able to ride them instead—to surf, as it were. This is the desire to know the truth. Unfortunately, this desire is not enough. One also needs a teacher. Did you have a teacher when you went surfing?"

"Yes, I went with my mother's friend, Jason, out near Santa Cruz, California. He could really surf! He knew exactly which wave to choose for whatever kind of ride he wanted. He could surf the more powerful waves for a fast and frenetic ride, but he could also ride waves that appeared to me to be no more than swells, which would give him a longer, slower ride almost to shore. I marveled at the way he could make the wave take him exactly where he wanted to go. Even when I could stand up on the thing I still had no control over where I would end up, which was usually right back in the water ten feet from where I started!"

"Would you say that Jason was a master surfer?" Thorn inquired.

"I don't know about that," answered Paxton. "Certainly he was very good at it. Sure, I guess he was a master. Why?"

"Because that is exactly what a spiritual master can do. Each time a soul enters the cycle of birth and death it gets to choose an energy wave to ride for that lifetime. Until one gets good at the choosing, one is in for a lot of surprises, often being dumped on one's head by the wave, or being taken in a different direction than one envisioned. A powerful wave can be very appealing, but it is also very dangerous, especially if one 'wipes out.'

"A long, slow ride is generally more conducive to spiritual growth, though this is not always true either. Spiritual masters are adept at the choosing of their energy waves. They can choose the right wave to take them exactly where they need to go in any given lifetime. I, myself, have chosen pretty calm waters for this lifetime."

"Are you a spiritual master then, Thorn?" Paxton asked.

"I would not presume to call myself a master. You can make that determination for yourself after you've gotten to know me a little better. I have amassed a great deal of knowledge about the spiritual quest that humans have been on since they could think clearly enough to ask the question, 'Why?' Whether or not the conclusions I've drawn are based upon truth remains to be seen. Regardless, I still have more to learn on this plane of existence, or I wouldn't have chosen to come here at all."

"If we are allowed to choose the circumstances of our births," challenged Tucker, "how is it that you ended up a tree?"

"Another excellent question! I knew you two wouldn't disappoint me! All I can figure is that there must be some spiritual insight to be gained from being a tree. I may not have lived as dynamic a life as either of you two, but I have grown more spiritually as a tree than I ever could have grown as a man. You have too many distractions in your world. I have spent countless hours in meditation and contemplation of the metaphysical, and although I certainly don't claim to have all the answers, I have been able to answer most of my questions to my own satisfaction."

"Speaking of satisfaction," said Tucker, changing the subject, "how about some lunch? I'm starving."

"Sounds great!" Paxton replied, stretching out his sore legs and crawling the few feet to his discarded backpack.

"What have you got there?" inquired Tucker.

"Some bread and cheese. And wine!" said Paxton, taking the bottle of red wine and the corkscrew from his backpack. He opened the bottle and filled the two plastic wine glasses that he kept in his cupboard for just such an occasion. He extended a glass to Tucker.

"Oh, that tastes good!" exclaimed Tucker, after touching the dark red fluid to his lips. "Toss me the cheese and I'll cut it up."

"Sorry we can't share this with you, Thorn," Paxton apologized, as he tore a large hunk from the round loaf of wheat bread he had just extracted from his pack.

"By all means enjoy your sustenance," invited Thorn. "I have been feeding myself almost continuously during our conversation. Besides, I can enjoy the wine and bread through your taste buds."

This last admission seemed to startle Tucker, who turned his head abruptly to look at Thorn, before turning back and meeting Paxton's questioning gaze. Paxton merely shrugged and continued to eat heartily. Neither man spoke as they stuffed their mouths full of bread and cheese and Thorn also remained politely silent. In this relative quiet, Paxton's mind began to ponder over all that Thorn had just told them.

Paxton had read about most of the world's religions by the time he was a teenager, when Mary deemed him old enough to begin to attend church in whatever town they happened to have spent Saturday night. She wasn't about to go with him, nor did she really want him to go, but she finally gave in to his pleading and was later happy that Paxton had found an outlet for his insistent questioning about the nature of God.

Paxton worked his way through the different Christian denominations as though he were at a spiritual smorgasbord, from the strict Southern Baptists to the ritualistic Catholic masses and onward toward the more libertarian Universalist churches. He had been frightened by the notion that you only get one chance at this lifetime and that at the end of it you are judged by a stern, albeit just God, as to your merit and assigned either a place in heaven, or in hell, for all eternity. His mother had never taught him to feel guilty and he had a hard time processing the news that he was born a sinner and somehow needed to be saved. After many sleepless nights pondering over all he had learned in the various churches he had attended, Paxton made the decision to replace the old, curmudgeonly judge with a God who loved all that he created and would never condemn one of his own sons or daughters to perpetual agony.

Paxton had called himself a Buddhist throughout college, more as a way to distinguish himself from his fellow students, than from any deep commitment to the precepts of Buddhism. When he started practicing yoga and meditation on a more regular basis in Africa, he began to fully appreciate their benefits and he studied the religion more closely. He read everything on Buddhism that came his way as the limited Peace Corps traveling library made its rounds amongst his fellow volunteers.

He favored many of the Buddhist beliefs to their Christian counterparts, and he liked the relative simplicity of the religion, but the individuality of Buddhism appealed to him most strongly. He could practice it on his own. He needn't be part of a larger church, and there was no one to tell him what he could and could not do. This also turned out to be a detriment to his development, because the more he practiced meditation, the more he felt that he had learned all that he could from books. Perhaps he needed to find a spiritual master to guide him, as Thorn had suggested.

Paxton favored the eradication of the concepts of heaven and hell and liked the idea that we work on our spiritual selves across lifetimes, but it was hard for him to believe in the non-existence of a supreme being. For these reasons he had never openly converted to Buddhism, though he still called himself a Buddhist when asked as to his religious bent.

"What kind of a loving God would base a decision as important as where an individual soul is going to spend all of eternity, upon the actions of one lifetime?" asked Thorn, reading Paxton's mind. The two men had finished eating and were lying prone on the grass, their heads almost touching.

"That would be like a mother sending her child off to an orphanage because he spilled milk on the carpet," he added. "What are sixty, or eighty, or a hundred years compared with infinity?"

"I agree completely, but why come back at all?" countered Paxton. "Isn't the spiritual plane a better place than this earthly one? Our souls must reside somewhere when we are not on this physical plane. Why not just stay there?"

"When you went surfing, how many waves would you say you rode?" inquired Thorn.

"How many did I ride, or how many did I attempt to ride?"

"Either one."

"I must have tried to ride over a hundred waves, but I probably only got up on the board a couple of dozen times, or so. Why?"

"After riding one, what made you turn around and paddle back out into the waves rather than head toward the beach?"

"It was fun!" Paxton replied. "And I was challenged. I kept getting a little better at it with each subsequent ride and I kept thinking that the next ride was going to be a really good one."

"There's your answer, Paxton."

After a few seconds of silence, Paxton asked, "Would you care to elaborate?"

"This world is a learning ground for our souls and each lifetime another lesson. If we are sincerely trying to seek out the truth, then we grow a little bit closer to enlightenment with each subsequent lifetime. This in turn gives us the desire to continue the search in the next lifetime.

"But equally as important—it's fun! Life was never meant to be a serious, heavy thing. We are born into the physical plane to educate ourselves, to be sure, but also because it is a diversion from the spirit world. Eternity is a long time, whether you're in heaven or in hell, or simply in limbo. One must do something to pass the time!"

"What do you suppose the surfboard represents in spiritual terms?" Thorn asked, after waiting a moment for Tucker to refill the wine glasses.

Paxton propped himself up on one elbow and took a sip of his wine. He responded without confidence, "God?"

"Why would you say that?" asked Thorn.

Paxton thought a moment before answering. When he did speak he began to wave his wine glass this way and that to accentuate the points he was trying to make.

"Because just as the surfboard keeps you afloat, God lifts you up above the human condition. Without a surfboard, you are in danger of drowning or being eaten by sharks. You have no sense of direction or purpose, but are just tossed about by the waves. Without God there is chaos and our lives are ruled by random chance. God gives meaning to our lives and divine order gives us direction."

"That's a good answer, Paxton," said Thorn, noncommittally.

"But not the right one."

"I don't know that there is a right one. It's not that kind of question. Certainly the surfboard is God, but so are the waves and the beach. God is the ocean and the sky and also the surfer. God is All."

"The surfboard does hold the surfer up above the waves," Thorn continued, "even as God helps the spiritual seeker to rise above the tumult of the sensual world. But the surfer has some level of control over the surfboard, based upon his or her level of mastery. Does the spiritual seeker control God?"

"Of course not," answered Paxton. "If anything, it's the other way around."

"Is it? What do you think, Tucker?" asked Thorn.

"I don't know what the surfboard represents, but I disagree with Paxton's answer on a more fundamental level. I don't think that there must, of necessity, be a Supreme Being to instill our lives with meaning. I don't know if there is a God or not, or what happens to us when we die. It's comforting to think that there is some sort of order to our world, but I think it's just as likely that we evolved from the first one-celled organisms which were created by random chance when lightning struck a pool of water filled with the rudimentary building blocks of life. It's nice to think that some part of our individuality will survive past death, but it may very well be the case that when our lights go out we just cease to exist."

"Well put, Tucker. We don't know the answer to any of these questions. That's where faith comes in. Belief in a higher power or in life after death can have a very profound transformative effect on the individual or the group."

"Yes, but is that transformative effect necessarily a good one?" Tucker pressed. "Many atrocities have been committed, and many wars fought in the name of religion."

"Strictly speaking, religion and faith are not the same thing. One of the major benefits of organized religion is that it helps to promote faith. Religion is really your only forum for spiritual education. Unfortunately, once they are created, most religions soon begin to take themselves too seriously. They forget that they are the paths and not the goals of the spiritual quest."

"That's it!" interjected Paxton. "The surfboard is faith! Faith holds us afloat and helps steer us toward the shore."

"That's true, Paxton. Increased spiritual awareness cannot happen without either faith or else some form of divine intervention, and there have been few documented cases of the latter."

"Have there been any documented cases?" asked Tucker. "The Bible is a great storybook, but did all of those things actually happen? I certainly have never been witness to any form of divine intervention in my lifetime."

"My doubting Thomas," Thorn repeated for a second time in as many days. "Your lack of faith is precisely why you haven't been able to learn to surf, spiritually speaking, of course. You have chosen a good wave for this incarnation, but you still need to get up on your surfboard and ride, or else be tossed about in the spray."

"Maybe I like it here in the spray," argued Tucker. "What if I have no desire to learn to surf?"

"There's nothing wrong with that, Tucker, but you might change your mind after you've heard everything I have to say. You've spent your life being tossed about by the circumstances which have befallen you. Sometimes you're floating high above sea level on a large, lazy swell of water. Other times you're turning somersaults and getting hammered into the sand by a rogue wave, such as the one that heralded the death of your family."

Tucker gasped aloud at the mention of Annie and Camden. He rose to a sitting position and pointed a finger at Thorn, "Are you telling me that I could have prevented their deaths?"

"Not at all! But if you had a little faith you wouldn't have spent the past year underwater. Being able to surf does not mean that you won't encounter turbulence, but you will be able to ride through the rough spots a little more easily."

"And I suppose *you* can teach me to surf?" Tucker asked in disbelief.

"I think I can teach you a lot about your spirituality," Thorn answered, seemingly oblivious to the increasing sarcasm in Tucker's voice. "But the desire to learn must come first. Then you'll need a surfboard, and lots of practice. Riding cosmic waves requires great balance and discipline, and to become adept at it requires practice. That is why Paxton practices yoga and meditation every day."

Wanting to ease the growing tension between Thorn and Tucker, Paxton took this cue to break back into the conversation.

"I've enjoyed this surfing analogy, Thorn," he said, "but that wasn't really what I was getting at when I asked you how Tucker and I fit into the story. How is it that you can communicate with us, and have you ever had this type of connection with other human beings?"

"Oh, is that what you wanted to know? I guess I never did finish my story, did I? Remember when I said that I couldn't communicate with the loggers? That wasn't completely true. There was one lumberjack with whom I was able to connect, though I couldn't actually talk to him in English. He came up here to see me on a number of occasions during the months that the loggers were camped out upon the slopes of this hill.

"The first time I saw him I was sure that he had come up here to cut me down. I was terrified, and began to summon all the forces of nature that I could muster to my defense, before I realized that he was empty-handed. Something about his demeanor told me that he meant me no harm and I relaxed my defensive posture. He sat up against my trunk, in the same spot Tucker sat during my story, and promptly fell asleep. I found that I could get inside his head while he was asleep, though I couldn't begin to understand all the things I found going on in there.

"He started to come up here as often as he could after his work hours. Those days the loggers lived in the woods all week and returned home to their families on the weekends. He used to sit against my trunk, smoking cigarettes and daydreaming about an easier life for his family. I couldn't speak to him in words, but I tried to exude peacefulness, which is what he sought beneath my shelter.

"One day there was an aura of sadness about him as he climbed the top of my hill. Even with my limited understanding of human behavior, I knew that he had come to say goodbye. The loggers were moving on to another stretch of woodland and he would be traveling with them. I had no idea how dependent I had become on him as a window into a world of which I still had much to learn. I considered him a friend, though he had barely an inkling as to my presence inside this tree. I felt so helpless as I watched him crush his last cigarette beneath his big boot and turn his back to me. Had I possessed tear ducts, I would have used them for the first time that day. As it was, my emotion caused me to shake so violently that some of my still green leaves began to fall to the ground.

"There was little or no wind that day, and he turned around at the sound of the commotion I was creating. I cried out, and he could hear my wordless entreaty inside his mind, though he knew not from where it had come. It scared him, I think, because he hastened down the mountain as quickly as he could after that. Our strange farewell also served to pique his curiosity enough to bring him back to this place, though it was many years later.

"I had long since mastered the human language before I saw him again. He brought his wife and family up here one Saturday afternoon for a picnic, which they ate beneath my shade. I connected particularly well with his youngest son, and we held a conversation in his mind after their lunch, while his siblings played in the meadow. I found that I could hear and understand the thoughts of every member of the family, but it was only the littlest boy who could hear me back. He told his family that he was talking to the tree, but they all scoffed at him, except for his father, whose ears perked up for a moment before he was distracted by a call from his wife to come to the edge of the cliffs and check out the view.

"I told the boy that it would probably be best to keep our friendship a secret, and I made him promise to come back to see me again. He has visited me infrequently ever since, mostly to find peace in times of trouble or to seek advice about some important decision he had to make. One day, at my bequest, he brought his own son up here, and that was the day I met you, Tucker."

It took a few moments for Thorn's words to sink into his head before Tucker asked, "You can talk to my father?"

"Yes, Tucker, and he's not the ogre you paint him out to be, although his priorities may be a little skewed. Once it was apparent that we could communicate, I had hoped he would come to see me more often, but he chose the material world over the more ethereal one which I might have introduced to him.

"I became much more interested in you, Tucker. As I've already told you, the first time you came up here your soul's frequency preceded you like the headlight of an oncoming train on a moonless night. It awoke me from a sound sleep when you were still many miles away. I was fascinated by how clearly your thoughts were translated to me and I was intrigued by the fact that you didn't seem to be aware of my presence, whatsoever. I tried repeatedly to contact you that day, and in the months and years that followed. Having tuned into your strong signal, I have been able to receive it to varying degrees ever since that first day, though I could never broadcast in such a way that your conscious mind could receive my messages. After many failed attempts, I found that I could communicate to you in your dream state, but that you didn't always remember these encounters, nor did you interpret any of them as meaningful. I always felt that when the time was right I would be able to reach you, and I believe that the time is now right."

"Right for what?" asked Tucker.

"That we shall see," Thorn replied.

"What about me?" asked Paxton.

"I originally thought that my connection to Tucker and his father and grandfather, was rooted somehow in their bloodline, as they were the only humans with whom I had ever been able to communicate. Then you and Annie entered the scene, and I discovered your frequencies to be only slightly less distinct than Tucker's. Even so, I couldn't make either of you hear me, except for that afternoon the three of you took psychedelic mushrooms."

"What do mushrooms have to do with it?" asked Tucker.

"Certain drugs have the power to foster changes in consciousness. These superconscious states can be achieved naturally, through spiritual practices, but under the right circumstances they can be brought about through the use of mind-altering drugs.

"Paxton and Annie and I held a long conversation that day, though neither of them believed it to be rooted in reality when they awoke the next morning. After that, I was reduced to talking to them in their dreams, too."

"How is it that we can talk to you now, then?" Paxton asked.

"I don't know for sure, Paxton. My latest theory is that our destinies are intertwined and that we are approaching the defining moment in the story we are weaving together. I think you and Tucker and I, and Annie, for that matter, are soulmates."

"Can you have more than one soulmate?" asked Paxton. "I always thought that we each had only one soulmate."

"In the common romantic usage of the term, you're absolutely right, but I view soulmates as the souls with which you have formed strong bonds that span across lifetimes, and I think that you have many of them. Perhaps soulmate is not the correct term, but friend doesn't quite cover the connection I'm talking about, either. *Cosmic family* might be a better way of describing the bonds of which I speak. I think we are in the same cosmic family."

"Hold on there," interrupted Tucker. "I have enough problems dealing with the family I have now. Don't tell me I have another one!"

"Yes, but you get to choose your cosmic family, over millennia of incarnations. Haven't you guys ever wondered why you are so close, or why you both held the same feelings for Annie?"

Paxton and Tucker looked at each other briefly, before Paxton blushed and Tucker turned away, reaching for the bottle of wine. He refilled his glass, though it was still half full. After taking a large swallow, he asked, "Are you saying that Paxton and I are in the same cosmic family?"

"Yes, along with Annie and Claire, and others."

"Wow!" exclaimed Paxton. "That's wild to think about!"

"We're just getting started, Paxton. If you liked my surfing analogy I've got another one for you. I have developed a way of thinking about this which I call my chord theory. It's not mine originally, but I think I have taken this particular train of thought, or thread, as it were, further than any of your human philosophers. Would you like to hear it?"

"Sure," replied Paxton.

"I'm game," said Tucker. "But first I have to go to the bathroom."

Without waiting for a response, Tucker rose to his feet and started walking in the direction of the rocky cliff on the eastern face of Blueberry Hill.

"I'll be right back," he called over his shoulder.

SIX

The Weaver

An old woman sits at Her loom
In the corner of a dusty attic room
Weaving the Tapestry of Life

The Past courses through Her delicate fingers
Collapsing in a crumpled heap at Her feet
There for the scholar to unfold and examine

The threads of the Future float freely
Upon cosmic currents flowing through the open window
Forming patterns in the secret silence of Her mind

The heartbeat of the living Present is marked
By the constant motion of the harness
As Her shuttle spins Future into Past.

She works tirelessly into the long night
Her aged back bent over Her labor
Brow furrowed in deep concentration

In the morning She examines Her creation
With the critical eye of the artist
And smiles, for She knows that it is good.

A s Tucker walked toward the eastern edge of Blueberry Hill, his mind was awash with the vivid imagery Thorn had painted upon its canvas. This picture was soon enhanced by the colors of Fall's latest fashion show, which began to unfold beneath him. The trees undulated slowly on the slight breeze, sporting the latest in foliage. Oranges, yellows and dappled patterns were in this year.

Tucker stopped only when the ground before him dove over the edge of a steep, rocky face. From this vantage point he could clearly see the string of rolling hills which straddled the eastern horizon, stretching away toward the outside corners of his eyes. This view also included a few small lakes, which looked more like islands in the sea of trees surrounding them.

Watching the wind play its wave patterns upon the trees made him think of surfing, which brought him back to the conversation the three of them had been having all morning. Although he was interested in what Thorn had to say, he certainly wasn't buying into any of it. He was more interested in determining how Thorn came into existence, than in pondering over metaphysical conundrums.

Tucker was raised in a Catholic home and had taken his turn, alongside his siblings, at all of the coming-of-age sacraments, such as First Communion and Confirmation. But he later realized that he was just going through the motions and he was never able to summon the faith that he saw exhibited in varying measures by the rest of his family. He had given up going to Mass as soon as he entered college and had never looked back, even during the tribulations he had experienced over the past year.

Paxton and Annie had repeatedly tried to get him into practicing yoga and meditation with them in the apartment they had shared together. He was capable of the concentration necessary for a deep state of meditation, and he enjoyed the peaceful feelings which accompanied that state, but he likened it to a recharging of the mental batteries, similar to the health benefits of a good night of sleep. Ever the realist, Tucker believed the post-meditation high to be caused by physiological factors, such as the release of endorphins in his brain as a result of the self-hypnotic state, rather than some supernatural phenomenon.

Tucker watched the golden arc of his urine splash upon a large rocky outcropping twenty feet below him. That protrusion of dirt and granite was the last real obstacle a climber faced in ascending the eastern face of the mountain. He and Paxton had climbed up this way in their college days, when they were both in better shape.

Tucker had tried real mountain climbing in the Rocky Mountains near Bozeman, Montana, where he spent most of the previous autumn. His climbing buddies called him fearless, though in truth he was still reeling from the loss of his family and was reckless and ambivalent about his own well-being. The short but steep climb on the eastern side of Blueberry Hill was nowhere near as challenging as the Rockies. He and Paxton used to climb it free form, though he doubted whether he trusted himself to climb it without gear now.

Having finished what he came there to do, Tucker hesitated a moment before returning to his old friend. Something seemed strange about how easily Paxton had accepted Thorn's presence inside of the oak tree. Perhaps Paxton was in on the joke after all. But their conversation had been too spontaneous to be staged, and it had taken place almost entirely in their minds. What was he having such a hard time believing? Taking a deep breath and one last look at the beautiful countryside spread out beneath him, he turned back toward the tree and the man lying prone beneath it.

"Feel better?" Thorn asked, as Tucker entered the circle of his shade.

"My bladder is empty," Tucker responded, "but I'd still like to know what the hell is going on here."

"Wouldn't we all," commented Thorn. "Why don't you get comfortable and I'll explain the gist of my chord theory. That may shed some light on your understanding."

"Alright," muttered Tucker, dropping to the ground next to Paxton. They prepared for Thorn's next lesson in their own ways. Paxton raised himself to a cross-legged position while Tucker set aside his wine glass and lay down in the grass. He rested his head inside the cradle of his interlaced fingers and stared into the shadows dancing from leaf to leaf above him.

"Imagine your soul as a thread," Thorn began, "a single strand of pure energy, stretching in opposite directions as far as the eye can see. You can think of it as your umbilical cord to God, intersecting your present form right below your navel. We'll stay with your concept of linear time for the moment, and imagine that the thread floating freely in front of you is your future, while that portion of the thread behind you is your past. The thread behind you does not float freely but has been interwoven with countless other, similar threads, into a tapestry depicting the history of the universe.

"Imagine God as a weaver at Her loom, taking these strands of energy and interlocking them into the patterns that form the tapestry. Each time The Weaver adds a new cross-thread, another small piece of each soul-thread is anchored firmly into the scene, as the present gives way to the past. The only dynamic part of this process takes place in the here and now, where the decisions are made as to how each individual thread will become enmeshed with the other threads of the tapestry.

"While in theory, an infinite number of choices are possible to each thread at any given instant, in practice these threads travel rather predictable paths. For example, it's possible that the two of you could wake up on the beach in Barbados tomorrow morning, but that's probably not going to happen. It's much more likely that you'll wake up in the tent that Tucker carried up here, though I predict that you'll wake up tomorrow morning in pretty much the same positions you are in right now. But that's beside the point.

"For the most part, each thread naturally takes the path of least resistance as it winds its way into the future. Threads that are already interwoven together tend to stay together, especially in the short term, as the process continues. A thread can be stretched to a different section of the tapestry, or broken and reattached elsewhere, but it takes a larger influx of energy to do so and it doesn't work aesthetically, although a stray strand here or there doesn't confuse the larger picture of the tapestry.

"As each thread finds its way into the pattern, it knows but a small piece of the overall picture being embroidered on the tapestry. Only The Weaver has the benefit of viewing the tapestry as a whole. The Weaver has an overall design in mind, but the final form of the tapestry is as yet unresolved. New directions are spontaneously chosen, strands break and new ones are added and even flaws are formed. But from the viewpoint of The Weaver, the tapestry still tells the story which She has envisioned, despite any flaws or broken threads which might be seen under higher magnification.

"The spiritual quest is the desire to see more of the tapestry, the desire to know why the universe has unfolded the way it has and in what direction it is headed. If one is viewing the tapestry from a higher vantage point, one can gain more insight into the larger picture. This enables predictions into the future, with it again being much easier to predict in the short term because the possibilities open to each thread are much more constrained. My prediction as to where you will wake up tomorrow was not that challenging, given the circumstances leading up to the present. Predicting where either of you might wake up a year from now becomes a more difficult proposition. A glimpse as to what the tapestry will look like much later requires a much larger view of the whole.

"Likewise this higher vantage point enables one to look farther back into the past, either as a whole, or in a more personal sense. These threads remain unbroken, for the most part, from one lifetime to the next and one could glimpse into one's past lives with a little more perspective. Higher states of consciousness, which can be achieved through spiritual practices, amongst other methods, give one that larger perspective.

"You've no doubt been picturing this tapestry as a flat surface. Let's add another dimension to it. Picture the thread that is your soul being braided together with the threads that are nearest to it. Just as fibers are braided together to form stronger rope, your soul is intertwined with other souls to form a stronger energy strand. The other souls, intertwined with your own, are your soulmates, and they are linked with your soul across lifetimes.

"These strands composed of several souls are then joined by other similar strands to form even larger ropes of energy. You live in a neighborhood, which is part of a society and culture, contained in a country, on a continent, on this planet called Earth. This process of braiding strands together to form ever larger ropes of energy continues eternally, growing in magnitude with each successive step.

"Consider the Earth as a strand of energy unto itself, interwoven with the strands of the other planets that make up this solar system. Our solar system is interwoven with the strands of other solar systems to form the strand of our galaxy. Other galaxies are then interwoven with this one. Your scientists are developing better and better techniques for studying and quantifying these larger energy systems, but as this increase in magnitude is an infinite process, there are infinitely many larger systems that have yet to be discovered. The magnitude of these larger systems is incomprehensible, and so they become one of the many unexplained phenomena of human experience. Religion calls this collection of mysteries God.

"Each soul is in turn composed of strands of energy, of which the mind and body are a part. These can then be broken down into smaller energy strands, each one again a system which can be broken down into its smaller strands. The body is composed of muscles and organs and bones, which in turn are made up of different cells, which are composed of molecules and atoms. Your scientists have explored these realms, also, and have discovered some very minute energy particles. Neutrinos are so small that billions upon billions of them pass through your body every second without interacting with any of the atomic particles of which your body is composed. And yet these neutrinos can be broken down into infinitely many smaller strands of energy. These minuscule energy systems are not quantifiable to the common awareness at this level of energy, and so they also become a part of God's workings.

"These larger, and smaller, energy systems cannot be adequately explained by humans, yet that is a very dissatisfying answer, so explanations are continually attempted. Science observes and quantifies so that the mind might theorize, while religion meditates and intuits so that the spirit might sense. They both seek to know the nature of God, though neither can fully attain this enlightenment without the other. A complete understanding of God requires both the mind and the spirit. Even so, they each draw their own conclusions and then shout proudly that they have discovered the answer!

"Much of the pain and suffering on this planet has been caused by various groups of humans who claimed to have discovered the truth and subsequently defend or enforce this truth to the death. On the other hand, the evolution of the human race would not have happened without the desire to know this truth. This quest is really what sets you apart from other animal forms, for good and for ill.

"Almost every human being on this planet has his or her own perception of God. Some think God sits on a throne and judges each soul upon the death of its physical vessel. Others believe God is a kind and loving father. Still others believe God to be not one but many different personas. Some choose not to believe in God, whatsoever, which is just as valid an explanation as any other. The personas that are invented for God are learned, sadly, for children are much closer to understanding God before parents and teachers tell them who *He* is.

"God is predominantly male, these days. This was not always the case, however. What you would consider more primitive humans thought of God as a woman—the Earth Mother. Life was much more peaceful under her reign, despite the harsh realities of Mother Nature. Patriarchal society took over the common consciousness by force, and has proceeded to rule by force ever since. I can foresee a time, however, when its stranglehold will be loosened and The Mother will once again come to the forefront.

"Be that as it may, any of these concepts is as good as another, insofar as none of them even hint at the enormity which is The All. But there is some value in having a working concept of God, insofar as it serves to remind the collective awareness on this energy level that there is something more out there. God gives the individual soul a yearning for the truth, which propels it on its spiritual journey. This is a striving to reach higher levels of energy, and lower ones, so as to be able to see more of the tapestry that The Weaver is creating."

"But I am completely down a side trail at the moment and we need to get back to the main path," Thorn continued. "The main path leads to a place I go to meditate, that I like to call The Chords. I'm not sure if I created this place out of my mind, or if it exists in and of itself, but it is there that I began to think of the universe in this way. From within The Chords I am able to view the tapestry of the cosmic dance. The past is recorded in pictures on the tapestry. One can view it as if watching a movie, but on a much grander scale. The picture of the future is much more hazy, the chords disentangling themselves as they stretch outward from the loom.

"The higher I am able to project my consciousness above the present's tiny point on my individual thread, the more I am able to glean about the past and the future. Imagine a half-finished tapestry on a loom. Suppose you are looking at the hind legs of a horse. If the tapestry is to be formed into a coherent picture, which hasn't necessarily been established yet, one would assume that the front half of the horse would follow, as The Weaver continues her work. If you could look at more of the tapestry you might see other horses in the picture, with soldiers astride them. Higher still, you could see that some sort of battle is going on and you might predict the outcome of the battle, based on the fact that there is an overwhelming majority of red uniforms in the picture. With a more expanded view you could see the causes and effects of the whole war. Then you might have some notion as to its probable outcome.

"This is how I *see* into the future. My foresight is not infallible, however. When the tapestry unfolds it might reveal twice as many blue uniforms in opposition to the red army. Through my spiritual practices I have been able to see increasingly larger portions of the tapestry. Consequentially, I've increased the accuracy of my predictions steadily over the years. What confounds me is that I am unable to glimpse much of anything about my personal future, or past.

"I can see both of your threads clearly, and mine as it has been interwoven with yours during this lifetime. I can follow your threads into your past lifetimes to a point, but I lose track of mine in the space before I was conceived as an acorn seed. I can also see a little into your futures, but I cannot see my own. I think that perhaps we aren't supposed to know too much about our personal futures, because that knowledge can rip the cosmic fabric. The reason I can't see yours very clearly, either, is because we have become too far enmeshed at this point and to see your futures would necessitate seeing my own.

"I cannot discern why I am unable to follow my own thread before this lifetime, though. I catch fleeting glimpses of a past which seems to be somehow connected to me, but I can't fit these pieces together. It could be that I don't have any history before this lifetime, but I can't accept that. I'm hoping that one of you might be able to follow my thread further back in time to determine if I do, in fact, have past lives, as do all of the other chords in the tapestry. How would you like to travel The Chords with me?"

"We can do that?" asked Paxton.

"I'm pretty sure that you can, Paxton, but I have my doubts about Tucker."

"Why is that?" asked Tucker, defensively.

"You are much too rooted in your version of reality, Tucker, and you have neglected your spiritual practices. If you are to accompany Paxton and me into The Chords you will need to do so from within a deep meditative state. I'm not so sure you can get there, but I'm willing to help you if you're willing to try to keep an open mind."

"*I think my mind is quite open enough,*" Tucker thought to himself, and then realized they had heard him when Paxton chuckled. He was still getting used to having Thorn and Paxton inside his head.

"Yeah, right," Paxton thought back to him in a good-natured way.

"Your resistance is going to make it harder for you," Thorn admonished.

"I'll give it a try," Tucker said aloud under his breath.

"Good," Thorn responded. "Let's get going!"

"I want you both to sit up against my trunk," Thorn began, waiting for them to crawl the few feet to his base and find comfortable seats. Paxton sat cross-legged, his hands resting on the two massive roots extending outward from Thorn on either side of his knees. Tucker chose his customary seat, straddling a root which arched upward before tunneling below the surface of the Earth.

"Relax," Thorn directed. "Shake out your shoulders and your neck. Rest your head and back against my trunk and feel the tension from your bodies being carried away by my roots into the ground beneath you. Concentrate on your breathing. Bring your awareness to the tip of your nose. Feel the breath as it enters and leaves your nostrils. Note that it is a little bit warmer on the way out than on the way in. With your next exhalation, draw your stomach as far into your body as possible. Now slowly let it back out as you inhale. Feel the tension you've stored there being discharged from your body through your breath. Count the length of each inhalation and exhalation, but don't otherwise try to control them. Just breathe naturally.

"If a thought enters your consciousness, acknowledge it, and then let it go, as though you're watching leaves float past you on the surface of a brook. When your mind has wandered, bring your awareness back to your breathing, without comment. Do not chide yourself for having lost your concentration. Do not congratulate yourself for having remembered to once again listen to your breathing. Just be aware of your breath. The mind can grab onto any thought and run with it, forming new ideas and branches of thought with the rapidity of a trip hammer. Once you've anchored your awareness back into your breathing, it's easier to keep it there if you don't immediately give the mind more fuel to burn. Follow your breath. I'm going to be silent for a few minutes so that you can find your quiet mind."

Tucker struggled to maintain his focus. The sounds of the active, afternoon forest distracted him momentarily, and he wondered if the animals, and the trees and plants, for that matter, knew of Thorn's extraordinary presence. Was it even extraordinary to them? Could they all communicate with each other in this fashion? Yet Thorn could communicate with Tucker in his mind, and he had never before observed this phenomenon in nature. Thorn was probably with him in his mind right now.

"Is this whole encounter created out of my mind?" Tucker thought.

"More so than you know," he heard somewhere inside his head, "Everything that you experience is created inside your mind. But that is a lesson for another time. Now bring your awareness back to your breath!"

"Feel your back against the rough bark of my trunk," said Thorn, continuing to guide them deeper into themselves. "Imagine your spine melting into my trunk and your spirit expanding into my boughs. Your consciousness is going to merge with mine. Imagine your legs becoming roots and diving into the earth. Your outstretched arms become your growing branches, leaves springing forth from your fingers.

"As you inhale, feel your roots pulling up the rich, brown earth energy into your body. Feel this energy making you grow and expand as it travels up the spine of your trunk. This energy is then exhaled through your outstretched branches into the sky. With your next inhalation, pull the fresh, mountain air energy into your leaves and down your branches to your trunk. Exhale it back down into the earth through your roots. In this way you become a link between heaven and earth. "Once again pull the dark brown, earth energy into your body through the roots at your feet. Exhale this energy into the sky as a fountain of green. Inhale the sky through your crown and let gravity pull it down through your limbs and body. Feel your roots grow stronger as you exhale this blue energy back into the earth. Imagine yourself becoming a tree. Be a tree."

Tucker awoke suddenly, as if from a dream. Darkness lay draped across his shoulders and hung heavily upon his eyelids. He tried to open his eyes, but he couldn't find them in the darkness. He tried to reach out and touch his legs, but found he had no awareness of arms or legs. In fact, he couldn't feel any part of his physical form. He knew only that he was in a dark place, alone.

After his initial shock wore off, Tucker discovered he was not frightened. On the contrary, he felt very much at peace. He had no awareness of his body or any of his five senses, yet he was still somehow connected to his mind and he began to wonder where he was. How long had it been since Thorn had ceased to speak?

"Thorn? Paxton?" he cried out in his mind. The sound of his voice echoed away from him, as though he were in a large cavern. He listened for a response, but heard only the low hum which his fading voice had become. The sound persisted, and grew slightly louder as the atmosphere around him turned almost imperceptibly lighter. Tucker began to feel a sense of motion, though he knew he was not propelling himself. It seemed as if he was being tugged forward by some unseen force. The darkness gave way to a thick tangle of stringy shadows, which closed in upon him as the light in the cavern increased.

"Snakes!" thought Tucker in horror, recoiling deeper inside himself to escape their serpentine shadows. His forward motion took him directly into their midst, but his bodiless form passed right through them. He relaxed once again, when he realized that the snakes surrounding him were nothing more than thick chords, interwoven into loose braids. The chords grew thicker and the weave got tighter as he traveled, and eventually all the strings around him spiraled together to form an even thicker chord. The chord vibrated and Tucker realized that the low tone he heard buzzing in his head was a result of this vibration.

The last thing Tucker could remember before coming to this place was the image of his body merging with Thorn's wooden one, and he reasoned that he must now be inside Thorn's trunk. The strands he saw all around him could be long strings of tree cells joined together. He called out to Thorn again, and again there was no response. He was still moving forward and decided he would just relax and enjoy the ride. Perhaps he was in the tree's transport system and he was heading towards its leaves. What would happen then?

The chord upon which he was traveling was once again met by similar chords and they wove themselves together into a stronger, braided rope. The light continued to increase steadily as he was propelled forward, and he began to see this new chord in more intricate detail. Images came flooding into his mind, as though he were watching a video running on fast forward. He began to recognize scenes from his own childhood. His siblings were there, playing in their old backyard. He saw friends and teachers from his grade school. His mother and father jumped busily in and out of the frames flashing before him, and he marveled at how young they looked.

The scene shifted to their house in Cape Elizabeth and his siblings had become teenagers. He saw Cindy Kessler, puckering up to give him his first kiss. Then he was on a football field being chased by a gang of blue and white jerseys. He suddenly realized that he could not see himself in any of these scenes, but rather was viewing them through his own eyes as they had happened in the past.

Tucker continued to watch this accelerated version of his life story and began to wonder whether or not he was still connected to that life. He had read about people who have come close to death, and their accounts of being in a dark tunnel, watching their lives being replayed before them as they head toward a distant light. He recalled that they all reported an extreme sense of peacefulness during this process, which was exactly what he felt as he watched himself dance at his high school prom. If this was death, he felt much too good to be worried about it at the moment.

As the atmosphere around him lightened even more, he started to see other chords in his peripheral vision. They converged upon the chord he had come to identify as his own personal essence. As they drew nearer, he recognized Paxton, and Annie. He saw his father, and then Camden. At the same time, the scenes now playing themselves out before him began to include these characters, and several others. He saw Paxton walking carefully across the top of the train trestle. Annie popped into his vision, laughing at Camden, who sat across from her in a high chair, his face covered in spaghetti. Pictures of Thorn in various seasons began to flash before him in what was now becoming more of a slide show than a movie. He saw Annie and Camden on the only plane trip Camden had ever taken. Shortly thereafter both of their chords became dark, though they continued to interweave themselves with his own chord as he was pulled ever forward upon his journey.

Tucker found himself sitting in a booth across from a stunning woman with long black hair, two cups of steaming coffee between them. It took a moment for him to recognize Claire, and he immediately realized that he was no longer viewing a past event. He caught fleeting glimpses of Beth in the slide show, and another little girl whom he had never before seen. He saw himself at a funeral which he assumed to be his father's, judging from his mother's tear-stained face beside him. The scenes began to change more rapidly, and contained more people whom he had never met and places in which he had never set foot. At the same time, the pictures lost their sharp quality and began to fade to white around the edges.

He was dimly aware that the larger chord upon which he was now traveling was being joined by other, similar-sized chords. He viewed the hazy scenes now appearing in front of his awareness at a greater distance, as if he was no longer a character in them, or at least not the main character. He strained to make some sense from the disappearing images, which increasingly dealt with scenes of destruction and war. He thought he caught a glimpse of some large city, abandoned and overgrown with vegetation, before the light surrounding him had intensified to such a degree so as to reduce his vision to a blinding field of white.

Now that he could no longer see, Tucker became aware that the tonal quality of the ever-present vibration in the chords around him had changed. Although still completely in harmony, it had grown lower and louder, increasing in intensity to rival the light as potentially damaging to his sense organs, had he possessed any sense organs in his present state. The sound grew so intense as to preclude all thought. Tucker lost his identity momentarily as he experienced the most profound sense of peace he had ever known.

Just when it seemed that he would be consumed into the oblivion of this magnificence, his forward motion slowed to a halt. He stopped only for an instant, however, before he felt himself moving backwards, as if he had been thrown into the air and had reached the top of his arc and was now descending back towards the Earth. Indeed, it felt as if he was falling, gaining momentum as both light and sound began to diminish. He felt no fear, but only sorrow, that he was now moving away from this brilliant presence.

The chord upon which Tucker was now traveling began to unravel as he fell back down its length. Eventually he came into contact with his personal strand and the slide show which was his life started to play again, this time in reverse and at a much more accelerated pace. He watched friends and family grow younger, before being thrust into the darkness of his mother's womb. This subsequently gave way to a more complete darkness which admitted neither light nor sound.

The movie suddenly began again, though Tucker recognized none of the actors and actresses. Most of the characters were old, though they grew younger at an astonishing pace. At some point he came face to face with Albert Einstein, who was sitting across from him at the dinner table. Albert remained in the story a few frames before being replaced by a younger man, and then by school children. Once again the screen went dark.

Tucker was falling much faster, now, and he began to grow a little concerned. His personal chord had frayed and split into several smaller chords, one of which he was still trailing as he fell. Dark objects flew past him at incredible speeds and the silence he had experienced mere seconds ago had given way to a chorus of high-pitched screams. This cacophony rose in frequency and volume as he sped onward, wishing he had some way to block the noise from entering his consciousness. He looked down the trail of the thread he was traveling upon and saw that it disappeared into a small, black circle. The circle grew larger as he neared it, and it seemed inevitable that they must soon collide. The dark orb now filled his field of vision completely, but just as impact was imminent, Tucker awoke with a start.

He was disoriented when he opened his eyes, for they were met with a darkness similar to the one he had so narrowly escaped. As they began to focus, he could see the twinkling of countless stars in the sky above him, and he remembered where he was, though how it could have grown so late he hadn't a clue. He propped up his head on his elbow to look for Paxton, and spotted his sleeping form several yards away from him in the open meadow. Sleep tugged insistently at the corners of his consciousness and he lay his head back down upon Thorn's protruding root, pulling his coat a little closer around his curled up body. He was asleep before he could form any hypotheses as to what had just befallen him.

SEVEN

Don't Grow Up Too Fast

Don't grow up too fast.
It won't be long before, "Watch me!"
Becomes, "I need my privacy."
Before, "Come play with me!"
Becomes, "You're embarrassing me."
Before, "Can I go to Katlyn's house?"
Becomes, "Can I go to Kevin's house?"
Soon toys will give way to books
    then books to boys and beers.
Then to toys again as you play
    with your own daughter.

My life is far richer
    for having you a part of it.
Is your life richer for having me?
It is a privilege for me
    to view the world through your eyes.
To become excited again
    about things I have seen
        countless times before.
To laugh and dance
    and sing and play with you.
To collect fireflies
    and color pictures
        and eat ice cream with you.
You keep me young.

I am very blessed
    to have you in my life.
Are you equally as blessed
    to have me in yours?
You may not think so,
    when you get older.
But you like me well enough now.
So don't grow up too fast.

"Time to wake up!" Claire heard, as if from far away. She tried to ignore the proclamation and sink back into the dark tomb in which she had become ensconced, but soon it was repeated, this time accompanied by a gentle but insistent tug at the sleeve of her nightshirt. She stirred slightly, rolling slowly toward the sound of the child's voice.

Claire was accustomed to working late into the night. As soon as Beth had fallen asleep, she had begun poring over the mountain of paper she had collected in her research for the upcoming hearing, barely noting the passage of time until the night was nearly over. She had been anxious to get at those files since her return from Chicago. She had much work to do before Friday, and she had *lost* a whole day yesterday, taking care of Beth.

Not that Claire had minded spending the day with Beth. In fact, it was the best day she could remember having had in many years. In the morning, they had gone on a long walk in the woods surrounding her small country home. Having lived the whole of her short life in Chicago, Beth had been amazed by the natural world in which she found herself. She had asked many questions, some of which Claire could not answer easily. Beth had been especially curious about the trees. She had wanted to know how they grew so tall and why there were so many different kinds.

In the afternoon, they had begun to paint Beth's new room pink, until Claire discovered firsthand the potential damage that could be caused by a paint brush in the hand of a three-year-old. They left that particular job half-finished in favor of watching the Disney movies they had rented earlier in the day. Beth fell asleep on the couch and Claire had tucked her in there, afraid that she might wake her up if she tried to move her into the bedroom.

"I saw that man again," Beth stated, climbing up onto the bed next to Claire.

"What man?" asked Claire, groggily. Her eyes were still closed, but she was now fully aware of her surroundings. Beth had climbed into the bed beside her and Claire now reached an arm up to cuddle her.

"From the other night!"

"Who? Paxton?" asked Claire, stretching her free arm out in front of her and emitting a long, loud yawn.

"No, the other one."

"Tucker?"

"Yeah, Tucker!"

"Really? You saw Tucker?" Claire asked as she opened her eyes and focused them on the smiling face of the child lying in the crook of her arm. "Where?"

"We were talking to a tree," Beth explained. "The tree said that something really bad was going to happen."

"That sounds scary. You must have been dreaming, sweetie."

"It wasn't scary," Beth replied. "The tree told me not to worry, I would be just fine. And I could see a man in the tree."

"A man in the tree?" Claire repeated. "Was he trapped?"

"No. He just lived there."

"What did he look like?"

"I don't know. He was kind of fuzzy. The sun was shining in my eyes."

After a few moments of silence Beth added, "Tucker and I had a picnic under the tree. I like him. Can he come over today?"

"I don't think so," Claire replied, a shadow passing over her face as she recalled her last encounter with Tucker. It was quickly replaced by a bright, red flush as Claire remembered the details of her own dream.

She had woken shortly before daybreak, sweating and aroused from a dream in which she was making love, to Tucker. Her hand had already found its way beneath her cotton panties, and she brought her pleasure to completion, shifting the focus of her fantasy to Paxton with a certain amount of concentrated effort. She had lain awake briefly afterwards, disturbed that Tucker had found such an intimate pathway into her thoughts, before sleep once again reclaimed her languid form.

Claire hadn't been with a man since Michael had left her. Having learned to deny her desire as well as her desirability, she had only recently begun to think of Paxton in a sexual way. Now that Beth and Tucker had entered upon the scene, however, it was going to be much harder for them to find the time or space for that kind of intimacy.

"I'm hungry. Can we eat breakfast?" Beth burst the bubble of her thoughts.

"Sure, sweetie. What would you like?"

"Pancakes!"

"Okay."

After Beth watched Claire whip up a batch of Bisquick pancakes, they took their breakfast into the living room. The only furniture in evidence was the white-pillowed couch and television on opposite sides of a throw rug which concealed about half of the hard wood floor. The room was suffused in the early morning sunshine streaming in through the big bay window facing toward the south. She had chosen this house over similar ones because of the large amounts of natural light which filtered into almost every room. The two bedrooms each had a skylight and one whole wall of the kitchen was formed by the two large, glass-paned doors leading out onto the back porch.

Although she had been in the house for almost two years, it still looked as though she were in the process of moving in. The walls were bare, as most of her pictures and other knickknacks were still packed away in the boxes lined up against one wall of the living room. She had meant to unpack the boxes on more than one occasion, but something more important always presented itself. Claire did not spend much time in her house, so its adornment had never been a high priority for her.

She turned on the television and searched through the channels for a show that would interest a three-year-old. Beth spoke out in favor of Animaniacs when they flashed across the screen and Claire consented. Beth sat staring at the screen, mesmerized by the cartoon images parading across it, but Claire was distracted. She kept looking at the little girl seated next to her, eating pancakes with her hands, and wondered about the strange turn of events that had brought Beth into her life.

Claire had been close with her sister, Hannah, with whom she talked on the phone at least twice a month. They used to have lunch together in downtown Portland quite often before Hannah got married and moved away to Chicago. Since then she had only seen her sister a handful of times. The newlyweds had returned to Yarmouth for their first Christmas together, and Claire had flown to Chicago to participate in Beth's baptism as her godmother. The last time she had seen her prior to the accident was at their family reunion two summers ago. The gangly toddler she had carried on her hip most of the weekend had grown into the fully-functioning, tiny human being now sitting next to her, giggling at the antics of the Animaniacs.

Having had limited exposure to children, Claire had no basis for comparison, but it seemed to her that Beth was intellectually advanced for her age. She had a remarkable vocabulary and had no trouble at all communicating verbally. Claire continued to be amazed by some of the pronouncements that had come from those three-year-old lips over the past couple of days. Beth was also well beyond the scribble drawings of other children her age, which Claire had seen tacked up on the cubicle walls of her employees' offices at SPAWN. Yesterday Beth had crayoned her old apartment house complete with interlocking brick walls and plants on the window sills.

Claire realized that she needed to go shopping sometime soon, as she watched Beth smear her syrup encrusted hand down the front of her shirt. She had brought as many of Beth's things on the plane as she could, but that amounted mostly to clothes and her few favorite toys. Movers would be bringing along the bulk of her things in a few days, but she needed some child accessories in the interim. Claire had been forming a mental list since they had come home, to which she now added wet-wipes. She reached over and swathed Beth's hands and face with a damp washcloth.

There were other things which needed to be done right away. Claire was going to have to arrange for some sort of day care for Beth. She had been able to convince Beverly, a friend with two children of her own, to babysit for Beth this week, but that was only a temporary solution. She also needed to find a good pediatrician, and a lawyer who could advise her about Beth's adoption. Of more immediate concern, she and Beth needed to go grocery shopping together so that Beth could help her pick out some things she would eat. She had ordered pizza last night, after her vegetarian fare was flatly rejected, but that certainly wasn't a habit she wanted to encourage.

As Claire thought about taking a shower, she recognized the need for child-proofing her house as yet another item on her growing list of things to do. She hadn't left Beth alone in the house as of yet. They had taken a bath together yesterday, and Beth had been at her side throughout the day. She wondered if she dared leave her alone for the ten or fifteen minutes it would take her to bathe. She decided that the cleaners under the kitchen sink were the only really dangerous things she had outside of the bathroom itself, and if she moved them under the bathroom sink she might feel comfortable enough to take a quick shower.

"Elizabeth, honey," Claire started, trying to break the TV's hold on her attention. "I'm going to take a quick shower. Will you be okay here alone for a few minutes?"

Beth nodded her head, but Claire wasn't convinced she had really heard her. She picked up the remote control and clicked off the television.

"Hey!" Beth complained, looking up at her.

"I need to talk to you for a second," Claire explained. "I want to take a shower. If I let you stay in the living room and watch TV, I need you to promise me that you will stay right here until I get back."

"Sure, Mommy!"

"I mean it! Don't move from this couch."

"Can I color?" Beth asked innocently.

"I guess that would be okay," Claire replied, gathering up the breakfast dishes and carrying them into the kitchen. She located the paper and crayons on the kitchen table and brought them in to Beth, who was now sprawled out on the floor.

"Is it okay if I stay on the floor?"

"Yes, but don't go anywhere else!" Claire said as forcefully as she could muster, handing over the paper and crayons. "Promise?"

"I promise."

Clicking on the TV, Claire patted Beth on the head and said, "I'll be right back."

As the hot water sprayed across her body, Claire thought about the three-year-old she had left alone in the living room. They had been together less than two weeks, yet it seemed as if she and Beth had known each other for much longer than that. Why had Hannah picked her to raise Beth? She was both flattered and frightened at the same time. Surely there were better choices amongst their other sisters. What had she ever done to instill that kind of confidence in her capabilities as a mother? And why had Hannah never discussed this decision with her?

Claire didn't know the first thing about being a mother. How was she going to be able to take care of that little girl? She had always been good with kids, but they were always somebody else's kids. After playing with them for an hour or two, she could send them back to their parents and shift easily back into adult mode. She had never spent any amount of extended time with a child, nor had she ever had anyone so completely dependent upon her.

On the other hand, it was so very easy to take care of Beth, at least up to this point. Whatever child-raising strategies her sister had been using must have been effective, because Beth seemed to be a very well-adjusted little girl. And although it still sounded strange to her, it was so endearing to have Beth calling her mommy. She only hoped that she would be able to live up to that billing.

Who was she kidding? She didn't have time for a child! This next week was going to be hell! She had an enormous amount of work to do to get ready for the hearing. She couldn't be expected to just drop everything she had worked so hard to achieve and tend completely to her new charge, could she? For a few fleeting moments she considered asking her mother to come help her out for a week or two. But then she remembered the last time her mother had come for a visit and decided that she would just be exchanging one type of stress for another.

Feeling more than a little overwhelmed, Claire's tears began to join the streams of water already coursing down her body. She had always considered the shedding of tears a sign of weakness, but she excused this lapse in self-control as a byproduct of the motherhood which had so recently been thrust upon her. Whatever the cause, she had cried more in the past two weeks than in the past ten years.

"What are you drawing?" asked Claire as she walked into the living room in a green robe, a towel wrapped around her hair. She left a slippery trail in her wake and continued to drip water onto the floor as she stood over her prone adopted daughter. Claire had been relieved to see Beth's socks raise their pink heads into view from behind the couch as she entered the room hurriedly. Everything seemed to be in its place and it appeared that disaster had been averted, at least temporarily.

"A tree," replied Beth curtly, intent upon her work.

"And what a beautiful tree it is!" Claire complimented her truthfully, as she glanced down at it. Beth had filled up a page of her sketch book with the colors of a tree in all its autumn glory. Claire was amazed at the detail to the drawing. There was texture to the bark of the tree, and an entire network of branches spreading out from its broad trunk. Green, red, yellow and orange crayons, in different combinations, had been used to place clusters of leaves at the ends of the branches. The only portion of the drawing which belied her age was the whimsical smiling mouth and dot eyes she had placed in black amongst the leaves.

"It's the tree from my dreams," said Beth, rolling over on her side and beaming at Claire's praise.

"Have you seen this tree in your dreams before last night?" asked Claire, more interested now than she had been when she had just woken up.

"All the time," Beth answered, rolling back onto her stomach and continuing her creation.

"And the tree talks to you?"

"Yep."

"What does it say?"

"Lots of things. He told me my mommy and daddy died, and they're in heaven. That was the first time."

"It's a boy tree?" inquired Claire, catching Beth refer to the tree with a masculine pronoun. "What's his name?"

"Thorn."

"What else does Thorn say?"

"He told me you were my new mommy."

"Really?"

"And Tucker is my new daddy."

"What?!"

"Tucker is my new daddy," Beth repeated.

"When did he tell you that?"

"Last night."

Remembering how Beth had greeted Tucker the other day, Claire asked, "Did he tell you that before last night?"

"Yep."

"When?"

"Back in Chicago."

"And you recognized him?"

"Yep."

"Listen, Elizabeth," said Claire seriously, squatting down so that she could make eye contact the girl lying at her feet. "I don't know what's going on with these dreams of yours, but Tucker is *not* your new father. Do you understand?"

"Yes, Mommy."

"I don't want you to say that anymore, because you might hurt somebody's feelings."

"Who's feelings?"

"I don't know . . ." her response was cut short by the ring of the telephone. Claire jumped up and ran into the kitchen to answer it.

"Hello," Claire spoke into the receiver.

"Hello, Claire. It's Darcy. I hope I didn't wake you."

"No, we've been up for a while over here."

"How are you doing?"

"Okay, I guess. Actually I'm pretty tired. I was up late last night working on that case. What's up?"

"The girls would like to know if Beth can come over and play this afternoon."

Darcy Hamilton lived with her husband and three daughters in an old farmhouse on Route 222, about five or six miles west of Bangor. Claire's house was another quarter mile farther from town. Beth had met her girls while they were out walking yesterday, and she had gotten along particularly well with her youngest, Katlyn, who was not much older than Beth herself. The girls played dolls together for the hour it had taken Claire to fill Darcy in on the situation.

"Really? That would be great!" Claire responded to her offer. "I have a ton of things I need to do this afternoon. Let me ask Elizabeth if she'd like to do that."

Claire cupped her hand over the mouthpiece of the phone and shouted, "Elizabeth!"

"What?" came the reply from the living room.

"How would you like to go over to Katlyn's house this afternoon?"

"Yeah!" Beth answered enthusiastically, running into the kitchen shortly thereafter.

"She'd love to. What time do you want me to bring her over?"

"We're going to ten o'clock mass," Darcy replied, "and then we'll need to get some lunch. How does one o'clock sound?"

"Sounds great. Thanks Darcy, we'll see you then."

Beth had been holding onto Claire's shirt and looking up at her expectantly since she had come into the room. After hanging up the phone, Claire picked her up and rubbed her adopted daughter's nose with her own.

"I'll take you over there after lunch," stated Claire.

"Awww, why can't I go there now?"

"They're going to church this morning," answered Claire, carrying Beth into the living room and sitting down on the couch with Beth still in her arms. "And they didn't invite you for lunch."

"Can we go to church, too?" asked Beth.

"I don't go to church," Claire told her.

"Why not?" pressed Beth, her innocent question catching Claire by surprise.

"How do I answer that?" she thought. Had Beth been an adult she would have told her that she just didn't believe in organized religion. She had been raised in the church, and continued to go sporadically throughout college, but had stopped completely when her study of the law began to consume her life. She had never really given her self-excommunication a second thought, nor did she feel as if anything in her life was missing because she wasn't a practicing member of a church.

"I haven't found a good church to go to," she said finally, feeling as if she was being at least partially truthful.

"I went to church in Chicago," Beth said. "Every Sunday."

"Really?"

"Will you take me to church, Mommy?"

Claire's heart melted at the sincerity in Beth's plea. She wondered, as she looked into the girl's silently imploring eyes, how she would ever be able to say 'no' to her, either now, or in the future.

"We can't go today, but maybe we'll go next Sunday," she compromised. "I'll have to find one around here, first."

"Why can't we go to Katlyn's church?"

"Maybe we will, honey. Maybe we will."

After dropping Beth off next door, Claire returned home to work on her case against B & G Lumber. She sat at the kitchen table with her files fanned out before her, a legal pad and pen in her hands. She listed the strongpoints of her case, putting a check mark next to those items which were ready for presentation to the judge. The rest needed more supporting evidence, which she hoped her team could gather by the end of the week.

The hearing had been granted on the strength of a two thousand signature petition, started by the residents of Dover-Foxcroft. They had asked Claire to represent them, and she jumped at the chance to directly oppose a clear-cut. Now that she had won her day in court and assumed the burden of proof, it had become increasingly apparent to her that she didn't have a case. She thought about the false bravado she had shown to Tucker the other night and regretted it. Why had she let him get to her like that?

She had done everything she could think of to prepare her offense. She had amassed all the statistics she could find about the damaging effects of a clear-cut, which she was prepared to name in excruciating detail. She had persuaded Dr. Lawrence, a forestry professor from the University of Maine, to attend the hearing to add some credibility to her facts and figures. She could also illustrate this damage with thirty color slides of the scars of past clear-cuts, taken from all over the northern Maine woods.

"Twenty-seven 8 by 10 color glossy photographs with circles and arrows and a paragraph on the back of each one explaining what each one was . . ." she remembered from an old Arlo Guthrie song, chuckling.

She had sent volunteers into the woods, mostly under the cover of darkness, to measure the size of the proposed clear-cut and its nearness to neighboring lakes and roads. She had also sent forays into the remains of forests already clear-cut by B & G Lumber, to search for improprieties in their logging practices. Had she been able to show that B & G had already stepped outside the bounds of the law, she would at least have been able to argue that they were more likely to do so again. Such was not the case.

All of her search parties had returned with the same bad news—B & G was clean. Whoever was running the show over there was being very careful with the law. Which is where the battle really needed to be fought, Claire realized. Unless they could get the existing laws changed, the systematic clear-cutting of Maine's forests would continue unabated. Unfortunately, they had already lost the first skirmish in that war when the citizen initiative entitled 'The Act to Promote Forest Rehabilitation and Eliminate Clear-cutting' was defeated by vote on the 1996 ballot.

"If only we could have convinced the people of Maine of the long-term damage caused by clear-cutting" Claire daydreamed, but not for long. Soon her mind was once again focused on the task at hand.

She had butted heads with B & G once before, over a clear-cut they were planning north of Monson. She had won that decision without ever having to go to court, because a pair of nesting bald eagles had been found on the site. Bald eagles were protected as an endangered species in the state of Maine. Claire had been lucky in that instance, but she couldn't expect that kind of luck to surface again.

"There must be some angle I haven't considered," Claire reasoned. "But what?"

Claire tossed the legal pad down on the table and began to rub her temples with her fingertips. Her thoughts turned to Beth, and she wondered what they were doing next door. Images from the past two weeks she had spent with Beth began to flood her mind and her motivation to argue this case waned.

"Is it really that important?" she thought. "I have a child to take care of, now. Why am I in here alone, working, when I could be outside playing with her?"

Then she remembered Beth's excitement as they walked through the forest the previous day.

"Will there even be any forests left in Maine by the time Beth gets to be my age?" she mused. "What kind of world will I leave her as my legacy?"

Realizing that her cause was even more important now than ever before, she was suddenly imbued with new resolve. She owed it to Beth to continue fighting for a reasonably clean planet and healthy environment in which she could grow to adulthood and raise a family of her own.

"But I still don't have a case," she told herself, her new resolve not strong enough to completely ward off the gnawing gnats of self-doubt which assailed her. "The law is pretty clear-cut."

Claire laughed at the pun, though she found no humor in it. She was exhausted, she realized, and rose from the table to make herself a cup of coffee. Just as she was about to turn the burner on, she changed her mind and decided to rest her eyes for a few minutes. She strode into the bedroom and collapsed upon the bed, not even bothering to take her shoes off. In minutes she had fallen into a deep slumber and an even deeper dream.

In her dream she and Beth were walking at twilight through the same woods they had explored the day before. Beth was uncharacteristically quiet, and she held tight to Claire's hand as though she were afraid of losing her in the growing darkness. They heard a wolf call in the distance and Beth squeezed Claire's hand even more tightly.

"Do not be afraid!" said a booming voice which seemed to come from somewhere behind them. "I am with you always."

The voice sounded to Claire like Hollywood's version of the voice of God, and she stopped in her tracks. Glancing nervously over her shoulder, she saw nothing but the trees and fallen leaves she could see in every other direction.

"Did you hear that?" she asked Beth.

"It's just Thorn," Beth answered with confidence. "C'mon, I'll show you."

She pulled Claire along behind her as she broke into a tottering run. Claire needn't do much more than walk fast to keep up with her, but she allowed her new daughter to lead, even after she abandoned the trail and dragged her into the thickest part of the forest.

It had grown darker still and Claire was just about to assert leadership over their expedition once more, when they came to a clearing. In the center of the clearing stood an immense oak tree. The oak seemed to be illumined from a source all its own and Claire could make out the details of every branch and leaf at a single glance. She stopped short and Beth's hand slipped from hers as the girl continued forward to rest her hands on the trunk of the huge tree.

"This is the tree I told you about, Mommy," said Beth, smiling back at her.

"This is Thorn?" asked Claire.

"My beloved, Claire," she heard in that same otherworldly voice, although it wasn't nearly as loud this time.

"Who is that?" Claire asked.

"My name is Thorn, but don't read too much into that. A tree by any other name would be as sweet."

"That doesn't even make any sense," said Claire, who had approached the tree and stood now touching the rough surface of the trunk opposite Beth.

"Does everything have to make sense?"

"I brought her up here, like you told me to," Beth's voice joined the conversation before Claire could answer.

"Good job, Beth," answered the deep voice of the tree. "You're a very sweet child. I've been wanting to talk to your new mommy for quite a long time."

"Talk to me about what?" Claire broke in.

"How is the court case coming along?" asked Thorn.

"Why do you want to know?"

"Look at me, Claire," the tree commanded. "You might say I have a vested interest."

"Oh," Claire exhaled, feeling foolish. "Not very well, I'm afraid. I can give the judge plenty of good reasons why he should stop the clear-cut, but I can't change the laws which say he should allow it."

"Did you know Tucker is going to be a witness for the defense?"

"Really?" Claire's interest was piqued. "In what sense?"

"He's a forester. He'll be testifying that the tree-cutters are doing everything by the book."

"Damn him!" Claire cursed loudly, and then remembered that Beth was close at hand. She covered her mouth instinctively as she began to circumnavigate Thorn in search of Beth.

"Don't be too hard on him, Claire. He's just playing his part, even as you are."

"Don't be too hard on him?" she shouted. "What do you mean don't be too hard on him? He's the enemy!"

"You may not always think so," Thorn replied, but Claire barely heard him. She had made a full circle around Thorn's trunk and still had not located Beth.

"Elizabeth!" she shouted. "Where are you?"

She moved around the tree again, in the opposite direction and running this time, just in case Beth was purposely trying to hide from her. There was no sign of her adopted daughter.

"Elizabeth!" she screamed, waking herself up from the dream. She sat bolt upright in bed, fully awake in an instant. Glancing at the alarm clock on the nightstand she noted that two hours had passed since she laid down. It seemed to Claire as if she had only just closed her eyes, though she had to admit that she no longer felt sleepy.

Swinging her legs over the edge of the bed, she pushed herself up and fairly ran into the kitchen to call Darcy. Beth was fine and playing outside with her girls. Darcy promised to bring her home within the hour. Relief washed over Claire as she hung up the phone. It was only a dream, she reminded herself. She cleared her files off the kitchen table, stuffing them into her briefcase before beginning her preparations for dinner.

EIGHT

Hunger Dance

Through my window, I hear their dance,
The stomping of feet, the beat of a drum.
A shadow on the desert, I make my advance.
I call out, "Nyai!" They answer, "Mum."

"Why do you dance here, Sister,
On this moonlit, Turkana night?"
"I dance my hunger, Mister,
I dance to forget, this is my plight."

Silently I watch, I am the outsider.
My satisfied stomach is full of food.
They see me solely, as their provider.
I'd feed them all, if I only could.

A girl pulls me up, to join in their dance.
The local brew has gone to my head.
Swaying hand in hand as if in a trance,
It's hours later before I'm home in my bed.

Long past midnight, time to sleep.
The dancers dance, the children weep.

D espite his training in meditation, Paxton had trouble clearing his mind for his first foray into The Chords. He thought about Claire and their changing relationship now that Beth had come upon the scene. He thought about Annie and Tucker, remembering them as they were when they had all been roommates, and the strange turn of events that had led Tucker back to this place. And he thought about the oak tree at his back, pondering over just who or what Thorn could possibly be and struggling to adjust the paradigm of his reality to include the existence of talking trees.

Suddenly Paxton was reminded of a paranormal experience he had encountered in the form of an acacia tree and his mind crossed both the Atlantic Ocean and the continent of Africa before alighting on its eastern edge in the small town of Lokitaung. It was here that he had spent two years of his life teaching mathematics to the Turkanans.

Turkana was the name given not only to the province in which he had lived in northern Kenya, but also to its inhabitants. Paxton had often wondered why anyone would willingly call this parched and rocky wilderness home, but the Turkanan people were fiercely loyal to their traditional tribal lands. Their thin bodies survived upon the meat of their equally thin goats, and the meager supplies they could garnish from the town's only store through the sale of these goats. With the exception of the children and his students, Paxton found the Turkanans to be an unfriendly sort of people. It wasn't until well into his second year that he was invited into the home of one of his students, though he had opened his front door upon many imploring eyes and filled many an open palm with rice before that time. He tried not to take their lack of warmth too personally, but rather blamed their collective surliness on the harsh realities of life in the desert.

For two weeks out of each month, while the half-moon waxed full and then shrunk into her opposite half, the Turkana would dance the night away beneath her watchful eyes. At first the constant drumming, which started as soon as the sun had set, kept him awake long after he had doused his lantern. Eventually he got so accustomed to the unchanging rhythm of the drums that the vacuous silence was almost scary on those nights when the moon kept her rounds with the sun. Paxton had never stayed awake long enough to hear their drums cease during the night, but they were always silent when he awoke at dawn.

Having never received an invitation to join their dance, Paxton had kept his distance until shortly before his Peace Corps tour was scheduled to end. One of the teachers had brought a case of beer up from Lodwar for his going away party and he had been drinking *pombes* all afternoon. When the drums began later that evening, the alcohol had given him enough courage to traverse the nighttime desert and seek out their bonfire.

The details of that evening were lost in an alcoholic fog, but Paxton's subconscious had elaborated upon his faulty memories with a recurring dream that differed only slightly in its various iterations. This particular dream usually began inside a small, earthen round-house in Kenya. He was seated upon a sturdy wooden bench, writing a letter of some sort by the dim light of a kerosine lantern, when the Turkana began their nightly drumming.

Paxton was immediately seized by the desire to join them at their moondance, but he was also frightened at the prospect of walking to their village in the dark. Finally, his curiosity overcame his fear and he went outside, but not before grabbing a flashlight to supplement the opaque light of the moon. He directed a beacon of light on the ground in front of his feet, searching the broken and rocky landscape for scorpions and snakes.

Guided by the light of their campfire, Paxton climbed to the top of a slight rise in the desert. Both the drumming and dancing stopped momentarily as his ghostly face appeared at the edge of their circle. He gave the customary greetings to the elders and then someone handed him a cup full of the local brew, and the drumming resumed. He sat next to the chief and drank two more *pombes* before the drums began to work their magic upon him.

The chief's words, which he could not understand, became more and more distant as the rhythm of the drums pervaded his consciousness. He could feel the pounding within his chest begin to amplify, and then synchronize itself to the timeless beat of those primordial drums. Soon he could contain himself no longer and he arose, stumbling into the circle of dancers.

The circle cleared and a beautiful, young Turkana woman danced into his field of vision. She wasn't much more than a girl, though her uncovered breasts were full and round and swayed seductively to the rhythm of her movements. Paxton couldn't take his eyes from her dark and shining skin, which reflected the light from both the campfire and the full moon. She gyrated toward him and Paxton joined in her stomping dance, his body mimicking her movements as the drums pulled the strings of his puppet limbs. Their dance became more frenetic as the drums picked up tempo, until they were twirling in tight circles and Paxton's head began to swim.

Here his dream changed scenes abruptly, and Paxton found himself walking home from their dance. He passed his favorite acacia tree, which grew in a dry riverbed at the base of the small hill leading up to his house. He sensed there was something very different about the tree as he approached it. Climbing into its lower branches he was immediately struck by the sensation that the tree was not only sentient, but malevolent.

He jumped down, landing hard on his right ankle, and recoiled as if he had been physically struck by the tree. Forsaking the winding path, he began to hobble straight up the hill toward his house, fear driving him onward. When he was about halfway up the hill, he stopped suddenly.

"You have set me free," he heard from behind him.

Turning around, he could see only the tree. He felt some sort of weight on his hurt ankle and looking down, he saw that a puff adder had coiled itself around his leg, rooting him to his spot on the hillside.

"What do we have here?" the timbre of Thorn's now familiar voice broke into his mind.

"Thorn? Is that you?" Paxton asked fearfully. Looking downward he could no longer see or feel the snake around his ankle. In fact, he was surrounded by an inky darkness that allowed him to neither see nor feel anything at all.

"Yes, it's me," answered Thorn. "Were you expecting someone else?"

"Where are we?"

"In The Chords," Thorn continued. "I have just left Tucker to his dreams and have come here just in the nick of time to save you from yours."

"I was dreaming about Kenya," Paxton confirmed. "I was remembering a certain acacia tree which grew out of a dry riverbed at the bottom of the hill near my house. It amazed me that it could grow there at all. The river only flowed for one month out of the year, during rainy season. I passed it every day on my way to and from school. It was my favorite tree. I actually felt like I communicated with it one night."

"What did it say?" Thorn asked, his interest piqued.

"It didn't *say* anything. We didn't communicate like you and I are communicating. I just felt a presence there. It gave me the creeps, actually. I passed it off the next day as being drunk. Even so, I never looked at the tree in quite the same way again after that night."

"Your drunken state may have opened up your mind to the experience," Thorn speculated, "but I wouldn't pass it off on the beer, completely. After all, you know, now, that it's possible for a tree to have a consciousness. Perhaps that acacia tree had one, too."

There was no mistaking the eagerness in the voice Paxton heard inside his head. He hated to squelch Thorn's hopes, but he didn't want to foster false ones, either.

"I think I must've imagined it," he said. "I only felt the presence that one time, and it happened as I stumbled home from a hard night of drinking with the Turkana. The tree never spoke to me in words, or answered any of my questions, as you are doing now."

"Sometimes words can be a barrier to real communication," suggested Thorn, undaunted. "Words might not have done justice to what you sensed about that tree with your subconscious mind. Or maybe it just couldn't communicate with you unless you made yourself available to the experience. I wasn't able to converse with you until you made the first move by opening up your mind to me."

"I suppose that's possible . . ."

"I'm going to try to find out," Thorn interrupted again in his excitement. "I've been searching for another of my kind for as long as I can remember."

"How are you going to do that?"

"Through The Chords, I hope. I have this idea that it might be possible for us to travel along each other's chords more easily than our own. If that's true, we may be able to learn more about each other's past lives. I haven't been able to glean much history, prior to my birth as this tree, from my own chord. It seems to me that this blind spot is a natural feature of The Chords, because I can travel more freely along other chords than I can upon my own."

"Haven't you already examined my past? You seem to know so much about me."

"I have up to a point, but the process of unraveling a single soul's strand from the tapestry is a slow and laborious one. Look around you."

Paxton did as he was told and was surprised to find that the total blackness in which he had so recently been immersed had given way to dim light and a tangled jumble of serpentine forms. It was as if he had been transported into a dense rain forest as the first rays of sunlight heralded the approaching dawn.

As his vision cleared, so too did his auditory system, and a low humming noise crept into his range of detectable frequencies. The sound continued to amplify and splintered into a multitude of soft, buzzing tones which gave Paxton the impression of being in the middle of a very large beehive.

"Great!" he thought. "Snakes and bees!"

"I rather like to think of it as the electronics of a supercomputer," commented Thorn. "The light and sound are caused by the flow of electrons through the wiring. Each wire plays its one small part in the calculation of some grand problem posed by The Programmer."

"Where is that noise coming from, really?" asked Paxton.

"Each strand you see vibrates with its own particular frequency, even as each string of your guitar has its own particular tone. And just as you combine certain notes to form a musical chord, the strands which intertwine together combine to form new frequencies. See if you can hear any."

Paxton listened carefully and thought he could discern a few more distinctive tones against the general buzz, but he couldn't be sure.

"As the chords join together to form stronger strands, the notes of the individual chords join together to form more complex musical chords. These chords then combine into more intricate structures— sonatas, songs and symphonies. When all of the chords come together as one, they form the universal tone which has been best approximated by humans as 'Om'. Spiritual aspirants chant 'Om' in the attempt to tune their individual frequencies to the universal frequency. If you could find and maintain that frequency indefinitely, you could find your Enlightenment."

"How are we supposed to find our way anywhere through this jungle?" asked Paxton.

"Making sense of The Chords requires patience and practice," explained Thorn. "To follow a single thread is like working your way through a giant maze. I think it will be easier with you here, though."

"Why is that?"

"Look at our two chords," instructed Thorn. "Do you notice anything different about them?"

Paxton was about to answer negatively when he caught an almost imperceptible shimmer of green light radiating along the length of what he could only assume to be his own chord, as it seemed to pass right through him. As he concentrated on it, the light grew stronger and he saw the trail it made through the impenetrable forest before him. Thorn's chord was next to his own, and it glowed even more brightly, with that same shade of pale green light.

"Why is your chord brighter than mine?" asked Paxton.

"I don't know," Thorn answered truthfully. "Maybe it's because I've been in The Chords many more times than you have. Did you notice how ours are the only two chords glowing this way?"

Paxton looked around him and verified Thorn's observation, but made no response.

"I noticed long ago that my own chord glowed, and I reasoned that it must have something to do with my presence here. That hypothesis was verified a couple of hours ago when I traveled The Chords briefly with Tucker. This glow should light a path for us as we travel down each other's chords."

Unconvinced, Paxton questioned Thorn's conclusion, "What if our paths diverge as we travel backwards? Won't our respective chords grow dimmer as we travel apart from them?"

"I don't know that either. I have a theory that our paths have crossed before this lifetime and if that is the case, we should stay close enough to continue to light each other's way. We can test that theory anytime you're ready to stop thinking and start moving."

"I'm ready right now," announced Paxton, slightly chagrined. "What do I need to do?"

"Concentrate your full attention on the light encircling my chord. Try to see that light to the exclusion of all else around you."

Paxton focused upon Thorn's thread, and the green light he saw along its length grew perceptibly brighter. Before long he could see only that one chord and he told Thorn as much.

"Now will yourself forward."

"I thought we were going backward."

"We are traveling into the past, but only because we are pointed in that direction. You will still feel the movement as a forward motion along the chord, even though the events you witness will be transpiring in reverse order."

"All right," Paxton said as he prepared to move. "I'll see you later."

"Yes, you will."

"Wait!" exclaimed Paxton. "What if we lose each other in here? How do I get out of The Chords?"

"I usually grow tired and fall asleep, just as Tucker did not long ago. When I wake up, I'm back inside my physical form. But I've also willed myself back into my physical form by concentrating my attention upon it. You should have no trouble doing the same."

"Okay," Paxton agreed skeptically, adding, "but you'll come and get me if I get lost, won't you?"

"Of course I will."

"Then I'm off!" Paxton announced, with as much enthusiasm as he could muster in the wake of his uncertainty. He focused his awareness on Thorn's chord, which had dimmed slightly during their conversation, and thought about moving forward along its length. He immediately felt the sensation of motion as he concentrated upon the path of light beneath him.

—

Thorn waited until he could barely feel Paxton's presence before beginning his trek into Paxton's past. Adept at traveling through The Chords, he accelerated his pace through Paxton's graduate education at the University of Maine. He was looking for something specific, and he had visited most of these scenes before.

Thorn had examined all of their chords—Paxton, Tucker, Claire and Annie—in as much detail as he could accomplish given the tangled mess they formed in either direction from the present's tiny point. Still, he had never discovered the acacia tree that Paxton had just told him about, even though he was familiar with most of Paxton's Peace Corps experience. Nor had he ever picked the details from his mind, and that bothered him. It was almost as if that information had been masked for some reason. He felt confident that he would be able to find the tree now, though, with Paxton's faintly glowing chord to light his way.

Thorn was moving so fast that he passed over the scene he was searching for before he had the chance to examine it. He turned around and moved back toward it in the forward direction.

He saw a circle of dancers around a campfire in the Turkana desert, beneath a full African moon. The blurry quality of the scene he was witnessing reminded him that Paxton had been drinking. This thought was confirmed when a hand holding a dirty brown bottle came into view at the bottom edge of his vision, and the starry night sky replaced the dancers momentarily as Paxton took a swill.

A young Turkana girl danced into his field of vision, which had become even more out of focus. She danced before him for a long time, almost as though she had been presented to him as a personal gift. Then she reached her hand out to Paxton, who staggered to his feet. Here the picture Thorn was watching began to move wildly about and he reasoned that Paxton must have been attempting to mimic the girl's dance. This went on for quite some time before the girl reached her hand out to Paxton again and he stumbled behind her into a small hut made of interwoven sticks.

Once inside the hut the scene blacked out, and Thorn could do nothing to make it come back into focus. He accelerated until the screen was illuminated once again by the brilliant eye of the full moon. Paxton was walking across a rocky footpath toward a darkened hillside. As he drew nearer the hill, an acacia tree sprouted out of the rocks and grew ever larger. When the thin branches and wispy leaves of the tree had formed a canopy overhead, and the trunk of the tree dominated his field of vision, Paxton's hand reached out to touch the smooth bark.

"How are you doing, old man?" Thorn heard Paxton's voice over the distant background drumming.

"Much better, now, thank you," came the gravelly response, as if the noise had been dredged up from the rocky depths of some immense underground cavern in the center of the earth.

"I wish you could talk to me," Paxton continued, obviously unaware that the tree had spoken to him. Branches swam through Thorn's field of vision as Paxton climbed into the tree.

"Ah, but I can, if only you could hear me."

Thorn could hear the deep and rumbling voice plainly, but it was clear that Paxton could not. The picture had stabilized once again as Paxton found a seat in the acacia's branches.

"Would you tell me the secrets of the universe?"

"I could. And maybe someday I will."

"What would you say?" slurred Paxton slightly, still talking to himself.

"Thank you, Father. You have set me free."

This time it appeared as though Paxton had heard the voice, because the scene Thorn was viewing froze for a moment, and then changed abruptly as Paxton jumped down out of the tree and was now looking upward into its branches. He stayed there but a moment before turning and limping quickly up the hill toward the large brown structure at its crest. Thorn surmised that Paxton must have injured himself as he jumped out of the tree. When he was about half the distance to his house, Paxton turned and gazed once more upon the tree, before resuming his hurried walk home.

A quick but thorough search through the rest of the Lokitaung footage convinced Thorn that the tree had only contacted Paxton once, but that one contact had been clear and definite. He replayed the scene several times to convince himself that it had actually occurred.

The acacia tree had a consciousness, too! Thorn was no longer alone! Were there other tree-souls out there? How could he possibly contact them? He thought about the implications of his discovery, and the tree's cryptic message, while Paxton's life proceeded backwards slowly, unnoticed for the time being.

—

As Paxton journeyed backwards along Thorn's chord, the images which flashed before him changed so rapidly that he felt as if he were viewing a slide show presentation rather than a moving picture. He saw Thorn from above and in the next instant he was amongst Thorn's branches looking down upon himself. He viewed the tree from the ground level and then Thorn was nowhere to be seen amongst the sea of green trees sliding past beneath him. Many of the scenes began to repeat themselves with slight variations and Paxton remembered that Thorn's 'eyesight' was made possible by borrowing the eyes of the creatures around him.

Once he found his bearings and the abrupt changes weren't so distracting, Paxton became aware of other senses as well. He found he could hear birds in Thorn's branches and the distant rumble of an eighteen-wheeler down Route 15. He felt the wind and the heat from the sun. Paxton soon began to experience a oneness with the natural world around him, and he was content just to be a part of it until he watched a bird fly past him, backwards. This recalled him to his mission and he concentrated a little harder on his motion along the chord. Soon the days were changing into nights much more rapidly.

He was mesmerized by the unending string of sunrises and sunsets, until the movement of three figures below him caught his eye and he slowed his progress to a standstill. In the center of his vision stood Paxton himself, his guitar strapped over one shoulder, while Tucker and Annie were frozen in comic postures, their naked bodies glistening in the sunlight. Paxton reversed direction with some concentrated effort, and heard himself begin to sing 'Uncle John's Band' as Tucker and Annie danced around him laughing and tossing long blades of grass on his head and shoulders.

Paxton watched the scene with rapt attention, though he knew exactly what was going to happen even before he took his guitar off his shoulder and joined them, naked on the blanket. He watched as the three of them made love together, beneath the oak tree. It seemed to him now that it was a completely natural extension of the love he could feel emanating from their bodies, as if it were a tangible force. He remembered this as one of the most transcendently beautiful experiences of his life, even if it did precipitate Tucker and Annie's marriage and his departure for Africa.

Paxton stared at the movie screen until their passion had run its course and they lay sleeping in a tangled heap beneath Thorn's boughs. It was then that he remembered he was watching the scene through Thorn's viewpoint. His nostalgia was replaced quickly by embarrassment, which in turn galvanized him into movement and he found himself traveling backward along Thorn's chord once more. Not wanting to watch the three figures below him make love again, Paxton tried, and succeeded in picking up his pace. Soon the days were flying past him as though he were watching the light at the top of a lighthouse turn night briefly into day as it rotated upon its axis.

This went on for a long time before the screen he was viewing suddenly turned black. After he had adjusted to the darkness, Paxton could make out the glowing trail of Thorn's chord passing beneath him. He concentrated on this faint line of light, because it made him dizzy to watch the other chords whip past him as he dove deeper into their midst.

The light returned to the screen before him as quickly as it had winked out and Paxton's field of vision was flooded with the light-brown color of parchment and a hand which seemed to be erasing the words written on each sheet. Although the pages were being turned very rapidly, Paxton could see enough to realize that the author was not using the English language. He guessed that the characters being annihilated were Arabic, but he couldn't be sure.

The scene shifted from time to time, as the writer moved about the room and slept, but the movie Paxton was viewing was dominated by the frenetic motions of that hand as it unwrote pages and pages of parchment. The author of those volumes lived in a small, square room with earthen walls and several narrow slits for windows. He rarely saw the landscape revealed by those windows, but occasional glimpses of sun and sand convinced him that he was in the desert, on the edge of a vast sea or lake.

Paxton originally thought he was seeing through the eyes of some type of monk, but as day after monotonous day rewound he felt more like a prisoner. This was confirmed when the setting changed to a more obvious prison cell within the same compound. This new room was much more crowded, and his manic cleansing of parchment was periodically interrupted as he tended to the care and comfort of the other prisoners. Paxton gradually became mesmerized by the repetitive daily routine to which he was witness and he began to lose focus upon the chord he had been traveling. His mind drifted slowly away from this particular scene and he fell into a deep sleep full of dreams about exotic peoples and faraway lands.

"Wake up, Paxton!" Tucker shouted, as he shook him forcefully by the shoulder. Paxton sat up abruptly, opening his eyes, and then he sank slowly back down to the earth, a huge yawn escaping his lips.

"That was some dream you were having," added Tucker, when Paxton looked up at him. "You were tossing around all over the place."

"It was that indeed," Paxton agreed, not offering to elaborate. "What time is it?"

"Judging by the sun, I think it's right around noon," answered Tucker.

"How can it be noon?" Paxton responded. "It was after that when we closed our eyes."

"It's noon on Sunday," Tucker added.

"What a trip!" Paxton exclaimed, before another forceful yawn escaped his lips. He stood up and reached his arms skyward and then bent at the waist to touch his toes. Looking sidelong at Tucker he asked, "How long have you been awake?"

"Long enough to figure out that we've been here almost twenty-four hours!" replied Tucker.

"That doesn't seem possible!" returned Paxton, straightening up. "I haven't slept this late since we were in college together!"

"Me either! What happened to us last night?"

"You took your first trip into The Chords," Thorn finally joined their conversation. "What did you think of it?"

"It was wild!" exclaimed Paxton. "I feel as though I have been having the strangest dreams all night long!"

"Some were dreams and some weren't," interrupted Thorn. "You both were in The Chords for a long time, but eventually your consciousness returned to a more normal sleep state and you dreamed more normal dreams."

"There was nothing normal about them," countered Tucker. "But you're right about one thing, while I was in The Chords it was more like I was watching a movie than having a dream. Sometimes I was a character in the movie, and other times I was a member of the audience. I watched the movie of my life, or rather, I re-acted it. But the images began to grow lighter and more indistinct as I approached the present, and I wasn't able to see much of anything into the future.

"No, that isn't true," he continued after a momentary pause. "I saw a lot of scenes from the future, but I was just a member of the audience at that point. What a future it was! Cities reduced to rubble. Famines. Earthquakes. An army so big it could be seen from outer space! I had visions of Armageddon!"

"So you're finally coming around," joked Paxton.

"I don't know about that," said Tucker, "but the visions were so real. Don't tell me you didn't see the same thing!"

"As a matter of fact I didn't," Paxton admitted. "Thorn and I traveled into the past on each other's chords."

"And what did you see of my past?" asked Thorn eagerly.

"You were indeed a man in your previous life," Paxton confirmed.

"I knew it!" Thorn shouted within their minds. "Tell me what you saw!"

"There isn't a whole lot to tell," began Paxton. "You were living in a desert. I thought it might be somewhere in the Middle East, judging by the garb that you and your contemporaries were wearing. You spent most of your time indoors writing. You were a prolific writer. I couldn't read the characters because they were in another language— Arabic, I think.

"The more I watched, the more I got the impression you were under house arrest. You weren't in a jail cell, but you seemed to be confined to your house nonetheless. Your life was pretty monotonous, at least what I saw of it. So much so that it put me to sleep. After that my mind was all over the place."

"Hey, wait a minute!" Tucker interrupted. "Why did you two guys ditch me?"

"I was with you the whole time," objected Thorn. "I didn't join Paxton until you were already asleep."

"You were with me the whole time?" asked Tucker in disbelief. "Why didn't you answer me?"

"I wanted you to draw your own conclusions. Besides, I was too busy dragging you around."

"It did feel like I was being drawn ever upward," Tucker remembered, "until you dropped me like a hot potato!"

"You were in the presence of The All," explained Thorn. "At your current level of awareness I could only allow you a few moments of such close proximity without sustaining some damage to your psyche."

"By The All do you mean God?" asked Paxton. "Because when I was in The Chords I felt closer to God than at any time during the last ten years of spiritual striving."

"Yes," Thorn answered, "and no. I believe that God is everywhere and everything, which is why I usually refer to the universal consciousness as The All. God is not only present in The Chords, but God *is* The Chords. God is composed of each and every chord in the cosmic tapestry, and when you can get to a vantage point where you can view a larger piece of the tapestry, you will see more of God. You will come closer to understanding the immensity that is The All."

"I thought you said God was The Weaver," Tucker reminded him.

"The Weaver is also part of The All. There is more than one way to imagine God. Humans have conceived of a myriad of ways to conceptualize God, each claiming to be the one and only truth when, in fact, they are all true!"

"How can everyone's beliefs about God be true when many of them contradict each other?" asked Paxton. "Each religion has its own prophets and its own image of God. Hindus believe in many gods. Jews and Muslims don't believe Jesus was the Son of God, but Christians do. Even amongst Christians there are vastly differing viewpoints as to what God is like."

"God is all of these things, and none of them," Thorn replied cryptically. "No one on this planet knows who or what God is, for sure, but we all like to think we do. I've been telling you my ideas about God, but they're just ideas. They're no more or less valid than either of your own concepts of God."

"I can definitely identify with the immensity you describe," Tucker broke in, "having felt it in The Chords myself. When I was at the pinnacle of my trajectory I caught a glimpse of the tapestry. In fact, it filled the scope of my vision completely. The edges of the tapestry seemed to stretch toward infinity in every direction. My own personal thread seemed so small and insignificant against that backdrop."

"Small, but far from insignificant," countered Thorn. "Your level of significance is relative to where your awareness happens to reside amongst the chords. You felt insignificant in relation to the larger picture of the tapestry, yet if your awareness happened to reside on an electron, say, you would view the inhabitants of this planet as gods, with the power of life and death over your world."

"Does an electron have awareness, then?" asked Paxton.

"Every chord in the tapestry has awareness, as every chord is a part of The All."

"But is an electron aware like I am aware?" pushed Paxton.

"And just how are you aware?" Thorn countered.

The question left Paxton stymied for a few moments, nor was an answer forthcoming from Tucker. The first thing that popped into Paxton's head was, 'I think, therefore I am,' but he suspected Thorn would not be satisfied with that oft-used Descartes quote.

"You're asking me to answer a question that humans have been wrestling with since the dawn of time" he stated, finally.

"Probably not for that long, Paxton, but you're right. That's not a fair question. Not yet, anyway. I'll let you ponder over that one for a while."

"I've had enough pondering for now, I'm hungry," said Tucker, emphasizing his point with a rumble from his empty stomach.

"What a bad host I am!" exclaimed Thorn. "By all means, eat some breakfast."

"I don't think we have much of anything left," said Paxton, moving toward his backpack. He rummaged through its contents a few moments before extracting a granola bar and an apple.

"Which one do you want?" he asked Tucker, holding them up.

"I'll take the apple."

Paxton tossed it to him. Tucker bobbled and dropped the apple, which rolled several feet behind him. As he turned to retrieve it, he saw yesterday's wine bottle standing upright in the grass nearby.

"Hey, we still have some wine!" Tucker said excitedly, as he stooped to pick up the bottle.

"There can't be much of that left, either," said Paxton.

"What are you talking about?" Tucker replied. "It's still three-quarters full."

"It can't be," said Paxton, moving toward Tucker. His eyes widened with surprise as he reached for the proffered bottle and saw immediately that Tucker's estimate had been correct. "I had three or four glasses of wine yesterday. How many did you have?"

"About the same," Tucker agreed.

"This bottle should be empty!" Paxton observed. "Did it rain here last night?"

"Not that I know of," replied Tucker. "Taste it."

After raising the bottle to his lips, Paxton passed it back to Tucker, who promptly did the same.

"If this is water," Tucker commented, "it's the best-tasting water I've ever had!"

"Why don't you have some blueberries with your wine?" asked Thorn, interrupting their wine-tasting ceremony.

"Did you bring any blueberries, Paxton?" asked Tucker.

"No, the only thing we have left is a granola bar and an apple."

"Look in the field below you," prodded Thorn. "It's full of blueberry bushes."

"You know as well as I do that blueberry season is long over . . ." said Tucker, whose voice caught in his throat as he turned to follow Paxton's incredulous gaze. The low blueberry bushes in the field below them were full of fruit, their tiny leaves a robust green in contrast to the more typical yellows and browns of the autumnal meadow.

"How can this be?" asked Tucker, walking toward the nearest island of green, followed closely by Paxton. The last of this year's blueberries should have been gone by the end of August, at the very latest. "I didn't see any blueberries in this field yesterday."

"There weren't any there, yesterday," said Thorn.

"How did they get here, then?" asked Tucker.

"Who cares?" mumbled Paxton around a mouthful of blueberries. "They're delicious."

Tucker tried one without comment, but Paxton clearly heard his friend's stomach rumble in anticipation of more. He lowered himself to the ground next to where Paxton had already taken a seat and began to gather blueberries, popping them into his mouth as fast as he could pick them.

"Eat your breakfast," said Thorn. "We'll talk more when you're done."

Tucker stammered a feeble protest, but Thorn's presence was already gone from their minds. He looked at Paxton, who merely shrugged his shoulders and then went back to the serious business at hand. It was only a matter of minutes before the two of them had picked clean the few bushes surrounding them and had moved to an even thicker stand of blueberries further out into the meadow.

NINE

*O*nce

Once an explorer set sail for the sea,
    to seek and discover new worlds,
        to be free.
What treasures he found,
    what secrets uncovered,
        what worlds are there left
            for us now to discover?
Today an astronomer peers at the sky,
    billions of worlds in the blink of an eye.
What does he suffer
    what passion, what pain,
        what does he risk,
            what does humankind gain?

Once a brave knight
    rode his steed off to fight,
        great fearsome dragons
            lighting up the night.
What battles he fought,
    what legends were told,
        what dragons are left
            for us now to behold?
Today a young man can't get up off his bed.
He's fighting the dragons
    inside his own head.
Alone in the room with a gun in his mouth,
    what does he care
        when the bullet screams out?

Once the hunter trekked the jungle primeval,
    valets pulled the cage
        meant for tiger retrieval.
How many tigers
    have we left to capture,
        to place in our zoos
            for the kids to enrapture?
Today a boy sits on his grandmother's knee.
She tells him about
    the way things used to be.
She tells him a tale of the beautiful tiger,
    across the big water
        and the land of the Niger.
And it's as if she's telling him of dragons
    in some land so far away,
Where the forests were green
    and the water ran clean
        and we weren't afraid of the day.

Once, we had it all,
    convinced ourselves we could never fall.
Perched on the pinnacle of the food chain,
    with opposable thumbs
        and an oversized brain.
Now we struggle just to survive,
    barely a handful, just barely alive.
Out of space, out of time,
    humanity in decline.

"Ｈow did those blueberry bushes bear fruit overnight?" asked Tucker, when they were once again seated beneath Thorn's outstretched arms.

"I thought you two might be hungry when you woke up this morning. The blueberry bushes just happened to be available, so it was easier to induce them to fruit than to order you up bacon, eggs and coffee."

"Easier to induce them to fruit?" repeated Tucker incredulously.

"But *how* did you accomplish it?" wondered Paxton.

"I just told you," it was Thorn's turn to repeat himself, "I *thought* them there. Thought creates reality. Have you learned nothing from your Zen training, Paxton?"

"'As you think, so you become,'" Paxton quoted. "But I always took that to mean that you should cultivate a positive mental attitude in order to find happiness."

"Of course," Thorn agreed, "but it means so much more. Our thoughts literally create our world, both individually and collectively. Let me ask you a question. Of what is the known universe composed?"

"Are we talking subatomic particles here?" Paxton asked for clarification.

"You guys are losing me now," Tucker chimed in.

"That would be matter," Thorn elucidated, ignoring Tucker for the moment. "What else?"

"Energy," Paxton answered with confidence.

"And under which of these two would you categorize thought?"

"Well it's clearly not matter," Paxton began, "so it must be energy."

"Precisely," agreed Thorn. "Thought is brain wave energy, and this energy can be converted into matter."

"Hold on there, Thorn," Paxton broke in. "I thought that it only worked the other way around, that matter can be converted into energy but not vice versa. I may only be a fledgling physicist, but even I know that matter can neither be created nor destroyed."

"Do you believe that to be an immutable physical law? At some point in the not too distant past, humans believed that the sun revolved around a decidedly flat planet Earth. Your understanding of the physical world continues to grow and evolve."

"Energy can most certainly be converted into matter," Thorn continued. "Your physicists have long since speculated as much and are even now building large particle accelerators to prove it. However, many spiritual masters from the past have already beaten them to the punch."

"What do you mean?" asked Tucker.

"Take Jesus the Christ, for example. How do you suppose he fed the multitudes with five loaves of bread and two fish? He changed water into wine, though I suppose you'd argue that this miracle was only a transmutation of matter rather than the creation of it."

"I would argue," countered Paxton, "that these miracles were performed by some divine power in answer to Jesus' prayers."

"You could say that, in a way," Thorn responded coyly. "There are so many things the universe is willing to grant you, if only you learn how to ask. Which is exactly why you must be careful what you ask for because you just might get it!"

"Can you teach me how to master this trick?" asked Paxton eagerly.

"That and much more, Paxton, but it will take some time. My *magic* comes from my spiritual knowledge, which I've acquired through one hundred years of meditation. I certainly can't impart all of that knowledge to you in one afternoon."

"Speaking of turning water into wine," interrupted Tucker, "did you also refill our wine bottle yesterday?"

"I may have had something to do with that," answered Thorn, enigmatically. "I'm afraid I'm showing off. I haven't had an audience for a long time. I also don't want you to have any doubts about what you've seen and experienced here."

"I don't doubt the validity of this wine," said Paxton, pouring himself a glass and tasting it. "Nor the blueberries, they were delicious. Thank you, Thorn."

"You're welcome."

"Yeah, thanks," said Tucker aloud, adding, "*I think*" in the silence of his mind. If Thorn caught this unspoken statement, he did not let on.

"*Who is this being?*" Tucker continued thinking to himself. The fact that Thorn had produced blueberries and wine, seemingly out of thin air, was even more fantastic to him than the fact that he was communicating with a tree. All doubts about Thorn's existence were now gone from his mind. This display of supernatural power also served to enhance the credibility of Thorn's spiritual teachings and Tucker began to reexamine their conversation with less skepticism.

"That's the million-dollar question, isn't it?" Thorn answered Tucker's unspoken query. "Paxton caught a glimpse of my previous life in The Chords last night. Soon we may be able to decipher exactly who this Arabian writer was."

"All this talk about physics reminds me of something I saw in The Chords last night," said Tucker. "At some point I was watching another life rewind and I distinctly saw Albert Einstein's face pop in and out of the picture. There was no mistaking that wild, white hair!"

"Interesting," Thorn commented.

"Do you think Tucker was Albert Einstein in a past life?" asked Paxton.

"Probably not," Thorn reasoned. "If he was seeing Einstein then he might have been an acquaintance or colleague, unless he was looking in the mirror, of course. Very interesting."

"It was all so garbled," Tucker admitted. "And it was hard for me to focus upon anything after witnessing all of those scenes of destruction!"

"I've also seen the approaching cataclysm in The Chords, Tucker," said Thorn after a brief silence.

"You have?" asked Tucker, in disbelief.

"Are these events going to come to pass sometime soon?" broke in Paxton.

"That is a surprisingly difficult question to answer, Paxton."

"Why is that?" challenged Tucker.

"First of all, as you may have already noticed, time in The Chords is not analogous to the time you're used to keeping here. You were in The Chords for twelve hours, Tucker, and Paxton was there longer than that. Did it seem that long to you?"

"I was surprised that it was nighttime when I awoke," admitted Tucker.

"How long was I in The Chords, Thorn?" asked Paxton.

"Somewhere between twelve and twenty-four hours," Thorn replied. "You were still there when Tucker returned, but your subconsciousness shifted into its more familiar dream state at some point before Tucker woke you up this morning. I'm not sure exactly when you made the transition, because I fell into dreams of my own during the night."

"I never would have guessed that I was in there for a full day," Paxton commented.

"In the same way that it is hard to gauge time in The Chords, it is also hard to estimate when any of the events you might witness there will occur in linear time," Thorn explained. "And just because you see something in The Chords, doesn't necessarily mean that it will come to pass. At least, that has been my experience. I have seen countless scenes played out upon The Chords, but relatively few of them have played themselves out in Earth's history.

"That's the trouble with predicting the future. There are an infinite number of paths leading from this point forward. Sometimes many of the paths point in a certain direction or in similar directions. Inferences can be made about future events based upon the number of paths that point in the same direction. But unless *all* of the paths lead to the same destination, which I have never seen happen, then there is always the possibility of making the wrong prediction.

"Of course, attempting to view all of the paths presents its own problems. You need a much higher perspective of the tapestry for that. If you could see the bigger picture, you could attach a probability to your predictions. Determining the likelihood of the occurrence of a certain event is a problem in statistics, though. Right up your alley, Paxton."

"It's not my specialty, but I've always been intrigued by the study of probability. Of course, when you're dealing with infinite sample spaces, things get a little tricky."

"Predicting the future is tricky business," agreed Thorn.

"You guys are starting to lose me again," Tucker complained.

"Let's say you have one hundred slips of paper in a hat," offered Paxton. "Ninety-nine of them are blue and one is red. You're going to reach into the hat and pull out a slip of paper, without looking. I would predict that you will pull out a blue piece of paper. In fact, I'd be willing to bet a lot of money that it will be blue."

"You don't have a lot of money," said Tucker.

"That's true," Paxton laughed, "but I could make a lot on this game. Still, I couldn't guarantee that you would pull out a blue slip. It's still possible for you to get a red one, it just isn't very likely."

"In the same way," Thorn began, "if many paths lead in a certain direction, one can be reasonably sure what events might transpire in the future, but rarely do you have such lopsided odds as the game you've just described. There are too many variables involved to predict future events with a high degree of accuracy. And the further into the future you look, the more inconsistencies you throw into your system and the harder it becomes to see anything but a tangle of disjointed paths.

"Consider the average weather forecast. What do meteorologists do but predict the future? They have a good deal of success in predicting weather patterns in the near future, say a day or so. It becomes a much harder problem to do an extended forecast of more than a few days, and these predictions tend to be a lot less accurate."

"Why is it that I could see future events concerning the fate of the Earth, but I could see little or nothing concerning my own personal future?" asked Tucker. "I could only catch bits and pieces of the direction in which my own strand appeared to be going."

"I don't know the answer to that one. As I've already told you, I don't think it's good for an individual soul to know too much about its own destiny. It hinders the learning that each soul birthed itself into this plane of existence to accomplish. Knowledge of the future may cause the individual to tamper with the natural weave of the tapestry, which can tear the fabric. Also, it is even harder to foresee the future of an individual soul than it is to see the future in a larger sense."

"Really?" stated Paxton. "I would have guessed it to be the other way around."

"Consider this," said Thorn. "Let's say you're rolling marbles down a staircase. The end result of this experiment is relatively easy to predict. You will have a pile of marbles at the bottom when you are done. Predicting the final resting place of an individual marble becomes a much harder problem. You have some idea what will happen. It will move down the staircase towards the bottom. But where will it stop? On top of the pile or off to the side? It's even possible that it will not make it all the way to the bottom, but stop on one of the stairs."

"That makes sense," Paxton said, "but if you know something more about your system, such as the initial angle and velocity of the marble, and the coefficient of friction of the staircase, you should be able to get a good idea where the marble will stop."

"Right again, Paxton. Knowing something more of the system is tantamount to seeing the bigger picture of the tapestry, of which you've recently gotten a glimpse. Knowing the initial angle and velocity of the marble is equivalent to tracing the thread of your soul back to its source, which resides in The All. These things are possible, but not without some amount of difficulty."

"Something about this example doesn't quite jive," Tucker interjected. "As soon as the marble leaves the person's hand its course is set, provided it doesn't encounter any outside influences on its way down the stairs. Are you saying that once we are shot forth from God's hand, our paths are completely predetermined? Do we have no freedom to make choices which will affect the course of our trajectories?"

"Good point, Tucker. This analogy is deficient in that sense, because each individual soul does have the freedom to chart its own course, whereas the marbles do not. This freedom of choice makes it even harder to predict the course of the individual soul.

"The choices made by individuals are much more erratic and unpredictable than those made by societies or countries as a whole. For example, tomorrow you might spontaneously decide to

pick up and move to another state or another country, change careers, adopt a child or even take your own life. Any of these decisions would cause drastic changes in your life, the latter one ending it, but none of them are going to affect the global economy."

"One person can't make a difference, is that what you're saying?" asked Tucker.

"On the contrary," Thorn replied, "one person can make a huge difference. Look at the way in which the world was changed through the life and death of Jesus Christ."

"Be that as it may," offered Tucker, a few moments later, "you've neatly avoided Paxton's original question."

"What question was that?"

"Whether or not we are going to see the End of . . ." Tucker caught himself, "*The Metamorphosis,* in our lifetime."

"Do you mean this present incarnation, or at some time before you achieve Enlightenment?" This time there was no mistaking the humor in Thorn's response.

"Let's stick with this present lifetime."

"You want an answer? Then the answer is yes, I believe you will."

"I knew it!" stated Paxton, triumphantly.

"You sound excited," chided Tucker. "Just can't wait to watch the destruction of our world, huh?"

"Yes, well no, of course not, when you put it that way," answered Paxton, "but it is an exciting time to be alive!"

"That it is, Paxton," agreed Thorn. "Humanity is in for one wild ride!"

"You two speak of this as if it's some great adventure!" accused Tucker. "If what you say is true, a lot of people are going to die!"

"That is true, Tucker, but death is merely a transition. An ending and a beginning, just like The Metamorphosis itself. There will be some human pain and suffering involved, for sure, but the transition itself will be effected over a relatively short period of time, a geologic wink, if you will."

"What will be the cause of all of this?" asked Paxton. "World War III?"

"Believe it or not, war isn't the cause, at least not initially. The Earth is on the brink of some cataclysmic changes that have nothing to do with politics."

"What kind of changes?" inquired Tucker.

"Environmental changes. Earth is poised for some major renovations. Your scientists have already begun to study the precursors and symptoms. They've made their diagnoses, but your governments are unwilling to pay for the cure, so the illness progresses. And the worst is yet to come.

"The signs of disease are everywhere. Certainly you've noticed the brown pine trees dotting the hillsides all around us. Brown is not a natural color for a pine tree. Acid rain is killing them slowly and insidiously, like a cancer upon the forest. Just as with human beings, if the cancer is not diagnosed and treated early after onset, it becomes too late to save the ecosystem."

Paxton and Tucker both looked out over the miles of forest spread before them. Tucker was very aware of the damage caused by acid rain, but he doubted whether Paxton had noticed. Even he hadn't realized until recently that the problem had become so widespread. There were more than just a few brown trees dotting the hillside. Tucker estimated that half of the pine trees he could see were turning brown in varying degrees.

"I knew the brown pine trees were caused by acid rain, but I never knew there were so many of them," commented Paxton, either reading Tucker's thoughts or simply concurring with them. "We're in the Maine woods, for God's sake. We're not even that close to any big cities."

"Exactly, Paxton," said Thorn. "Imagine what's happening to forests which are closer to major sources of air pollution, like the Adirondack Wilderness of upstate New York."

"So you're telling me that our civilization is going to be wiped out by acid rain?" Tucker asked, skeptically.

"Don't be silly, Tucker. It is merely one of many symptoms of the decay caused by the various forms of pollution being introduced into the environment. Acid rain is a relatively minor problem compared to the widespread deforestation taking place in many parts of the world."

"Now you're going to start in on me, too?" asked Tucker. "Trees are a renewable resource. The trees we cut down here will be replaced by seedlings."

"You can replace the trees, but you can't replace the forest."

"It sounds as if you've been talking to Claire," Tucker complained.

"I have been, but she hasn't been listening."

"You can communicate with Claire?" Paxton asked.

"She's somehow involved in all of this, too."

"Then I'll tell you the same thing I told her," offered Tucker. "There are countless acres of forest in the state of Maine."

"They are definitely countable, Tucker, and disappearing at an alarming rate. But I'm not merely picking on you or your small logging company. The most serious damage is happening in Central and South America and Southeast Asia, where major tracts of rain forest are being cleared for lumber, and to make way for farmland. These trees are not being replaced."

"I'm all for saving the rain forests, Thorn," said Paxton. "But what does their destruction have to do with the Metamorphosis?"

"I don't need to tell either of you about the important symbiotic relationship shared by the animal and plant kingdoms."

"But you will," guessed Tucker.

"If you insist, Tucker. This topic is near and dear to me, as you might well imagine. Now that I'm on my soapbox I do have a few things I could tell you, if you'll indulge me for a moment."

"Of course we will," said Paxton eagerly. Tucker let out an exaggerated sigh, but did not say anything.

"Most humans don't realize how important trees are to their environment. Sure, we're nice to look at, especially in this season. We can also provide shade, form windbreaks and help to stop erosion. But we perform a much more important function, every day. We filter the air which you breathe. In some sense, we help to create that air.

"Both animals and plants need air to breathe. Plants breathe in carbon dioxide and breathe out oxygen. Animals, of course, do the opposite. There is a delicate balance in this planet's atmosphere that is being drastically altered by the removal of the rain forests. With this balance upset, there are going to be a lot of out of breath humans running around."

"Is that it then, Thorn?" asked Paxton. "We're going to asphyxiate ourselves by depleting our rain forests?"

"Certainly that's one possibility, Paxton. The destruction of the rain forests, coupled with the ever-increasing levels of toxins being discharged into the atmosphere, is seriously affecting the quality of the air which you breathe. Even so, the death of this planet's animal life forms by asphyxiation would be a long, slow process, and I believe the coming changes will be much more dramatic."

"What kind of changes?"

"Haven't you noticed an increase in the frequency of natural disasters, lately?"

"I have noticed it!" Paxton agreed. "That's one of the predictions in The Book of Revelation as a precursor to the Second Coming!"

"Is the frequency of natural disasters increasing," Tucker questioned, "or do we just hear about more of them nowadays because mass media has increased our awareness of world events?"

"A little of both, to be sure," replied Thorn. "But make no mistake about it, the frequency and intensity of natural disasters has been increasing steadily and will continue to do so. The balance that the Earth's natural environment has enjoyed for tens of thousands of years has been upset by humankind in only the past few hundred. The balance of which I speak is a delicate one. Small fluctuations on the global scale can result in large and even catastrophic changes in our ecosystem. The loss of a few degrees of warmth exterminated the dinosaurs."

"How do you know that?" challenged Tucker.

"I don't, for sure. It's just one of many theories concerning the extinction of the dinosaurs, but it's the one I find most plausible."

"I think they were killed by a massive asteroid," interjected Paxton.

"That may be what caused the temperature fluctuation," agreed Thorn. "After the asteroid collided with this planet, the Earth was blanketed by a dust cloud for many years."

"The small changes that have been occurring in our global environment over the past two hundred years are beginning to accumulate," continued Thorn, steering their conversation back to the present. "The Industrial Revolution has introduced more carbon than our depleted ecosystem can easily remove. The greenhouse effect caused by the increasing levels of carbon is raising the surface temperatures on our planet. This global warming is causing airstream and tidal flows to shift, along with existing weather patterns. The polar ice cap is melting, which not only results in rising sea levels but also diminishes the biggest solar reflector on the surface of the Earth, creating a positive feedback loop which raises temperatures even further.

"The Earth is slowly being poisoned by humankind and soon she will decide to purge herself of these toxins. Mother Nature is about to shrug her shoulders, and when she does there will be little or nothing that humans, in all their technological glory, will be able to do to withstand her." "You make it all sound so dire, Thorn," said Tucker. "Scientists have been documenting these environmental changes for years, yet none of them are raising an alarm of impending doom."

"That's not entirely true, Tucker. There are scientists raising an alarm, but their voices are being drowned out by the largest campaign of disinformation the world has ever known. Who do you think stands the most to lose if steps are taken to curb global warming?"

"Industry?" guessed Tucker.

"The oil companies!" asserted Paxton with more confidence.

"Every economy in the world would suffer," observed Thorn noncommittally. "Those who benefit the most from strong economies do not want to see their wealth affected by environmental concerns. They pay good money to prevent those concerns from ever surfacing. Until the changes taking place in our environment are commonly perceived to have dire implications, neither effort nor resource will be expended toward finding and implementing solutions. Your race is still in a stage of denial, and by the time you realize how serious are the problems threatening your survival, it may be too late."

"You said it *may* be too late," reiterated Tucker.

"There are possible solutions, Tucker, but putting these solutions into effect becomes a problem in and of itself. At the heart of the matter is the overpopulation of the Earth. This world has its carrying capacity, as does any finite ecosystem. Consider mold growing in a petri dish. The mold will continue to grow at an exponential rate until it has consumed most of the food in the petri dish, at which time it will go through a stationary phase and then begin to decline."

"I know there are places in the world where people die of starvation, but don't we still have plenty of food, and the resources to grow more if need be?" asked Paxton.

"For the moment, Paxton, but you're overlooking a more important resource that does not come in unlimited supply. Your current population explosion has been fueled largely by the oil and other fossil fuels you became clever enough to extract from the ground and learn to use to your advantage. Not only do you rely on these fossil fuels for energy, but they are used to manufacture everything from the plastics so prevalent in your world to the fertilizers you use to mass produce food for the masses. What do you suppose will happen when the oil wells run dry?"

"It would be catastrophic!" agreed Paxton. "But no one is touting the end of fossil fuels. If anything, we are urged in ways large and small to consume them faster and faster."

"It's not entirely true that no one has raised the alarm. Geophysicist M. King Hubbard correctly predicted that your country's oil production would peak and then begin to decline in the 1970's. He also predicted that world oil production will peak shortly after the turn of the century. As your fossil fuels go into decline, so too will human population, though it will lag behind, dependent upon your ingenuity and how quickly you can convert to an alternate power source."

"Surely you can't be saying that we've reached the carrying capacity of the Earth," said Tucker in disbelief.

"No, Tucker, under ideal conditions the Earth could sustain twice the number of people now inhabiting it. But the present environmental conditions on Earth are not ideal, and they are getting worse every day.

"The carrying capacity of an ecosystem can be affected by outside influences as well. Earth's carrying capacity is being drastically reduced by the pollution being introduced into the environment, and the massive deforestation occurring around the globe, amongst other factors. The growth in human population and the decline in the carrying capacity of the Earth are rushing towards each other, and when they meet, the population must of necessity be reduced until the ecosystem once again reaches equilibrium."

"So we're going to wipe ourselves out through overpopulation!" said Paxton excitedly, as if he'd finally figured it out.

"Not exactly, Paxton," Thorn informed him. "Overpopulation and the general decline of conditions here on Earth are chasing each other around the wheel of cause and effect. Is the deterioration of our environment causing overpopulation or is it the other way around? Your overcrowded cities are growing steadily outward, creating larger amounts of garbage in all of its forms. More and more of Earth's natural environment is either being covered in concrete or corn. Tigers are in danger of becoming extinct not because they are still being hunted, but because their natural habitat is being turned into farmland. As conditions become more crowded, tensions are more likely to erupt into violence. Take the genocide that occurred in Rwanda during the first half of this decade, for instance."

"I thought the conflict in Rwanda was an ethnic clash," Paxton interjected.

"Ethnic tension existed in Rwanda, and was exploited for political gain, but the underlying dissatisfaction of the Rwandan people which made the genocide possible was caused by the country's overpopulation. Before the genocide, Rwanda was one of most densely populated countries in the world, second only to Bangladesh. Land had been divided up so many times amongst the family units that fathers no longer had any more plots of land to give to their sons upon their marriages. This led to a whole generation of disenchanted youths, who were then very receptive to any idea which would result in them having land of their own, even if it meant they must take it from their neighbors by force."

"I never thought that overpopulation was such a major concern," said Paxton, "considering all of the other global problems we're faced with. I guess I thought it would come into play much further down the road in Earth's history. From what you've been saying I gather it's going to be a real problem in the nearer future."

"As opposed to all of the fake problems Thorn's been telling us about?" Tucker kidded him.

"What I mean is that the other problems that we're faced with don't seem insurmountable to me. We can stop poisoning our environment and we can stop cutting down our rain forests, but can people really be expected to stop procreating?"

"You're absolutely right, Paxton. Humans in general are reluctant to even broach the subject, let alone try to explore possible solutions. China has one of the worst problems of overcrowding in the world. Her government, which is trying to curb China's population growth by levying heavy penalties on families with more than one child, is meeting with all kinds of resistance, not only from within her borders but from without. This latter self-righteous outcry comes mostly from religious institutions, which feel this policy contributes to the practice of abortion."

"Don't even get me started on abortion," said Paxton.

"Really," agreed Tucker, "don't get him started."

"That may be a topic better left for another day," said Thorn, heeding the warning.

"But . . ." Paxton started, pointing a finger as if he was about to launch into the subject anyway, before he held himself back. He asked instead, "Is there nothing that can be done to save ourselves, Thorn?"

"On the contrary, there are an infinite number of possible futures for this planet and hence an infinite number of solutions to all of the problems now facing humanity. However, implementing solutions to the crises now facing humankind would require, first of all, that these crises be acknowledged as such.

"Finding solutions to a problem presupposes the knowledge of the existence of the problem," continued Thorn, back on his soapbox. "Even had you the solutions to your environmental problems in your hand, however, convincing the governments of the world to adopt these solutions would be a formidable task. World powers don't want to upset the precarious balance of their economies by imposing too many restrictions on their industries in order to protect the environment. Third World countries are too obsessed with development to be concerned with the lasting damages they are inflicting in their own, and the world's, natural resources.

"Putting solutions into effect would require cooperation and sacrifice on the part of all of the peoples of the world. Your race is not yet ready to lay aside political boundaries for the common good, nor are your peoples willing to implement solutions which might infringe upon their quality of life.

"Consider the problem of the vanishing rain forests. Governments harvest the wood because it boosts their economies, but it is also good for the homesteader. Big corporations cut logging trails into formerly impenetrable rain forest, thus making it easier for individuals to come in after them and clear more of the forest for farming and grazing. It doesn't matter to them that the world needs those trees, they have families to support.

"Take the average Brazilian country family living in the Amazon River Basin. They need to clear some forest in order to farm so that they might not starve to death. In clearing that forest, they are killing themselves in another fashion. But it takes a lot less time to die of starvation than it does to die from lung cancer caused by the poisoned atmosphere, or dehydration caused by global warming, so of course they're going to opt for survival in the short term. The irony here is that as the rain forest goes, so goes the rain which was in large part created by that forest, making it much more challenging to grow crops on the newly cleared farmland. It's one big catch-22."

"Surely there must be some way to convince these people that it's not in their best interest to cut down the rain forest," stated Paxton hopefully.

"Why don't you start by trying to convince Americans to give up their morning cup of coffee? What do you think is being grown on all of this new farmland? There's a market for the coffee, and cocaine for that matter, being grown in South America. You can't fault Juan Valdez for trying to feed his family, unless you are also going to fault John Smith for feeding his. Here in this country forests are also being clear-cut. The only difference is that here the battle for the right to clear-cut forest land is being waged not over the creation of farmland, but over the preservation of jobs in the lumber industry. You're a perfect example, Tucker."

"What are you talking about?"

"Why do you cut down trees?" Thorn pressed.

"I haven't cut down any trees," Tucker answered.

"But you're getting ready to."

"*I'm* not going to be cutting them down," Tucker defended himself.

"But you work for the company that will be doing the cutting," accused Thorn.

"Which trees are going to be cut?" interrupted Paxton.

Tucker rose and pointed in the direction of the sun, which was sinking inexorably toward the western horizon. "Most of the woods to the west and north of this hill will be gone," he said, unemotionally. "Also some of the woods to the south of us."

"I can't believe you guys are going to cut down this forest," Paxton reproached, following Tucker's pointing finger with his eyes. "What about Thorn?"

"What about him?" Tucker returned, anger beginning to rise from somewhere deep within his gut. "It's not like we're going to cut down Thorn!"

"Are you sure about that?" Thorn asked.

"Positive. The upper slopes of this hill are too steep to bring any heavy equipment to bear. The skidders won't be coming anywhere close to this hilltop."

"You seem worried, Thorn," Paxton observed. "I guess I would be, too."

"I've been having these dreams, lately," Thorn admitted, "about being cut down. I know it's not very likely, but I've come to trust my dreams over the years. They've proven to be remarkably accurate."

"I think you're being paranoid, Thorn," scoffed Tucker. "It would make absolutely no sense for anyone to come up here and cut you down."

"I hope you're right, Tucker. I really hope you're right."

TEN

Freedom

Freedom.
What does that mean?
The state or condition
of being free.
Free from what?
Ourselves?
Is that where our
true slavery lies?
Slaves to our thoughts
and conceptions.
Slaves to the narrow view
of our experience.
Slaves to our egos.

Freedom from prison?
Our bodies are already
our prisons.
Freedom of speech?
Our words are limited
by the outreach of our minds.
Freedom from persecution?

Our most vicious attackers
are our own inner critics.
Freedom of religion?
Our infinite gods
are trapped within
our finite heads.
Freedom of choice?
Or divine order?
Which is it?

How do we become free
of ourselves?
Must we merge our energy
into the infinite
essence of the cosmos
to find true freedom?
An energy which can
neither be created
nor destroyed.
Is death merely
the beginning of life?

"Something is bothering me about this whole idea of predicting the future," said Tucker, seated several yards away from Thorn's broad trunk so as to feel the late afternoon sunshine upon his face. He had poured himself a glass of wine and was lazily running his finger along the plastic rim, his brow knit in concentration.

"What's that?" asked Thorn.

"It seems to me that there exists a paradox between free will and predestination."

"I'm pretty sure I know what you're getting at," Thorn said, "but could you state your paradox a little more clearly?"

"I was taught from an early age to believe in an omniscient God. I was also taught that God gave us free will, the power to choose between good and evil and to shape our own destinies. I don't understand how these two things can coexist. I can't fully rationalize it. For if God really is all-knowing, then He knows past, present and future. He knows not only every action I will perform throughout my life, but the actions and interactions of everything on the planet as the future unfolds. How can I, or anyone else for that matter, have freedom of choice, if those choices are already known to God? On the other hand, if I really do have the power to shape my own future, then that future must be variable, in which case neither God nor anyone else can know in advance what I'm going to do in a day, or a month, or a year from now."

"I can see you've given this a lot of thought," mused Thorn.

"Ever since my childhood, really," replied Tucker. "This issue has always been a stumbling block to my faith in a higher power. I've talked with many people over this very question, from ministers to friends to children, yet I still haven't determined a satisfactory explanation."

"You may not find mine satisfactory, either, but I'll take a shot at it."

"I'm all ears."

"What color was Annie's favorite dress?" asked Thorn, seemingly changing the subject.

"White," answered Paxton and Tucker simultaneously.

"What was so special about that dress?"

"That's a good question," answered Tucker. "I don't really know why she was so attached to that particular dress."

"Her dad gave it to her for Christmas when she was a senior in high school," interjected Paxton, as if that explained it.

"She wasn't much for wearing dresses, actually," Tucker said, glaring at Paxton. He found himself suddenly jealous of Paxton's knowledge of this detail of Annie's past, though the emotion dissipated almost as quickly as it had come. "She liked to wear her white dress for special occasions. She used to always have this big dilemma over what to wear when we were stepping out. She would lay her few dresses out on the bed and hold them up in front of the mirror. I used to laugh at her because after all of her parading around the bedroom she would invariably choose the white dress."

"Did you ever try to influence her decision?" asked Thorn.

"No, not really. If she asked for my opinion I usually told her to wear whichever dress had been hanging in her closet the longest, but I knew that it was a moot point because she would eventually choose the white one. Boy, did she look good in that dress."

Paxton nodded his head and began to verbalize his agreement before he caught himself. His eyes met Tucker's for a moment and then looked quickly away.

"So you knew in advance that Annie would be wearing the white dress to whatever function you happened to be attending," Thorn reiterated. "Does that mean she didn't have the freedom to make that choice for herself?"

"I see where this is leading, Thorn. I had a good idea which dress she would choose, but I couldn't be one-hundred percent sure that Annie would always choose the white dress. In fact, once she surprised me by coming downstairs with nothing on at all, and we decided just to stay in for the night! I based my predictions on past observances and by virtue of the fact that I had gotten to know her so well."

"The All has been acquainted with you for a lot longer than the six or seven years you knew Annie. You have been a part of the All for many lifetimes. You're pretty predictable by now, Tucker, which is not to say that you're not capable of some surprises, also. After all, you do still have freedom of choice."

"There's the flaw in your logic!" said Tucker excitedly, jumping up from his seat and stepping within the circle of Thorn's shade. "If I am still capable of surprising God, then God cannot be omniscient. It still seems to me that the two things cannot coexist."

"Take it easy, Tucker. You've found a flaw, to be sure, but it's a flaw in your paradox rather than in my logic. You're right that free will and an omniscient God cannot coexist, logically. You've been trying to determine which one is true and which one is false, when in actuality they are both false. The All is not omniscient, nor do we have complete freedom of choice. In fact, there are very few absolutes in this universe. You need to rethink your concepts, not only of God, but of what it means to have free will. Better yet, you need to stop thinking about them."

"Are you asking me just to accept everything on faith?" asked Tucker, disappointedly.

"I'm not asking you to accept anything, Tucker, but don't underestimate the power of faith. I just said you should stop thinking and start meditating. Meditation is nothing more than the attempt to quiet the mind so that you can establish a connection with The All."

"Which is much easier said than done," Paxton observed.

"You're right, Paxton," agreed Thorn. "Meditation is not easy. That's why you practice it every day. If it were easy there would be a whole lot more spiritual masters on this planet, and it would be a much more peaceful place. Thinking is a part of the human condition. It sets you apart from what you consider to be the lower animal forms. It also serves to prevent you from connecting with The All."

"Any attempt to define The All puts limits upon something which is limitless, and as such is doomed to failure. Ever since humans have perceived of some higher power, some sense of divine order, you have been attempting to define it. Each culture and religious tradition has developed its own interpretation, each believing its way to be the correct way, when in truth none of them have even the slightest inkling into the nature of The All."

"So you're saying," interrupted Tucker, "that since we can't hope to understand God, we should stop trying?"

"No, Tucker. What I'm saying is that you cannot hope to understand The All with your thinking mind, alone. You must also seek this understanding through your spirituality. To understand The All more completely you must first learn to disconnect from your mind. Unfortunately, I'm going to have to do precisely that, very shortly."

"Do what very shortly?" asked Paxton.

"Disconnect from your minds. It's getting late and I'm getting sleepy."

Both Paxton and Tucker were surprised at how late it had become. Although it was still over an hour until dusk, a close cloud cover had moved in from the east as they were talking, causing a premature twilight.

"How did it get so late?" wondered Tucker aloud.

Before Thorn could respond, Paxton asked, "Trees get sleepy?"

"Of course we do! We're gearing up for our long winter's nap, even now. More specifically, this conversation has made me weary. It takes great amounts of energy for me to be able to communicate with you in this fashion, and even more to make blueberry bushes fruit out of season. I'm tired."

Paxton rose from where he had been sitting up against Thorn's trunk and stretched. He asked jokingly, "Are we being dismissed, then?"

"I guess you could say that," Thorn replied. "You can certainly come back, though. I'm not going anywhere."

Tucker began to gather their few scraps from the ground surrounding Thorn. He found the wine bottle lying on its side in the grass and upended it to be sure that it was now empty. Paxton drained the last few drops from his glass and handed it to him. After a cursory glance through the grass at their feet for anything they might have forgotten, both men shouldered their backpacks. Tucker raised his eyebrows to Paxton as if to ask, "Are we ready?" Paxton nodded.

Paxton took the few steps to Thorn's side, patted his trunk and spoke his farewell aloud, "We'll let you get your rest now, Thorn. Is it all right if I come back up here on Tuesday? I have my calculus class to teach tomorrow."

"I'm already expecting you," Thorn returned. "And I'll see you tomorrow, Tucker."

"What do you mean?" asked Tucker. "How can you know that? This is exactly what I'm talking about! If you already know what's going to happen tomorrow, do I have no choice in the matter?"

"There are always choices, Tucker, and an infinite number of possible paths you can take from this point forward. We've already talked about predicting the future. Let's just call it a hunch. We'll find out tomorrow if it turns out to be true."

"But . . ." Tucker started and then stopped, feeling Thorn's presence suddenly gone from his mind. "Good night, Thorn."

"I'll see you on Tuesday," Paxton said, turning to leave.

As they took their first few steps away from the tree, they each *heard* a clear but faint, "Good night."

—

"What are you thinking about?" asked Paxton, breaking the spell they had been under since leaving Thorn's side. They had hiked down the mountain as silently as they had journeyed up its slopes the day before. Paxton had been trying to eavesdrop on Tucker's thoughts as they drove home in the gathering darkness, but his mind's receiver captured only static, broken occasionally by a thought all his own. Apparently they would need to communicate by more conventional means.

"I was just going to ask you the same thing," Tucker admitted.

"I don't know what to think. Did that really just happen?"

"That's the same question I asked myself as I drove home on Friday. It all seems so fantastic."

"But it would be even more fantastic to think there was a logical explanation for all of this. We were communicating telepathically up there! Not to mention the blueberries and wine. And The Chords! Who do you think Thorn is?"

"It might be better to ask what he is," corrected Tucker. "He's certainly not merely a tree."

"Could he be some supernatural entity trapped inside the tree?"

"Like what?"

"I don't know. An angel, or a god?" guessed Paxton.

"Before today I would have said that I don't believe in either angels or gods. Now I'm not so sure. Maybe he's just another soul like you or me, except that he was born into a tree instead of a human body."

"Then how can you explain his miracles?"

"I can't. Maybe his powers are a result of his hundred years of meditation, just like he said."

"If that's true, I definitely need to learn how to meditate like that!" Paxton exclaimed. "I thought you didn't believe in the power of meditation, either."

"I don't. Or at least, I didn't. I don't know how else to explain everything we saw and heard this weekend."

"Maybe we can't explain it. Maybe it's beyond the realm of our understanding. Do we at least both agree that it happened?"

"Of course!" Tucker stated, definitively. "We were both there. If I was up there alone I would definitely be doubting my sanity right about now."

"I could've told you that you're insane!" laughed Paxton, breaking their somber mood. "What else do you want to know?"

Tucker punched Paxton in the shoulder good-naturedly, and then asked, "What did you think of The Chords?"

"That was wild! I definitely want to go back there! Do you realize the amount of knowledge stored in The Chords? The history, and the future, of the universe is written right there on the tapestry like a road map. I just need to figure out how to get high enough to read it."

"That's not usually a problem for you," offered Tucker with a grin, "getting high enough."

"That's true," agreed Paxton, grinning back at him.

"I never did get a decent view of the tapestry from where I was," Tucker admitted, "but I got a pretty accurate picture of my life while I was in there. I kept thinking that I was dead and seeing my life flash before my eyes. You know, like those near death experiences where people say they travel down a dark tunnel and meet up with a bright light at the end of it?"

"Maybe that's where you go when you die."

"Then how did we get back?"

"Thorn brought us back. He brought us in there, he ought to be able to bring us back out."

"Maybe the whole thing was just manufactured by Thorn."

"What do you mean?" asked Paxton.

"He knew a lot about us. Perhaps he just picked the details of our lives from our own minds and replayed them back to us."

Paxton remained silent for some time, thinking about this new possibility. Then another thought occurred to him and it was out of his mouth before his internal censor could stop it.

"Do you think Thorn knows about that day you, and Annie and I . . ." Paxton's voice trailed off to a whisper and then fizzled out altogether. He sensed that supplying any more detail would somehow make the recollection too vivid for them both.

"He must," Tucker stated with certainty, knowing exactly what Paxton was talking about. "He seemed to know everything else there was to know about us."

This time it was Tucker's turn to fall silent, nor did Paxton care to intrude upon his quietude.

"I'm not going back up there tomorrow," Tucker asserted finally, changing the subject.

Looking over at the determined set to Tucker's jaw, Paxton asked, "Why is that so important to you?"

"I don't know, it just is. I feel as if my freedom of choice has been taken away by Thorn's prophecy. Maybe I need to make sure I still have free will. More importantly, if Thorn can be proved wrong about that simple prediction, then I will feel much better about disregarding his more dire predictions concerning the fate of our planet."

"Many of those predictions can be found in the Book of Revelation. Thorn certainly didn't make them up."

"The Book of Revelation is no more than a book of poetry to me," countered Tucker, "with about as much predictive power."

"Blasphemy!" yelled Paxton in mock seriousness, pointing a finger accusingly at Tucker. "Burn the infidel!"

"Since when did you become the religious zealot?" Tucker laughed, shrugging off Paxton's finger.

"I'm not, but I'm not blind to the signs of the times, either. The wheels of Armageddon are in motion, man."

"I'm not denying that we couldn't blow ourselves up at any time, but I don't think we're going to do it in fulfillment of some master plan."

"Just wait," Paxton stated smugly, nodding his head emphatically. "You'll see."

"And you'll see that Thorn is not infallible, tomorrow. Frankly, I'm surprised he would waste his credibility on such an inane prophecy. All I need to do is call in sick and lie in bed all day long to prove him wrong."

"Why don't you just quit?" asked Paxton.

"Why would I do that? I love this job!"

"You've just had the most incredible experience of your life . . ."

"How do you know it was the most incredible experience of my life?" interjected Tucker.

"Name something more incredible," Paxton challenged.

"I can't think of anything offhand," Tucker grinned at him.

"You've just spent two days, no three days, talking to a tree, and now you're going to go right back out there and continue helping the people who are cutting them down?"

"We won't be cutting Thorn down."

"I don't care!" Paxton returned, his voice rising. "Didn't you hear a word that Thorn said about the damage being caused by deforestation?"

"I heard it, but I don't know that I believe it. If the problem were really that bad, somebody would have already put a stop to it."

"Like who?"

"I don't know, the government?"

"Yeah right," sneered Paxton.

"Maybe Thorn is just feeding us alarmist propaganda to try to get us to help him save his fellow trees."

"You don't really believe that, do you?"

"I don't know what I believe. I need to think about all of this some more. In any event, the destruction Thorn was warning us about is taking place in the rain forests. We're not clearing these trees for farming. We're going to replace them."

"You're incredible! How can you be so hard-headed, Tucker?"

"Look who's talking?"

They glared at each other across the cab of the truck until Tucker had to look back at the road to keep from veering off into the soft sand shoulder which accompanied many of Maine's rural routes. Neither of them spoke for a long time, thereafter. Tucker eventually broke the silence with a peace offering.

"I'll tell you what," he said. "I'll do some research on my own. If the deforestation problem is as bad as Thorn says it is, I want no part of it. But I'm not going to just up and quit the best job I've ever had, without some hard evidence. Besides, this job gives me the perfect excuse to go back up there and talk to Thorn. Not tomorrow, of course."

"All right," Paxton consented, only partially appeased, but not wanting to remain angry at Tucker. "Far be it from me to tell you how to live your life. But I'm going to do some research of my own, too."

"How about Pat's for dinner?" asked Tucker, as they turned onto Mill Street in Orono.

"Sounds great," Paxton agreed, rubbing his empty belly.

They split an extra-large vegetable supreme pizza and a pitcher of beer between them, and there were no leftovers of either when they finally arose from the table. Tucker insisted on paying the bill and Paxton left him standing in line at the cash register while he went out to the truck to collect his backpack. Tucker offered to give him a lift home but Paxton declined, saying that he wanted to walk the few blocks to clear his mind.

"Are you sure?" Tucker reiterated his offer. "I don't know about you but I'm beat. I didn't sleep all that well last night on the cold, wet ground. I can't wait to find my bed."

"I'm pretty tired myself," Paxton agreed, stifling a yawn. "I probably won't be too far behind you, but I've got a couple of things I need to do first. Good night, Tucker."

"Good night," Tucker responded, climbing into the cab of his truck. He honked twice before pulling out onto the road as Paxton hitched up his pack for the short walk home.

Despite his exhaustion, Paxton sat at his kitchen table for another two hours, grading quizzes for his calculus class. He was too excited to go to bed, but he was too distracted to muster the brain power for anything more mentally arduous than the mindless meandering of his red pen as it skittered across page after page of identical calculations. The chore took him twice as long as it should have, his mind quantum leaping between the crest of Blueberry Hill and the mathematical equations spread before him.

Even after he had crawled into bed and shut off the lights, the Sandman did not join him until long after midnight. When he did come, he told him bedtime stories of calamity and destruction, continually kicking him awake before he could sink into a deep and unencumbered slumber. The following morning he remembered one dream in particular, which had projected itself upon the screen of his subconscious in four or five parts, broken by short, wakeful intermissions.

In his dream he had been the commander of a fort, somewhere in the Midwest. The fort was very crudely put together from scrap metal, mostly used cars that had been crushed together in an interlocking brick-type pattern to form its walls. A tractor trailer, parked alongside one of the fort's walls, could be driven forward to block the only opening to the fort in case of enemy attack. A city of tents huddled together in one corner of the fort, with a few scrap iron buildings interspersed amongst them. The rest of the free space inside the fort was taken up by various machines of war, which included several troop transport trucks, a few tanks and a jet fighter. The rust that had overtaken its wings and tail, coupled with its two flat landing wheels, gave Paxton the impression that the jet was permanently grounded.

He guessed that he was somewhere in Kansas, because the land was so flat, yet the terrain looked nothing like the breadbasket of the America he grew up in. Wheat had given way to parched earth, and only a dirty, brown river, running next to the fort and stretching from north to south, broke the monotony of the landscape.

There were rumors of an approaching army which was laying waste to everything in its path. In this setting that seemed rather redundant, but it was also said that they were taking no prisoners. There was talk of flight, but no one was really sure where they could escape to. It was generally believed that there existed a mystical place somewhere across the sea where men and women still lived pretty much as they used to before the cataclysm. A place where the vast lawless hordes were still being resisted. But no one was sure where that might be, or even if it actually existed.

At sunset a rag-tag army approached the fort, trailing behind it a huge cloud of dust. A beautiful, white stallion pranced incongruously at the head of the unruly mob. As they neared the entrance to the fort, Paxton could see that the figure astride the stallion was Dr. Taylor, a mathematics professor at the University of Maine. He said that he was in search of the 'Land Beyond the Sea' and invited Paxton and his forces to join him. Paxton had declined, saying that he would take his chances right where he was. He regretted this decision almost as soon as Dr. Taylor had left, his foot soldiers straggling behind him.

Paxton was trying to decide what he most wanted to do with his last remaining time on Earth. He came up with many good ideas, amongst them throwing an 'End of the World' party with the last of their provisions, recording everything he could remember about his life or reconciling himself to God. He opted for the party, as was usually the case, rationalizing that there was still plenty of time to parlay with God.

No sooner had he made the decision than he woke up, briefly, and looked out the window to gauge the time by the rising sun. Though there was still an absence of light in the sky, he struggled to stay awake, not wanting to fall back into the same nightmare. He was unsuccessful on both counts, though he couldn't remember how this epic ended, upon waking for good in the morning.

———

The space inside Tucker's sleep was also filled with dreams, though they weren't quite as disturbed as his former roommate's. He remembered only the one which woke him up, and it stayed in his thoughts most of the following morning.

It began at a restaurant, where he was having dinner with a nondescript woman. He was sure he knew this woman but he couldn't quite place her in the dream, and indeed it seemed as if her features somehow shifted and changed throughout the course of their dinner.

They were clearly enjoying each other's company, drinking wine and alternately laughing and then staring silently into each other's eyes. At some point he realized the woman seated across from him wasn't Annie, and he felt suddenly guilty. He began to scan the room, expecting to see her seated amongst the other patrons of the restaurant. When he turned his eyes back to his dinner companion, Annie was standing behind the woman's chair, resting her hands on Claire's shoulders.

Tucker felt as if he had been caught in the midst of some illicit love affair. Rising out of his chair he said, "I can explain . . ." But he couldn't explain. His heart jumped into his throat at the thought that Annie might not love him anymore as a result of this indiscretion. But Annie was smiling. She lifted her hand slowly to her lips, "Shhh." Tucker rushed to her side and they embraced, the other woman completely forgotten.

"It's all right," she whispered in his ear. "I don't mind."

She smiled and planted a wet kiss on his lips. When she drew away from him, her expression had turned more serious.

"I have to go now, Tucker," she said sadly, pushing him gently away and lifting her hand in farewell. "We'll be together again soon."

"Where are you going?" he shouted after her, as her image faded slowly into the background, which also receded into the gathering white mist. Tucker waved goodbye, and as his hand passed in front of his eyes, it left trailers out behind it, as if he was watching the motion under a strobe light. He tried the other one, to the same effect. He held both of his hands in front of his face and when he took them away, the mist had vanished and he found himself outside and floating high above the ground.

A momentary panic ensued before he realized that he must certainly be dreaming. When it became clear that he wasn't going to crash to his death, he began to examine the terrain below him. At first it appeared as if he was looking at a never-ending, dark green shag carpet. As he continued to peer at it, he saw the tops of the tallest trees breaking free from the enfolding canopy below them and he realized he was hovering above an immense rain forest, broken only by the serpentine form of a large, brown river. Tucker found that by leaning to one side or the other he could project himself into motion. He leaned forward and began following the trail snaked out by the river.

He began to accelerate subtly and soon he was soaring quickly over the forest below. He tilted his head backward to examine the night sky above him. There was barely a sickle-moon low on the horizon and the heavens were ablaze in an infinitude of stars. When he looked back down, the rain forest had become an ordinary Maine forest, and the river he had been following had turned into a road, its accompanying houses spaced at odd intervals along its length. He began to recognize landmarks, and he realized he was following Route 15 toward Blueberry Hill.

Tucker found that he could maneuver himself quite easily, now, and he followed the old logging road toward the crest of the hill. When he was directly above Thorn, he hesitated a moment, unsure how to land. Thinking that he wanted to be on the ground, his body began to descend slowly through Thorn's branches and leaves, until his feet were once more firmly rooted to the earth.

The first thing he noticed was a huge orange ribbon tied into a bow around Thorn's trunk. The satin ribbon was about one foot wide and the bow, tied slightly askew, was easily four feet square. It was as if Thorn were some gigantic gift, just waiting to be opened.

"A present, for me?" asked Tucker, jokingly.

"Yes," he answered, "but you must share me with the rest of the world."

Tucker laughed and was about to respond when he looked at the ribbon again and it had changed into the listless plastic orange ribbon that circled the trunks of the trees along the borders of the proposed clear-cut. It finally dawned on him that this meant Thorn was also condemned.

"No!" shouted Tucker, waking himself up with the force of this subconscious scream. He was relieved to find himself in his bed, but he quickly jumped out of it, judging by the amount of sunlight in the room that he had overslept. His next thought was that he was going to be late for work and he began to dress himself hurriedly, his resolve to call in sick completely forgotten.

—

At the crest of Blueberry Hill, Thorn had a dream of his own. He was standing beneath a giant fig tree, staring upward into its interlocking branches. He watched himself reach up and pull down one of the ripe fruits and suddenly realized that he was in human form. He took a bite of the fig and immediately spit out the bitter fruit, though his stomach grumbled as if it hadn't been satisfied for some time. Looking down Thorn saw that he wore only a loincloth to cover his bronze skin, and he pulled a loose fold to the side to verify that he was, indeed, a man.

The fig tree seemed to beckon to him, and he sat down underneath its shade. Folding his legs beneath him, he rested his back against the trunk of the tree and surveyed the surrounding land. The earth directly beneath the tree was fertile and lush with green grass, but the ground outside this small oasis was parched and cracked for lack of water. He saw snow-capped mountains off in the distance, looming over the arid plain at their feet. A small cloud of dust began to form where the desert met the foothills, and grew steadily larger. As it drew nearer he saw a rider on a horse, trailing another horse out behind him.

The brown-skinned rider was clothed in a finely tailored uniform, a jewel-encrusted sword as his side. Jewels also shone forth in abundance from the saddles and bridles of the horses. The soldier pulled his horse to a stop a few feet in front of Thorn, and said, in a voice more pleading than commanding, "Come with me, please."

"I cannot," Thorn heard himself reply, though the words sprang from his lips through some will other than his own. "I am waiting."

A short time later another figure approached him. This time it was a woman, the sun glistening upon her naked arms. The white robe she wore did little to hide her ample, brown breasts and the curve of her hips. Her long, black hair cascaded off her shoulders, falling almost to her knees. She pierced him with her dark eyes and said in a sultry voice, "Come with me."

"I cannot," he said once again, this time a note of sadness in his voice. "I am waiting."

As her swaying form retreated toward the mountains, a smaller shape formed from her shadow and approached him. A young child walked right up to him and took hold of his hand.

"Come play with me!" the boy said excitedly, tugging his arm and smiling broadly.

Thorn disengaged his hand and said with remorse, "I'm sorry, I cannot. I am waiting."

He was still waiting beneath the fig tree as the sun's first rays broke through a gap in the clouds on the eastern horizon.

ELEVEN

Half of Everything

Half of everything,
How do you measure that?
Half a refrigerator,
Half a photograph.
I have half a mind
To meet you halfway.
I'd make a half-hearted attempt,
If this were any other day.

I'm half convinced
I own half of the blame,
Half the regret and
Half of the pain.
Cheering half-backs with half-wits
I was out half the night,
My flag at half-mast when
I came home in the half-moonlight.

Half in a daydream
I still call you my wife.
You were my better half for
Half of my life.
Half of all marriages
End in divorce.
Did we stand half a chance
Or was this just a matter of course?

Half of everything,
How do you measure that?
Half of a Buick,
Half of a cat.
I have half a mind
To give you half of all I got.
My half-pennies you may have
My half-pints you may not.

Roland Grenaud was a man besieged. The last year of the twentieth century had not been kind to him. A less tenacious man might have broken under the stress he'd endured over the past ten months. Roland seemingly took it in stride, though his recent setbacks had taken their toll on his health. He lived now with an almost constant pain in his gut, a pain that was only partially reduced by the ten or so TUMS he chewed daily. A peptic ulcer, the doctor had told him. It was by far the least of his concerns.

Alice, his wife of more than thirty years, had deserted him shortly after the start of the new year. In fact, she had told him she was leaving after the last of their guests had departed their traditional New Year's Eve party.

"I want to start my new life with the start of a new year," she had told him with conviction, although she had perhaps gained some courage from the wine she had been drinking. "It's been years, years stretching into decades, since you've been a husband to me. It's time we acknowledge the emotional distance between us with a physical separation."

Roland's response to this unexpected speech had been to smash his glass against the brick hearth. As the splintered shards fell to rest amongst the embers of the dying fire she turned to him and said, "I did truly love you with all my heart, Roland. I suppose I still do, but I can't live like this anymore."

Roland almost reached out to wipe the lone tear running down her still smooth cheek, but he couldn't force his leaden arms into motion. Nor would his pride let him go after her as she turned and wordlessly climbed the stairs to their bedroom.

Alice had always attached inordinate importance to the New Year and its accompanying resolutions. Sometimes she even made it to February before breaking them, although she had seemingly little trouble in keeping this one. Roland had never believed in resolutions. He busted his ass every single day of his life, he reasoned, how could he resolve to do more?

"Happy fucking New Year," he muttered under his breath, his face breaking into a sardonic smile. This had become his standard response whenever he thought about that night. Still, he could not blame Alice for wanting out of their marriage. His heart had not been in it for more than twenty years now. Her timing, however, could not have been any worse.

Roland sat behind his massive cherry desk, a steaming cup of coffee in one hand. He had purchased the desk shortly after taking over this office, and it had become his stronghold. Hunkered down in the large, black suede chair behind the darkly shining desktop, Roland felt completely in command of his company.

There was nothing obstructing the pathway from the door to his desk, and except for the grey filing cabinets lining one wall, the only other piece of furniture in evidence was a simple wooden chair in the corner, which vanished whenever the door was opened. Roland enjoyed having the visitors to his office stand before his desk as he peered upward at them from beneath his bushy eyebrows, and he rarely offered the chair to anyone. He was not a tall man, and so was accustomed to having to look up into people's faces, but doing so while seated behind the smooth and polished sides of his fortress gave him a feeling of power over the usually ill-at-ease person standing before him.

The powerful aura Roland exuded wasn't merely an illusion. He carried his stocky, five-foot four-inch frame with a confidence and self-assurance which belied his diminutive stature. His booming voice commanded attention, not only from the recipient of his directives, but from anyone else unlucky enough to be within earshot at the time.

Roland had the habit of peering directly into the eyes of whomever he was addressing, until that person was forced to look away uncomfortably. He judged a man's mettle by how long he held his gaze before Roland stared him down. He never lost at this contest, nor did he allow his opponent anything more than a brief respite before beginning the next round. Many wandering eyes, caught gazing at the light patterns dancing across his bald pate, were drawn suddenly and forcefully back within the radius of his piercing eye contact by the intrusion of his megaphone voice.

"Was the boss in your face?" his workers would ask one of their own who had just come out of his office after a particularly loud broadcast. It had begun as a joke about Roland's height, but anyone caught directly in front of that face, listening to those speakers at full volume, knew the real meaning behind the expression.

Reaching into the ashtray at his right elbow, Roland plucked a well-chewed cigar from its resting place and relit it. After drawing from it strongly, he watched the steady stream of smoke escape slowly through his pursed lips, his thoughts traveling backward to a happier time and place.

He had married Alice after his junior year of high school, which was to be his last. She was a year older than he and their wedding took place a few weeks after her graduation, much to the dismay of their respective parents. They had no money and no jobs, but they were young and in love, and determined to defy the odds stacked against them. Not wanting to subject themselves to their parents' disapproval on a daily basis, they went north to Houlton, where Roland joined the crew of a small lumbering company and Alice took a job as a waitress in a diner.

Roland rarely allowed himself the luxury of thinking about the past, but he had begun to examine his life with a more critical eye in the months since Alice deserted him. His mental meanderings invariably led him back to those first five years of marriage to Alice, the only time period of his adult life in which he was truly happy. He worked long, back-breaking hours in the northern Maine woods, but Alice was always waiting at home for him with a hearty meal and an even heartier embrace at the end of each exhausting day. Their lovemaking kept them warm throughout the long winter months, when Roland sometimes stayed home and made furniture from the scraps he collected at the sawmill. He sold his furniture to the limited tourist traffic which came through Houlton during the summer, when Alice's short-lived but prolific garden filled their pantry with fresh vegetables.

Jerry Crowley, the owner of the small logging company for which he worked, was impressed by Roland's bulldog tenacity. He unofficially adopted the young couple shortly after their arrival in Houlton. 'Old Man' Crowley had survived his wife by more than thirty years and having just buried the last of his three sons, he filled the empty space inside his aged heart with the laughter and warmth he found on the front porch of their wooden cottage. As the years went by he began to show up on their doorstep at dinnertime more often than not. The three of them would watch the sunset from the porch, the men playing cribbage and drinking beer while Alice worked at her needlepoint.

Toward the end of that first five years of marriage, two events occurred which changed the landscape of their lives irrevocably. Alice gave birth to the first of their two daughters, and two months later 'Old Man' Crowley stopped counting his years at eighty-two and bequeathed his logging company to Roland.

Roland soon became obsessed with the small company he had inherited. He was determined to show the many naysayers of his past that he could become a success in the only way that they could understand—by making lots of money. He began to work even longer hours in the woods and in his small office. His feet rarely crossed the threshold of his home until after Alice had put Abigail to bed, and usually after Alice was already asleep herself. He took to sleeping on the couch so as not to disturb them, and most mornings he was gone again before he ever heard Abigail's wake-up wail. Alice protested his absence at first, but she learned to assuage her loneliness with her developing child.

In the next five years Roland tripled the size of his crew and his land holdings. It was also during this time that Alice conceived another child, when an unusually wicked December snowstorm kept him homebound for nearly three days. These storms, which made Roland feel like a trapped animal, were welcomed by Alice with joyful celebration. She was perhaps the only Mainer who actually prayed for calamities of nature. Nine months later, she gave birth to their second daughter, Rachel, who promptly became as much a stranger to Roland as the first. Alice stayed home with the girls and saw increasingly less of Roland as his business took over his life.

It was a cold, January day that Carl 'Buddy' Belleview knocked on the door of Roland's office with a business proposition. Roland and Buddy had been good friends in high school, but they had lost touch after Roland and Alice had moved up north. They were reacquainted the previous summer at Alice's ten-year high school reunion, where they rediscovered their friendship over so many Budweisers that their wives had to drive them back to their hotels. They had vowed to keep in touch, a vow that had been forgotten until Buddy parked his Lincoln town car outside Roland's office window on that cold winter morning.

Buddy had inherited the management of his retiring father's saw and paper mills near Bangor. Although he wouldn't actually take ownership of his family's land holdings until after his father's death, he had complete control of tens of thousands of acres of forest in central and northern Maine. He proposed a merger between their two companies.

Buddy had never been interested in the day to day operations of the family business. He had other passions to pursue, among them women and horses. Having researched the success of Roland's lumbering operation, he wanted Roland to take over the helm of his father's company. Knowing that Roland would never come to work for him, he had conceived of the idea of a marriage between their two companies. He would be the silent partner, he explained. He would provide the financial backing behind Roland's expanding lumber business, and they would split the profits fifty-fifty.

Roland had his misgivings about Buddy, but the thought of once again tripling the size of his company had convinced him to accept his proposal, and B & G Lumber Company was born. Buddy handled the financial end of the business and Roland took control of everything else. The arrangement worked out marvelously for both partners until six months ago, when Buddy decided to cash in his half of the company. He left behind a note on Roland's desk, handwritten on their company letterhead:

Roland,

We've had a good run of it, haven't we? I guess I should say that you have, because I had little to do with the success of this company. Unfortunately, my gambling debts have caught up with me and I have pressing need for my rightful half of the business. What's left is yours, and I've signed papers with our lawyer to that effect. I'm sorry that our partnership, and no doubt our friendship, had to end like this, but I have no other choice. I know you'll land on your feet.

Buddy

Roland still hadn't fully assessed the damage caused by Buddy's flight, nor had the private detective he hired been able to locate his former friend and business partner. As near as he could figure, Buddy had been embezzling from the company for years. In the past few months he had sold half of their landholdings and emptied the company's bank account of all of its cash reserves. He also hadn't paid the mortgages on several of their mills during this time.

Buddy had indeed taken only roughly half of the company's assets, but the other half of the company was tied up in land, sawmills and heavy equipment. Taking a long draw off his cigar and exhaling forcefully, he cursed himself yet again for having trusted Buddy to the management of their finances.

Roland had taken out a loan to pay his employees and the mortgage company in that first month after Buddy vanished. B & G appeared on the brink of bankruptcy, but only for a short time. He had shored up his floundering company with a renewed attack on his only source of quick income, the trees. He began to clear-cut large tracts of land, a practice that he had previously used only sparingly. The saw mills ran around the clock and the influx of capital had kept B & G afloat, if only barely above the floodwaters Roland imagined rising all around him.

As if his present situation wasn't already awash with pitfalls and setbacks, he now had the environmentalists to consider. The rapidly changing landscape in central Maine had not gone unnoticed. Unlike the big paper companies, who could rape the northern Maine wilderness with impudence, most of Roland's land bordered more populous areas. Even though he was clearly within the law, his changing company policy had begun to attract attention. He had already been blocked by a local environmentalist group from cutting a profitable lot because of the discovery of a bald eagle's nest. Now he was being taken to court by the same group, over the right to log the hills along Route 15. It was a case he didn't intend to lose.

Roland's thoughts were interrupted by a barely audible knocking at his door. Looking up he could see a large silhouette framed in the opaque glass of the door and he realized that this was the knock for which he had been anxiously waiting since he'd arrived at the office just before dawn. He glanced at his watch and noted that Thomas Tucker was half an hour late for work, but decided not to confront him with his tardiness at this time. They had more important matters to discuss this morning.

"Come in!" shouted Roland above the noise of the saws.

"Good morning," announced Tucker, opening the boss's door. "David said you wanted to see me."

"Yes, come in, Thomas," Roland repeated, motioning for him to shut the door. The closed door lowered the decibel level in his office slightly, but it also accentuated the scent of stale tobacco which clung to everything in the room. "How is the job going?"

"So far, so good," Tucker confirmed.

"Any problems?"

"No, not really."

"Anything to report?"

"Well, I checked out that lot on Route 15, like you asked me to. I do have some suggestions, if you care to hear them."

"Yes, yes, of course I'm interested," lied Roland.

"If you restrict your cut to the foothills and valleys, you'll get much less erosion off the hillsides and the cut will be less visible from the road. And it'll be easier for the new seedlings to take hold in the lowlands. It would also be a good idea to . . ."

"Those are all good ideas," interrupted Roland, impatiently. "I'll tell you what, why don't you write a report outlining your findings so that I can give them due consideration."

"Sure," Tucker responded, slightly taken aback.

Roland apologized, "I didn't mean to cut you off. I just have a million things on my mind at the moment with this hearing coming up. Have you heard about the hearing?"

"I've heard a couple of people mention it."

"An environmental group is trying to block me from logging the woods you were examining last week. The hearing is scheduled for this Friday. I'd like you to testify on behalf of B & G."

"You want me to testify?" asked Tucker in surprise. "What do you want me to testify to?"

"To the fact that B & G is an environmentally friendly company. You're a forester. Your testimony will carry some weight."

"I don't know," Tucker hesitated. "I don't know that I can do that, Mr. Grenaud. I haven't really witnessed any of your logging practices. The only thing I've seen so far is the stretch of woods you're about to cut."

"That's true, Thomas, and that's why I want you to go to Monson with a crew I'm sending up there tomorrow. You can observe a cut first-hand and you can also check out a few of our old cuts along the way. We own quite a large area of woodland between Guilford and Greenville. Can you be gone for a few days?"

"I," stammered Tucker, "I guess so."

"Great! Can you drive your truck up there? I'll pay you for the mileage, of course."

"Sure, that's no problem."

"That'll help me out," Roland conceded. "There are too many passengers for one company truck and that's all I can spare at the moment. Besides, you may be coming back by yourself. The rest of the crew is going to stay up there for a few weeks."

"When do you want me back?"

"You'll have to return by Thursday night at the latest, if you're going to testify on Friday. Spend a few days with our guys in the woods. If you're still not convinced, I won't *make* you testify. Fair enough?"

"Fair enough," Tucker repeated.

"If you do testify," added Roland, "there'll be a big bonus check in it for you."

Tucker nodded, and then asked, "What do you want me to work on today? Shall I get started on that report?"

"There will be plenty of time for that another day," he replied. "I'm sending you back up to Route 15 with Wendell today."

"Okay," Tucker responded tentatively, "but I'm not sure what more I can do for you up there."

"I'm looking for an oak tree," said Roland, noting that Tucker's eyes snapped up in surprise at this statement.

"What for?" he asked, holding Roland's gaze longer than most, before turning to look out the window.

"I need some good, wide oak boards for my own personal use," Roland replied, somewhat irritated that he was explaining himself to one of his employees.

Alice had been after him for a new china cabinet for years. As her subtle hints evolved into not-so-subtle nagging, Roland insisted that he was looking for the right wood for it, but he had not looked very hard. Alice's desires were always very low on his list of priorities. She had given up eventually, and he had forgotten all about it until the day she left, when she had cited the cabinet as yet another example of his indifference toward her.

He had worn this indifference as a shield when she left him, keeping all other emotions at bay as he thrust himself ever more forcefully into his work. He tried to convince himself that he was better off without her, and he held onto this fallacy successfully until the death of his mother, shortly after Buddy absconded with half of his company's net worth. The doctors said it was the lung cancer that killed her, but it could have been any of a long list of ailments from which she had suffered the last few years of her life. Suddenly he felt as if everyone he had ever cared about had abandoned him. In his loneliness and depression, Roland realized that he still loved Alice and he wanted her to come back to him.

As with any endeavor he undertook, Roland devised a plan of action for winning back Alice's affection. Central to his plan was a china cabinet he planned to construct himself, from the best oak wood he could find. What better way to convince Alice of his commitment to her, and his resolve to stop taking her for granted? He hadn't built any furniture since the early years of their marriage, but he was convinced he still possessed the necessary skills. It would take time, but he had many long, lonely hours ahead of him, hours which could be spent in his basement, with the wood-working tools that had lain dormant for so long. He could almost picture her face as he presented it to her, almost feel her warm embrace as she forgave him and said that she still loved him and wanted to return to their home.

Roland was startled out of his daydream by Tucker's polite cough. Embarrassed, he searched for a way to cover his lapse in attention.

"You two had better get a move on," he instructed, looking at his watch. "It's already getting late!"

He enjoyed Tucker's discomfort as he waited for him to manufacture an excuse for his tardiness. He had no way of knowing that Tucker's unease had nothing at all to do with the fact that he had shown up late for work. After a long moment, and an equally long sigh, Tucker stopped examining his shoes and looked him straight in the eyes.

"Alright," he agreed. "Where can I find Wendell?"

"He's probably already waiting for you in the truck," offered Roland. Tucker seemed as if he had something more to say, but he turned and shuffled his leaden feet through the office door without another word.

Tucker stayed in Roland's thoughts long after he shut the door behind him. He had hired Tucker as a favor to the wife of an old logging buddy. Charlie Maynard had died many years ago, but Roland had continued to have his secretary send Christmas cards to Charlie's wife and he still visited her occasionally. Tucker just happened to be at his grandmother's house during one such visit. Roland liked the man immediately, and upon learning that Tucker had a background in forestry and was currently unemployed, he promptly offered him a job at B & G.

This spontaneous offer had arisen as a kindness in memory of an old friendship, but on the ride home Roland had determined that he just might be able to put Tucker to good use. With less than a month before his scheduled hearing with the environmentalists, Roland was searching for any advantage which might help to stifle the suit against him before it went to trial. Having a forester on his team to vouch for his logging practices could only serve to strengthen his case. He had driven home from that visit very pleased with himself, and wondering if maybe this was the beginning of a change in his fortunes.

He had kept Tucker in the office for the first week or so, observing him and trying to gauge his mettle. He found that his first impression of the man had been correct. Tucker was not only very personable but also a very hard worker. Unfortunately for Roland's plan, he also seemed to be a principled man. He doubted that he would be able to buy Tucker's loyalty, but he still believed that if handled correctly, Tucker could be convinced to testify for him at the hearing. He had kept Tucker in the dark as to the impending hearing for as long as he felt he could and he regretted his need to manipulate the man, but he felt he had no other choice. Without the revenue generated from this particular cut, his company could be in serious jeopardy. He was prepared to do whatever it took to keep that from happening.

Roland rested his forehead on his upturned palms and closed his eyes. He felt alone and abandoned. He wished he could talk to his mother, with whom he had been very close. He wished he could talk to his daughters, with whom he'd never been close. He wished he could talk to anyone who might care about what he had to say. He wished most of all that Alice would open the door for him when he returned home tonight. She was his only remaining human connection to his past, to his identity. He wished he could turn back the clock one year, so that he could take the steps necessary to avoid all of the trouble that had befallen him since last New Year's Eve.

This moment of self-pity was gone almost as soon as it had come over him. It was replaced by a firm resolve. Roland lifted his head from his hands. His eyes were narrow and his cigar, which had gone out sometime during his conversation with Tucker, was clenched in his teeth. He had never before in his life admitted defeat, and he was not prepared to do so now. He would save his company and he would somehow win Alice back, or else he would die trying.

—

Paxton glided his bike to a stop at the side entrance to Neville Hall and locked it to the bike rack squatting in the bushes nearby. He climbed the stairs to the fourth floor and tiptoed past the open door to Robert Taylor's office. He had just passed through the triangle of light which came spilling out of his doorway when he heard, "Good morning, Paxton," amidst the bleeps and whirs of Alien Invasion.

"Good morning, Dr. Taylor," Paxton replied, lengthening his stride now that stealth was no longer needed. He walked to the end of the hall and unlocked the door to the office he shared with three other graduate students.

It seemed to Paxton that Dr. Taylor was always at school. It was rare that Paxton arrived at the office before him and rarer still that Dr. Taylor left for home earlier than Paxton. He suspected that Dr. Taylor's long hours at the office were motivated not by his dedication to mathematical research, but rather by his overriding need to escape his wife, Maureen, about whom he complained almost incessantly.

Whenever Paxton stepped into his office, which he avoided as much as possible, Dr. Taylor was seated at his computer, surfing the Internet or staring intently at his latest computer game. He had long since been granted tenure and because he was only a few years away from retirement, the Math Department didn't expect much more out of him than the one or two classes he taught each semester.

Paxton had been assigned Dr. Taylor as his academic advisor upon entering graduate school. All incoming graduate students were given an interim advisor, to help them decide which courses to take and to steer them toward a field of interest. Once these students located the areas in which they wished to specialize, they chose an advisor with whom they wanted to work. Paxton had decided he was more interested in theoretical physics than mathematics, and he had chosen his advisor from amongst the Physics Department faculty.

Because the Mathematics Department had much better funding than the Physics Department, Paxton had elected to co-major in math and physics, at the advice of his new mentor. This allowed him to keep his mathematics teaching assistantship, which paid his tuition and expenses provided he live frugally, in exchange for his teaching one introductory math course each semester. This arrangement worked out well for Paxton, who both loved to teach and was accustomed to living frugally.

Paxton opened his door and set his backpack down on the chair beside his desk. The office was petitioned into four cubicles and Tucker could have chosen which one was Paxton's at a glance. It seemed as if every available space in his corner of the room was being used in some fashion or other. The walls were completely covered in pictures, postcards and posters. The three bookshelves along one wall were filled to overflowing with textbooks and journals. The mass of paper which had engulfed Paxton's desk had spilled onto the floor and was marching across the small walkway to mount an assault upon Jeffrey Wilson's cubicle.

A maroon, fake leather couch crouched in the corner under the window. It was almost totally buried in paper and books as well, but it was still possible to sit on the arm of the couch by wedging oneself into the corner. Paxton usually tried to leave the two chairs next to his desk empty, one for his students and one for himself. At the moment, his backpack was occupying the designated students' chair.

He sat down and opened the lowest drawer of his desk to retrieve his class roll so that he could record his students' latest quiz grades. He taught a nine o'clock section of freshman calculus this semester, which met three days a week. Paxton didn't like to teach so early in the morning, but he had to take his turn along with everybody else. Eleven o'clock was the perfect time to teach as far as he was concerned. Both he and his students were wide awake by then and lunch hadn't yet caused the flow of blood to be diverted from their brains to their stomachs.

"Did you see that game yesterday?" Dr. Taylor's familiar voice came booming from his doorway.

"What game?" asked Paxton distractedly. He continued to mark the last few scores on the spreadsheet before him, without looking up.

"The Patriots game, of course! They blew it in the closing minutes, but it was a hell of a game!"

"No, I missed it. I was gone all day, yesterday. What happened?" asked Paxton, looking up into Dr. Taylor's wrinkled face, now that he was done recording the grades.

"The second-string Miami quarterback threw the winning touchdown with less than a minute to go. It was a heartbreaker! Of course, I could've enjoyed the game a lot more if Maureen and her hen pals hadn't been in the kitchen cackling the whole time."

"I'm sorry I missed it," lied Paxton, hurriedly gathering up the stack of papers before him and shoving them into his backpack. He was going to be late for class again, but his students were used to that by now. He tended to run five minutes behind the rest of the world, and sometimes more than that in the morning.

"I still think the Pats will make the play-offs this year, don't you?" continued Dr. Taylor.

"Oh yeah," answered Paxton, not really sure what he was agreeing to, but guessing from the tone of Dr. Taylor's voice that agreement was expected.

"They may even make it to the Superbowl, if they can find a way to win these close ones."

"I've got to go teach class," stated Paxton, rising from his desk and shouldering his book bag. He was grateful for the excuse to get away so easily. Dr. Taylor was harmless, but he had an infuriating habit of coming into Paxton's office in the morning to recite the daily news. Paxton wasn't interested enough to read about it himself in the newspaper, and he certainly didn't need to hear Dr. Taylor's particular bent on current events. He had taken to excusing himself to go to the bathroom as a means of cutting off his lengthier news reports. He pushed past Dr. Taylor and into the hallway, closing his office door behind him.

"I'll see you later," said Paxton, over his shoulder.

"Ayuh," he heard from behind him, as he entered the stairwell.

"I'm sorry I'm late," Paxton recited the four words with which he usually began his lectures, walking briskly to the front of the classroom.

"Dr. Taylor again?" asked a coed from the front row.

"Who else?" Paxton agreed, though it hadn't really been his fault. He set his backpack down heavily upon the desk in the front center of the room and reached inside it to retrieve their quizzes. Before he could begin the process of passing them back one by one, a rather well-done, chalk-rendered piece of graffiti caught his eye. He set the quizzes down on his desk for a moment and picked up an eraser from the ledge beneath the chalkboard. With back and forth motions of his right arm he removed the moniker *Paxton Saves* from the lower right corner of the board.

"I can assure you that the resemblance is purely physical," Paxton remarked sardonically, without turning around to show them his smile. It was not the first time he had been greeted in this fashion, nor could he deny that the long, brown hair falling past his shoulders and weaving itself into his full, year-round beard would give him every advantage in an audition for the lead role in *Jesus Christ, Superstar*. The tie-dyed T-shirts, bell-bottomed jeans and sandals that constituted the bulk of his wardrobe would seal the deal on that particular casting call.

Paxton stood five feet, nine inches tall, with a physique kept slim through his yoga practices and the pick-up basketball games he played as often as his schedule would allow. He moved and spoke with a certain dramatic flair, so much so that he sometimes seemed to be performing when he stood in front of his class with chalk in hand. His penetrating blue eyes could be used to express anger or joy equally well, though most of the time they seemed to be laughing in accompaniment to a smile which was always ready to spring forth from his face, especially at the most inopportune times. He flashed this disarming smile to his students as he turned around to face them.

"It seems I can't quite save you from yourselves," he joked with them. "These quizzes were awful!"

After returning their papers and answering their questions, Paxton began his lecture on derivatives. He was more distracted than usual as he paced back and forth in front of a board filled with algebraic symbols and mathematical equations. His mind was still on top of Blueberry Hill and his lapses of attention became increasingly obvious to his students.

"Mr. Stevens?" a young, male voice interrupted his musings after he had dropped his chalk hand and adopted a far-away look in his eyes. He immediately snapped back to attention and wrote a five-digit number in the upper corner of the chalkboard.

"What's that?" asked the same student.

"It's the answer to a problem I've been working on for days!" he exclaimed with a wink, returning to the half-finished example on the board. Most of his students laughed at his attempted humor and Paxton succeeded in finishing his lecture without further incident.

"When will we ever use this stuff?" came the question from the back of the room as Paxton was writing their homework assignment on the board.

This particular question always made Paxton cringe. He usually answered flippantly that they would definitely need to use it on their next test. He took a deep breath and looked at the clock hanging upon the back wall of the classroom. There were only a few minutes left in class, so he decided to wax philosophic.

"How can we possibly know when any of our past remembrances will come in handy? We'd need to be able to predict the future. What profession will we choose? Who will we marry? Where will we live? We merely walk through the present, making choices that will affect our future, while drawing on our knowledge of past experiences. This makes knowledge of any kind a 'good thing.' The more you know, the better prepared you will be to make good decisions."

His soliloquy was answered by a few knowing smirks, but met mostly with blank faces. One or two of the students in the front row were writing furiously in their notebooks, trying in vain to keep up with his speech. This caused Paxton's stoic expression to break into a wide grin, in spite of himself.

"I think that's about enough knowledge for today, don't you?" he asked. "I'll see you on Wednesday. Don't forget that we have a test in here on Friday!"

After erasing the boards and gathering up his things, he followed the few remaining students out of the building and into the bright light of an autumn sky full of cottony, cumulus clouds. Paxton still hadn't determined why many of the math courses were taught in buildings other than the one designated for mathematics, but he didn't mind the walk across campus on this beautiful fall morning.

He took his usual detour to the Damn Yankee for a cup of coffee before he needed to return to Neville Hall for his office hour. Paxton had scheduled his office hours directly following his lectures. This was done deliberately and partially for selfish reasons. His Real Analysis and Particle Physics courses both met on Monday, Wednesday and Friday afternoons, so he was completely free to work on his research on Tuesdays and Thursdays. But he also believed that it was most useful to his students to come for extra help while the calculus was still fresh in their minds. As he neared the Student Union, he could hear the trademark baritone voice of The Preacher, spouting his daily message of hellfire and brimstone.

"Our Lord, Jesus Christ, said, 'I am the way, the truth, and the life. No one comes to the Father, but by Me.' And we all know the alternative to Heaven is to writhe in agony in the flames of Hell for all eternity . . . ." shouted The Preacher, as he preened self-righteously in front of the entrance to the Student Union building. It was obvious to the seasoned onlooker that he hadn't quite worked up a full head of steam, perhaps preferring to save his best material for the inevitably larger lunch crowd.

Paxton stood for a few moments amongst the handful of hecklers to watch the show. Although there were probably some students genuinely interested in his message, the majority who took momentary pause at his sideshow were there to poke fun at him. It was sort of a game to see who could get The Preacher the most worked up. The game invariably ended in a shouting match, at which point The Preacher would spew a stream of Bible verses non-stop until the other person or persons got fed up and backed down. The Preacher would then do his victory strut, waiting for the next challenger to try to reason against his all-powerful Bible.

The Preacher had been delivering his message almost daily at the University of Maine since Paxton was an undergraduate. He wondered what The Preacher did for a living. Was he actually a preacher by profession, or was this just a diversion for him? He had to respect The Preacher's conviction in his beliefs and his courage to stand up against a hostile crowd, but this is about all he found to respect. For the most part, Paxton thought him a misguided fool, turning far more souls away from Christianity than the ones he saved.

Paxton never could watch the show for more than a few minutes without becoming exasperated. He had yet to fall into The Preacher's trap and be goaded into a shouting match, and it certainly wasn't going to happen today. He edged his way past a girl who was foolish enough to ask him a pointed question and walked up the steps to the front door of the Student Union, barely avoiding being struck by one of The Preacher's wildly flailing arms.

TWELVE

Lucid Dreamer

Falling further and faster
I scream
Clutching frantically
At everything
And nothing.

I stop my descent
In an instant
Hovering in midair
I'm dreaming, I realize
Lucid dreaming.

Having discovered this
I take flight
Soaring above the treetops
Into the clouds
And beyond.

I awaken from the dream
To find my soul ensconced
Within another dream
Which my body is playing
Upon this consciousness.

A moment of awareness
A fleeting pinpoint of lucidity
Descends upon me
And just as quickly
Vanishes.

There is more
To this life, I realize,
Than the knowledge
Of my senses
But how to proceed?

The lucid dreamer
Sleeps soundly
The following night
A character in another
Impossible situation
Yet playing the part
As if he were born to it.

The sometime sage
Walks cautiously onward
That same day
A character in a lifetime
Equally as strange
Yet playing the part
Because he was born to it.

The master lives lucidly.
Having pierced the illusion
He continues to draw breath
As do those around him
But he does so with a smile
For he knows
This is not real.

Tucker drove the company truck down Route 15 in the slanting autumn light of an October midmorning in Maine. Wendell Hawthorn was perched on the seat next to him. The steam rising from their cups of coffee filled the void between them much more completely than any words could have done. Tucker was slightly disconcerted by Wendell's silence, and the underlying hostility he sensed therein. He tried to pass it off as the characteristic reticence of many of the older Mainers he knew, but he wasn't fully convinced.

Looking over at Wendell, Tucker guessed his age at about sixty. He based this guess upon Wendell's wrinkled and leathery skin and stark white hair. Had he judged him by the strength he had seen Wendell display in and around the mill, he would have shaved ten or fifteen years off this estimate.

The only evidence that Wendell might be starting to lose his battle against aging was his incessant smoker's cough, which sometimes doubled him over and left him gasping for breath. Tucker looked away as Wendell launched into a violent fit of coughing which caused him to spill the better part of his coffee on his jeans. Wendell kept his silence afterwards, but rolled down the window far enough to spit out the phlegm he had dredged from his lungs.

Tucker became mesmerized by the scenes flashing across the truck's big screen windshield. The hills had opened and he could see autumn's patchwork quilt, the countryside nestled snugly beneath it. It occurred to him that he hadn't even appreciated the view from atop Blueberry Hill over the past few days, so distracted had he been by Thorn's presence. Partially to prevent himself from replaying their conversation yet again, and partially to alleviate the building tension in the cab of the truck, he broke the long silence.

"There's a lot more acid rain damage than I remember from my college days at Orono," Tucker cited his college experience to let Wendell know that he wasn't a complete outsider, but realized almost immediately that he had made a mistake.

"I don't have no fancy college degree," Wendell sneered, "but I damned-well know how to cut down trees. Been doin' it for more than thirty years, now. You ain't one of them god-damned tree-huggers, are you?"

"No," answered Tucker, truthfully. "But I am concerned about the environment."

"Good, because that's the last thing we need around here is some god-damned environmentalist tellin' us how to cut down trees," replied Wendell.

"I'm not here to tell you how to cut down trees," said Tucker, taken aback.

"Well what are you here for then?"

"That's a good question," chuckled Tucker. "As far as I can tell, Mr. Grenaud wants me to make sure that the trees are being cut down in such a way so that the environmentalists won't have anything to complain about."

"Are you shittin' me?" asked Wendell skeptically, jabbing another cigarette into his mouth and lighting it.

"No, why?"

"That's pretty funny," said Wendell, with anything but humor in his voice. "Don't you know he's plannin' on clear-cuttin' this forest?"

"I'm well aware of that," replied Tucker, "but there are ways to do it that are less damaging to the environment. I'm going to recommend that he restrict his clear-cut to the lowlands and valleys. That will reduce the erosion of the soil off these hillsides and it will also make the clear-cuts less visible from the road."

"The boss will never go for that. There's too much money to be made in these woods. My guess is he's tryin' to look good for that hearin'. Some group or other is takin' him to court to try to stop him from loggin' these woods. Damned tree-huggers are ruinin' this country, tryin' to take jobs away from decent, hard-workin' folks with their scare tactics. But I don't see that they have a leg to stand on. Mr. Grenaud owns this land fair and square."

"Yeah, he's asked me to testify at that hearing," interjected Tucker.

"Testify to what?" asked Wendell with a sneer. "You've been on the job all of a month!"

"I don't know . . ." began Tucker.

"There's a lot you don't know," groused Wendell, interrupting him. "How did you get this job, anyway? You gotta sleep with somebody to get a job in forestry around here."

"I haven't slept with anyone, but maybe my grandmother did. She's an old friend of Mr. Grenaud."

This made Wendell laugh out loud, and the tension was broken for the moment.

"Who's your grandmother?" drawled Wendell in his thick, Down East accent. Tucker noted that his accent was not that far removed from the drawl of a North Carolinian.

"Francis Maynard. She lives in Bangor now, but she raised my mom in Lewiston."

"Charlie's wife?" asked Wendell with genuine surprise.

"One and the same," Tucker verified. "Charles Maynard was my grandfather."

"Charlie was a good guy," Wendell admitted grudgingly. "But you don't sound like you're from around here."

"We moved around a lot while I was growing up. I was born in Bath, but my dad took us out of state as he worked his way up the corporate ladder. They're back in Bath, now. He's supposed to be retired, but he's doing some consulting work at Bath Iron Works."

Wendell took one last drag from his cigarette before flicking it out the window. He seemed to have softened toward Tucker somewhat, but Tucker was well aware that he still considered him to be *from away*. To an old-timer like Wendell there were only two kinds of people, those from Maine and those from away. They drove the rest of the way in silence, eventually turning down the unmarked entrance to the logging road, which was still cloaked in the shadow of Blueberry Hill.

"What are you lookin' at?" asked Wendell, as they ate lunch together on a fallen white pine tree. They were very close to the path that led to the top of the hill, and Tucker's eyes were continually being drawn to its hidden entrance.

"I thought I saw something moving through those trees," he replied, not wanting to divulge his secret.

They had spent what remained of the morning making slow but steady progress up the old logging road. Wendell needed to stop every twenty steps or so to alternately catch his breath or light another cigarette. In an attempt to curb his growing impatience, Tucker had removed his topographical map from his pack and used a black sharpie to mark the wash-outs that would need to be filled in before any heavy machinery could be brought to bear. Someone had already been up there to cut away all the blow-downs in the road. The wood had been chopped and stacked next to the road so that the men could use it for their campfires.

Tucker had the same map spread out upon his knees now, as he ate the Snickers he had packed for dessert. The southern boundary of the clear-cut was delineated with the same black marker from his foray in the woods on Friday, before his serendipitous meeting with Paxton and Thorn. Taking off his hat for the moment, he wiped the sweat off his forehead with his sleeve. A stray rivulet coursed down his cheek and fell onto the map, temporarily flooding the hand-drawn boundary line and causing it to branch off in three different directions. He blotted the excess water with his hat before tossing it into his backpack.

They had not found a suitable oak tree for Roland upon their morning hike up the hill, but to be fair, neither of them had put forth much effort into the endeavor. Wendell had been too busy coughing up a lung and although Tucker had scanned the woods on either side of them, he had not seen any out-of-the-ordinary trees of any variety in the immediate vicinity of the logging road. Tucker reasoned that most of the nice old-growth trees near the road had already been taken during the last selective cut on this land.

Although it seemed unlikely that Wendell would hike any further up the mountain from their present position, it made Tucker nervous to be resting so close to the trailhead which would take them to an all-too-suitable oak tree, whatever Roland might have planned for the lumber. He needed to find a way to direct Wendell's attention elsewhere.

"I want to walk the woods north of the road after lunch," said Tucker, pointing his finger away from the top of Blueberry Hill behind them.

"What do you want to go and do that for?" asked Wendell, suspiciously.

"I want to determine exactly which trees have already been marked."

"There's no need to go and waste your time doin' that. I can tell you which trees have been tagged. I done most of the taggin' myself."

He inched closer to Tucker on the log and peered down at the topographical map. Tucker could smell the stale cigarette smoke that clung to his hair and clothes, a residue from the gray wreath he perpetually wore about his head and shoulders.

"I marked the boundary from about where we are right here, down to this stream," he said, pointing to the thin blue line on the map, "and then down along the stream here until it crosses the road. Mr. Grenaud doesn't own the land on the other side of the stream."

Wendell then sat back, turned his head and spat, satisfied that he had put the matter to rest.

"Good," said Tucker. "Now I know where I'm going."

"What do you still need to go down there for? I just told you which trees I tagged."

"Aren't we supposed to be looking for a big, old oak for Mr. Grenaud?" pressed Tucker.

"You're not gonna find one down there. I've already been all over those woods."

"Still," Tucker hesitated, searching for a plausible excuse, "I want to get a feel for the lay of the land and the slope of this hill."

"Isn't that what your topo map is for?"

Tucker winced under the weight of his sarcasm, but he didn't give ground. He asked instead, "Are you coming?"

"No, I'm not. I'm gonna go further on down the road and get back to work markin' the boundary," Wendell grumbled. "But first I'm going to rest my eyes for a spell. I don't reckon we've used up our full lunch hour just yet."

It was a long-standing joke at the sawmill that Wendell spent a good part of his afternoons sleeping. Why the boss put up with it was anyone's guess, because he must surely be aware of Wendell's habitual siesta. Even Tucker had been at the job long enough to be in on the joke.

Tucker watched Wendell stretch his body out upon the ground and pull the brim of his faded Red Sox cap down further over his eyes. What should he do now? He had hoped Wendell would follow him back down the hill and away from Thorn. Should he leave him there and trust that he would sleep away the afternoon, or wait for him to wake and let Wendell take point upon the mission the boss had entrusted to them? As his mind debated over possible courses of action, Wendell's wheezing breath grew deeper and slower and began to sound more and more like snoring.

Tucker folded the map carefully and put it back in his own pack, along with the remains of his lunch. Since Wendell showed no sign of doing the same, Tucker gathered up his litter as well. He stood up and shouldered his pack, nudging Wendell's steel-toed boot with his own.

"Where should we meet later?" he asked in loud whisper. He didn't really want to wake Wendell, but he wanted some gauge as to how deeply his co-worker was sleeping. When he received no reply he raised his voice a notch and kicked a little harder, "Wendell!"

Satisfied that Wendell was fully asleep, Tucker turned on his heel and trudged not downward as he had told Wendell he would, but up the little rise that led to the concealed trailhead. Until that moment he had no intention of visiting Thorn, but now that the idea had taken root in his brain, the need to converse with the old oak had become more a compulsion than a desire. He took one last look at Wendell's prone form before parting the green veil and watching his big feet propel him upward upon the walking path it revealed.

Tucker made a point of taking in the view as he crested the hill this time. He could see in all directions from the top of Blueberry Hill, but he had to walk in a big circle around the oak tree to do it. The autumn foliage was spectacular, but his critical eye also noticed large patches of brown in amongst the fall colors and the contrasting greens of the pines.

He tried to imagine what the landscape would look like after the clear-cut. It would destroy the northern and western vistas, and eventually the view to the south, but the eastern side of the mountain was all government land, as far as he knew. He thought about what Wendell had said, and wondered if his recommendations for a limited clear-cut would fall upon ears deafened by the sound of jingling coins.

He walked another complete circle around the tree, as if to etch into his mind the full panorama of the pristine Maine wilderness, before it was irretrievably altered. Then he turned his attention to the old oak tree, and cut a path through the golden leaves which were already carpeting the ground beneath its boughs.

He waited until his hand made physical contact with the rough surface of the massive trunk in front of him before he asked out loud, "Thorn? Are you there?"

"Where else would I be?" came the response in the now familiar, masculine voice inside his head.

Tucker removed his hand and shrugged off his backpack, dropping it to the ground at his feet. He was relieved to determine that he could reconnect with Thorn, half expecting that the past weekend had been an elaborate dream and he would find himself on this beautiful, October afternoon with only his own thoughts to keep him company.

"You were right," he conceded, dropping his big frame to the ground as well. He shuffled his butt along the carpet of golden leaves until it nestled itself in a hollow against Thorn's base and aligned his own trunk with that of the tree, cradling his cranium in the interlaced fingers behind his head.

"About what?" asked Thorn innocently.

"About me coming back up here today," continued Tucker. "I was determined to steer clear of you, right up until Wendell fell asleep on the job, yet here I am. I just suddenly had the urge to come up here and speak to you."

"I'm afraid I may have inadvertently planted that seed," Thorn confessed. "I wanted to see you, as well, and I sometimes forget the strength of my mental projections."

"So you compelled me to come up here, against my will?" asked Tucker as tendrils of anger formed in his gut and began to climb upward along his spine.

"Relax," Thorn offered. "I would never compel you to do anything against your precious free will, but I can and often do offer suggestions."

"Are you in the habit of offering me *suggestions*?" questioned an unappeased Tucker.

"Not at all," answered Thorn in a conciliatory tone, "and not usually in your waking mind. Such things are much more effective in the dream state, where I can speak directly to your subconsciousness."

"So you've been talking to me in my dreams?"

"I've been talking, but you haven't necessarily been listening. I can transmit, as well as receive messages via your soul's particular wavelength. You have not been particularly receptive to my transmissions, but it is easier to get through all of your static and make the connection with your mind when you're dreaming. It's really no different than the way in which we're communicating right now."

Tucker suddenly realized he had not spoken his last few questions aloud and they had begun to converse completely in his head. It was still an uncomfortable feeling, and he shook his head vigorously, as if to expel the tree's voice from it.

"So now you've invaded my dreams, too?" he asked out loud, his anger honing the edges of his words. He was not at all sure he liked the idea of sharing the quiet space inside his mind, and was beginning to resent the tree's presence there.

"Hardly, Tucker," Thorn replied, ignoring his anger. "Most of your dreams are merely movies being played by your subconsciousness, but they can be so much more. The dream state is a vast, untapped resource of the human psyche. Prophecies, messages from the spiritual realm and hidden psychic talents are also a part of the dream state. The trick is being able to differentiate between the more meaningful dreams and the plays enacted by your own mind."

"If you've been coming to me in my dreams, why don't I remember it?"

"You don't lend any credence to your dreams. Remembering and interpreting dreams requires some mental effort on the part of the awakened dreamer."

"Why should I believe in them? As you've just said, dreaming is like watching a movie. If it's a good movie, it can capture my attention and I do commit it to memory. But then I wake up, the movie is over, and my real life begins again."

"Who's to say that this is your real life? Many great sages throughout history have taught that this life is like a dream. Your spiritual life is your real life, they would say, and each reincarnation into the physical realm is a dream you are having on the spiritual plane. It seems very real at the time, when you're here for those sixty years or so, but when you die and come once again to know your own soul, you see the illusion for what it was. The wise ones are those who are able to shatter the illusion while they are still here—to lucid dream, if you will."

"What does that mean, to lucid dream?"

"To lucid dream is to connect your present consciousness, what you would call your real life, with your subconsciousness, which presides over your dream life. Haven't you ever had a dream in which you realized that you were dreaming?"

"Just last night I did!" exclaimed Tucker. "I was flying above an immense rainforest, which eventually turned into this forest. Whenever I have dreams of flying, I know that I am dreaming, but that realization usually makes me start to fall back to the earth."

"But not last night?" Thorn asked, though it was more a statement than a question.

"Exactly!" Tucker answered, too excited to realize that Thorn knew a little too much about his previous night's dream. "I continued to float, and once I realized I wasn't going to fall I had fun learning to propel myself all around these hillsides."

"That's the beauty of lucid dreaming," began Thorn. "Once you realize you are in a dream, you don't expect that the laws of this physical world, like gravity, need apply to you anymore. That's where the fun begins! Teleportation, telekinesis, conversing with persons long since deceased, all of these things and more become possible. Of course, I would contend that these are all possible here in this physical world as well, once one realizes that this life is but a dream."

"How does one come to that realization?" asked Tucker.

"How indeed!" laughed Thorn inside Tucker's head. "I'm still working that one out for myself! We're talking about nothing less than the quest that spiritual aspirants have been conducting for millennia— spiritual enlightenment! In the course of human history, relatively few have found the way there, and your various religious traditions have sprung into existence as a result of the paths these few have taken.

"I personally believe that everyone must find his or her own path, rather than trying to follow in the footsteps of another. Certainly one can learn from the mistakes and successes of the spiritual seekers who have come before us, but ultimately we need to draw our own conclusions and find our own connection to The All. But whatever way one chooses, the path is narrow and steep and it is very easy to become distracted and lose one's way."

"You're getting way ahead of me there, Thorn," Tucker interrupted him. "I don't aspire to enlightenment. I was merely asking you to enlighten me about lucid dreaming."

"The two are interrelated, Tucker. That's my point. Lucid dreaming is not an easy technique to master. You dream with your subconscious mind, which is much more receptive to alternate realities. In your dreams you find yourself in situations that your conscious mind would deem impossible, yet you play them out in your dream as if they were real. Hence the relief you feel when you wake up from a nightmare in which some hideous monster has been chasing you, or the regret when you realize you are not actually dating Hollywood's latest bombshell.

"Learning to live your conscious life lucidly is even harder. Spiritual masters spend many years of their lives in meditation and prayer to be able to see through the illusion of this physical plane of existence. It can be done, but it requires patience and discipline. Most humans find that too steep a price to pay and choose to blunder through this dream as if it were real, until upon death they awaken into their souls and realize that they've been dreaming once again. In a similar fashion this may bring the soul relief or regret, depending upon whether or not one deems this lifetime a nightmare or a lark."

"To foster lucid dreaming one must learn to bridge the gap between the conscious and subconscious minds. To learn to live lucidly one must bridge the gap between the conscious and superconscious minds. Once that is accomplished, all things become possible."

"Hold on a minute, Thorn. I can buy that these supernatural powers are possible in the dream world, but it's not like I'm ever going to be able to fly in real life!"

"It is precisely your doubt that is holding you back. Wasn't it Jesus who said that you need only the faith contained in the tiniest of mustard seeds to be able to move mountains?"

"He was speaking metaphorically . . . ." Tucker began, even as he felt his body begin to rise slowly up and off the ground. "What? What is going on here, Thorn?"

"I don't believe gravity holds complete sway over our universe," stated Thorn simply. "So for me it does not. And for the moment, neither does it govern you!"

Tucker continued his gentle ascent, using his arms to guide himself through the maze of Thorn's branches until he was head and shoulders above the tallest foliage. Fearful of rising any further he pleaded with Thorn to put him down. Thorn was only too happy to oblige and he perched Tucker upon the highest forking branch which would bear his weight.

"You've proved your point, Thorn," Tucker conceded. "Now how am I supposed to get down from here?"

"What's your hurry?" asked Thorn. "You have a great view from up here!"

He had to grant Thorn was right about that. He could see in all directions from his vantage point, though the twisting of his torso to see behind his back caused the branch he was sitting upon to dip precariously. He was reminded of last night's dream and his descent through these same branches.

"There's the answer to your question," offered Thorn, reading his thoughts. "If you want to get down, will yourself down, just like you did last night."

"Yeah, right," Tucker returned, too freaked out by his erstwhile flight to take offense at Thorn's intrusion into his thoughts. "Or I suppose I could just teleport?"

"It's possible," Thorn allowed, "though probably beyond you at this point."

"Was it you who caused me to fly in my dream as well?"

"I didn't raise you up, but I did hold you aloft once you realized you were dreaming. That's the critical point for any lucid dreamer. Once you realize you're dreaming the conscious mind tries to take over. For your dreams of flight that usually means you begin to fall and then somehow wake yourself up before you hit the ground. I held you aloft so that your lucid dream could continue. Do you remember how it ended?"

Tucker closed his eyes and recounted what he could dredge from his memories, "You had a big orange ribbon tied around your trunk. You told me that I had to share you with the rest of the world."

"You do remember!" Thorn applauded in his mind. "And what do you suppose I meant by that?"

"You want me to tell other people about you?" Tucker guessed. "Like whom?"

"For starters, you could tell Claire and Beth, as Paxton seems reluctant to do so."

"Nor is it my place to be the one to tell them," Tucker pointed out. "As if they'd even believe me!"

"Beth already knows of me!" Thorn admitted. "I've been visiting her in her dreams as well. Claire will take some convincing, however. You and Paxton should bring both of them up here when you visit me this weekend."

"How do you know we'll be back up here . . ." began Tucker, catching himself. "Never mind."

He was lost in his own thoughts for moment before he continued, "There's one person I won't be telling about you—my boss! He's looking for a big oak tree for a *personal project*. I've no doubt he'd love to get his hands on you, but I still contend it would be way too costly to get you down this hill! Wendell and I . . . . Oh my god, Wendell! I've got to go!"

Tucker began to gingerly pick his way amongst the largest branches he could find, alternately lowering each foot to the next available crook of the tree. He picked up speed as the branches became thicker, talking all the while.

"I came up here with a co-worker," he said aloud, starting to breathe more heavily, "an old guy named Wendell Hawthorne. He took a siesta after lunch and I just left him where he fell asleep, down near the trailhead. I have no idea where he is or what he's up to, but it wouldn't do for him to find me up here."

"I can take a look for you," offered Thorn, just as Tucker jumped from Thorn's massive lowest limb, landing heavily upon the ground. He barely had time to shoulder his pack before Thorn returned to his mind.

"He's right where you left him," Thorn confirmed, "sound asleep."

"That's good to know," said a relieved Tucker. "Even so, I should go. We still haven't found that oak tree for the boss, and I'm sure Wendell will want to get back to the mill before quitting time."

"Absolutely," agreed Thorn.

"I don't know when I'll be able to come back up here. Mr. Grenaud is sending me to work with a crew up in Monson tomorrow."

"I'll see you on Saturday," said Thorn with conviction.

"That's probably about right," agreed Tucker, not wanting to argue the point. "Then I guess it's goodbye for now."

"Goodbye, Thomas," Thorn's voice echoed in his now empty head. He had taken but a few steps away from the tree before the now familiar voice came back for a last piece of advice.

"Follow your heart, Thomas. Each of us needs to decide for ourselves what is right, and what is wrong."

"What is that supposed to mean?" asked Tucker, turning around to face the old oak tree.

"You'll know when the time comes," answered Thorn cryptically.

"If you say so," he replied. When there was no response forthcoming, Tucker turned back around to renew his descent of Blueberry Hill, and he did not stop again until he reached the prone form of his sleeping companion.

—

Wendell had indeed fallen into a deep sleep by the time Tucker returned to their lunch spot, but he hadn't been sleeping all afternoon. Tucker's gentle kick and questioning as to where they should meet up had pulled him back from the verge of a lovely afternoon nap. Not only had this pissed him off, but when he had finally opened his eyes to deliver his sarcastic response, he saw Tucker's form disappearing into a thicket on the south side of the old logging road in direct opposition to his stated intentions. Both curious and suspicious, Wendell had rousted his fifty-eight year old frame from the forest floor and shuffled after him in not-so-hot pursuit.

Once he had established the path leading up the hill he had been in no hurry to catch up to Tucker but had followed along behind at a leisurely pace. He was careful not to enter the meadow upon cresting the hill, but rather seated himself behind a stunted blue spruce which allowed him to peer into the clearing atop the hill without being seen.

Tucker was already seated beneath the oak tree upon his arrival, with his feet at a ninety degree angle to Wendell's line of sight. He was talking out loud, but Wendell could not hear the words clearly enough to decipher them, nor did there seem to be anyone else up there but the two of them. Thinking that he had been discovered, he was about to give himself up and confront Tucker when the enormity of the tree under which Tucker sat finally imprinted itself upon his brain. Wendell had never seen such an enormous oak tree, and he had spent most of his life in the Maine woods.

Struggling to listen to Tucker's soliloquy more closely he finally surmised that he was either talking to the tree, or talking to himself, which was disturbing either way. Then his rambling ceased altogether and Wendell figured he must have fallen asleep. He waited for something else to happen, long enough that he almost fell asleep himself, before he reluctantly turned quietly away and slunk back down the trail to locate his previous napping spot.

He hadn't stuck around long enough to witness Tucker's flight through Thorn's branches, but he had seen enough to condemn Roland's newest employee as a slacker at best, and at worst a crazy person. He couldn't wait to share this discovery with the boss, let alone to be the one to take credit for the oak tree he was so keen on finding.

Wendell was very pleased with himself as he lay down for his later than usual afternoon nap, and in no time at all he had drifted off into a deep and dreamless slumber.

THIRTEEN

The Mole

The mole
spends most
of its life
in dark
subterranean
tunnels
hiding from
death.

A man
spends most
of his life
in the dark
tunnels of his
sensory perception
hiding from
himself.

Blind
to the sunlight
he forages for food
beneath the stars
feasting on
earthworms
and grubs
rutting in the
dead and decaying
compost carpeting
the forest floor.

Blind
to the Light
he searches for
economic security
feasting on
mass produced meat
and beer
raising a family
amidst the refuse
spilling over
the local landfill.

It's not a bad life
for a mole
what knows he of
sky and stars
of art or music
of television
airplanes or
gravity?

It's not a bad life
for a man
what knows he of
the universe
of Heaven or Hell
of life after death
omnipotence or
immortality?

Ignorance is bliss.

Ignorance is bliss.

Paxton strolled leisurely through the center of The Mall, confident that for once he wasn't late for his weekly meeting with his advisor. He hadn't lingered with the handful of students seeking clarification on the lecture from his Real Analysis professor, preferring instead to spend a few stolen minutes outdoors on this beautiful Indian Summer afternoon. He had bounded hurriedly up the stairs to his office and just as quickly packed his backpack, before he could be sucked into the daily game of Nerf basketball that his officemates had raging in the aisle between their cubicles.

The Mall was a long, rectangle of grass which stretched from the front of the library to the fieldhouse. On nice days it was littered with bodies at rest and in motion—sunbathers, picnickers and students playing every outdoor game imaginable. It was too late in the season for the sunbathers, but Paxton passed several small groups of students huddled together over their dinners or their studies. He joined a hackeysack circle for a few minutes before continuing towards the Physics building, which squatted next to the fieldhouse at the far end of The Mall.

He walked quietly down the stairs and along the dark hallway in the basement of Bennett Hall, stopping at about the halfway point, in front of an unmarked wooden door. He rapped his knuckles twice upon the door, waited a second and then rapped once more, using the secret knock he had been given to signal his identity. Dr. Browning did not like to be disturbed at his work and he chose not to answer the majority of the knocks he heard at his door. Paxton didn't imagine that he had too many visitors down here in The Dungeon, but he accepted the secret knock as he had accepted all of his advisor's little idiosyncrasies.

The basement of Bennett Hall was primarily laboratory space for research being conducted by the physics professors and their graduate students. Dr. Browning was the only professor to have an office there, by choice rather some oversight on the part of the Department of Physics. He had told Paxton that he preferred to be with his experiments and as far away from office politics as possible. His anti-social behavior had not gone unnoticed and his colleagues had taken to calling him The Mole.

Paxton was about to try the secret knock once more when he heard shuffling footsteps and the door was opened upon a well-lit but windowless room.

"Come in, Paxton!" said Dr. Browning enthusiastically.

As Paxton was confronted with the smiling face before him, he was reminded that there was more to his advisor's nickname than the fact that he spent his days in the dark hole beneath Bennett Hall. Dr. Browning's eyes were inset deeply into his face and sat a little too close to each other. The thick glasses perched upon his bulbous nose magnified his eyes to twice their normal size, and when he took his glasses off it appeared, by contrast, as if he had no eyes at all. The smoothness of his bald pate was matched by the almost wrinkle-free skin of his face, which belied his fifty-three years. Only the gray patch of hair at his temples gave away his age.

After hearing that moniker one too many times Paxton had asked him, "Are you aware that there are some people in the department who call you The Mole?"

Dr. Browning had laughed, "Yes, I'm aware of it. That's been going on for years."

"And it doesn't bother you?"

"It did at first, but now I kind of like it. It's rather fitting, don't you think? Besides, I'd much rather be a mole down here than take part in the academic squabbling that goes on above me every day."

Paxton had been surprised to learn his advisor wasn't offended by this nickname, and he gradually came to be able to hear it in the upstairs hallways and offices without cringing. He even began to refer to him as The Mole in conversations with his friends, though this was done with some measure of affection rather than the derision which it was meant to convey.

"Have you ever been faced with an impossible situation?" Paxton asked The Mole, opening their conversation.

"There are no impossible situations," he answered, tersely.

"What about traveling faster than the speed of light?"

"You got me there," admitted The Mole. "Let me amend my statement. There are no impossible occurrences. It is possible, however, to construct an impossible hypothetical situation."

"What about Jesus walking on water?"

"If that event did, in reality, occur, then the fact that it occurred proves it is possible. Perhaps Jesus knew more about the laws of physics than we know today."

"What does physics have to do with it?" asked Paxton.

"Everything in the physical world is governed by the natural laws of the universe. An event which seems impossible to us is not unnatural or supernatural, but merely beyond the realm of our understanding of those laws."

"What about talking to a tree?" Paxton prodded further.

"Although that might be deemed unnatural behavior, it certainly doesn't go against any natural law."

"What if the tree talked back?"

"Now that would be a strange occurrence, indeed. How would the tree accomplish this feat? Does it have a mouth and vocal chords?"

"No," admitted Paxton, feeling suddenly silly for having broached the subject at all. "It communicates through mental telepathy."

"I see," said The Mole, skeptically. "Then the tree in question must have consciousness, and if the tree can think then it must have some type of brain function. You're talking about a pretty special tree."

"It is that," muttered Paxton under his breath.

"Where are you going with this, Paxton?"

"Nowhere. Never mind," Paxton answered, deciding that he wasn't ready to share the experience with his advisor's cold, analytical intellect. "But since you brought up brain function, is it possible that brain waves are a form of energy?"

"The brain controls all of the other functions of the body," answered The Mole after a quiet moment of reflection. "There's your kinetic energy, but there's also an enormous amount of potential energy stored within the brain. Every human endeavor that has led to the creation of the world in which we live started with a thought which was formed in someone's brain."

"And is it true that energy can be converted into matter?"

"Yes, Paxton," confirmed Dr. Browning. "Many experiments have confirmed that a large enough concentration of energy can create unstable subatomic particles, but this isn't a process that occurs in nature. Researchers are even now building a massive particle accelerator on the border of France and Switzerland to explore this phenomenon. Subatomic particles will be accelerated to almost the speed of light and then collided against each other to release their kinetic energy. It is commonly believed that when this kinetic energy is freed by these collisions it will be transformed into matter."

"Then is it possible that the energy contained in brain waves could be converted into matter?"

"Highly unlikely," countered The Mole. "The key to transforming energy into matter is in the concentration of energy. Did you get burned by the sun on your walk over here today?"

"Of course not," Paxton replied. "It's not nearly that hot!"

"Yet if we walked outside right now," continued The Mole, picking up a magnifying glass from his cluttered lab table, "I could burn you pretty good by focusing the sun's rays upon the surface of your skin with this magnifying glass.

"These particle accelerators I have been talking about concentrate an enormous amount of kinetic energy into tiny subatomic particles. Even so, the amount of matter produced by these colliding particles is also subatomic and highly unstable. The energy present in brain waves is much too diffuse to be converted into matter."

"But what if brain waves could be concentrated as well?" Paxton continued to engineer his present train of thought. "What if we could focus our thoughts, much as the light is focused through your magnifying glass? Would it be possible to *think* matter into existence? Could this be how Jesus fed the multitudes with two fish and five loaves of bread?"

"This is the second time you've mentioned Jesus this afternoon," observed The Mole. "I had no idea you were so religious, Paxton."

"I'm not," said Paxton, "but I've been thinking about miracles a lot lately. If these miracles have their basis in the laws of physics, then these spiritual masters throughout human history were nothing more than masters of physics, and it should be possible to replicate their miracles."

"I agree with everything you've just said, Paxton, except that I don't believe in miracles. Have you ever actually seen one of these miracles with your own eyes?"

"As a matter of fact . . ." Paxton began, but then thought better of his response. He decided once again that he wasn't ready to have this conversation with The Mole.

"No, I haven't," he lied, "but I've read plenty about them."

"I'll wager you've read the Greek mythologies as well," commented The Mole.

"Yes, I have."

"And do you believe that Hercules strangled the Nemean lion with his bare hands, that Theseus found his way through the labyrinth to slay the Minotaur or that Orpheus played the flute so beautifully that he was allowed into the Underworld to retrieve his lost love, Eurydice?"

"Well, no . . ." admitted Paxton.

"Then what makes the stories surrounding Jesus any more valid? What used to be the religion of the most advanced civilization of the times has now been relegated to a collection of bedtime stories for children. Will more advanced human beings scoff at our current religions in another thousand years?"

"I take your point," said Paxton, "but Jesus was an actual historical figure and there were eye witnesses to the miracles he performed."

"And these stories were written many years after the fact. Stories are embellished, especially if the aim of the storytellers is to establish a fledgling religion. Did Jesus walk on water, or were the desert heat waves creating the illusion of water? Did he raise Lazarus from the dead, or did he merely come out of a coma? Water into wine? How hard would it be, really, to replace a bunch of water jugs with wine jugs when no one was paying any heed?"

"So your take is that these reported miracles are just stories, and that miracles don't exist?"

"On the contrary, there are plenty of miraculous occurrences in the physical world, all around us, every day. I just don't need to go looking for my miracles in a church, or synagogue or temple. The fact that you and I are here today, having this conversation, is a miracle in and of itself.

"Consider the astronomical odds against the formation of life on this planet in the first place, and the billions of years of evolution that led to the creation of homo sapiens. Then, of the millions of sperm released into your mother's womb, the one that created you was able to swim the distance through her fallopian tubes and fertilize that month's particular egg. Then we must consider all of the decisions that I have made in the last fifty-three years that have led me to be here, in this office on this particular day, not to mention all of the decisions you have made in your, what, twenty-five years?"

"Twenty-six," Paxton corrected him.

" . . . in your twenty-six years that have led you here. The conversation we are having right here, right now, is a miracle. Hallelujah!"

When Paxton remained silent for an uncomfortable length of time, The Mole brought their focus back to the original reason for Paxton's visit to his office.

"Do you have any questions for me concerning the reading I gave you last week?"

Paxton's research was still in its infantile stages. The Mole had been giving him a wide range of papers to read, most of which dealt with relativity and its applications. Paxton read the papers and then came to his advisor's office to discuss them. It was expected that he would eventually choose an area of specialty in which to concentrate his research upon, but he had yet to narrow it down.

As far as Paxton knew, The Mole had little or no experience working with graduate students. He had worked in a government think tank for most of his career, until that project lost its funding. At the University of Maine, Dr. Browning was valued for his research capabilities and he typically taught only one course per semester. He didn't encourage his students to seek him out, nor did many of them choose to come back to his office after their first visit.

Paxton was the exception. He visited The Mole in his office after the first day of his class in general relativity. Despite his instructor's brusque attitude, Paxton persisted. When The Mole recognized Paxton's genuine interest in relativity he softened his stance. After the course was over, he agreed to become Paxton's advisor, provided Paxton was willing to work hard.

The Mole had not reneged on his promise to make him work. He had been giving Paxton two or three papers to read each week since he had taken him under his tutelage, and he fully expected Paxton to return for their weekly meetings with meaningful questions about the material he had been assigned. They typically met on Monday afternoons, though Paxton would occasionally seek him out later in the week if he was stuck on a particular thought.

"Actually, I don't have any other questions at the moment," admitted Paxton sheepishly. "To be honest, I didn't get through all of the reading you gave me last week. I was gone all weekend."

The Mole remained silent, but the enormous eyes dominating his puzzled expression stared across his desk into Paxton's own, demanding, "Then why are you here?"

Paxton got the message. He stood up to leave, saying, "I'm sorry to have disturbed you, Dr. Browning. I thought you might wonder what happened to me if I just didn't show up today."

"You haven't disturbed me," lied The Mole, also standing up and moving around his desk to show Paxton out. "Why don't you come back and see me when you're done with the reading I gave you?"

"I'll do that," muttered Paxton on his way out the door.

"Goodbye, Paxton."

"Goodbye," he replied, to a door which was already closing behind him.

—

The late afternoon sun slanted through Roland's office window, illuminating the layers of smoke drifting lazily about the room. It was quitting time for the first shift, but not for Roland, who could only look forward to several more hours in his office. He had no motivation to do otherwise. What did he have to go home to? He lacked the skills to feed himself a proper meal. That had always been Alice's responsibility. Nor could he stand the utter quietude which waited tirelessly for him to come home.

Although he had long since lost the capacity for meaningful communication with his wife, he found he missed her presence and its accompanying background noise. He missed the easy laughter he heard as she talked with friends in the kitchen or over the phone. He missed her body in his bed, even though its springs rarely complained of anything other than a slightly stirring sleeper. The choice between the oppressive silence of his so-called home or the singing of his saws was not a difficult one for Roland. He waited anxiously, now, for the saws to recommence their song, signifying the changing of the guard. Instead, he heard a tentative knock at his door.

"Come in!" shouted Roland, his amplified voice hardly necessary, given that the mill was still couched in silence. He half-expected to see the foreman of the second shift come to inform him there was a problem with one of the saws.

"Evenin', Mr. Grenaud," said Wendell, stepping into the smoke-filled room. He closed the door behind him but remained standing next to it, his hand resting lightly on the knob.

"Come in, Wendell," repeated Roland, glad for the distraction from his musings. "How'd it go today?"

"Okay, I guess," Wendell responded. "I think I found the oak tree you been lookin' for."

"Really?" Roland asked, sitting up. "Where?"

"On top of Bald Mountain. Must be a hundred years old. The trunk's a good six feet in diameter and you could get some good twelve-footers out of the lower limbs, too. It's goin' to be a bitch gettin' it down from there, though."

"Can it be done?"

"Ayuh, you get enough man power up there. You can only get the skidders in so far, but we could get up to the top with the four-wheelers. You'd have to come up there and see for yourself if it'd be worth the trouble."

"I might just do that," muttered Roland, more to himself than to the man standing before him. "If I can ever get out of this god-forsaken office."

He imagined the oak cabinet he would build for his estranged wife. In his mind's eye it was eight feet tall and two feet deep, with four glass doors on the upper half and pull-out drawers beneath. He would use basic, round wooden knobs for the drawers and stain the finished product slightly darker than its natural color. Maybe he'd invite Alice over for coffee and ask her to get the good china cups and saucers from their dining room. Once there, she would be blown away by her new oak china cabinet.

Wendell lit a match with his thumbnail and the sudden flare of light dispelled Roland's daydream. He refocused his eyes and looked up at the old man leaning against his office door.

"Did Thomas get in your way today?" he asked, raising his voice involuntarily above the noise of the saws, which had begun to sing their nightly song.

"He wasn't so bad," stated Wendell cautiously. "Where'd he come from, anyway?"

"He's the grandson of an old friend," answered Roland. "You remember Charlie Maynard. Anyway, he needed a job and you know I always got a job opening."

The strength of B & G Lumber, and the secret to Roland's success, rode firmly on the backs of his workers. Over the years Roland had employed many natives of central Maine in his mills and on his lumbering crews. Despite his company's current financial status, Roland had hired even more workers over the past few months to handle the larger volume of lumber coming into his mills.

Roland was known to be a fair boss, quick to reward hard work and loyalty and equally as quick to punish laziness and disrespect. He tolerated mistakes, provided those responsible were willing to work hard to remedy them. He was generally well-liked by his work force, especially by those who had worked with him for any length of time.

Sensing Wendell's reluctance to speak, Roland gave him the opening, "I don't know the boy from Adam. You can speak your mind."

Wendell took a long drag from his cigarette, before his caution flew away with the white cloud he exhaled, "I don't want him tellin' me how to cut down trees. He comes here with his high-flutin' college degree but he don't know jack-shit about lumberin'."

Roland laughed, understanding what this was about. "Take him with a grain of salt, Wendell. He's not your boss. But I do have him working on something important to me."

Wendell looked up from the baseball cap he was holding in one hand and smiled, "He's weird, too. I think he's one of them tree-huggers."

"Why do you say that?" asked Roland, his interest piqued. He sat up straighter in his chair and laid his chin on the triangle formed by his upper arms and interlaced fingers.

"He was the one that actually discovered the oak tree, if he didn't already know it was up there. We split up after lunch. He said he wanted to walk the northern boundary, even after I showed him the trees I tagged on his map. Only he didn't go to the northern boundary, he went up to the top of Bald Mountain.

"He slipped away when he thought I wasn't lookin', but I saw his red shirt disappearin' over a ridge on the south side of the road. Now I was really curious, 'cause he wasn't goin' where he said he was goin'. I figured he was up to something, so I followed him.

"There's a clearin' at the top and that giant oak tree is smack dab in the middle of it. And do you know what he was doin' when I got up there? He was talking to that tree."

"No," Roland interrupted in disbelief. "Wendell, are you sure?"

"Sure as I'm standin' here. I watched him from a distance on account of I didn't want him to know I was spyin' on him. He was either talkin' to the tree or he was talkin' to himself. I don't know which one 'cause I was too far away to hear what he was sayin'. After a while his lips stopped moving and I figured he must've fallen asleep. I was sittin' there for so long watchin' him that I fell asleep there towards the end, too."

"Are you sure you didn't just dream the whole thing up while you were sleeping, Wendell?" asked Roland. He was aware that Wendell spent a good part of his afternoons alone in the woods sleeping. Under normal circumstances such an employee would be fired without consideration, but Roland kept him on as a reward for the loyalty he had shown the company over the years. As long as Wendell got his work done, he was entitled to a little rest and relaxation on company time.

Wendell had worked in the woods since he was old enough to heft an ax, trudging in the footsteps of his father and brothers. He had originally worked for Old Man Crowley. When Roland took over the company he had stayed on, moving from site to site, single-handedly cutting large swathes across the landscape of northern and central Maine. Roland had given him the job of tagging trees over a year ago, as partial compensation for the slight bow Wendell's back had acquired during the forty years he had spent humping his chainsaw through the thick, Maine forest.

"I'm sure, Mr. Grenaud," stated Wendell with an emphatic nod of his head. "He was talkin' to that oak tree before I fell asleep. Besides, I don't dream no more. Stopped doin' that years ago."

Roland wasn't convinced, but he decided to let the matter drop. Wendell was beginning to fidget nervously and looked as though he were anxious to get out of the office and onto his favorite corner barstool at Lucky's Tavern.

"Good work, Wendell," he said. "I'll have to have a talk with that boy. In the meantime, why don't you keep an eye on him for me?"

"Will do, Mr. Grenaud," muttered Wendell, "Have a good night."

"You too, Wendell."

As Wendell turned to leave, Roland remembered something else, "Hey, did you see any eagles up there?"

"No, sir. But I'm keepin' a look out for them, just like you told me to."

"*Sure you are,*" thought Roland, but he said, "Good job. See you tomorrow."

—

Paxton crossed the Stillwater River on the small sidewalk allotted to pedestrians and climbed the hill toward downtown Orono, if one could, in fact, assign the term downtown to the handful of stores and shops huddled together at the first intersection across the bridge. Taking a left onto Mill Street, he ambled past Pat's Pizza, one of the few fixtures in this college town's ever-changing landscape. He ate breakfast at Pat's whenever he was hung over, a condition he experienced much less frequently as a graduate student than he had as a college freshman. The morning special, consisting of eggs, bacon, homefries, Texas toast, juice and coffee had gone from two dollars to three in the interim.

Paxton watched an absent sun change the colors at the fringes of the clouds in front of him as he placed one foot in front of the other along the gentle downslope of the road. He found himself drawn to their old tenement and he chose to detour slightly from his usual path home in order to take a walk down memory lane.

The old tenement looked as if it hadn't changed much in the years since he had signed his name to the lease. The white vinyl siding seemed to be holding its own against the weather and there was a gravel driveway where they used to park upon the grass. He wondered what the current tenants were like, and concluded that they probably weren't much different from the young college kids that he, Tucker and Annie had been when they had lived in this house.

He could picture the three of them out there on the front lawn, drinking beer and playing hackeysack. They would be talking and laughing between tries, the sack spending much more time on the ground than it did in the air. Life had been so much simpler back then, before they had ever discovered that huge, old oak tree atop Blueberry Hill; before that fateful afternoon the three of them had tripped on mushrooms beneath its branches; before their trio became a married couple and then morphed back into a couple of old friends; before that old oak had turned out to be so much more than just a tree.

A blue Toyota Corolla, with a Mean People Suck bumper sticker attached to its rear window, pulled into the driveway of the house that Paxton was staring at so fixedly, jarring him out of his daydream. The young man who jumped out of the vehicle glanced pointedly in Paxton's direction. They locked eyes for a brief moment before

Paxton gave him an embarrassed smile and turned to continue his trek homeward. From the corner of his eye he watched the young man check his mailbox and then bound up the still rickety stairs and disappear inside.

A short walk further found him standing on the porch of a small, square house, checking his own mail. He opened the door into a large, well-lit room with a hardwood floor partially covered by a tattered, maroon and white Persian rug. Most of the rest of the floor was blanketed in books and paper. There were homework papers in various stages of grading from the course he taught at the university. Papers displaying poetry, sheet music and half-written letters lay lightly on top of every free surface that could hold them, as if the room had recently been dusted with snow.

Bookshelves of various sizes stood against the wall opposite the front door, their lower shelves spewing a collection of hardback classics, textbooks and paperback novels onto the floor. To the casual observer, Paxton's living room looked as if it had been ransacked by someone who had tried desperately, but failed to locate some vital piece of information. Paxton, however, could lay his hands on a specific document in a matter of moments, from the grade reports of last semester's calculus class to a particular poem he had written years ago.

The remaining walls were completely covered in photographs, drawings and posters, which added to the general chaos of the room. Many of the drawings were done by Paxton, though there were also several surrealistic prints and twelve Escher pencil drawings with last year's calendar printed on their flip sides. Albert Einstein stuck his tongue out from one wall at himself, smiling from the other. Einstein had only recently banished Jerry Garcia to the bedroom. Paxton had taken a course in relativity the previous spring semester and had become enthralled with the possibilities it entailed. Since then he had taken to reading anything he could find written by or about Albert Einstein. Many of the unshelved books lying strewn about the floor were somehow related to relativity.

Apart from paper, the room was very sparsely furnished. Two chairs and a brown sofa sat in conversation across a small coffee table. There was no television in evidence, but a boom box crouched in one corner next to a crate full of cassettes. A guitar lay in an open case in the corner, its strap coiled on the floor like a sleeping serpent. Paxton had picked up the guitar as a freshmen and devoted more of his time that year to the study of music than mathematics. He had further honed his skills in Kenya, where he found ample time to practice during the long, lonely hours between dusk and dawn.

Paxton took off his dirty green knapsack and laid it in its customary spot next to the front door. His backpack was forest green, not army green, though it looked as if it had been through a war. It had been overstuffed on countless occasions with everything from clothes to textbooks to camping gear to firewood. It had traveled all over Kenya and into the Himalayan mountains with him, and although it had a broken strap and none of the zippers were still functional, he couldn't bear to part with it. Its duties these days were limited to carrying a few writing materials and an occasional picnic lunch. The brunt of his usually heavy paper loads were toted by the new L.L.Bean book bag his mother had given him last Christmas.

He sat down on one end of the sofa, causing a whole stack of homework papers to lean precariously over the edge, and began to leaf through his mail. Determining that it was all junk-mail, as it seemed to be on most days, he tossed it casually over his shoulder onto a pile which, although it looked no different from any of the other piles of paper lying about the floor, was earmarked for the garbage can.

Paxton arose and strode into his bedroom to change into some loose-fitting clothing for his daily yoga session. His bedroom was a smaller version of his living room, the sofa being replaced by a mattress on the floor, which was covered in clothing rather than paper. The only room in the small house which he bothered to keep clean was his meditation room. It had housed a roommate the previous year but now stood empty except for his yoga mat and an overturned milk crate decorated with a yellowing newspaper and an odd assortment of incense sticks and accompanying detritus. He lay down lengthwise on the mat in the corpse position, concentrating on his breathing as he began to try to quiet his mind.

He was only about halfway done the familiar routine when the phone rang, recalling him instantly to his surroundings. He chided himself for forgetting to disconnect it and debated whether or not to let it keep ringing until the caller got bored and hung up. His phone rang so seldom these days that he decided it might just be important and he dragged his relaxed body from the floor to the living room. He located the receiver beneath his sketchbook and picked it up on the eighth ring.

"Hello?"

"Paxton? Hey, it's Tucker."

"Tucker, what's up?"

"I'm just calling to let you know that I'm going to be gone for a couple of days."

"Really? Where are you going?"

"Up north to Monson. The boss wants me to join a crew working up there."

"So you're finally going to get to be a lumberjack," joked Paxton.

"I don't think I'll be cutting down any trees," Tucker replied. "I'm just an observer. Mr. Grenaud wants me to learn more about the business."

"Sounds like he's grooming you to take over his job."

"Hardly," laughed Tucker. "Anyway, I think I'll be back on Thursday or Friday. Are you up for climbing Blueberry Hill again on Saturday?"

"Sure!" Paxton agreed immediately. "But I'll probably go back up there a couple of times by myself between now and then."

"Be careful!" Tucker warned him. "A guy I work with, Wendell Hawthorne, will probably be tagging trees somewhere in those woods this week and you're just the type of long-haired hippy freak they don't want running around up there right now."

"Hey! I resemble that remark!" Paxton feigned offense.

"I'm serious! Wendell is harmless enough, but he'd certainly give you an earful if he caught you traipsing through those woods. I was up there with him today and he gave *me* an earful!"

"What were you doing up there?" asked Paxton.

"Working, same as always," Tucker replied, "but I did get the chance to talk with Thorn a bit."

"You didn't bring Wendell up there, I hope!" Paxton exclaimed.

"Of course not! He fell asleep after lunch and I took the chance to sneak off and see Thorn."

"He was right!" exclaimed Paxton, remembering Thorn's prediction. "He said he would see you today!"

"I know," conceded Tucker, grudgingly. "I was thinking about calling in sick to work, but then I dragged myself out of bed and one thing led to another."

"What did you guys talk about?"

"Dreaming, mostly," answered Tucker. "He was trying to convince me that this life is a dream that we're having from some other plane of existence."

"Did it work?"

"Well, it definitely caught my attention when he lifted me up and put me on his highest branch."

"What do you mean he lifted you up?" asked Paxton. "He grabbed you with his branches?"

"No, nothing like that. I was sitting on the ground with my back against his trunk when all of the sudden I became weightless and started rising up off the ground. I kept going slowly upward and I used my hands to maneuver in and around his branches until my upper body broke free of his foliage and I could see in all directions!"

"That's incredible!" exclaimed Paxton. "How can he do that? Why would he do it?"

"I was telling him that in my dream last night, I flew bodily up the hill to see him and he was showing me that flight is just as possible in this waking life."

"I can't wait to get up there tomorrow! What else did you two talk about?"

"Nothing much. He said that he wants us to bring Claire and Beth with us when we go up there this weekend."

"Why Claire and Beth?"

"I don't know. Why don't you ask him yourself?"

"Good idea."

"It might also be a good idea to prep Claire beforehand, if we indeed decide to bring them with us."

"I'll have to think about it," stated Paxton.

"You do that, buddy," Tucker exhorted him. "I'll give you a call when I get back to town."

"Alright. Good luck in Monson."

"I won't need it, I'm sure. I'll talk to you soon."

"Goodnight," said Paxton, before replacing the receiver back upon its cradle.

Paxton lay awake in his bed, pondering over Tucker's latest revelations. How was it possible for Thorn to defy gravity? Was that any more miraculous than creating blueberries and wine out of thin air? Probably not, he surmised, and then accepted this new wonder as though he had seen it with his own eyes. It was Tucker's more innocuous disclosure that had him tossing and turning well past midnight.

What did Thorn want with Claire and Beth? What could he even say to Claire to convince her to come up to Blueberry Hill with him? The truth? There was no way she would believe him, not without proof of Thorn's existence. And he couldn't provide that proof until she consented to the hike up the hill. Claire was not predisposed to jaunts through the Maine woods, for all of her interest in protecting them. Spending a whole day hiking, together with Tucker, was not going to be an easy sell.

When Paxton's conscious mind finally powered down for the evening, he dreamed of the four of them having a picnic beneath Thorn's shade, complete with a red and white checkered blanket on the ground beneath them and a wicker basket filled with homemade pastries, fruit and wine. Something wasn't quite right, however.

The adults were getting along marvelously, which would have been quite a stretch in the real world given how Tucker and Claire's last meeting had ended. The three of them laughed and told stories over glasses of wine, while Beth stood in the middle of the meadow flying a kite. Only she wasn't alone.

A dark-skinned boy, barely taller than herself, stood next to Beth with the string of another kite in his two hands. Paxton watched as he tied the kite to a stake in the ground and then came running toward them. He didn't slow at all as he approached the blanket but flung himself into Paxton's lap, spilling what wine was left in his glass all over the trunk of the oak tree.

"Come play with me, Father!" exhorted the child enthusiastically, extricating himself from Paxton and grabbing at his hand.

The dreaming Paxton did not question the validity of the child's paternity but instead jumped immediately into an upright position and allowed himself to be led to Beth's side. The boy stooped to untie his kite, exclaiming back over his shoulder, "Watch this, Father!"

Paxton peered skyward in time to see the boy's kite transform itself from a painted picture into a live, brown hawk which immediately attacked the pink and white kite next to it and tore it to pieces. Beth screamed as the hawk swooped downward to alight upon the boy's heavily-gloved arm. The strange, little boy beamed a white-toothed grin expectantly up at him, but Paxton chose instead to run after a hysterical Beth who was now making a beeline for the tree.

Beth passed around behind the tree, momentarily out of Paxton's field of vision. He followed her to the other side of the huge, oak tree and instantly forgot all about Beth, which was just as well since she was no longer in evidence.

The picnic blanket had been deserted too, except for the pile of clothes heaped off to one side and spilling onto the brown grass of the meadow. He heard their moans of passion even before he turned to see Tucker's naked backside pistoning back and forth from between Claire's outspread legs as he held her naked form up against the trunk of the tree. Neither made a move to curtail their lovemaking, though it was obvious that Paxton had startled them out of their rhythm. He took a step toward them screaming, "Noooo!"

The shock was too much for his subconsciousness to retain its hold upon his mind and he kicked himself awake, his heartbeat racing within his heaving and sweaty chest. The covers were knotted around his arms and legs as he sat bolt upright in bed. He slowly extricated himself from their embrace so that he could walk the short distance to the bathroom and do his best to shake the remains of the dream from his mind before coming back to bed.

FOURTEEN

Pro Cre Ate

The rational mind,
shining the spotlight
of intellect into
the dark corners of
Universal Consciousness,
searches for answers.

What caused the Big Bang,
and what will be left
when the universe ceases
to expand and crumbles
in upon itself?

Can God travel faster
the speed of light?

What is the
Base Building Block
of molecular structure?

How did Buddha
attain Enlightenment?

Where does
Gravity reside?

How did Christ
defeat Death?

What happens
to each of us
when we die?

Why continue
the Search
for meaning?

Let go the
rational mind
and plunge
into the jungle
of the irrational.

Does Absolute Truth exist,
or is the universe
governed rather by Chaos?

Are we merely
a collection of genes
preprogrammed
to replicate?

Is our Divine Mission
nothing more than the
preservation of species?

Is there a
Fifth Dimension
beyond the world
we experience
with the Five Senses?

See the sunset
feel the pain
taste the wine
smell the fear
hear the pounding
rhythm of the drums
beating in our loins.

Pro cre ate
Pro cre ate
Pro cre ate

T he frost gathered quickly on Paxton's boots as he trudged along the path. They would be soaked by the time he reached the top. He watched the dark patches on them grow as he climbed, needing to look down to navigate over the rocks and roots lying in the old trail.

Paxton tried to practice a form of walking meditation as he hiked up the mountain, focusing his attention on his breathing and timing it with his steps. He had been able to control his breathing for most of the climb, alternately inhaling and exhaling for six steps each, but he found this increasingly difficult to maintain as the trail steepened. With the disruption of his breathing pattern he also lost control of his mindfulness. Thoughts of last weekend's conversation with Thorn, and their trip into The Chords, came flooding into his awareness.

That Tucker had seen visions of Armageddon was not surprising to Paxton. He had been anticipating such an eventuality for years. At the moment he was more interested in their exploration of the past. Who had he been in his previous life, or lives, if Thorn was to be believed? For that matter, who was Thorn? His venture into Thorn's past seemed to indicate that the consciousness now housed inside the oak had once been human. Paxton had uncovered clues as to Thorn's previous identity, but not enough to make a positive identification possible.

He recalled what it had felt like to see the world through Thorn's *eyes*, or rather the eyes of the myriad creatures in close proximity to the tree. He had found the constantly changing perspective to be distracting at first, until he had gotten used to it. Then he remembered the scene he had witnessed yet again, though it was quite a different experience, seeing the video of the three of them making love together as though it was shot from a camera directly above them.

"Why does it always come back to that?" he thought to himself, reexamining the turning point in their relationship for perhaps the hundredth time.

"Don't be ashamed, Paxton," Thorn's voice invaded his thoughts.

Paxton stopped in his tracks and his eyes shot upward. He had broken free of the shadowy edge of the forest and into the bright light of the meadow. Thorn was now plainly in view, though still twenty or so yards away.

The old oak tree was resplendent in the early morning sunlight. Diamonds glinted off the frozen dew clinging to the orange and yellow leaves, both on the tree itself and blanketing its roots. For a moment

Paxton imagined the tree covered in snow. He had seen Thorn only once in the dead of winter, when he and Tucker had walked through waist-high snowdrifts to reach the top of Blueberry Hill. Thorn looked much the same to him now, except that he was still clothed in fall foliage.

"I'm not ashamed," Paxton was quick to reply, his red face belying his response.

"It was a natural extension of the love you all felt for each other. I thought it was a beautiful thing."

"Nevertheless, everything changed after that," Paxton thought, more to himself than to Thorn.

"I have observed that amongst your species," Thorn commented, reading Paxton's unguarded thoughts as easily as the ones which were directed at him. "The biological reproductive function has a way of changing your relationships which I've never been able to fully understand."

"How could you understand? You're a tree!" Paxton thought once more to himself. This time he made a conscious effort to shield his mind from Thorn's intrusion. He had no idea whether or not his attempt at privacy had been successful, but Thorn remained silent as he searched for some way to change the subject.

"You never told me what you saw along my chord the other day," he observed. He was genuinely curious now that he had broached the subject.

"I went back to the night you spoke with the acacia tree in Africa," Thorn began. "You were right about the tree trying to communicate with you. It spoke to you, but you couldn't hear what it was saying."

"What did it say?" asked Paxton excitedly.

Thorn detailed their conversation. Paxton had forgotten that he had talked to the tree out loud and he was surprised to learn that the tree had been answering him, but his heart skipped a beat when Thorn told him the acacia tree's last comment.

"Then it said, *'Thank you, Father. You have set me free.'* You seemed to have heard this last statement because you immediately jumped down out of the tree and looked at it very strangely, before limping back up to your house."

"I must have heard it," Paxton confirmed.

"Why do you say that?"

"Somehow it must have gotten into my subconsciousness. I have been having a recurring dream about that night ever since. The details change from dream to dream but they always end with me talking to the acacia tree and the tree saying those exact words to me. Usually there's a snake involved, too. Puff adders were pretty common out there, especially at night. But I don't remember seeing one that night."

"Nor did I see one in The Chords."

"In my dreams the snake usually coils itself around my right ankle, the one I hurt jumping out of the tree."

"You did land pretty hard," Thorn commented, "but you still hustled up the hill afterwards, as though you were scared something was after you."

"My ankle was sore for a month after that night. It swelled up to the size of a soccer ball! I'm surprised I made it back up to my house at all!"

"You probably didn't feel it at the time," Thorn speculated. "You were pretty drunk."

"I'll say," admitted Paxton. "I don't even remember all of the details of that night. I drank too much of the local brew and my tolerance for alcohol was way down. *Pombe* didn't come to Lokitaung very often. The owner of the store there was a Muslim and he didn't drink alcohol, at least not when his wife could find out about it."

"But the contact you made with the tree was not a product of your intoxication," Thorn assured him. "That acacia tree really did have a consciousness. I'm sure of it. And now I know that I'm not a singularity. There are others like me!"

"I wouldn't say that the acacia tree was like you, Thorn. Maybe it had a consciousness like yours, but didn't you sense that there was something evil about it?"

"I'm not sure that *evil* is the right way to describe it, but I know what you mean. I got the feeling that the soul which communicated with you was not very happy about being encased in that acacia tree. It's got to be a hard life, searching endlessly for water and nutrients in a desert."

"I never thought about it like that," Paxton admitted, and then pressed Thorn further, "What else did you see in my past?"

"I spent the rest of the time that we were in The Chords together going over your Lokitaung footage in excruciating detail. I wanted to see if that acacia tree tried to make contact with you at any other time."

"Did it?"

"Not that I could tell," admitted Thorn, "but that one time was unmistakable."

Thorn seemed content to drop the subject and Paxton remained silent as he began to walk in Thorn's direction. He glanced toward the patch of blueberries he and Tucker had sat in and dined upon the last time they were here. He could not find even one speck of blue peering out from beneath the frost, nor did the blueberry bushes give any inkling of the rich, deep green they had so recently sported. He nodded his head in their direction, asking "What happened to the blueberries?"

"The birds ate most of them," Thorn responded. "Squirrels and mice took the rest."

"But how did the bushes lose their color again so quickly?"

"The energy that was coalesced to produce those blueberries has dissipated, freeing the plants to return to their slumber."

It certainly wasn't any more startling to Paxton that the blueberry bushes had lost their color, than it was that Thorn had induced them to fruit out of season in the first place. Still, he wondered about the physics behind Thorn's miracle.

"Where did the energy come from?" he asked. "And what type of energy is it?"

"I won't be able to answer those questions to your satisfaction, Paxton. I lack the words and concepts to explain the phenomenon in a physical sense. When I want something, I wish for it to occur. The air around me becomes supercharged, similar to the way a large electrical charge accumulates prior to a lightning strike. The more my desire runs contrary to the laws of physics as you know them, the larger the buildup of energy surrounding me and the longer the time span of meditation and intense concentration which is necessary to fulfill that desire. But I can't explain the science behind the miracles. Perhaps that will be your job someday."

"What do you mean?"

"It is rare to find a teacher who is adept at both science and spiritualism. Who better to expound upon the science of spirituality?"

"The science of spirituality?" Paxton repeated. "What do science and spirituality have in common?"

"A lot more than you might think. Both science and spirituality seek answers to the same basic questions. Why are we here? What is the meaning behind our existence? How does the universe work and what is our place in it? Both disciplines seek the Universal Truth, they differ only in their methodologies. Science takes nothing on faith but must have physical evidence to substantiate any claims upon the Truth. On the other hand, spirituality is based completely on faith. The spiritual search presupposes the existence of The All and then attempts to explain that existence.

"Operating apart from each other, neither can provide the complete picture of the Truth. Both provide adequate answers in their own realms of expertise, but deny the findings of the other precisely because they cannot explain them from beneath the umbrella of their own dogma.

"Many Christians still maintain that the theory of evolution is a myth because it runs contrary to their belief that the universe was created by their God. They accept the words in the Bible as literal truth and deny everything which does not conform to this truth. Just as many scientists would claim that the alleged miracles performed by Christ are merely myths. The laws which govern their physical world cannot explain how Christ walked on water, or rose from the dead, for that matter, so they assume that it couldn't have happened."

"I just had this conversation with The Mole yesterday!" exclaimed Paxton.

"I know," Thorn admitted. "Now that I have tuned into the frequency of your brain waves I could probably connect with your mind from anywhere on the planet."

Paxton thought this admission to be a little creepy, but he pressed forward with his current train of thought, "You're talking about extremes, Thorn. The Mole on the one hand and religious zealots on the other. There are many more people whose beliefs lie somewhere in between."

"Precisely my point, Paxton, and you're a perfect example. The realms of science and spirituality have always overlapped, though the staunch adherents to either one continue to deny their commonalities. In this age they have begun to merge in the collective consciousness, and as they continue to merge, all manner of new insights into the age old questions will present themselves. You, in particular, must make yourself available to these new insights."

"Why me? I'm adept at neither science nor spirituality."

"That may be true, Paxton, but you're a student of both, and you're learning at an incredible rate."

"I'm learning more about the physical than the metaphysical at the moment, I'm afraid. I sometimes get discouraged about the lack of progress in my meditation."

"Why do you feel as if you haven't been making any progress?"

"In all the years that I've been practicing meditation, I have never had a vision or extrasensory perception or any experience which I would consider to be outside the realm of reality. Until the other day, that is, but that was fostered by you."

"That's what spiritual teachers are for, Paxton. I want to introduce you to the worlds of possibility that exist beyond your physical reality. But I merely opened the door upon The Chords, you passed through it on your own. Your years of practicing meditation have not been in vain, but have prepared you for this meeting. Why did you keep practicing if you felt you weren't making any progress?"

"I enjoy the sense of peace and well-being I feel after a yoga or meditation session. I always feel as if everything is all right with the world and that I am doing exactly what it is I'm supposed to be doing in it. Of course, that peace is usually shattered the moment I reenter life's mainstream."

"But those moments of clarity were enough to keep you coming back for more," Thorn observed. "The process of spiritual growth is a slow and laborious one. It's generally measured in lifetimes, not in days, or even years. You have progressed a lot farther than you think, Paxton. Your body is much healthier and more limber than it used to be, and your mind is quieter. Still, you can only get so far on your own. Reading and practicing are important, but so too, is the guidance of a spiritual teacher. Are you studying relativity on your own?"

"No," Paxton admitted. "You know I've been working with Dr. Browning."

"Why haven't you sought a teacher to assist you in your study of spirituality?"

"Where am I going to find a Master in Orono, Maine?" Paxton defended himself.

"Why not Orono?" Thorn queried. "The little town of Bethlehem was not holy until after the nativity."

"Are you my guru?" Paxton asked, suddenly realizing what Thorn was trying to tell him.

"In the flesh. Or should I say, in the wood? But perhaps it is more apt to say that we are each other's gurus, for I believe I have some lessons to learn from you as well. Your striving for spiritual growth has made this meeting possible. The rest is up to us."

Paxton tried to assimilate all that was being said to him. Could he really have found his guru, in the guise of a tree? It all seemed too incredible to him. Was he losing his grip on reality?

"You've got a lot more work ahead of you before you'll be able to do that," his newfound guru said, listening to his thoughts. "You're still much too grounded in the world of your senses to transcend what you deem to be real. You must first understand the relativity of reality."

"The relativity of reality? What does that mean?"

"Tell me what you know about relativity," Thorn demanded, by way of answer.

"That could take all day," Paxton chuckled.

"Don't flatter yourself," Thorn replied, joining in on the joke. "Let me be more specific. Explain Einstein's theory of special relativity to me."

"You mean there's something you don't know?" Paxton teased.

"There are many things I don't know," Thorn admitted, "but this isn't one of them. I'm interested in your interpretation of the theory."

"I'm not sure where to start."

"Why don't you start at the beginning?"

Paxton thought for a moment and then responded, "There is a much used example concerning a boy and a ball on a train. I could tell you that one, but you're probably already familiar with it."

"That would be fine," Thorn allowed. "I'm all knots!"

Paxton looked at Thorn's trunk and burst out laughing. He was enjoying the light-hearted atmosphere that had developed between them. It seemed to Paxton that he had known Thorn for much longer than the past couple of days.

"Picture a train traveling at fifty miles an hour," Paxton began. "There is a child on the train who is bouncing a ball up and down and catching it. From the child's viewpoint, looking straight down upon it, the ball appears to be a single point in space. Now imagine that his sister is sitting across the aisle watching him. She would describe the ball's motion as a vertical line extending from the child's hand to the floor and then back up again. There is yet another way to describe the ball's motion. Imagine there is a man in a car, waiting for the train to pass by his intersection. He can see the bouncing ball through a window of the train. He would describe the motion of the ball as a series of arcs as the ball travels both vertically and horizontally in front of him."

"Which one describes the ball's motion correctly?" asked Thorn.

"They are all correct!" Paxton responded with confidence. "That's the essence of relativity. There is not one correct way to describe the ball's motion. It cannot be described as an entity unto itself. Its motion can be described only in a sense relative to some other object, which is also in motion."

"So what you're saying is that, even though all three people have their own conflicting versions of reality, each one is correct?"

"Yes, well no," stammered Paxton, no longer so sure of himself. "The ball really is moving both horizontally and vertically, so the man's version is the only one based upon reality. The other two are viewing optical illusions, based on their limited viewpoints of the motion of the ball. If they could see the whole picture they would be able to describe the ball's true motion."

"Who sees the whole picture?"

"The man in the car does."

"Really?" Thorn sounded skeptical. "What if you were an astronaut on the moon with a powerful enough telescope to view the ball's motion on the surface of the Earth? Wouldn't you describe not only the horizontal and vertical motion of the ball, but also the circular motion it picks up as a result of the revolution of the Earth around its axis?"

"What if you're an alien viewing the ball's motion from another galaxy?" Thorn continued. "Then you'd have to factor in not only the elliptical motion caused by the Earth's orbit around the sun, but also the relative motion between the two galaxies. What is the whole picture?"

"Now I see what you mean," stated Paxton, "but I don't have the answer to your question."

"Who has the only complete view of the entire universe?" pressed Thorn.

"God?" guessed Paxton.

"Exactly, Paxton. Only The All can see the totality of reality. All other versions of reality are necessarily flawed and completely relative to the viewpoint of the observer. In that sense there are six billion different versions of reality on this planet, none of which are completely correct, although each one is not only meaningful, but essential to the individual who harbors it.

"No two humans live in the same reality. Though they may experience the same sequence of events, each interprets them from within the framework of their own knowledge and beliefs, their own biases and prejudices, their hopes and fears. Each one's reality is relative to their point of view."

"But," Paxton argued, "their interpretations of the event do not change the event itself. There is one overriding reality, one absolute truth."

"That one Absolute Truth is The All. And since we don't understand the nature of The All, we must work from within the frameworks of our own separate realities."

Paxton remained silent and Thorn waited a few moments before asking, "How do you explain the miracle of the boy catching the ball?"

"What miracle is that?"

"How fast is the ball traveling?" Thorn asked.

"Well, to the boy it's only traveling up and down at a few miles per hour."

"Lucky for him," Thorn asserted. "Didn't we just decide that the ball was hurtling through space, blasted outward from the Big Bang, at millions of miles per hour? Why doesn't that reality kill the boy?"

"Ahh," Paxton exhaled, rubbing his hands together. "Now we're back into my kind of relativity."

"We never left it."

"The speed of the ball is also relative to the position of its measurement," Paxton continued, ignoring him. "The man measures the ball's speed as it passes him at fifty miles per hour. The boy's hand measures only the slight upward velocity of the ball as it bounces back into his palm. His point of reference negates the train's speed because he is also traveling forward at fifty miles an hour."

"So the speed of the ball is different in each of their realities?" Thorn feigned ignorance. "Who is right?"

"They both are right. The speed of the ball cannot be measured absolutely. Each of their interpretations is correct for their own situations. Picture the boy walking forward in the direction of the moving train at five miles an hour. His sister watching him walk away from her measures his speed at five miles an hour, but the man watching from his car measures the boy's speed at fifty-five miles an hour because he also factors in the speed of the train. If the boy turns around and walks back to his sister at the same speed, she still measures his speed at five miles an hour, but now the man in the car measures it at forty-five miles an hour."

"So you're saying we can't measure the speed of anything absolutely?"

"Anything except light. Light moves at the speed of 670 million miles an hour regardless of where the measurement is taken relative to the light source."

When Thorn said nothing Paxton continued, "Now let's say that the boy is carrying a flashlight while he walks forward. You would expect that the man in the car would measure the speed of the light at 670 million plus fifty-five miles an hour. Similarly, if the boy turns around and walks back, you would expect the man to measure the speed of the light at 670 million minus forty-five miles an hour in the opposite direction. In reality, the speed of light is measured the same in either case and it remains constant at 670 million miles an hour. Nor can anything travel faster than the speed of light."

"Nothing can travel faster than light?" Thorn mused, playing the part of the student. "What is so special about light?"

"If I knew the answer to that I'd be a famous man," Paxton commented.

"No doubt," Thorn agreed.

"Scientists are still trying to figure that one out."

"So are holy men," Thorn returned, "and women."

"Why would holy men be interested in the nature of light?"

"God is Light! Your spiritual texts are full of references to this fact. You can see the Light, be filled with Light and head toward the Light as you ascend toward The All, while Black Magic is dubbed The Dark Arts and the evils of humankind are done in the darkness of sin, banishing the evildoers into the dark, depths of Hell for all eternity."

"But God isn't actually light," Paxton reasoned. "It's just a religious allegory."

"How can you be so sure?"

"In the beginning God said, 'Let there be light!'" Paxton quoted the Bible. "God created light."

"The Bible also says that God created Adam and Eve, Methuselah lived nine hundred and sixty-nine years and the entire gene pool of the current world was carried upon and then released from Noah's ark on Mt. Ararat. Do you accept these as the Absolute Truth?"

"Touché," granted Paxton, raising his imaginary sword in salute.

"The Bible is a storybook, certainly inspired by The All, but written by humans nonetheless. But you're right, it might be better to say that 'Light is God,' or at least a part of The All."

Paxton had adopted the pose of The Thinker, except that he was seated cross-legged on the ground at the base of Thorn's trunk, oblivious to the melting frost he was absorbing through his jeans.

"The Absolute Truth lies with The All, just as Absolute Speed is a property of the Light, at least as far as your scientists can surmise. In seeking out the nature of light they are seeking the nature of The All. They are seeking the Absolute Truth about the universe in which they find themselves."

"But we are getting off the subject, here. We have plenty of time for theological debate," Thorn not so subtly directed the conversation. "You were just about to tell me how the theory of relativity was born."

"That's right!" Paxton took his chin off his closed fist and looked up at Thorn thoughtfully. "How did you know that?"

"Our conversation was quite logically leading up to it," Thorn replied innocently.

"Yeah, right," Paxton grunted aloud, trying to break Thorn's hold on his mind. He felt suddenly squeamish about having Thorn so intimate with his thoughts. Thorn was silent as Paxton eyed him suspiciously.

After two long minutes Paxton asked, "Why are you so quiet?"

"You shut me out of your mind," Thorn answered. "That's the only way I am capable of communicating with you."

"I can do that?"

"Sure. All you have to do is concentrate and close the mental door to . . ."

Paxton tried it again, and again he turned Thorn's volume down and then off.

"I feel a little bit better now," he admitted. Perhaps Thorn wasn't able to probe the far reaches of his psyche.

"Don't worry," Thorn popped back. "I'm not opening your mind's dusty, closet doors. I'm only connecting with that part which is readily accessible to me. Now, you were saying?"

Paxton struggled to regain his lost thoughts, and then said, "Einstein's genius was not that he came up with the concepts of which we've just spoken. Scientists have been studying relativity as far back as Galileo, and Copernicus, and farther. His genius was that he came up with a new way to tackle the problem.

"The scientists of Einstein's time were studying the properties of light as a way to understand how its speed could be unaffected by relativity. Einstein decided the answer lay not with light, but with the way in which we measure speed.

"Speed is a measure of distance, or space, divided by time, and this has been readily accepted for thousands of years. That was what was so radical about Einstein's approach. He reasoned that there was something wrong with our conception of speed, which meant there must be something wrong with the way in which we thought about space and time."

"Einstein was a free thinker," Thorn interrupted. "That is really where his genius stemmed from. He was also one of the greatest students of both science and spirituality that this world has ever known."

"That he was a great scientist is self-evident," Paxton commented, "but I was unaware that he was also interested in spiritualism. I mean, I know he was a philosopher. I've read some of his more philosophical works. But he never really received any recognition for them."

"Is one's greatness a product of the acclaim of one's peers? Would Einstein have been any less of a great thinker if he had never shared E equals m, c-squared with the rest of the world?"

"Of course not," admitted Paxton, "but we wouldn't know of his greatness, and we never would have progressed as far as we have, without that knowledge."

"You may also have never developed nuclear weapons."

"Einstein didn't work on the Manhattan Project," said Paxton in his defense.

"True, but it was his knowledge that enabled the technology to develop the atomic bomb, something he felt guilty about for the rest of his life."

"Surely you're not saying that we'd be better off without the theory of relativity."

"It's a moot point," stated Thorn noncommittally. "The evolution of the Earth and its inhabitants is taking place exactly as it should be.

What I am saying is that just because Einstein didn't walk on water, doesn't mean that he wasn't spiritually adept. He was one of the great humanitarians. His non-conformity and free-thinking intellect was not limited to the realm of science. Einstein was a pacifist and an internationalist long before those movements became popular.

"Far from being an atheist, Einstein believed the workings of the natural world were synonymous with the mysteries of The All. Physics and mathematics books were his scriptures and calculations his prayers. Similar to Buddha sitting in meditation under the fig tree waiting for Enlightenment to resolve the duality of human existence, Einstein sat in his own form of meditation in his office at Princeton University for more than twenty years, waiting for the synapses in his brain to converge upon the one theory which would resolve the duality of natural laws into unity."

"Except that Buddha found his Enlightenment, while Einstein did not."

"Did he? The physical manifestation which the world has come to know as The Buddha, was just one of many of that soul's incarnations. Was it the last one, or will He come back? Has He already come back?"

"Why would Buddha come back if he's already found Enlightenment?"

"Why indeed? On the other hand, who's to say that Einstein didn't find his Enlightenment?"

"He never did come up with the Unified Field Theory."

"Not that you know of," Thorn responded cryptically. "Maybe after witnessing the destruction caused by E equals m, c-squared, he decided that the world was not quite ready for Unified Field Theory. Regardless, he was a man at peace at the time of his death."

"How do you know that?"

"I connected with him," answered Thorn. "Not like we're connecting now, but I could enter his subconsciousness through his dreams. I have also been able to locate the thread of his soul in The Chords."

"Really?" asked Paxton, not sure which admission he found more incredulous.

"What took me decades, Tucker accomplished in only his first journey through The Chords."

"What's that?"

"He connected with the thread of Einstein's soul as he traveled backwards through The Chords the other day."

"No way!" said Paxton aloud, and then thought, *"Why Tucker? I should have been the one to hook up with Einstein's chord. Tucker couldn't give a rat's ass about Einstein."*

"I was surprised, too," Thorn replied, reading his thoughts easily, although they weren't directed at him. "Tucker must have been somehow connected to Einstein in his previous life."

"I find that hard to believe," Paxton scoffed, more than a little jealous. "If Tucker can do it, so can I. Can we go back into The Chords, Thorn?"

"Not until you get your motivations straight," admonished Thorn. "Your jealousy will prevent you from passing through the portal to The Chords. Let's wait a while. Besides, I want to hear more about the relativity of space and time."

"I can't tell you any more than you already know," said Paxton sulkily.

"That we shall see, Paxton."

FIFTEEN

The Space Inside A Second

So many people killing time.
Don't kill any of mine.
Don't you think that there's
    enough killing going on?
Animals, trees, our enemies,
        even children
            are under the gun.
Tell me,
        do we have to kill time, too?

So many people wasting time.
Don't waste any of mine.
Don't you think that there's
    enough wasting going on?
We've poisoned our seas,
        the air that we breath.
Our sky lets in
        too much of the sun.
Tell me,
        do we have to waste time, too?

So many people spending time.
Don't spend any of mine
What's the precious gift that
        you're hoping to buy?
Heavens keys? A cure for disease?
Or something that
        won't let you die?
Tell me, is it worth the price
        that you're paying?

I'm more interested in stretching time.
I'm more interested in trying to find,
The space inside a second.
For time is elastic, time is expanding.
Time is a relative thing.
And as I sit in contemplation,
Searching for some realization,
Practicing procrastination,

Another year passes away.

"Let's revisit the train example," said Paxton, standing up to stretch out his legs. He felt foolish explaining what Thorn probably knew better than he did himself, but he had accepted the mantle of teacher for the moment. "Suppose there is a light clock on the train."

"What's a light clock?" asked Thorn, playing his own role.

"I'm just about to tell you. Suppose the boy sets his flashlight on the floor, pointing it up at the ceiling. On the ceiling is a mirror which reflects the light back down to the floor. The unit of measurement for this light clock is the time it takes for the light to make the round trip."

"That's a pretty accurate clock," Thorn observed.

"I'm not saying it's feasible to make such a clock. We're just conducting a thought experiment, for which Einstein was famous. He couldn't test his theories directly, at least not at first, so he used thought experiments instead. In this one we shall examine the path of the light beam as observed by the boy on the train and the man in his car.

"The boy sees the light beam travel straight up and then back down in a vertical line. The man's perspective allows for the motion of the train. Just as he sees the ball bouncing in arcs before him, he sees the light beam travel upward at an angle and reflect back down to the floor at the same angle. The path traversed by the light beam appears to him as the upper two sides of a triangle."

"Would he really see that much of a difference with the train going so slow, relative to the speed of light?"

"Good point, Thorn. We need to also imagine that the train is traveling close to the speed of light."

"Fast train," Thorn commented, and Paxton thought he detected a trace of humor in the voice he heard inside his head.

"The point is, under these circumstances, the path that the light travels according to the man is longer than the one the boy observes. Remember that speed equals distance divided by time. Since the speed of light is a constant, if the distance the light travels becomes longer, then it must also take a longer amount of time to get there. The man perceives the boy's clock as running slower than an equivalent, but stationary one. Einstein's theory of special relativity predicts that as an object approaches the speed of light, time slows down."

"That was a good explanation, Paxton, and I agree with your conclusion, except that you don't need to go nearly that fast to slow down time."

"That's true, but at slower speeds the time differential is so small that we don't have clocks accurate enough to measure it."

"Forget about your clocks!" Thorn stated forcefully. "You can slow down time, or speed it up for that matter, without moving at all."

"You're going to have to explain that one to me."

"Consider the people involved in your thought experiment. Imagine that the man waiting for the train to cross his path is in a hurry. He is late for work yet again and this is causing him stress. He is thinking about what excuse he will use for his tardiness, and what he will do for a job if this train doesn't hurry up and get out of his way. The five minutes it takes for the train to pass by seem more like twenty to him.

"The sister is thinking about the boyfriend she left back home. She will be gone on this trip for a month and she's missing him already. She barely sees the ball she is staring at so fixedly, as she reminisces over the last time she saw him, and how he had kissed her goodbye. She is completely unaware of the five minutes that have just passed as she daydreams scenes in the passing countryside. For her those five minutes are no more than five seconds.

"The boy is engrossed in his play. He watches the ball bounce, down and then back up again. He times it in his head. In fact, he measures time with the beat of the ball, bouncing up and down. To him the five minutes are five minutes, no more, no less. Who, of the three, has the correct conception of time?"

"I would have to say the boy," guessed Paxton, "because he measures the five minutes as exactly five minutes."

"So the boy, then, is the only one living in reality?"

"They are each living their own separate realities, based upon their different perspectives of that five minutes," Paxton answered, sure he was on the right track this time.

"Exactly, Paxton. They are each living their own *relative* realities. Just as the motion of the ball cannot be measured as an entity unto itself, time cannot be measured solely in seconds, minutes or hours. It can only be measured in relation to a certain perspective of its passage. Time is also completely relative to one's perspective."

"But that's not the same type of relativity I was talking about!"

"Oh?" Thorn sounded skeptical. "What's different about it?"

"Einstein predicted that time itself would slow down at speeds close to the speed of light. In your analogy, actual time isn't affected. Five minutes have passed for all three of them. Their perception of time is different in each case, but the time itself isn't distorted."

"Isn't it?" Thorn asked. "If one's perception is that an hour has passed, isn't that the reality experienced by the perceiver, regardless of the actual number of revolutions made by the minute hand of a clock? The clock is a modern invention, as is the concept of linear time. Modern humans invented these things to better understand their relativity to the universe, yet they have become enslaved to them."

"I am not enslaved by time," Paxton defended himself. "I don't even wear a watch."

"Yet you keep one in your backpack," countered Thorn. "I heard it beeping not too long ago."

Paxton glanced at the crumpled, green heap, lying several yards away where he had dropped it upon greeting Thorn.

"I need to know what time it is when I'm teaching," Paxton justified. "That's why I keep one in there. Otherwise, I don't use it much."

"Which is why you're always running late."

"Hey! How do you know that?"

"Don't you find it stressful to be forever arriving for class out of breath and apologizing for your tardiness?" interrogated Thorn further, ignoring Paxton's own question.

"I'm usually pretty flustered when I get to class," Paxton admitted. "It takes me a few minutes to settle down and get into the flow of the lecture."

"You get *stressed out* precisely because you can't escape time's boundaries. Boundaries you yourself have imposed."

"I don't impose those boundaries," Paxton retorted, "society does!"

"That's partially true, yet you choose to live within the boundaries imposed by your society."

"What other choice do I have? Where could I possibly go to escape time's boundaries? Are there places on this earth unaffected by time?"

"Not unaffected," Thorn replied, "but there are places where the rhythm of life runs much more slowly than in your society's well-oiled machine."

"Like where?" Paxton asked, his defensive posture gone in the wake of his curiosity.

"Take, Kenya, for example. Did you need a watch when you were in Kenya?"

"Pah!" Paxton laughed to himself. "About as much as I needed a hair dryer! In Kenya they have a saying: 'Time is elastic.' Kenyan's aren't that concerned with keeping precise time. Meetings at my school were scheduled for 'the morning' or 'the afternoon' and just sort of started up spontaneously after everyone had arrived. I used to get so pissed off! I'd get there first thing in the morning and wait sometimes three hours for my colleagues to straggle in. Once I figured out their system and adopted it I became much more relaxed. By the time I left Kenya I was showing up for meetings as late as everyone else and bringing a book or my journal with me so that I wasn't stressed out waiting for the other teachers to arrive."

"And yet you weren't completely free of time, either."

"No, I guess not. Someone rang the bell at school when it was time to change classes, so someone had to keep track of time. Even so, my fellow teachers used to disregard the bell. That made me angry at first, too. I would go to my next classroom at the sound of the bell with my forty minute lecture prepared, and wait impatiently for fifteen minutes while the teacher ahead of me finished his own lesson. I was forever battling the other teachers over the rights to my forty minutes, even interrupting their lectures when it was my time to teach."

"Did it do any good?"

"No," admitted Paxton. "I couldn't make the whole school adopt my rigid time schedule, so I eventually adopted theirs and became much happier. Rather than ending my lecture on time, I still used my forty minutes and made the next teacher wait for me. Actually, the teacher after me was never in a hurry to get started with his lesson, so it was a non-issue."

"You brought that time stress with you to Africa," Thorn commented, "because you were still conditioned to the frenetic pace of this country. You weren't able to relax your rigid rules about time until you could break your entrainment to that faster rhythm."

"What do you mean by *entrainment*?" Paxton asked.

"You can think of entrainment as synchronicity. Objects in motion naturally tend toward the same patterns or rhythms. Two pendulums of equal length, started at different times, will eventually move back and forth as one. People walking together in a group will tend toward walking in rhythm or in sync, left and right legs stepping forward in unison. Several women living together will eventually realign their menstrual cycles so they all start and end their periods at the same time each month. All of these are examples of synchronicity, or entrainment.

"Your modern world moves quickly, especially compared to your tiny village in Kenya. You can travel to almost any other point on the globe in less than twenty-four hours. Spoken messages to the other side of the earth take mere seconds. Even in your village in Kenya you had a phone with which you could call your mother."

"Yeah, but that took longer than a few seconds. Try a few hours!"

"Even so, you could make that contact." Thorn pointed out. "You have more information at the tips of your fingers than any one person could possibly ingest in a lifetime. Things happen fast in your culture, and when you live in it, you get used to things happening fast. You become entrained to the pace at which time travels in your society, just as you entrain to different rhythms in music. Rock and roll fills you with energy and makes you tap your foot to the drumbeat, while classical music makes you quiet and reflective. In a similar way you can entrain to different senses of time."

"That reminds me of a funny story," Paxton chuckled, still thinking about Kenya.

"Go on," urged Thorn, when it seemed as though Paxton would keep it to himself.

"I brought my coffee travel mug with me to Kenya," Paxton reminisced, "and I used to fill it up with *chai* every morning for my walk to the school. The villagers pointed at me and laughed as I power-walked the half kilometer to my school every day, sipping my chai. I was pretty self-conscious about it at first, wondering if I was dressed inappropriately, or otherwise breaking some local custom. I finally figured out that they were pointing to my travel mug and laughing at me for drinking chai on the fly. A Kenyan would sit down and enjoy his cup of chai in the morning before setting about the business of the day. After a while, I abandoned my travel mug and did the same."

"Were you happy in Kenya?" Thorn inquired seriously, after a short silence.

"Yes, I was happy," Paxton answered just as seriously and without hesitation, "once I relaxed into their culture and learned how to slow down. It was one of the happiest times of my whole life, or at least the most peaceful."

"Which is not to say there weren't also hardships," he continued. "I had no running water or electricity in my house. I carried water from school for my cooking and bathing needs, and I used a kerosine lantern to light my house at night. I did my dishes and my laundry by hand, using as little water as possible. I went to the bathroom in a hole and took my 'splash-baths' in a bucket. I also had to deal with loneliness and find new and interesting ways to entertain myself."

"Yet you just said that it was one of the happiest times of your whole life."

"It was! I felt good about the work I was doing and I learned so much, not only about Kenya but about myself as well. I taught myself how to play guitar. I learned about astronomy through direct observation of the night sky. I kept a journal and I wrote several hundred letters in that three years. I practiced yoga and meditation almost every night before I went to bed. The simple lifestyle I lived there suited me well and I was completely at peace. Well, maybe not completely, especially at first, but I had a hard time leaving when my service was over."

"One reason you were so at peace in Kenya was because you were able to slow down the pace of your life. You were living in an older place, governed by older rules. The pace of modern life is much faster than it was ages ago, and continues to accelerate at an alarming rate. Today you can take trips in a few hours that used to take days or weeks. You can compute in an afternoon what used to take mathematicians whole lifetimes to compute. You have the capability to obliterate whole cities in an instant. In times past it would have taken weeks or months of siege to do the equivalent."

"So what if our pace has accelerated? Maybe that's not always such a bad thing!" interjected Paxton, feeling as if he needed to defend modern humankind. "Here I don't have to spend three hours doing my laundry by hand, which frees up my time for more important things."

"Does it really? Are you still practicing yoga and playing guitar and writing in your journal every day like you did in Kenya? How many letters have you written since returning home?"

"Not very many," Paxton confessed. "I can't find the time for such things every day, anymore."

"Why is that?" pressed Thorn. "You have an oven and a microwave to cook your food quickly, not to mention fast food restaurants of every conceivable variety to choose from. You can ride your bicycle or your car to work instead of walking and you no longer have to carry water to your house. You have a dishwasher, a washing machine, and a vacuum to help you clean, not to mention a computer to write all your correspondence. What do you mean you can't find the time?"

"I'm much busier here than I was in Kenya."

"Why does everybody in this day and age complain that they don't have enough time?" asked Thorn, before Paxton was done with his feeble excuse. "Is there less time in the modern world? Where did all of the extra time go?"

"I guess everyone is a lot busier these days," said Paxton, sticking to his original answer.

"I'll grant you that," Thorn conceded, "but what I want to know is why?"

"I have the feeling you're about to tell me why."

"When modern conveniences like washing and sewing machines were first invented, they were touted as great time savers. They were going to save the housewife so much time that she'd be able to relax and enjoy her day. Do modern housewives or house-husbands get to relax and enjoy their days?"

"I don't know, I've never been one!"

"Or do they use the extra time for doing even more chores? Mass production was going to enable the population of the industrialized world to work less. Twenty hour work weeks could produce more than forty or sixty hour work weeks used to, so everyone would have more free time on their hands for more pleasurable pursuits. Do the workers of today work any less than workers did fifty years ago, or do they just produce more?"

"But we're better off than we were fifty years ago!"

"Better off in what sense? Are you happier, more relaxed or more fulfilled? Or do you just have more things?"

"You can't be saying it would be better to go back to the time before the Industrial Revolution!"

"No, human evolution is following its natural course. What remains to be seen is whether you're heading toward enlightenment or destruction. Which of your inventions will turn out to be more significant—nuclear power or nuclear bombs? Let me ask you this. What do you consider the most important invention of humankind?"

"Of those two?"

"No, in general."

"Let's see," thought Paxton. "The lightbulb? The combustion engine? How about the computer?"

"Each one of these inventions tampers with time. The lightbulb extends the daylight, making it possible to fit more activities into a single day. Automobiles, trains and airplanes allow humans to move faster, which reduces travel time. The computer lets you perform a year's worth of calculations in an hour. My point is that all of these inventions were designed to save time. Time conservation is the great motivating factor of the human race."

"I thought that it was money."

"Time is money. Money may not be able to buy you love, as the Beatles so aptly put it, but it can buy you time."

"In what sense does money buy time?"

"With enough money salted away you could conceivably stop working and enjoy your time, though it seems that humans have trouble determining what constitutes 'enough money'. Money allows you to fly to your destination, rather than traveling overland or oversea, thus saving time. With money you can afford all of your modern conveniences, reducing the amount of time spent on life's everyday chores. You can also purchase life's luxuries, thus making the most of your time. Money will buy you the best health care possible, adding years to your lifespan, which is quite literally buying time. Money is the currency of time."

"Money is time, time is money," muttered Paxton, nodding his head in agreement.

"Time is this and much more. Think of all of the common references to time in your language. You can waste time, push time, kill time, work overtime, take your time or take a time out, spend time, manage your time, make time or make the most of it, mark time, serve time, be on time, have a good time, arrive ahead of time or fall behind the times, save time, stretch time . . . . Now there's an interesting idea."

"What's that?"

"Stretching time. Your Kenyan friends were right. Time is elastic. It stretches."

"Can you make time stretch, Thorn?"

"Yes, but so can you. You do it all the time."

"When do I stretch time?"

"Remember when you first started to meditate?"

"Yeah," Paxton replied, tentatively.

"How long were your sessions then?"

"I tried to sit for fifteen minutes, but I seldom made it. In the first five minutes my back would start to ache. I would open my eyes to check the time after what seemed like half an hour, only to discover that I had been sitting for just ten minutes."

"You see," Thorn reiterated, "you also have the ability to stretch time."

"I guess so," Paxton spoke tentatively, as though he wasn't completely convinced.

"Do you think that if you had been making love for those ten minutes you would have even noticed the passage of that time?"

"I see what you're getting at, Thorn, but I'm only stretching the time in my own head. I can focus on the passage of time or become oblivious to it. In either case, the time itself remains constant. My watch ticks off ten minutes, regardless."

"But that ten minute interval can be as ten seconds or ten hours to you, depending on your perception, and regardless of the ticks of your clock. If you've been waiting for what seems like an eternity for a loved one to return home late at night, what comfort does it bring you to look at a clock and verify that, indeed, only ten minutes have gone by? Likewise, if those ten minutes have gone by in an instant, what clock can give you back that *lost* time? Is your reality based upon your perception of time or upon the strict laws laid down by your Almighty Clock?"

"My personal reality is based upon my own perception," answered Paxton, "but the collective reality shares a common perception of time, which is measured in fixed increments."

"What is the collective reality? You've already told me that Kenyans don't share this society's concept of time. Who keeps the correct Universal Time?"

"God does!" Paxton replied with enthusiasm.

"That's both right, and incredibly wrong, at the same time."

"How can that be?"

"The All keeps Universal Time, which is not limited to the linear time you're so fond of keeping on this planet."

"How else can you keep time?"

"There are endless variations on time. Your ancient forebears kept circular time. They were more concerned with the cycles of nature and believed that time always circled back to its point of origin. Parallel time would allow for the concurrent existence of an infinite number of worlds. Which world houses any individual consciousness would depend upon the choices one makes in each present moment. Time in The Chords is rather like a motion picture where one can rewind and fast forward, even though one isn't actually traveling through time. The time kept by The All encompasses each of these concepts, yet espouses none of them. I like to think of The All as existing in timelessness. Time is the antithesis of The All."

Thorn waited a few moments for Paxton to reply. When no response was forthcoming he continued, "Do you remember your travels through The Chords the other day?"

"How could I forget?"

"When you gain a higher perspective of the cosmic tapestry, you also gain a higher perspective of time. You were able to glimpse the bigger picture and so could see more of the interlocking threads of past and future as they connect to the present. Because you were viewing the tapestry from this higher vantage point, time passed much more slowly for you. Twelve hours went by in the place where you left your physical body, but you felt it to be no more than an hour or two."

"It seems as if you're contradicting yourself," Paxton observed. "If I only perceived those twelve hours to be two, wasn't time going more quickly for me?"

"It all depends on your point of reference. Imagine that both your body and your consciousness had clocks during that time. Your body's clock measured twelve hours while your consciousness measured two. Your body's clock was moving faster relative to that of your mind. Your consciousness succeeded in slowing down time."

"But the actual time went faster," Paxton argued.

"Which one is *actual* time? Which one is the *real* you, your body or your consciousness?"

"I would have to go with my consciousness."

"Then the actual time being kept by your consciousness while you were in The Chords was moving more slowly than the time experienced by your physical form. Consider what would happen if you continued your flight above the tapestry even higher. When viewing time on this macroscopic level, hours, days, and even lifetimes would be as seconds to you. How far above the tapestry is The Weaver? Centuries pass in the blink of her eyes. She is far enough above the tapestry that she lives outside the boundaries of linear time. She is Past, Present and Future. She exists in each instant, yet lives into eternity. She is everywhere and everything—all at the same time.

"The first key to enlightenment is to step outside the boundaries of time. The desire to be closer to The All is the desire to be free of time, for The All resides in timelessness. If you ever hope to become enlightened you are going to have to rethink your conception of time."

"How can I step outside the boundaries of time?" asked Paxton, finally. "I have a feeling that it's easier said than done."

"You're absolutely right, Paxton, but you have the advantage of having witnessed a slower way of life in Kenya, although you've forgotten most of the experience now that you've become entrained once again to your faster modern life. You find it difficult to step out of that entrainment, but not as difficult as do most of your contemporaries, who have never been out of sync with modern time.

"To become free from time one must learn to slow time down and eventually stop it altogether. This can be achieved by either accelerating the rhythm of your life, or by slowing down that rhythm."

"How can you slow time by accelerating the rhythm of your life?"

"Isn't that what Einstein's theory was all about? You told me earlier that as you approach the speed of light, time slows down. Your world is attempting to slow time by accelerating the rate at which you move. In that sense, human evolution is proceeding in the right direction, spiritually speaking. But it will be many eons before you can achieve collective enlightenment in this fashion. When you can travel at the speed of light, you will become Light."

"But it's impossible for anything but light to travel at the speed of light! Einstein's theory of special relativity also predicts that as you travel faster, your mass increases. As you approach the speed of light you approach infinite mass which means you'd need infinite power to accelerate any further."

"Then I guess you've got your work cut out for you if you're going to approach The All from that direction. Maybe that's why more traditional spiritual aspirants have chosen to slow down time by slowing down themselves. And those that have been able to achieve it have been revered throughout the ages as spiritual masters. Imagine the miracles you could perform if you could slow time down. Perhaps Christ didn't walk on water so much as he slowed his fall to the point where it appeared as though he was stationary on the surface of the lake.

"What if you could stop time, or travel time, or disregard it altogether? Enlightened masters can do all of these things and more. Teleportation, appearing in two places at the same time, prophesying, healing the sick or raising the dead—all of these powers would be within your grasp."

"Can you teach me to do those things, Thorn?"

"Those are very advanced techniques, Paxton. I'm not saying you couldn't eventually learn them, but you must first learn to slow down time. You must first break your entrainment to the fast pace of your society. You can't approach The All from both directions at once. Entraining to the fast modern pace leaves little time for more traditional spiritual pursuits."

"How can I break out of that entrainment?"

"You already know how to do it, you just need more practice. Meditation is one way to slow down time. When you are in a deep meditative state, your heartbeat and breathing slow, and your brain wave activity tapers off. In short, your own internal clock slows down, relative to time measured on a more standard clock. Five or six hours of *real* time might pass in what your mind and body measure as an hour of meditation. This is why a yogi can sit in meditation for days at a time. Shiva Bala Yogi meditated twenty-three hours a day for eight years of his life, and then twelve hours a day for another four years. After almost twelve years of meditation, he awoke as if from an afternoon nap, except that he awoke enlightened."

"Wow! Is that what it takes to become enlightened?" Paxton asked, amazed. "That's so extreme! I mean, I know enlightenment is a noble goal and everything, but it seems to me that Shiva Baba . . ."

"Shiva Bala Yogi," Thorn corrected.

"It seems to me that Shiva Bala Yogi didn't *live* during those twelve years. Aren't we also here to explore our human natures?"

"I'm sure that's not why I'm here!" Thorn kidded him. "But I see your point. To live an austere life one must forsake the sensual pleasures of this world and set aside one's human nature. That's a steep price to pay, which is why there are few humans who choose the path of austerity. There are also no guarantees that this path will lead to enlightenment in this lifetime. Many spiritual seekers spend their adult lives in monasteries but are never recognized as spiritual masters. Have they lived their lives in vain, then?"

"I suppose not," Paxton answered hesitantly. "I believe that if you live a good life, you will ultimately be better off in the next one—closer to enlightenment."

"Now we're getting somewhere, Paxton. You need to change your perspective on time. Granted, if this life was all there was, spending it in a monastery might be considered a waste of your precious human time, especially if it didn't result in achieving enlightenment. But if you put this lifetime in its proper perspective, as just one of many lifetimes, then these sixty, or eighty, or one hundred years are merely a brief swing in the endless universal playground of time. If that lifetime spent in austerity brings you closer to The All, was it not then worth it?"

"Are you saying that I should become a monk?"

"Not at all, Paxton. All souls are moving toward The All at their own rate. Any progress you make in this lifetime will carry over into the next one. While a life spent in meditation might speed the process along, it's not apparent to me that monkhood is to be your destiny in this lifetime. What I am telling you is that you should practice slowing down time and that meditation is one way to do this. Another is the practice of mindfulness."

"Yeah, but practicing mindfulness is just as hard as practicing meditation," Paxton complained.

"Harder, in fact, but who ever said sainthood was easy? When you sit in meditation you shut the rest of the world out as you seek self-actualization. Mindfulness means trying to sustain this meditative state throughout the course of the rest of your day, through all of the distractions of your everyday life. Mindfulness is meditation in action.

"By concentrating on whatever task you find before you, whether it be work or play, to the exclusion of all else is to live in the present moment, forgetting both the past and the future. The extent to which you are successful in living in the present moment is precisely the measure by which you can slow time. Could you live completely in the present you would be able to make time stop. It is there that you would see the face of The All.

"So much of your conscious thought is spent on the future or the past. You wonder or worry about what you will be doing in an hour, or a day, or a year from now. Or you think about what has befallen you over the course of the day, or yesterday, or last week. With the consciousness diverted by past and future, you miss out on what occurs in the *now*. We've been discussing relative realities. Can you be living in reality if you never live in the present moment? What is more real, the past, the future or the present? It is only through living in each present moment that you can fully experience life.

"By embracing each experience and then letting it go and jumping into the next one without reservation, you become free of time. The illusion of time is shattered as past and future merge into the present moment. Life is a necklace strung with moments. Moment after moment after moment, beaded upon the thread of time. Living inside each moment enables you to escape time's boundaries and approach that timeless space wherein resides The All."

"Be here now," Paxton summarized Thorn's long speech.

"Exactly," agreed Thorn.

"I've read as much in my study of Zen."

"This idea is central to Zen, though not limited to Buddhism. Christ alluded to this when he talked about the lilies of the field. 'Consider the lilies, how they grow. They neither toil nor spin, yet I tell you, even Solomon in all his glory was not arrayed like one of these. If God so clothes the grass which is alive in the field today and tomorrow is thrown into the oven, how much more will he clothe you?'"

"Are you quoting from the Bible?"

"Luke, chapter 12, verses 27 and 28. I know it by heart."

"But how?" wondered Paxton, momentarily forgetting the source of Thorn's knowledge.

"Christian radio and television broadcasts crowd the airwaves, not only in this country, but worldwide. All I need do is pay attention."

Paxton nodded his head slightly as if to acknowledge that he accepted this explanation, and then asked, "Isn't there more to that particular verse? Something about birds?"

"'Consider the ravens,'" Thorn quoted further. "'They neither sow nor reap, they have neither storehouse nor barn, and yet God feeds them. Of how much more value are you than the birds! And which of you by being anxious can add a cubit to his span of life?'"

"Do you live in the present moment, Thorn?"

"Everything in nature lives in the present. Look at the natural world all around you. All of the animals and trees you see are living in this present moment."

"Squirrels gather nuts for the winter," Paxton retorted, watching a squirrel scamper across the open ground at the edge of the clearing with an acorn in his mouth. It vaulted onto the trunk of a stunted pine tree and soon disappeared amongst its branches.

"Yes, but they do so instinctually, and without worrying about what will happen to them if they don't salt away enough. They live in each moment as they perform their gathering."

"Aren't humans also a part of the natural world?"

"Yes and no. Humans choose to set themselves apart, and above, other life forms. You view the natural world from behind the bars of the cage you have built out of time. You were separated from the natural world when you stepped out of the garden of Eden."

"I thought you didn't believe in Creationism, Thorn."

"I don't, but it is a good metaphor, nonetheless."

"You're avoiding my original question."

"Which one was that?"

"Do *you* live in the present?"

"In all honesty, no. Maybe it's because I have a consciousness similar to your own, but I am also caught in time's grasp. I used to live in the present almost exclusively, before I discovered The Chords and became distracted by future and past."

At the mention of The Chords, Paxton's head shot up, "Can you take me into The Chords again, Thorn?"

"Yes, Paxton, but you should eat your lunch first. There's no telling how long we'll be in there."

Paxton tried to arise, but his legs complained at the sudden movement. He sat back down and stretched them out before him, massaging the blood back into them. When he had removed all of the pins and needles from his feet, he stood and walked the few feet to his backpack.

"What did you bring?" asked Thorn.

"Yogurt, carrots and sunflower seeds. Oh, and some iced tea. I wish I could share them with you."

"Why don't you pour some iced tea near the root next to your right foot?"

"You can taste it?" asked Paxton, looking quizzically up into Thorn's branches.

"Not the way that you taste it, but the sugar makes my roots tingle," Thorn replied. When Paxton's questioning look remained on his face, he added, "Things have been spilled up here before."

Paxton poured half of the plastic bottle on the spot Thorn had indicated, laughing at the absurdity of such a gesture.

"Cheers," he said, still laughing. He raised the bottle a few inches toward Thorn before taking a drink from it himself.

SIXTEEN

If Jesus Were Alive Today

I watched the news today, it was the same old story yesterday.
Our children are fighting and dying in lands so far away.
The price of gasoline is on the rise, we can't let this be our demise.
Launch all of the battleships, let our fighter planes fill the skies.
But our president says it's okay, 'cause every night before bed he prays,
To his Almighty God, who then shows him the way.

If Jesus were alive today, what now would he say,
About a people who love their flag but hate the man who's gay?
Would he take up arms, would he heed the call, would he be proud of our arsenal?
Or would he shed a tear for us at losing our own way?

I went to church today, and they asked me to pray.
In support of our soldier sons and the holy war they wage.
But in my Christian zeal, I made God one further appeal,
Grant us the strength of arms and a resolve forged out of steel.
Kill every woman, child and man, spill their blood all over the sand,
Prove to the infidel it's our army at Your command.

If Jesus were alive today, is this how he would pray,
Would he ask his Father to smite his foes, would he throw himself in the fray?
Would he draw a gun, if you struck his cheek, would he condemn all the mild and meek?
Or would he shed a tear for us at losing our own way?

I read the news today, I don't believe what those people say,
We're on our way to victory, we can win this war someday.
Now is not the time to cut and run, while old white men are having so much fun,
Playing games of world conquest and counting profits from running guns.
We'll get through to that heathen hoard, even if we have to water board.
But first we'll try our best to convert them to the Bible at the point of the sword.

If Jesus were alive today, what now would he say?
About a people who justify using torture to get their way?
Would he smile at the hypocrisy, would he castigate all the Pharisees?
Or would he shed a tear for us at losing our own way?

"**I**'d like to try something different in The Chords this time," stated Thorn, as Paxton finished eating the last of his meager lunch.

"What's that?" he asked aloud, around a mouthful of carrot pieces.

"I've actually glimpsed bits and pieces of the Middle Eastern scenes you saw along my chord the other day, but I could never be sure they were my own visions. It seems to me that they were being shown from another's viewpoint. I think that I may have seen them while traveling along *your* chord into the past. It's hard for me to remember because I have traveled so extensively throughout The Chords, but I think that's where I saw them!"

"What does that mean?"

"Don't you see? Perhaps this is not the first time that our paths have crossed. Our chords are so tightly woven together in the present that it only makes sense that we would have encountered each other in a past life. You and I are soulmates."

"Hold on there, Thorn. Are you sure?"

"No, but I think we can find out."

"How?"

"When Tucker and I were in The Chords last weekend, I was able to pull him along his own chord to places that I'm sure he couldn't have gotten to on his own. Perhaps if you and I travel together through The Chords we may be able to see each other, and ourselves, in the past."

"So what are we waiting for?" asked Paxton.

"We're waiting for you to put yourself into a state of meditation," instructed Thorn. "Then I'll take you into The Chords."

Paxton pulled his legs up under him into a cross-legged position and rested his hands palms upward on his knees. He shifted his weight a little to ease the strain on his back and took a good look around before closing his eyes. In the absence of sight, Paxton's other senses became more acute. He felt the roadmap of Thorn's rough bark against his spine. He heard the leaves above him whispering on the slight breeze which blew stray strands of hair from his face. A sparrow called to her mate, who answered from across the meadow. A light-hearted pine perfume floated lazily upon the acrid scent of decaying leaves.

Paxton explored his lesser-used senses for several minutes before he began to focus his mind on his breathing, centering his concentration on the portals of his nose. When a stray thought entered his consciousness he visualized it walking down his nose to the tip and jumping off, borne away by his exhaled breath. As his mind grew more and more quiet, he began to focus his awareness inward. He was searching for the source of his being, and in so doing he became less and less cognizant of his physical self.

Paxton had no idea how long he had been sitting there before he perceived Thorn's presence in the darkness surrounding him. The realization that he was no longer alone was accompanied by a tingling sensation which began at the base of his spinal column and walked slowly upward. He wondered if Thorn was somehow massaging his back, and was about to ask him as much before the movement along his spine reached the base of his skull, and his consciousness was suffused in a brilliant, white light. He lost all power to reason as he melted into the warm embrace of the light and an extraordinary sense of peacefulness permeated his whole being.

"I don't know where I am," he thought, after he had recovered the power to do so, "but I like it, a lot."

"Your body is right where you left it, leaning against my trunk," Thorn replied, "but your soul is in the presence of The All. Or more precisely, you are now aware that your soul is in the presence of The All. You never actually leave God's presence."

"This is incredible," thought Paxton, lost in the brilliance of that magnificent white light. He had felt ecstasy before, or so he thought, but this was rapture. He never wanted to be removed from the divine presence again.

"Alas, that is one of the drawbacks of incarnation. You are part of this world and so must remain in this world. But you can establish your God connection so that you'll be able to sit in the divine presence at will. That is something we can work on, but for now, we must go."

"Do we have to? Can't we stay just a little longer?" Paxton pleaded, as though he were a child asking his mother to let him stay in the swimming pool for five more minutes.

"You can stay a little longer," granted Thorn, "but no more than that. It is dangerous to remain here too long. In your unformed state, you may lose your sense of self."

"What's wrong with that? Isn't that the goal of meditation, to transcend the ego?"

"To transcend, yes, but not to annihilate it. That is not your destiny, at least not yet."

"Hey, I thought you weren't supposed to tell me about my future!" Paxton exclaimed. When Thorn remained silent he turned his full attention back to the radiance which held him in its gentle grip. He felt heat burning through the layers of his mind and he surrendered all control to the intense white light surrounding him. For a brief moment, he did lose himself into the infinitude of The All, but only for a moment.

As if the hand holding him had suddenly loosened its fingers, he felt himself falling away from the divine presence. The light began to flicker and then fade, losing only a fraction of its intensity at first, but gradually becoming dimmer as he receded from its source.

Paxton was disappointed but not distressed. The great peace he had so recently experienced lingered as a fingerprint upon his soul, until the light had been replaced by a darkness so complete that he began to fear he would never see light again.

"Thorn?" he called out tentatively. When there was no response he became more forceful, "THORN!"

"I'm right here," Thorn responded. "You don't have to yell."

"I can't see you. I can't even feel you. Where are we?"

"We're in The Chords, of course," replied Thorn. "You can't sense anything because the imprint of The All has been burned into your consciousness, similar to the way that the circle of the sun will burn itself into your retina if you look at it openly for too long. Your *vision* will clear up in a moment."

Paxton waited with as much patience as he could muster, until the darkness enfolding him began to melt slowly away, revealing the endless tangle of threads which could only be The Chords.

"How did we get here?" he asked, after trying unsuccessfully to reproduce the intensity of the sensations he had felt but a short time ago in the presence of The All.

"We fell backward through time, from that point in the future where all chords meet and become The All."

Paxton thought about this a moment before asking, "Why wasn't I able to see any future events?"

"You were temporarily blinded by the brilliance of The All, which is just as well. Knowing future events is not necessarily beneficial to your present stage of spiritual growth."

"You've said as much before," commented Paxton. "What are you so worried about? I wouldn't mind knowing what I'll be doing twenty years from now."

"Sure, it would be great to know you're still healthy and happy in twenty years," responded Thorn dryly, "but what if the prognosis weren't so cheerful? What if I told you that you'd be dead in twenty years? Or five years, for that matter."

"I'd make the most of those five years," Paxton responded flippantly.

"Would you? Or would you become so obsessed by death that you'd miss the opportunity to fulfill this lifetime's purpose? To know too much about one's future inhibits Tucker's precious free will."

"I thought you said the future could be changed."

"It can. The Chords show many possible futures. One future is usually more prevalent than the others and that one is the future most likely to occur, although I have observed exceptions."

"Then you could change a bad future into a good one."

"Bad and good are relative terms, too. It was no doubt *bad* for Jesus personally to be nailed to the cross, but Christians everywhere would agree that his sacrifice for their sins was a *good* thing. We are all changing and shaping the future with every decision we make, but to base those decisions upon knowledge of possible futures is to tamper with one's karma. Would you forsake the lessons you have set for yourself in this lifetime?"

"Yes," Paxton responded, unsure of himself. "Well, no. I don't know."

"Neither do I," admitted Thorn, "and for the moment, the point is moot. We are now traveling into the past."

Paxton looked downward and soon discovered a pair of green chords dodging and weaving amongst the other chords which composed the larger braid beneath them. He willed himself forward and they began to loom larger in his field of vision.

"Can we go back inside our individual chords?" he asked.

"We can, but I thought it might be better to wait until we encounter a previous life. We can travel much faster from up here."

As Thorn spoke, the light in one of their chords winked out and Paxton was no longer sure which one it had been. He asked, "What just happened?"

"We've reached a time before you were born. Your chord is still down there, it's just harder to keep track of now."

Paxton watched as single strands were separated from the braid periodically and others were wound into it. The weave of the larger chord had grown less tight as they traveled backward, but it still formed a cohesive braid amongst the myriad of loose threads surrounding it.

Light suddenly appeared in one of the individual chords below him and Paxton asked, "Is that mine?"

"Yes."

"Can I go check it out?"

"Let's go together. My chord is still playing out my existence as this tree."

Paxton's field of vision was instantaneously replaced by a movie screen upon which, if Thorn was to be believed, played images of his life before the one he now led.

It appeared immediately that Paxton had been some kind of teacher in his previous life as well. He spent his days in the office of a university he did not recognize, pushing mathematical symbols and equations across the pages of papers splayed over his desk. This activity was curtailed intermittently by the few lectures he delivered to packed and attentive classrooms.

"Are you sure this isn't my present lifetime?" Paxton asked.

"When have you ever had an audience like that for one of your lectures?" Thorn kidded him.

"Never," Paxton admitted, "but it looks like I was doing the exact same thing in my previous life."

"Certainly not the *exact* same thing, but the similarities are uncanny. That is not as surprising as it may seem. You've had countless lives prior to the one you are now leading and there are not countless human occupations. There is bound to be some overlap."

"Yeah, but back-to-back lives as a teacher?"

"The occurrence is not statistically significant, as you would say. It could be mere coincidence or there could be more to it. Maybe you were working on something you thought was important enough to spend another lifetime upon it."

"What could that be?"

"I don't know. Let's keep watching."

Paxton could not understand a word of the backward dialogues he was hearing. Indeed the reverse language the characters were using gave him an unsettling and eerie feeling. It reminded him of the time he had given himself the willies trying to listen to certain record albums backwards to hear the satanic messages they were supposed to convey. With a conscious effort he turned the movie's volume down and then off and was content to just watch the proceedings.

His daily routine did not have much variety. He rarely lectured more than once a day and many days he did not lecture at all. He worked at his office seven days a week, when he wasn't traveling to give lectures elsewhere. It seemed he also enjoyed walking, sailing and playing the violin. Eventually Paxton noticed a detail which gave him a clue as to his identity, although he found it very hard to believe.

"Did you notice that he has a closet full of gray suits?" he projected toward Thorn, whose presence he still felt nearby.

"Now that you mention it, I did think that rather odd."

"I'll bet that's what Albert Einstein's closet looked like. He didn't like to waste any mental energy getting dressed in the morning so he always wore the same style of suit. You don't suppose . . ."

"Why not? That would explain why Tucker saw Einstein in his previous life. You two have been soulmates for a long time as well."

"No way," said Paxton in disbelief, but even as he said these words he caught a glimpse of himself in a bathroom mirror. There was no mistaking the frizzled white hair upon his head and upper lip. "I can't believe it."

"What's so hard to believe?" Thorn asked. "Einstein was just a man. He was bound to reenter the cycle of birth and death like any other soul."

"He was an extraordinary man," Paxton corrected, and then added, "I guess *I* was an extraordinary man."

"You still are," Thorn commented. "You just don't know it yet."

Paxton was enthralled, watching the life that he had read about from so many different sources. Though it was confusing to watch it backwards, he recognized many of the events and people parading across his field of vision. Einstein's life at Princeton was based upon a strange dichotomy. He spent an inordinate amount of time alone working on his Unified Field Theory. When he was not alone, he was in conversation with some of the most important figures of the times, from scientists to philosophers to politicians. Paxton had seen their names in books, but he could recognize few of them by their appearances.

As they continued to watch the screen before them in silence, an old woman began to appear in his home life. Paxton recognized her from pictures he had seen in books as Elsa, Einstein's cousin and second wife. Soon after her arrival upon the scene they took a long boat ride across what Paxton could only assume was the Atlantic Ocean and they took up residence in Europe—Oxford, if Paxton remembered Einstein's biography correctly.

His tenure at Oxford was relatively short and marked by numerous lectures and meetings. His next stop was pre-Nazi Berlin, where he worked on his research at the Prussian Academy of Science. Here he remained for quite some time and Elsa was replaced eventually by his first wife, Mileva, and their two children. Shortly thereafter the scene changed to Zurich and then Berne, where Einstein had written his five famous papers while working for the Patent Office in 1905.

"There's his paper on special relativity," Paxton commented, "probably the most important breakthrough in Physics in the twentieth century!"

"I didn't know you could read German," observed Thorn.

"I can't, but I've seen a copy of that paper in its original German over the course of my research."

Paxton made a mental note to view this fascinating story as it unfolded in the forward direction on his way back to the present. He would still not be able to understand the dialogue for the first half of Einstein's life, but at the least he would see the events in their proper order.

As he watched, the scenes were overrun with young men and classrooms in which he received rather than gave the lectures.

"This must be the Polytechnic School in Zurich," Paxton pointed out. Eventually the scene shifted to another school in another city.

"And this is the Luitpold Gymnasium in Munich," Paxton continued his narration. When he received no reply he called out, "Thorn! Thorn, where are you?"

No answer came from the darkness surrounding him and he could no longer feel Thorn's presence at his side. A momentary panic engulfed him in which he felt lost and alone, but then he remembered that he had traveled The Chords by himself once before to no ill effect. He tried to concentrate on the story playing itself out backwards on the screen before him, but he was distracted by Thorn's absence and wondered where he had gone.

Paxton's mind continued to wander as his point of view shrank from that of an adolescent to a child and then a toddler. His attention was drawn back to the screen, however, when he suddenly found himself inside the womb of Einstein's mother. The screen had gone mostly dark, but he could see a surprising range of light from behind the veil of her skin. He could also hear voices quite clearly, though he still had no hope of understanding what it was they were saying. He was able to see and hear less and less as he continued his journey toward the point of conception. Soon the screen went completely dark and he found himself floating once more above the braid containing his soul's individual chord.

"Thorn?" he called tentatively. "Thorn, can you hear me?"

The sound of his voice seemed to be absorbed by the mass of strings through which he was traveling and he doubted if Thorn could hear his words unless he was right beside him. Looking more closely at the braid beneath him, Paxton realized that one of its chords was glowing. He willed himself toward it and passed through its outer edge.

"I think I've discovered my identity!" Thorn told him excitedly, almost as soon as the movie screen before Paxton had once again come to life.

"Why did you leave me all alone?" Paxton asked, ignoring Thorn's revelation.

"I had no choice in the matter. My consciousness was pulled back to my own chord when my past life overlapped yours. You were still in secondary school when I left."

Turning his attention to the movie screen Paxton asked, "What's going on here?"

"It appears as though I'm under some sort of house arrest."

"Hey!" Paxton exclaimed. "This is the same thing I saw the last time I was in The Chords."

"I recognized it from your description as well, except that now I'm pretty sure I know who I was during my last life."

When he offered nothing more Paxton asked, "And who would that be?"

"Baha'u'llah."

"*Baha* what?"

"Baha'u'llah. The prophet of the Bahai religion."

"The Bahai religion," Paxton repeated. "I've heard of that religion before, but I'm not familiar with it."

"I'm not as well versed in the Bahai religion as I am in other world religions," Thorn admitted, "but I do have an adequate overview of its history and precepts. The Bahai believe that Baha'u'llah was the Second Coming of Christ."

"Boy, you really go for it all when you speculate about your past life!" joked Paxton. "What makes you think you were the Bahalluah?"

"Baha'u'llah," Thorn corrected him. "That's what everyone keeps calling me. I've been going backwards and forwards along my chord so that I could understand some of the dialogue. Everyone has been treating me with great respect and calling me Baha'u'llah."

"It makes sense given my other circumstances," Thorn continued. "Baha'u'llah was imprisoned in Akka for the last 25 years of his life, although most of that time was spent under circumstances more closely akin to house arrest than traditional incarceration. He was also a prolific writer."

"You definitely spent a lot of your time writing," Paxton asserted, even as the hand on the screen unwrote pages and pages of what appeared to be a voluminous manuscript.

They watched in silence for a long time, viewing scenes that Paxton had already detailed. The monotony of the man's existence lulled Paxton into a state resembling sleep. When he had regained his focus, he noticed immediately that the man was now in a considerably less accommodating prison cell than the sunlit house he had lived in for so many years.

"Where is he now?" Paxton wondered groggily.

"If I am right about my identity, I'd say this is the Black Pit, a prison beneath the city of Tehran. It was here that Baha'u'llah realized he was a messenger of God."

"It looks like a pretty vile place," observed Paxton.

"It was notorious for its cruelty and virulent conditions," Thorn confirmed.

Paxton studied the prisoners through the shadows cast by the flickering torchlight. Most of them were shackled hand and foot, their emaciated bodies covered in bruises and open sores. Rats gnawed at the arms and legs of those prisoners who hadn't the strength to keep them at bay. The darkness was filled with the groans of hurt and dying men, and the wails of those being tortured, although he couldn't see any evidence of the latter in this particular cell.

"What did he do to land himself in here?"

"He was a follower of The Bab, or 'The Gate', who foretold of the coming of a new and divine prophet. The Bab preached against the Islamic backdrop of nineteenth-century Iran. The Muslim priests of the times did not tolerate any religion other than Islam in their jurisdiction and they systematically exterminated The Bab and his followers."

"Why didn't they kill Baha'u'llah?"

"He came from an influential family, so perhaps they didn't dare kill him outright. They put him in the Black Pit and when he did not die there, they tried to poison him. Still he did not die, and he later became the prophet for which the followers of The Bab were waiting."

"How long did he have to stay in this . . . ." Paxton began to ask, but his question caught in his throat as the screen before him suddenly changed and he found himself staring up at a perfectly blue sky.

Moments later he was on his knees and looking at the ground where he caught glimpses of several pairs of feet circling around him with flails trailing out behind them. Judging from the cries which he finally decided were coming from his own throat, he realized that the men surrounding him were causing him great physical pain. He couldn't feel the pain being inflicted upon his body, but he could see the spatters of blood on the ground and on their clothing, and he could hear the sharp cracks slicing through the air as their whips struck his back. He could also hear the jeers coming from the crowd of onlookers located a respectful distance away from his tormentors.

Soon he was being marched back underground and thrown into the Black Pit with the other prisoners. When he came face to face with Baha'u'llah, a second movie screen appeared before him. It was adjacent to his own screen and angled slightly inward. The bearded figures on both of the screens appeared almost identical. Both had metal hoops around their necks with two thick chains attached to them and both were hobbled around the ankles.

"What's going on here?" Paxton asked.

"The two of us are together at this point in time. We are seeing ourselves through each other's eyes."

"But if I just popped back onto my own chord, that must mean . . ." Paxton trailed off.

"That you were executed by the prison guards," Thorn finished for him.

Paxton had no idea how long the two men conversed in the timelessness of the Black Pit, but it was only a matter of a few minutes in The Chords before they were separated and the man Paxton had been was once again living in the daylight.

It appeared that he was a fabric merchant in some Persian town. He went home each night to a wife and three young children, who proceeded to grow even younger and then disappear as he traveled further into his past. Soon his wife was also gone and he grew younger himself. Paxton watched with great fascination as he got smaller and smaller and once again jumped back into his mother's womb. At the speed he was traveling it seemed only a moment or two before he was no more than a thought in his mother's mind, and he found himself once more an explorer of the chord jungle.

It took him a long time to find Thorn's still faintly glowing chord. He willed himself toward it and was just about to enter inside when its light blinked out as well and he felt Thorn's presence in the darkness.

"That was wild!" Paxton exclaimed, glad to have Thorn beside him again.

"It was that," Thorn shared in his friend's exuberance. "I'm certain I was Baha'u'llah!"

"But who was I?" asked Paxton.

"I'm not sure. I would have to examine your chord in more detail."

"It looked like I was some sort of merchant," Paxton offered. "It certainly didn't seem as though I had done anything to land myself in the Black Pit."

"Maybe you didn't do anything wrong. Maybe you were thrown in there because you were also a follower of The Bab."

"That would make sense," Paxton agreed, not wanting to believe that he was some sort of criminal in a past life.

As they were talking, one of their chords burst back into green flame and Paxton immediately wanted to go in for a closer look.

"Let's travel up here for a while," Thorn suggested. "I'd like us to push as far back as possible while you're still with me. I'm hoping I'll be able to follow the trail we're blazing on my own after you've gone."

"But I'd like to check them out, too," Paxton complained.

"You'll get your chance," Thorn told him, "but for now, our time is short."

Paxton was going to argue about it further, but they were already picking up speed. They followed the twists and bends of the larger chord through no conscious effort on Paxton's part. It was as though they were riding upon a roller coaster attached to tracks which would not let them be thrown off to the side, even as they negotiated the increasingly crazy angles of the turns. Paxton would have been battered and bruised if they did not pass right through the dangling vines which crossed their path in increasing numbers.

He watched the light in their individual chords blink on and off as they sped backwards. Occasionally they both were on at the same time, but more often than not there was only one chord illuminated at any given time. After a while Paxton could differentiate between the two chords by their slightly different shade of green light, but he had no idea which one was his own. One of their chords was lit up more often than the other. Just as he was about to ask Thorn which chord was which, they came to a point where their two chords diverged. Immediately their progress slowed and then came to a halt.

"What just happened?" Paxton asked.

"The larger braid which has encompassed our two chords for a long time has unraveled," Thorn replied.

They turned around and slowly approached the vortex where they could see that several smaller chords were twisted together to form the rope upon which they had been riding. Each of their green chords had belonged to a separate bundle before they were combined at this juncture.

"I guess this is far enough for now," Thorn concluded.

"What's happening here?"

"This is where our two souls first encountered each other," Thorn answered. "At least, I think that's the case. It could be that we merged and diverged before this point, but our chords are definitely coming from different directions here. This is a very important nexus in our relationship."

"Then let's go check it out," Paxton suggested again. This time Thorn consented.

In the next instant Paxton found himself in a small sailboat upon a large lake, straining to pull a net out of the water. A man dressed in a flowing brown tunic worked at the opposite end of the net. Eventually they heaved a small load of fish over the side and into the bottom of the boat. The man spoke to him and he replied, but Paxton could not understand the language they were speaking. Raising their small sail, they rode the strong wind back toward the shore of the lake.

Once upon the shore they bantered with other fishermen as they hauled their catch onto the beach and began to fill woven reed baskets with the still writhing fish. A commotion developed farther up the shore as a small crowd gathered around a stranger who had walked into their midst. A dirty white robe covered the man's body and well-worn sandals protected his feet from the broken ground upon which he walked. Although dressed similarly to the fishermen, this man was somehow different. He spoke with confidence, his words emphasized by graceful gestures of the hands extending outward from the folds of his robes.

"Can you understand what they're saying?" Paxton asked, but received no reply from Thorn.

The mysterious man walked up to him and laid a hand on his shoulder. Words were exchanged, followed by an embrace, and then he and his fishing companion followed the stranger away from the beach, leaving their catch behind.

"What is happening?" Paxton tried to project his thoughts with more force, but Thorn still did not respond. He continued to watch the scenes before him as he and four or five other men followed the stranger through the semi-arid landscape to the top of a small hillock. Here the man turned around and looked directly at Paxton with penetrating eyes.

Paxton could stand the force of his gaze for no more than a few moments before he looked at his feet. Movement in the corner of his eye had him turning to see that the number of stragglers in their make-shift procession had grown to forty or fifty men and a few women. He watched as they all took seats upon the ground before turning back uphill to see that their leader had already done the same. All was quiet as the man began to speak in soft tones which grew ever more strident as his passion consumed him. Paxton only wished that he could understand what was being said to them.

Paxton sensed that he was being drawn away from The Chords even before the scene before him began to fade. He felt a sharp pain at his shoulder and his consciousness fell back into his body with an almost audible thud.

"Wake up!" he heard from a source very close to his ear as he was shaken violently once more by the shoulder. A thumb dug into the crevice below his collarbone and Paxton's eyes flew open.

"Ouch!" he shouted, as his arm shot upward reflexively, jarring loose the vice-like grip which was clamped hard upon his shoulder. He blinked his eyes a few times to clear his vision and saw the weather-beaten face of an old man leering down upon him. Another man stood behind him and off to one side, his arms folded across his broad chest.

"What are you doing up here, Mr. Stephens?" demanded the man who was farther away, in an authoritative voice.

"Who are *you*?" Paxton countered, straining to see his face through the cloud of smoke which had just been exhaled from beneath the hostile eyes bearing down upon him. "And how do you know my name?"

"You're a pretty deep sleeper," said the man before him in a thick Down East accent. He tossed Paxton's wallet down into his lap forcefully, as he sent another cloud of smoke sailing at his face. Paxton coughed.

"That'll do, Wendell," voiced the man who was clearly in charge. The old man took a few steps backward as Paxton gathered his wallet from where it had bounced after striking his thigh. He took a quick look at its contents before putting it back into the right, rear pocket of his jeans, from where it must surely have been lifted while he sat in meditation.

"I own these woods," the slightly younger man spoke up again, gesturing forward with a lift of his chin and a short sweep of his right arm. "Are you aware I could have you arrested for trespassing?"

"This is private property?" asked Paxton, feigning ignorance.

"Damned straight," interjected the old man. "Tell me you didn't see the 'No Trespassing' signs on your way up here!"

"I didn't," lied Paxton. "What signs?"

"What are you doing up here?" repeated the man whom Tucker would recognize as Roland Grenaud.

"I was just out looking for a hike, a little exercise," stammered Paxton. "I must've fallen asleep up here."

"You were definitely asleep and this is definitely private property," continued Roland. "I'm not going to press charges but I don't want you to come back here ever again. I'll have crews in these woods by the end of next week and I don't want any accidents."

Roland said this last with a measured tone of menace, but his stance had softened somehow and he seemed ready to believe that Paxton was indeed a casual hiker who chose to ignore the 'No Trespassing' signs. He turned to his employee and began discussing other matters, as if Paxton had already been dismissed and was no longer of concern to him.

"Alright," Paxton agreed.

After the glare of their spotlight had been redirected, Paxton turned his attention to his body, which had moved only slightly during the entire exchange. He felt a dull ache in his lower back and then realized that he had no feeling in his legs whatsoever. He looked around him as he began to massage blood back into his thighs and was amazed to discover the sun above the trees in the west, only an hour away from nightfall.

Could he really have been sitting beneath Thorn for so long? It seemed hard to believe, but became easier as he tried to move his numb legs from beneath his body. He had to use his arms to pull them out straight and he grimaced at the pins and needles he felt as the blood began to flow freely back into his calves and feet. His stomach grumbled, reminding him that he had eaten precious little for lunch.

"Thorn?" he called out silently with his thoughts.

"I'm here," came the reply. "What do you make of these guys?"

"One of them is Tucker's boss, I think," Paxton reasoned. "I'm not sure who the old guy is, but he's starting to piss me off."

As if on cue, Wendell looked over at him and asked, "Well, what are you waiting for?"

Paxton looked away, saying through gritted teeth, "My legs are asleep."

Wendell grunted in response and turned back to his boss, who was talking about Thorn, Paxton finally realized.

"This will be more than enough wood for my purposes," Roland appraised the tree, "and I'll get a good price for the boards I don't use."

"You're not planning on cutting down this tree?" Paxton couldn't make up his mind whether he was asking a question or making a statement.

"That's none of your business. Get out of here!" barked Wendell.

"But it's an awesome tree!" Paxton argued.

"Yes it is," agreed Roland, looking straight into Paxton's eyes. He seemed to be sizing Paxton up again, as if he was reconsidering his decision to let him off the hook. "It'll be even more *awesome* in my living room as a cabinet."

"Thorn!" Paxton called aloud before he could stop himself. Both men looked sharply at him.

"What did you say?" asked Wendell.

"Nothing," muttered Paxton. "Except I think it's a shame you cutting down this old tree."

"We don't care what you think," spat Wendell, who then received a look from his boss which told him to let it go.

The pain in Paxton's legs had subsided, and he stood slowly, holding onto the tree for balance. His legs threatened to buckle underneath him, but they held his weight and slowly adjusted to his upright position. He peered up into the branches of the tree with his arms spread in an imploring gesture.

"Did you hear that?" he thought.

"I did," Thorn answered in his mind. "And I want to hear what else they're saying. You better get going, anyway. Come back up here as soon as you can, though."

"But . . ." Paxton trailed off, looking meaningfully at the two men talking ten feet away.

"Don't worry about them, just be careful."

"I'll try to come up again on Thursday," offered Paxton.

"Great, see you then."

Paxton stooped down and gathered his few belongings into his backpack. Neither man looked at him as he shouldered it and turned to walk away. When he reached the edge of the meadow where the dirt path began to descend more quickly, he turned back to the clearing.

"Good night, Thorn," whispered Paxton, raising his hand in farewell. Paxton thought for a moment that one of Thorn's huge lower limbs moved rhythmically up and down as though he were waving back to him, but he received no verbal farewell in reply. He turned back around and took a few tentative steps down the path before gaining confidence in his stiff legs and letting gravity pull him back down the hill to his car.

SEVENTEEN

Homefires

A thin line of smoke
is rising up into the air.
Mixing in the mist of dark grey
storm clouds that are gathering there.
The road winds
across the mountaintops
under the open sky.
Open like the shells of bombed-out
buildings that are passing by.
Tell me, my sister,
when the war machine came through.
Tell me, my sister,
what did they do to you?
Or even better yet I wish that
somebody could tell me why.

A soldier stops us on the road
he wants to know just who we are.
He looks through our possessions
searching for articles of war.
I open up my backpack
I've got nothing I need to hide.
Except the secrets of my soul
I've buried deep down inside.
I'll tell you, mister soldier-man,
exactly where to start.
Look into the battlefields,
the scars upon your heart.
Or is there something there
you're hoping no one will ever find?

Homefires are burning for me.
Homefires are burning for you.
Homefires are burning here too.

Ascending to your perch
a hundred children tramping on behind.
How many of these children
have been orphaned by this genocide?
A quest for hope to find you here
among these ancestral hills.
This valley where mankind was born
where ancient god are living still.
Tell me, my father,
how did you survive?
Tell me, my father,
what it means to be alive.
And how did you
escape the closing walls
between this clash of wills.

I ask you to explain to me
how you could let this happen here.
This beautiful green countryside
now ruled by torment, death, and fear.
You look at me with strange eyes
you tell me I don't understand.
My ways are not your ways
I come from a foreign land
I'll grant you my, my brother,
that I may not comprehend.
This war and all its killing
are they signals of the end?
How can you speak of reconciliation
that gun in your hand?

Homefires are burning for me.
Homefires are burning for you.
Homefires are burning here too.

Wednesday, October 20, 1999

It's almost 3 PM and I'm sitting on a massive, fallen oak tree in the middle of the woods about five miles southwest of Monson. It's unfortunate that this particular tree has already decomposed past the point of harvest or it would have been perfect for Mr. Grenaud's purposes. Even so, I have seen plenty of good-sized, live oak trees over the past couple of days. I should have no problem diverting his attention away from the top of Blueberry Hill. None of the ones I have seen here are as beautiful as Thorn, of course, but they're all within a skidder's reach of the road, which cannot be said of Thorn.

I was able to get away for a couple of hours by telling the guys that I wanted to walk the boundary in this sector. I don't even know what that's supposed to mean—'walk the boundary.' It sounded good when I said it to Wendell the other day and no one has called me on it, so I'm going to keep using it. It means I'm walking through the woods looking for the perfect oak tree, that's what it means.

I guess this won't be an official entry after all. I need to sit down and write a full report for Mr. Grenaud, at some point. I'm just trying to get my thoughts together at the moment. I'll have to make sure that no one from work gets hold of this field notebook.

I still haven't figured out if I'm going to testify on Friday. I keep going back and forth. If clear-cutting is bad practice, why haven't they already outlawed it? I've seen some places they've clear-cut and replanted and the new trees are coming up just fine. I certainly think there is a limit to the number of trees that should be clear-cut, but have we reached that limit? I wish I knew the answers to these questions, before I have to decide what to do on Friday.

I guess I'm leaning toward testifying. If they were doing something illegal out here, that would be one thing, but they're within the law. More importantly, it seems as though they're within tolerable limits as far as the impact to the environment is concerned. There's no question that clear-cutting is bad for a forest, but the great thing about forests is that they grow back. As long as a reasonable amount of care is taken, and not too large an area is cut, I'm convinced the environment can handle it.

I am curious as to why the company switched to clear-cutting in the first place. The forest has healed quickly from the selective cuts they've shown me, some of which were done as recently as one year ago. It's got to be economic. The foreman said that the company was in some sort of financial trouble, but he didn't offer to elaborate. Everyone here has been pretty tight-lipped. I think they're all a little suspicious of me. I wonder if Mr. Grenaud has said anything to them about why I'm here.

For my part, I still feel like I have to watch what I say and do. I don't want to ask any stupid questions, and I don't want them to think I'm not on their side. These guys in the woods, and in the mill, for that matter, are great—really down to earth. Definitely men's men, though.

I really like this job. I'm doing what I got my forestry degree to do—work in the woods. I could see myself staying here for a long time. And if I want to keep my job, I better testify on Friday. Roland hasn't come out and said that my job depends on it, but testifying seems the surest way to stay in his good graces.

I'd also like the chance to go head to head with Claire. For some reason she raises my hackles, and I don't know exactly why. She thinks she has all the answers and that the rest of us are all a bunch of idiots. Arrogance. That's what I don't like about her. And she knows she can get away with her arrogance because she's so damned gorgeous. Paxton sure knows how to pick them.

Regardless of whether or not I testify, I've got to keep the boss well away from Thorn's hilltop. And what of Thorn? How is it that he can communicate with us? How is it that he can create blueberries and wine out of thin air, or lift me bodily off the ground? I've gone through all the logical explanations I can think of and none of them make any sense.

For whatever reason, that old oak tree has a consciousness. What if there are other trees like him out there? What if every tree in this forest has a consciousness? How can I ever condone the cutting of another tree? But Thorn said he hasn't been able to talk with any of the trees around him. Is he a rarity, or have the other trees just not learned how to communicate with humans? I really need to talk to Thorn about all this before I make my final decision on whether or not to testify. But when? The hearing is only two days away.

For now, I'd better get back to the trucks. They were already joking that they'd leave me out here if I wasn't back by quitting time, and I have a pretty long hike ahead of me. I'm not sure if I'm any closer to making a decision about testifying, but I feel a little better about things after getting some of these thoughts down on paper. I should write in here more often.

Tom

—

Paxton peered out over the stack of half-graded homework assignments on his desk, his attention focused on a lone, dark red maple leaf that floated lazily to the ground outside his office window. The red pen in his right hand involuntarily tapped out the rhythm to a Grateful Dead song that only he would recognize as *Sugar Magnolia*. Because he was even more distracted than usual, he had chosen to devote his afternoon to classwork rather than his recently neglected research, but even the mindless grading of papers proved to be too much of a demand upon his concentration. He could not stop thinking about Thorn and what he had seen and experienced in The Chords.

Was he actually in the divine presence not twenty-four hours ago? The intense emotions he had felt only yesterday had already faded in his memory and the whole trip through The Chords had taken on a dream-like quality. Was Thorn really the prophet of the Bahai faithful in his last incarnation? He had certainly seemed convinced. Thorn had given Paxton no reason to doubt his knowledge of world religions, but Paxton resolved to research the matter further, nonetheless.

Then there was the revelation of his own past incarnation. If The Chords were to be believed, he was the reincarnated soul of Albert Einstein. How was such a thing even possible? Was his desire to get a PhD in mathematics some kind of compensation for Einstein's shortcomings in the subject? Was he somehow trying to continue Einstein's research into Unified Filed Theory? If he was able to access Einstein's knowledge from within The Chords, Paxton could literally pick up where the great scientist had left off. Now there was an idea worth exploring. He was excited by the possibilities and began making a mental list of all of the questions he wanted to pose to Thorn.

Paxton regretted that he hadn't gotten the chance to talk to Thorn about what they had seen in The Chords after they had been so rudely pulled out of them yesterday afternoon. He couldn't wait to get back up there tomorrow, but he also felt some trepidation over the possibility of coming face to face with that nasty old man again, or anyone else from the lumber company who might be up there. Hiking up Blueberry Hill was going to have to be a covert operation from now on.

"Let's go have a beer!" a familiar voice called to him from the open doorway to his office, startling him out of his reverie.

Paxton whirled around in his chair and was immediately dumbstruck, not only by the beauty of the woman smiling down upon him, but by the unlikelihood of her unannounced appearance at his office door in the middle of the afternoon. Claire stood leaning against the doorjamb, her arms folded across her chest and her black hair hanging freely about her shoulders. In her faded jeans and dark blue, University of Maine sweatshirt, she could easily have been mistaken for one of Paxton's calculus students, until closer examination revealed the slight crow's feet she had begun to develop at the corners of her eyes.

"What are you doing here?" he asked, incredulously. "I thought you had a ton of work to do before Friday."

"I do," she replied curtly. "But I've been at it for three days straight and I needed a little break. It looks like you could use one, too."

Paxton looked at the clock on the wall above his office-mate's desk and then back at Claire, saying, "I still have twenty minutes left on my office hours. I extended them today because they have a test on Friday. I told my students I'd be here until four."

Claire peered at him from beneath her raised eyebrows as if to say, "What a lame excuse!"

It took Paxton only a moment longer to agree with her. He picked up the papers he had been balancing upon his knees and tossed them onto the top of the pile of papers which already covered his desk. Grabbing his coat from the back of his chair, he followed Claire into the hallway, closing his office door behind him.

—

As Claire sat in the dimly lit booth of the Bear's Den, waiting for Paxton to return with their drinks, her thoughts were focused upon the reason for her unexpected visit to the campus in the midst of one of the busiest weeks she had ever encountered. The trip to Chicago had really set her back, and then there was Beth. Now, of all things, she had to deal with Tucker.

She had received a phone call early yesterday morning from His Honor Henry Granville, who informed her that a witness had been added to the defense. She had objected to the late change, but the judge said he had decided to allow it, since she was calling an expert witness of her own and it was only a preliminary hearing. She had asked for a postponement, but that had also been summarily denied. Then she had to ask him to repeat himself when he told her that the name of the surprise witness for the defense was Thomas Tucker.

How could Thomas Tucker testify for that logging company? He had only been in Maine for a few weeks! What did he know about the situation? And that's where she found her edge. The key to discrediting his testimony was to discredit Tucker himself. To do that she would have to know as much about him as possible. Who better to give her that information than his best friend?

She had discovered, after talking on the phone with Paxton last night, that he knew nothing about Tucker testifying for the defense at the hearing. He had called as she was putting Beth to bed, and they hadn't talked for long. It wasn't until later that evening that she realized neither of them had mentioned the hearing at all, although Paxton had informed her that Tucker was out of town for a couple of days.

Now, as she watched him walk toward her from the bar, she wrestled with her dishonesty. It would be much easier to get Paxton to talk about Tucker if he wasn't aware she planned to use the information against him at the hearing. Convincing herself that it was merely a lie of omission, and that her cause justified her means, she decided to proceed with her plan.

"How are things going with Beth?" Paxton asked, sliding into the bench opposite her. He pushed a glass of red wine across the table and raised his bottle of Samuel Adams in the air in a mock toast before taking a gulp of its contents.

"Great!" answered Claire enthusiastically, taking a sip of her wine. Setting her glass down she added more soberly, "I guess. I mean, it's great having her around, but I don't know if I'm doing such a great job taking care of her. I wish I could've taken this week off to spend some time with her."

"Where is she now?"

"At Beverly's house. I guess I'll have to put her in day care, once I get the chance to look around for a good one. She was going to a day care in Chicago, so she's already used to it."

"How are *you* doing? You look exhausted."

"I haven't been getting much sleep lately, but other than that I'm doing all right. I'm not dealing with anything at the moment, emotionally. I'm just trying to get through the week and win this case."

"How's it coming?"

"It doesn't look good for the home team," Claire admitted. "So far I haven't been able to prove that they're breaking any laws. And I've only got two more days until the hearing."

"You'll turn up something. You always do."

"I wish I could share your optimism. I have my doubts about this one."

"Let me know if there's anything I can do to help."

"You're sweet," she said, reaching her hand across the table and resting it on his, "but I don't think . . ."

"No, I'm serious," Paxton interrupted her refusal to accept his offer. "Whatever you need to get done. I'm not above being a gofer. You have to save those woods!"

"Why are you suddenly so interested in this case?" Claire asked, startled by the urgency in Paxton's voice. She had realized from the start of their friendship that Paxton did not share her zeal for protecting the environment. In fact, she was flattered when he kept coming back to volunteer at SPAWN, after it became obvious that he was doing so only as an excuse to see her. He was so cute when she confronted him with her suspicions. He had denied her accusations at first, but then his face had turned bright red and he had admitted his attraction to her, a sheepish smile splayed across his lips.

"I was up there yesterday," Paxton said simply, not bothering to defend any previous lack of interest.

"Up where?"

"On Blueberry Hill."

"Did you find your thrill?" she teased him.

"Not without you there," he answered, winking at her. "I don't know its actual name. We just always called it Blueberry Hill, but it's a part of that section of land they're going to clear-cut."

"What were you doing up there?"

"I used to go up there a lot when I was in college," he answered after an uncomfortably long silence.

"You're still in college," Claire reminded him.

"The first time I was in college," he continued, rolling his eyes. "It's so beautiful up there. I had no idea that it was Blueberry Hill you were fighting to save, until Tucker told me so the other day. I wanted to go back up there and take a look before they cut it all down."

Claire's cringed involuntarily at the mention of Tucker's name and there was a hard edge to her voice as she asked, "So you don't think I'm going to win either?"

Paxton was immediately apologetic. He held up both hands saying, "No, that's not it at all! I know you can win, but you just said that it doesn't look good."

When Claire remained silent, Paxton proffered a peace offering, "I should really take you up there, sometime. You'd love it. Have you been in those woods?"

"I've driven by, but I haven't hiked through them."

"Maybe we can go this weekend, after the hearing," offered Paxton. He seemed eager to say more, but then thought better of it.

"Maybe," Claire agreed absent-mindedly. "I can't think that far ahead at this point."

"Yeah, it'll be great!" pressed Paxton. "We could pack a picnic lunch and head up there for the day with Beth and Tucker . . ."

"Tucker!?!" Claire almost spat out the sip of wine in her mouth. "Why would I go anywhere with Thomas Tucker?"

"Sorry," Paxton apologized. "I forgot you don't like him very much."

"He's the enemy!" she wanted to shout at him, but she managed to keep her cool.

"He's not the enemy, he just works for them."

"Same thing."

"If you got to know him I think you'd really like him."

Grateful for the opening, Claire inquired, "Why don't you tell me more about him, then?"

"What do you want to know?"

Claire looked into Paxton's soulful eyes and hesitated a moment. She regretted the need to lie to the only man she had been attracted to since her divorce, but she knew that she was going to do it. This was too important.

"You told me you met him in college, right?"

"That's right."

"What was he studying?"

"He was in engineering when we met, but he switched into forestry right away. His willpower amazed me. Or maybe it was his stubbornness. He worked his ass off to put himself through school, when his father would have paid for it."

"Why didn't he take his father's money?"

"His dad wanted him to be an engineer and follow his footsteps up the corporate ladder. When Tucker said he wanted to study forestry instead, his dad told him that was fine, but if he wanted to waste his time in school he could also waste his own money."

"How did you pay for college?"

"Lots of scholarships and financial aid. One of the benefits of being poor . . . and brilliant!" Paxton raised his almost empty bottle of beer in another mock toast. Claire smiled, but made no move to raise her own glass.

"What did Tucker do after graduation?"

"He married our roommate, Annie, and they moved down to North Carolina. That's where she was from."

"Did you ever visit them down there?"

"No," Paxton paused a moment. "The truth is, we had a falling out after graduation."

"What kind of falling out?" Claire asked eagerly, her interest aroused.

"We had sort of a love triangle going on that last year of college," Paxton admitted, too embarrassed to look her in the eye. "Tucker and I both loved Annie, and I believe she loved both of us as well. We all left our feelings unnamed until Tucker asked her to marry him. It was an impossible situation that was bound to end badly. I just happened to be the odd man out."

"Paxton, that's awful," Claire sympathized, taking both of his hands in her own. "How is it that you two can still be friends?"

"It was awful at first, but time has a way of making you forget all but the good memories. Now that Annie is dead I kind of feel sorry for Tucker. It makes it easier to like him again."

Claire wanted to ask what Annie was like, but she knew that if she didn't press her interrogation to its conclusion, she'd miss her window of opportunity. Instead she asked, "What did Tucker do for a living in North Carolina?"

Paxton laughed and then shared the joke, "If you ask him, he will say he was a landscape architect, but basically he mowed people's lawns . . ."

"You mean he didn't work in forestry?" Claire interrupted.

"No. He said it was impossible for an outsider to get a job with the Forestry Service down there. In fact, this is the first job he's ever had where he is using his degree. That's why he likes it so much."

"And he's been at this job how long?"

"Three weeks? Maybe a month."

"How did he get this job if he has no experience?"

"His grandmother knows the owner of B & G Lumber. I'm sure that had something to do with it."

A smile had formed upon Claire's face as she realized that Paxton had just given her all the information she needed to discredit Tucker and his testimony.

"What's so funny?" Paxton asked, wanting to share in the humor showing plainly upon her face.

"Nothing," she replied, but then added, "I thought that Tucker knew what he was talking about when we debated the clear-cut the other night."

"Don't let his inexperience fool you," Paxton defended his friend. "Tucker is very knowledgeable when it comes to forestry."

"I'm sure he is," Claire lied, still very much pleased with herself.

Paxton went on to sing Tucker's praises both as a scholar of the forest and in the unrelated realms of fatherhood and basketball. Claire heard little of this diatribe. Her mind had already turned back to the hearing and she began plotting her course of action over the next couple of days. She was brought back to the present when Paxton had to ask her twice if she wanted another glass of wine.

"No, I can't," she answered. "I have a lot of work to do tonight."

"You haven't heard a word I've said for the past five minutes," stated Paxton. "Have you?"

"I'm sorry. I was just thinking about my case. I'm really going to be glad when this one's over."

"Do you want to get together this weekend and celebrate?"

"There may not be anything to celebrate."

"Either way, it'll be over."

"That's true. I'll have to see how I feel. I really want to spend some time with Beth this weekend. I feel like I've been neglecting her since she got here."

"She's not the only one," muttered Paxton.

"What do you want me to do?" Claire asked him angrily. "There's only one of me to go around."

"I'm sorry," Paxton apologized. "I didn't mean anything by it. I just miss you, that's all."

"I miss you, too. C'mon, why don't you walk me to my car."

They walked the short distance to Claire's car hand in hand. Claire was about to open her car door when she turned around spontaneously and threw her arms around Paxton's neck, favoring him with a lingering kiss which he returned wholeheartedly.

"That will have to tide you over for a few days, I'm afraid," she gasped, after they had stopped to take a breath.

"You better let me have another one then," Paxton demanded, leaning in to her again. He kissed her once more through the window, as the engine of her Subaru sputtered to life.

"Good luck on Friday," Paxton offered.

"Thanks, I'm going to need it."

"Be sure to call me afterwards."

"I will. And maybe we can get together this weekend. We'll just have to see."

"All right. See you later."

"Bye."

Claire felt a jumble of tangled emotions as she made the left turn onto Stillwater Avenue and headed for home. Paxton's sweaty man-smell lingered in the air around her and she was still physically excited from their kissing. By the time she crossed the Stillwater River, her arousal had been replaced by guilt. She hadn't been up front with Paxton and she had the sinking feeling that her dishonesty was going to come back to bite her in the ass. She was more attracted to him than she would care to admit and the thought of losing him gave her a sick feeling in the pit of her stomach.

As she merged into the traffic moving southward along Interstate 95, her thoughts had turned back to the hearing and she smiled in spite of herself. Paxton had given her the first real break she had found in this case. At the least she should be able to nullify Tucker's testimony, which would be doubly satisfying considering how annoying he was. But it wouldn't win her the hearing. She set her jaw in grim resolve as she realized that she had a lot more to do before Friday's hearing.

Claire worked for several hours after she put Beth to bed. When she could no longer hold her own head up, she left her case on the kitchen table and shuffled into bed, only to pick it up once again in her dreams.

She dreamed she was in the courtroom, trying her case. The jury-box contained its requisite dozen and the gallery was filled with people. Tucker was on the stand and Claire paced the floor in front of him, firing her pointed questions with the accuracy of a sniper.

"Do you consider yourself an expert in the field of forestry?" she asked.

"I don't know that I'd call myself an expert."

"But certainly you have a working knowledge of the subject, or you wouldn't have testified for the defense."

"That's correct."

"What are your qualifications?"

"I received a Bachelor of Science in Forestry from the University of Maine and I'm currently working as a forester for B & G Lumber Company."

"What was your grade point average at the University of Maine?"

"I don't remember," stammered Tucker.

"Let me refresh your memory," Claire offered, handing him a piece of paper. "Will you tell the court what it is that you're holding, Mr. Tucker."

"This is my transcript from the University of Maine."

"And what is the overall GPA on your transcript?"

"A two-point-five," he whispered.

"Can you speak up, please?"

"It's a two-point-five," he said more loudly, "but that's because . . ."

"Just answer the questions, please," Claire interrupted him. "Can you tell the court what grade that GPA corresponds to?"

"It's between a C and a B," Tucker responded, sulkily.

"A solid C average," Claire corrected.

"Objection, Your Honor," came from somewhere behind her. "She's leading the witness."

"Sustained."

"How long have you been working for B & G Lumber?" she pressed.

"About a month."

"Where did you work before that?"

"I've moved around a lot over the past couple of years and worked a variety of odd jobs."

"Were any of these odd jobs related to forestry?"

"Not exactly."

"Have you ever worked as a forester before the past month?"

"Not in the strict sense of the term, but . . ."

"I have no further questions, Your Honor," Claire stated with finality.

"Well I have some questions," Tucker spoke up from the stand, causing Claire to turn back toward him. She waited for the judge to reprimand him, but he stared down at her from behind the bench instead.

"Is it not true that your ex-husband left you because you are barren?"

"I don't see what this has to do with . . ."

"I'll allow the question," broke in the judge in an imperious voice.

"Yes, it's true that I am barren, but I left my ex-husband because he was cheating on me."

"And how did you come to be infertile, Ms. Harrison."

"This is highly irregular, Your Honor," pleaded Claire, looking hopefully toward the judge.

"You will answer the question," he commanded.

"I contracted chlamydia while in college," Claire spat the words at Tucker.

"Chlamydia. Isn't that a sexually transmitted disease?"

"You know very well that it is."

"Did you contract this disease from a boyfriend?"

"No."

"Is it not true that you got chlamydia from a man you slept with only once?"

"Yes."

"Did you make a habit of one night stands while you were in college?"

"No, it was only that once. Your Honor, this is ridiculous. I'm not on trial, here."

"I'm afraid that you are, Ms. Harrison."

As the judge spoke those words Claire noticed that she had traded places with Tucker and was now seated on the stand herself.

"Is it not true," Tucker continued, "that you gave up your chance to be a mother, for one night of sexual pleasure?"

"No," Claire screamed at him.

She searched the sea of faces in the courtroom for signs of an ally, but found only indifference, or open hostility. Someone in the room shouted, "Yes!" This was taken up as a chant by those looking on, most of whom pointed their fingers at Claire in accusation. Their chanting rose in volume until Claire could hear nothing but that one condemning syllable, "Yes!"

Claire sat bolt upright in bed, immediately relieved that she had been dreaming. The covers had all been kicked onto the floor and she shivered as she reached over the side of the bed for them. She was about to pull the comforter over her when she saw the clock on the nightstand, its first digit a glowing red five. She decided to get out of bed instead, though she still pulled the comforter around her as she walked into the kitchen to get some coffee started.

—

Paxton dreamed he was on the back of a lorry on his way to his Peace Corps site. What made this particular trip stranger than usual was that he was the only passenger. Vehicles to and from Lokitaung were scarce, and he had never been on one that didn't have a closely-packed human cargo. He held onto the bars overhead and swayed back and forth as the big truck lumbered over the rocky road.

As they reached the outskirts of Lokitaung it also seemed strange that there were no children running out of the roadside huts to greet the lorry. In fact, Paxton saw no one in evidence until they arrived at the only store in town and Yusef, the Pakistani owner of the small *duka*, came out to unload his supplies.

"Where is everyone?" Paxton called down to him.

"All gone," Yusef shook his head sadly. "I am the only one left."

"What do you mean they're all gone?"

"See for yourself," Yusef invited, "but hurry back. The lorry will be returning to Lodwar within the hour."

Paxton climbed down from the bed of the dump truck and stretched back muscles which had been jarred mercilessly on the trip across the desert. Then he took off at a fast walk toward the school compound. As he crested the small hill which would give him a view of the entire school grounds he stopped short, a gasp of surprise escaping his lungs.

Where the school used to be stood several large piles of crumbling, whitewashed bricks. A deep and jagged gorge now ran through the center of the parade grounds, extending all the way to the base of the hill upon which he had lived. He scanned the horizon for his house, but saw only another small pile of rubble, crowning the hillock king of this barren wasteland. Also missing from the foreground was the acacia tree he passed every day to and from school. The rent in the ground seemed to end on the exact spot the tree used to occupy.

Paxton felt suddenly lonely and turned back toward town. He was relieved to see the lorry still parked outside Yusef's store, although neither he nor the driver were in sight. Paxton found Yusef drinking a warm soda inside the *duka* and he grabbed an orange Fanta of his own as he walked past a case which had just been brought inside.

"What happened here?" he asked.

"Earthquake," Yusef answered simply.

"How long ago?"

"About a year after you left, maybe longer. Those that weren't killed in the quake were taken by the soldiers. Even the Turkanans packed up their huts and moved to some other place."

"Why haven't you left?"

"I've lived here most of my life. This is where my homefire burns, bwana."

"But how can you stay in business?"

"The soldiers have to eat," he answered, "and drink."

Noticing the cases of *pombe* for the first time Paxton chided him, "Are you selling beer now? What's your wife got to say about that?"

Yusef shook his head sadly in answer, just as the lorry outside fired up its engine.

"I better get going!" Paxton announced, rising quickly from the table. "*Bahati nzuri*, Yusef!"

"Good luck to you, too," he heard from behind him as he ran out the door. The lorry was already an impossible distance away for such a slow moving vehicle.

"Wait!" Paxton shouted. He tried to run after it, but his leaden feet wouldn't allow him to move any faster than a lumbering walk.

As the lorry disappeared over a ridge in the road, Paxton sat down to catch his breath. Putting his head in his hands he whispered, "Wait."

Epilogue

On the top of Blueberry Hill, Thorn dreamed he was in human form, sipping cappuccino at a black, wrought iron table outside a small French café, surrounded by a host of historical figures. Across the table from him sat a man he could not place, although he had no trouble naming all of the other patrons of the café.

Plato and Socrates were having a heated philosophical debate with Rene Descartes at the table to his right. Next to them sat Albert Einstein, Marie Curie and Leonardo Da Vinci. Benjamin Franklin and Thomas Jefferson were getting cozy with Josephine Baker to his left as Mahatma Gandhi and Martin Luther King, Jr. looked on from their own table next to the café's double doors. Marie Antoinette served them all pastries and coffee in a skimpy waitress uniform which did very little to hide her long legs and ample breasts.

The man now staring intently at him from over his large bulbous nose wore a goatee, and a smile which seemed incongruous with the penetrating blue eyes which bore down upon Thorn. He appeared to be waiting for a response of some kind as he rested his chin on his interlaced fingers, but Thorn had no idea what question had been posed.

"You know I'm right," the man stated self-confidently, without lifting his head from his hands.

"I know nothing of the sort," Thorn responded, trying to remember the thread of their conversation.

"They're lost without us," the man continued, "searching in vain for order amongst chaos; for logic within insanity; for identifiable patterns amidst random chance."

"I'm sure I don't know what you're talking about," Thorn said truthfully.

"Ahh, but you do. That's why you feel obligated to light a candle in the darkness. You don't trust them to find the answers on their own. And I'd say your instincts are right on target. Without you to guide them, humankind would still be mired in the primordial ooze they think they've left so far behind, bickering about which of their tiny little windows on the universe presents the most complete picture."

As if on cue, Descartes rose quickly from his seat, pounding his table with both fists. He almost knocked Thorn's chair over in his haste to leave, screaming back over his shoulder at his Greek counterparts, "I think! I think! I think!"

"See what I mean?" the man asked him, drawing his attention away from the backside of the departing philosopher. "Each one of them believes the lie told to them by their senses. Each believes his or her own perception of reality to be the correct one, when in truth none of them even have a clue."

"But it is in the asking that they define themselves," Thorn found his voice, suddenly remembering what it was they were debating. "It is in the asking of the great metaphysical questions that they set themselves apart from the other life forms that share their existence."

"They only think they are set apart. Because they can reason, they believe that they do not share the fate of those other life forms. They think they will somehow be spared the death which awaits each and every one of them."

"Death is only the end of their physical existence."

"It is the end of their lives as they know it. What good does it do them to know that their energy will survive, if their personal essence does not?"

"But it does survive, and is reborn again into another physical manifestation."

"Small good that does them," scoffed his companion, now raising his head and leaning back in his chair. "They don't remember anything of their past. They might as well have been sent to that blissful oblivion."

"Each one will remember in his or her own turn. You and I did."

"And now it's our job to enlighten others. Is that it?"

"Not exactly . . ."

"Which brings me back to my original point—they'd be lost without us."

"I think you're wrong."

"How about we try a little experiment, then?"

"What kind of experiment?" asked Thorn warily.

"Let's remove ourselves from the equation for a fixed period of time, say a hundred years."

"What is that going to prove?"

"Let's see if humanity moves collectively forward or backward in our absence. Will they progress toward your precious enlightenment or climb back into the primeval jungle trees from which they descended not so long ago."

"That's all well and good, but how can I trust that you won't interfere during that time?"

"We could both go away for a while, take a vacation to another galaxy."

"I'd want to witness what was happening in our absence."

"I've got an idea! What if we were both reborn as trees? In that form we will still be able to observe, but we will be powerless to interfere. We could go to opposite sides of the Earth if you like, and allow ourselves to become reincarnated as trees for the next one hundred years."

"I don't know about that . . ."

"What have you got to lose? Are you afraid they'll blow themselves up in your absence?"

"Well, no, but . . ."

"Put your theory to the test. Let's see if they truly will evolve onto a higher spiritual plane without our interference. You'll be back in time for your precious millennium."

"You've got yourself a deal," Thorn finally consented. "But I get to choose where we each will take root."

"Fair enough," said the man opposite Thorn, standing up. "When do we get started?"

"There's no time like the present," Thorn answered.

"Give me a day or two to get my affairs in order," said his companion, turning to leave. Thorn watched his shrinking form until it was no more than a black dot in the mist that had begun to absorb the details from the edges of his peripheral vision. Soon the only thing he could see was Marie Antoinette standing in front of him with her tray.

"More cake?" she asked him, before bursting into a bout of maniacal laughter. He could still hear her laughing as he returned to his conscious mind, and the wooden frame which had housed it for the past hundred years.

THE STORY CONTINUES IN BOOK TWO:

Thorn:

The Prophet